# KILLING FIELD

★★★★★★★★

At that moment there appeared, almost noiselessly, the dark circular shape of a hoverer. Rifle fire ripped downward, tearing into the throng. Men tried to run. Slave girls screamed. Otto seized Julian and flung him to the ground. Princess Gerune huddled on the dais. Julian freed himself from Otto's grasp and, fighting his chains, struggled to the dais. He grabbed the Princess, thrusting her beneath the platform's timbers.

"Who holds the key to your chains?" Otto called.

"There!" cried Julian. "There!" He pointed to a body, one of Ortog's yeomen. Otto reached the corpse, and tore the wallet at its belt. In moments he had Julian free.

"We must flee!" said Otto.

"Not without the Princess," said Julian.

Gerune looked at him wildly.

Atop the flaming, blackened dais, King Ortog stood alone, cursing, firing his pistol into the air...

# THE CAPTAIN

# JOHN NORMAN

WARNER BOOKS

A Time Warner Company

WARNER BOOKS EDITION

Questar is a registered trademark of Warner Books, Inc.

Cover illustration by Dorian Vallejo
Cover design by Don Puckey

Warner Books, Inc.
1271 Avenue of the Americas
New York, NY 10020

 A Time Warner Company

Printed in the United States of America

First Printing: September, 1992

10 9 8 7 6 5 4 3 2 1

This book is dedicated
to all who disapprove of censorship.

## · · · **PROLOGUE** · · ·

*"And then the ships departed, leaving behind them ashes."* —*The Annals.*

Again I have chosen to begin with an excerpt from the Annals. It is an excerpt not untypical of the dark and troubled times.

One who has lived in, or knows only, times of sheep will find it difficult to understand times of wolves.

In this account is continued a story, drawn from the dark and troubled times.

The dark and troubled times were times of wolves.

Again, it must be clearly kept in mind that I do not write to edify or instruct, nor to praise or blame, nor even, really, to explain, or understand. I am not sure, you see, what are the criteria for understanding, how I might, so to speak, know if I understood, or only thought I understood, and perhaps did not really understand. Who can understand himself, or others, truly? Surely, at least, it is hard for the heart, as for the eye, to look upon itself. It is always, so to speak, behind its own back. Too, perhaps, in the end, there is no understanding, no more for us than for the tree, or rock, only that we think that we understand, that we have that illusion, that natural, comforting illusion, much as sap might flow in the tree or molecules sleep in the rock.

In short, know, dear reader, whoever you may be, that you are loved, but know, too, that I strike no bargains with you. It is not my business to tell you what you want to hear, nor to reassure you *that the cosmos, and time and space, and substance, and right and wrong, if they exist, are tidy, safe, and cataloged upon your shelves. I do not know the measure of man, nor can I, unlike so many others, weigh his soul, and mark out the boundaries of his heart. I do not know what is best for him, nor if what is best for him is right or wrong, nor if right and wrong, in their thousands, are something that he has not yet decided, or something that was decided for him, long ago, by the movements of molecules in the primeval nebula. So it is not my business to assure you that the world is as you would like it to be. It is not I, you see, nor you, but the world that has the last word on such matters.*

*So let us, given these cautions, and reflections, reverencing reality, and expecting no more than it is willing to give, patient with mystery, resume our story. It takes place, as we noted, in the dark and troubled times, in a time of broad-winged vultures, and long-maned lions, of processions, of marches with arms, of dark ships, soft in the night, and fires, and ashes, in a strange and dreadful time, a turbulent time, one when life was harsher and more terrible, and perhaps more real than now. This is a time when men lived by their wits and strength, and cunning and skill, a time when marches were long, and weapons so sharp that, as it was said, they could draw blood from the wind. In this time there were men, and women, and other creatures, and it was a time of endings, and beginnings, of battles and cities, of harvests and burnings, of taverns and brothels, of long voyages and bustling markets, in many of which beauty had its price, and times, too, here and there, well worth remembering, today so far from mind, of fidelity, of discipline, and honor, and courage. Doubtless it was a dangerous and terrible time in which to live, that of endings and beginnings, and yet, interestingly enough, nowhere, in all the Annals, and contemporary documents, not in the letters, the heroic lays, the skaldic verses, the chronicles, the tracts, the myths, the tales, the saints' lives, the accounts of captains, the songs of chieftains and kings, the treatises, the sagas, the simplest commemorative inscriptions, nowhere that I can determine, do I find regrets expressed that one lived then. Nowhere, as far as I can determine, did anyone express a desire that they might have existed in another time.*

*How inexplicable is so simple a thing!*

*One wonders how such a thing may be.*

*In a time of sheep men may fail to notice that they are alive, or, at least, may take it muchly for granted, or not pay much attention to it, but, it seems, that is not the case in a time of wolves.*

*And the dark and troubled times were, as we have noted, such a time, a time of wolves.*

*In such a time, if nothing else, men and women were alive.*

**Note:**

Earlier, in a previous manuscript, we included certain commentaries and speculations having to do primarily with historiographical matters, which it would be inappropriate to reiterate here. At this point we will note only that the chronology of the accounts seems obscure. There are, of course, many difficulties in dealing with the problematicities of time. Similarly the multiplex labyrinths of space, it is occasionally speculated, perhaps idly, may enfold one another, or retrace their passages. It is possible, too, one supposes, that there are dimensions other than our own, and that the tiers of reality may exceed our horizons, which we take, naturally enough, like the rodent and insect, to constitute the termini of being. Perhaps there are parallel, or intersecting, universes, or dimensions. This possibility, absurd though it may be, suggests the possibility of points of connection with our own world, perhaps even "corridors" or "gates." Too, some speculate that the Telnarian world, in some obscure sense, may be our own world, and not another, that it lies somehow in our own past, or, perhaps, future. Perhaps it was once our world, and has grown apart. Perhaps we are branches on the same tree, and as we grow toward the stars, or doom, we can hear, from time to time, the rustle of one another's leaves in the darkness. But such speculations are doubtless absurd. Therefore we dismiss them. Lastly I might mention that we have, on the whole, followed the chronicler's, or chroniclers', if that should be the case, divisions of the manuscript.

# · · · CHAPTER 1 · · ·

"Remove her clothing," said the connoisseur.

"I see," said the connoisseur.

"She is not mine," said Julian, of the Aurelianii, speaking to the connoisseur. "I would like, as a favor, for a friend, as a surprise for him, to have her informed, enlightened."

"Trained?" asked the connoisseur.

"Well trained," said Julian.

"Exquisitely?"

"Surely."

"Until she becomes fully what she is, explicitly, manifestly, and can be nothing else?"

"Yes."

"One wonders," mused the connoisseur.

"It is my expectation," conjectured Julian, "that she might prove acceptable."

"That seems possible," said the connoisseur. "Is she alive?"

"I do not know," said Julian.

There was a sudden, soft, startled, involuntary, timid, shamed, helpless cry.

"Keep your hands at your sides," said the connoisseur.

There was an intake of breath. Then there was another small cry, suddenly, much like the first.

"She will moan well," said the connoisseur.

"Excellent," said Julian.

"Kneel, with your head to the floor," said the connoisseur. "She will require attention, and frequently," he said.

Julian looked down at her.

"I leave the matter then in your capable hands," said Julian. He then turned about and left."

# • • • CHAPTER 2 • • •

"Look!" cried a citizen.

Fellows about him laughed.

"It is a bumpkin from an ag world," cried the citizen.

"Where did you get those frocks!" cried another."

The giant raised his hand to his forehead, and, with the back of his hand, wiped away the rage of sweat. This was not, of course, Telnaria, the home world, but was a summer world.

Flies swarmed about his face.

*It was different in the cool, dark forests of his tribe, taken to be that of the Wolfungs. It was one of five related tribes, the others being the Darisi, the Basungs, the Haakons and the Otungs. The Otungs was the largest and fiercest of these five tribes. It was also considered the parent tribe of these five tribes. It had been muchly devastated, long ago, as had its brethren tribes, in wars with the empire. We may think, collectively, of these five tribes as constituting the nation. There were many such nations, composed of diverse tribes. This particular nation, in which the Wolfungs, the Otungs, and such, figure, was a nation not regarded, at that time, as one of great importance, particularly after its defeat in various wars. This particular nation was that of the Vandals. Few people, at that time, had heard of it. The etymology of the name has been elsewhere discussed. The expression 'nation' is here used advisedly, but not, I think, inappropriately. The expression 'folk' or 'people' would doubtless be more judicious but we are here dealing with political matters and in such a case it seems more apt, for our readers, to speak of "nations." Too, there is a tendency, perhaps now too ingrained to be ignored with impunity, to speak of "nations" in these matters. There are some differences, however, which are not unimportant. In particular, the relation a member of one of these tribes has to the tribe, or the people, or folk, or nation, is not to be understood as being identical to that of a citizen to his state, though there are doubtless similarities. The state, in a sense, is an artificial nation, a contrived nation, a legal construction, relying upon conventions acknowledged, and observed, a theoretically voluntary organization, though, to be sure, it may confront the citizen with all the practical irrefutability and implacable solidity of a given datum, a condition of being, a law of nature, a family or species. The relation of a citizen to a state is usually construed, at least in theory, as a contractual one, either implicitly or explicitly, as in uttering oaths of allegiance, and such. The relationship within the tribe, on the other hand, is not contractual, neither implicitly nor explicitly, no more than that of being brothers. One does not participate in a tribe, but one is of the tribe, much as one finds oneself, through traditions of blood, one of a family, or line. Tribes consist of clans, and clans of families, and thus one is speaking, here, when one speaks of tribes, of complicated and extensive networks of human relationships, and predominantly blood relationships, though in many cases of an extended and tenuous sense. The state rests upon law, and the tribe on blood. One cannot, in the ordinary course of things, cease to be a member of tribe, any more than one can cease to be the son of one's father. To be sure, certain caveats must be entered. For example, one may be accepted into a tribe, and then one is truly of the tribe; and one may be cast out of the tribe, and thus be no longer of the tribe; and one may repudiate the tribe, and thus remove oneself from it. Here, in such considerations, we find that the tribe bears analogies to, for example, the obtaining of citizenship, the loss of citizenship, the repudiation of citizenship, and such. The tribe is thus, in a sense, analogous to a biologically founded state. It is thus, actually, not simply biological, not simply a matter of blood, and, at the same time, it is more than an abstraction, a matrix of legalities, a creature of convention, profound or otherwise. There are, of course, many other differences, and many other commonalities, as well. It may be useful to mention some, as it may render more intelligible some portions of what follows. Custom is important in the tribe, and law in the state, though it is a matter of degree, for the state, too, has its customs, and some tribes, at least, have their laws, though usually the laws in such tribes are unwritten, and are the province of the law-sayers, who must, in many such tribes, memorize the law, and are responsible for reciting portions of it at gatherings, to keep it in living memory, usually a third of it at each annual gathering. Thus the men in such tribes will hear the law as a whole, from its sayers, once every three years. In many tribes, on the other hand, the court of law is the hut of the chieftain, and its statutes and codices are his whims. Better put, perhaps, in such tribes there is no law, but there is the will, the decision, of the chieftain. Citizens are often literate, while tribesmen are less often so. But, of course, there are illiterate citizens and literate tribesmen. Men who can read and write are often kept, like interpreters which, in a sense, they are, in tribes, to aid in the conduct of business, and in transactions with other communities. Although tribes are diverse, as are men, and hanis leopards, it is frequently the case that a distinction is drawn within the tribe between what we may think of as the aristocracy and the yeomen, so to speak, between the high families and the ordinary free men. In the empire, distinctions obtain between, similarly, the honestori and the humiliori, the higher, honored classes and the commonality. Within the honestori falls the patricians, which includes the senatorial class. These relationships are more volatile, and more subject to mobility, than those within the tribe. For example, one may ascend to the honestori by appointment or acceptance, an appointment or acceptance often consequent upon unusual service or merit, or, in some cases, it is rumored, consequent upon the provision of favors, moneys, and such. The coloni, or tenant farmers and laborers, fall, obviously, among the humiliori. So, too, do individuals bound to certain occupations or to the soil, whose numbers were increasing in recent times, due to the needs of the state to stabilize the population, primarily to assure a continuation of necessary services and, more importantly, a reliable, locatable tax base. Slaves need not be mentioned here, no more than cattle, and sheep, as they, too, are domestic animals, a form of livestock, some of which are quite lovely. There are many other differences, and similarities, between states and tribes, but it would be tedious, and impossible, to attempt to enumerate them in a genuinely useful manner, as the factors are numerous, and as states differ among themselves, as do tribes. A last remark or two will, however, be helpful. Some think of the tribe, or folk, or people, as having a certain mystical aura. Doubtless it does. But the reality here is doubtless far more profound than any trivially conceived mysticism could perceive, as it rests upon genetic profundities, whose origins lie in the immemorial past, long before*

*shambling creatures began to shape stones and scratch their
dreams on rocks. What may lend the tribe, or folk, or people, its
somewhat mystical air is that tribality has presumably been selected for, biologically, bonded groups, mutually supportive, and
such, tending to have a considerable advantage over more anar-
chic social aggregates. In war, for example, in times of fear and
danger, would one rather have at one's side a stranger or a
brother? We have spoken of the tribe as being rather like a
biologically founded state. It would be more accurate, perhaps, to
think of the state, or at least the successful state, as being rather
like an artificial tribe. Consider the attempts to induce, artificially,
a sense of tribality, of community, or brotherhood, among dispa-
rate individuals, the reliance on symbols, on conditioning, on
myth, and such, anything to increase and consolidate devotion to,
and loyalty toward, a given set of practices and institutions,
anything to increase social bonding. And then, of course, there are
the clever individuals who manage, after a time, to see what is
obvious, and then exultantly denounce such tribality altogether.
This is the shallow rationality, but not the deeper rationality. What
is not understood is that belonging, community, tribality, such
things, lie within the nature and needs of many men, and that to
mock these things, or to deny him these things, and, indeed, many
others which are as much a part of him as his backbone and heart,
is to deny him, to rob him, of a part of himself, without which he
cannot be whole or human. He who has no people, no unit, no
brethren, no tribe, so to speak, no loved ones, no family, what can
he be? One requires more to be a man than the ability to add and
subtract with rapidity. To the side of history, forgotten, lie the
bones of scoffers, and shallow mockers, together with those of the
groups to whose disintegration they dutifully and gladly contributed. What can one be without a unit, without a tribe, without a
people? Must one not then be more than man or less than man?
Surely such a one, one so alone, if contentedly so, must be either a
god, or beast. But there are other men, men alone, of course, and
many of them, men with no place, no state, no tribe, those who
have asked directions of gods, and failed to receive them, those
who have interrogated beasts, but could not obtain guidance. They
do not know who they are; they do not know if there is a place in
which they belong. They are not the scoffers, the mockers. They
are far from such lost, weak ones. They are strong ones, and some
are terrible ones. They are rather the far walkers, the wayfarers,
the searchers. It is not that they repudiate their brethren; rather, on*

*long roads, and in distant places, they search for them, But such reflections are gloomy. Let us leave them*

"Ho, behold the bumpkin!" cried a fellow, pointing to the giant.

The giant did not think it would need chains to hold the fellow. A cord would suffice, as it would with a woman.

The giant followed his companion through the streets.

Aromatic herbs, in this district, had been crushed and scattered on the stones. The emperor was now in residence, here, on this summer world, in one of the many summer palaces. Indeed, it was just that many-walled domicile, with its polychromatic, labyrinthine geodesics, which constituted the destination of the giant and his companion.

"Lout, boor!" called another fellow.

But they did not approach more closely. It was easy for them to be bold, at a distance, and, too, for the guards, a squad of nine, with rifles, who accompanied the giant and his companion through the streets. Perhaps they thought that the giant was a prisoner. But he was not such. Had that been wished, it might easily have been managed in other places, and at other times, on the first ship, for example, on which they had taken their leave from the Meeting World.

"Cur, clod!" cried a man.

The giant wondered how the fellow might stand up against an ax attack.

"It is not far now," said the giant's companion.

In this district, near the summer palace, no vehicular traffic, save for official vehicles, usually armored, was permitted. It would have been too easy to approach the walls, and the metal of the vehicles might have masked the metal of weapons, and the vehicle might have served as a launching weapon, or as the weapon itself.

The giant enjoyed walking, and movement, and running, as after bark deer in the forests, for sport. One could pursue the delicate beast for hours at a time, and then, at the end of the hunt, when they lay helpless, gasping on the leaves, lungs heaving, unable to move, eyes wild, one could kill them, or let them go. Sometimes one carried them back to the village, on one's shoulders, to pen them and see to it, later, that they were mated, thence to be released, pregnant, to the forests, later in soft glades to deliver wet, awkward fawns, destined in time to be the swiftest of the swift. The eggs of hunting birds, too, were sometimes stolen from nests, to be hatched by vardas in their coops, the hatchlings later to be trained to the wrist and thong. Many were the pastimes, and sports, of the forests. And high among them, one of the most pleasurable, was the mastery, and use, of female slaves. These, too, at the master's discretion, could be judiciously mated.

"Lout, peasant!"

His large frame had been cramped in the seat cubicles of the snakelike limousine which had brought them from the hostelry near the port to the *pomerium* of the sacred district, within which lay the summer palace.

"Soil worker! Peasant!"

The giant had indeed, at one time, been a peasant, a denizen of a small village, a *festung* village, the *festung* village of Sim Giadini. It is in the vicinity of the heights of Barrionuevo. This range is located on the world of Tangara. He did not understand why the work of the peasants, or the peasants themselves, should seem so scorned here, and by such a dirty, ragged swarm. Did they not eat? Did they not owe their lives, in a sense, to the labor of such as he once was? Were they so much better than they upon whose labor they depended? Did they think it easy to guide the plow, to turn heavy soil, to harrow and disk the fields, to judge seeds, to plant properly, in suitable times and places, to toil long hours, when one's back was nigh onto breaking, to resist a relentless sun, to hope for rain, which might not come, to be so hungry at times, to have to yield the tithes to the lofty *festung* of Sim Giadini, almost lost in the clouds of the heights?

"Get back!" cried his companion, gesturing toward one of the bolder of the unsolicited escort. But he did not care to touch him. "It is not that they believe you are a peasant," he said to the giant. "It is merely a term of abuse."

They continued on their way.

The peasant had not been born in the *festung* village. He did not know where he had been born.

He had left the village after killing a man, one named Gathron, who had been his best friend. He had broken a post over his back, and watched him die, at his feet. Gathron had attacked him, and Gathron had been his best friend. This was something which the giant often remembered, that one does not always know, really, who is one's friend and who is not. The squabble had been over a woman. That, too, had never been forgotten by the giant, that it had been because of a woman that the business had come about. He regarded women as dangerous, untrustworthy, and tantalizingly delicious. They were to him as another form of life, one excruciatingly desirable, one against whom one must always be on his guard, one which must be managed, controlled, and kept strictly in its place. The place of woman, such delicious, dangerous, precious, despicable, desirable creatures, was at the feet of man, rightless and powerless. This was the decree of nature. Free, out of nature, they will bite at you, and scratch at you, and diminish you, or destroy you, owned, within nature, on the other hand, deprived of power, no longer dangerous, they find themselves suddenly with a different vocation, that of, with trepidation, and zeal, in fear of their lives, devoting themselves eagerly to your service and delight. The answer to the riddle of woman, and the key to her happiness, is the chain and whip. She must never be allowed to forget whose hand it is that holds the leather over her.

"It is rather," said the friend, "that they see you are different, that you are clad differently, that you carry yourself differently, that you walk differently, that you look about yourself differently."

The giant nodded, and brushed away flies. They tended to move toward the eyes, which were moist, and sparkled. Sometimes they encircled the eyes of babies in their cradles, tilted there, peering within those flickering orbs, like restless, tiny, winged crusts.

The giant supposed that he did seem different. It is often that way with animals, he knew, that one which is different, the goat among sheep, the hawk among vardas, the lion among wolves, is marked out for abuse, to be bitten, or driven away. Such things were doubtless owing to the mysteries of being, to those cruel principles or laws without which life might never have emerged, amoral and hungry, from prehistoric colloidal films.

"Bumpkin!" cried another fellow.

"See the clothing!" cried another.

And so a strange beast, among other beasts, is viewed askance.

"Lout!" cried another.

"Who is your tailor, bumpkin?" called another.

His clothing, true, a rough tunic, of pelts, belted, with leggings, was not of the city, but fit rather for the forests of his world, affording its protection against wind, and cold, and brush, that between the meadows and the depths, and, with its mottled darknesses, like shadows, permitting him to stand unnoticed within five yards of the bark deer, that lovely, delicate sylvan ungulate. The pelts were those of the forest lion. Such came sometimes even to the edges of the fields, and, in the winter, softly, to the palings of the stockade itself. The giant had killed the animal himself, with a spear. He had gone out alone. This is not intended to elicit surprise. It was not that unusual. Indeed, in many tribes, a young man was not permitted to mate within the tribe unless he had given evidence of skill and courage, until he had demonstrated his worthiness or prowess to experienced older men, hunters and warriors. One way of accomplishing these things, or providing such evidence, was to slay such a beast, or, in daylight, an alerted foe. Sometimes the young man comes to the hut of the father, to sue for the hand of a daughter. "I hear a lion in the forest," says the father, if he approves of the young man, though there may be no such sound. The young man then rises gladly and leaves the hut. He does not return until he brings with him the pelt of such a beast. Thongs from the pelt will be used to bind the wrists of the daughter in the mating ceremony. The mating, you see, is understood as a binding of the woman, and it is done that she may understand her relationship to the male, as, in effect, that of a captive to her captor, that she is to please him, and such. As she is a free woman, her wrists are usually bound before her body. This is to honor her, and show her importance, for it is common to bind those of a slave behind her body. Upon the pelt, of course, the mating is later consummated. In such fashions, with many variations, with diverse tests, and such, do the Wolfungs, and many similar tribes, take care to supervise the breeding within the nation.

"Bumpkin!" cried the fellow, running at the side.

"Do not mind him," said Julian.

About the neck of the giant was hung a rude necklace, of the claws of the lion he had slain.

It was but one of many which had fallen to his spear.

"Boor, lout!"

"It is not just that you are different," said his companion. "They fear you, for they have heard of the troubles at the borders, the loss of stations, the incursions which have reportedly taken place, though denied officially."

"I am not of the cities," said the giant.

"I offered you silken robes, even a uniform of the guards," said his companion.

"It is hot," said the giant. He pulled at the laces of the tunic, opening it, baring his chest.

"Sherbets and ices will be served in the palace," said his companion.

"I do not like being without a weapon," said the giant.

"Only authorized personnel may carry such in these precincts," said his companion. "Too, do you think that small blade would protect against the blast of a rifle?"

"No," said the giant, thoughtfully. But he knew that men such as he, in places, men not so different from himself, had such weapons.

Let those of the empire consider that.

There was considerable obscurity having to do with the antecedents of the giant. Though he had been raised in a *festung* village, he did know that he was not of the village, only that, somehow, he had been brought there, as an infant. Neither he himself, nor his companion, knew his origins. His body, it might be noted, was quite unlike that which one tends to associate with the peasantry. That was of interest. It did not have the same heaviness, or dullness, or stolid massiveness that one tends to associate with those who, for generations, have grown congruent with the life and demands of the soil. Whereas the bodies of the peasants might be likened fancifully to rocks or trees, patient and weathered, his seemed, if one may fancy things so, more bestial, more feral, or leonine, enormous perhaps, but yet supple, agile, subtle, swift. It was capable of movement as sudden and unexpected as that of the vi-cat. Similarly his mind was quite unlike that of the typical denizen of a *festung* village. It was inquisitive and active, complex and subtle. It was not patient; it was not accepting, not unquestioning. It was the sort of mind which wonders where roads lead; the sort of mind not content with close horizons. Too, the emotional makeup of the giant had little in common with that of the peasants. It was high-strung, touchy, fiery. He was not patient. He was quick to anger, and, when angry, could become quite dangerous. Lastly, perhaps most interestingly, and most surprisingly for one raised in a *festung* village, he seemed to have a kinship with weapons, taking to them, and handling them, as naturally as the lion might make use of its teeth, the leopard of its claws, the hawk of its beak and talons. These things seemed in him a matter of instinct, or blood, rather than one of training. It was as though his heritage might have been, oddly enough, shaped by skills with such things, rather as the swifter and more terrible, the more agile and ferocious beasts, those most successful in their pursuits, their hunts and wars, survive, to master and rule, and to replicate themselves, thus transmitting, casually, thoughtlessly, in a moment's pleasure, such significant, terrifying genetic templates to succeeding generations. How is it that the duck can swim, that the bird can fly, and that some men can seize a wrist, or parry a blow, or instantly, exactly, without the least hesitation, strike? In any event, it does not seem that the giant was of peasant stock. His, it seems, was a darker, more terrible, blood.

"Soon, at the end of this street, then the plaza," said the companion of the giant.

To their right, as the group, consisting of the companion of the giant, the giant, the officer of the guard, and the guards, advanced down the street, it approached a pair of women, one dark, one fair, well-bangled, richly silked, with golden sandals, lounging against a wall.

"Handsome guardsmen!" called one of them, the fairer one.

"Recollect us!" called the other, enticingly.

The fairer one drew back her silks, a little, as the group approached, that an inviting flank might be glimpsed.

"Slaves?" asked the giant of his companion.

"Prostitutes," said his companion.

Then the group had passed the women.

"Then they will keep their own earnings?" said the giant.

"Yes," said his companion.

The giant had thought perhaps that they might have been slaves, put out by their masters, to be beaten if they did not bring back coins. But then, it was true, they were rather overdressed for slaves, and they were not collared. And slaves thusly put out might have a small coin box, metal and locked, chained about their neck, or ankle, into which their earnings, destined for the master, would be placed.

"They should be slaves," said the giant.

"Certainly," said his companion.

"Begone! Back to your pigs, peasant!" cried a fellow, growing bolder. It was he concerning whom the giant had wondered how he might stand up to an ax attack.

As they made their way through the streets the giant looked into various windows, where shutters might be open, or curtains spread. These windows were well above the street level, like most in this city, but one could form some conjecture of the riches of the compartments, from hangings and such. Here and there, too, a shelf might be espied, on which reposed vessels of silver and gold.

The world from which he had come but months before, and Tangara, on which he had been raised, where lay the *festung* village of Sim Giadini, at the foot of the heights of Barrionuevo, were poor in such things. This was a rich world, exceedingly rich it seemed to the giant, and it was only a summer world, not Telnaria itself.

And there must be many such cities, and worlds, within the empire.

"Hold," said the officer of the guard, lifting his hand, near a barrier. A guard station was there.

"Permission must be obtained, for weapons to be carried from this point to the edge of the plaza," said the giant's companion.

"Even those of our guard?"

"Yes."

"At the edge of the plaza?"

"We shall there be met by guards from the palace, to escort us farther."

A woman was to the right, near the wall of a whitewashed building.

Richly was she garbed, in embroidered *leel*. Wealthy then must be her station. No prostitute she.

The giant, with a glance, stripped her in his mind, removing the *leel*, cutting the straps of the undergarments, pulling them away. She was not then different from the other women. He would put them all on the same chain. He did not think that there would be much to choose between them, when each, in turn, ascended the slave block.

Such look well, he thought, carrying vessels, collared, naked, their hair not permitted binding, serving warriors at their feasts.

She spun away, angrily. She did not walk badly, he thought.

In a moment the officer of the guard had cleared the group for its progress.

It again moved down the street.

The giant looked back, and noted that the woman had stopped, and was standing there, angrily, her robes pulled closely about her, and was looking after them.

The most insistent, most insulting fellow, he who seemed the leader of the jeering, petty, pestiferous escort, he concerning whom the giant had conjectured of cords and axes, with others, one pressing closely behind him, competing with him for attention, inserted himself into even greater proximity. He was perhaps emboldened by the guards' seemingly straightforward attention, renewed now in the march, which ignored, or seemed to ignore, him and his fellows, Not so much as a rifle butt had been raised against him. Perhaps, he was now emboldened, too, by an aegis of citizenship, recently awarded universally on this world as a gift of the emperor, on his visit.

The apartments in this area, closer to the plaza, and to the palace, were even richer and more lavishly appointed than their only somewhat more distant predecessors.

The giant wondered what occurred in such apartments. Muchly were they different from the huts of the forest, many of mud and sticks.

The giant was not overly enamored of material possessions, saving as females slaves counted as such.

He was interested more, though he would not have said so at this time, in the riches of power.

He who rules those with wealth is richer by far, you see, than those he rules.

Yet the giant was not insensitive to the beauty of precious stones, nor that of rare, glittering metals, no more than to that of owned women.

In his way, thus, he was not insensitive to riches.

And he knew that many men, those deprived of them, were far more sensitive to them than he.

And they meant power.

Too, for some reason, it seemed there was some sort of odd prestige connected with them, as though those who possessed them thought themselves somehow superior to those who did not.

The giant did not like that.

"Lout!" cried the fellow, almost intruding himself among the guards.

"Do not mind him," said the companion of the giant.

The giant, seemingly not noticing, marked the fellow's position. It was casually done.

Riches cannot, in themselves, be a sign that one is superior, thought the giant, for it seems obvious that many who possess them are not superior.

"Bumpkin!" cried the man.

Do those of the empire regard themselves as superior to us because it is they, and not us, who possess such things?

"Lout, lout!"

Perhaps, thought the giant, wealth, the rule, riches, such things, should belong to those who are superior, but, if that is the case, then surely they should not belong to men such as these, running along, harrying us with their ridicule, shouting, carrying on like smug, arrogant, invulnerable rats, <u>thinking</u> themselves so safe within the walls of the empire. Perhaps, rather, riches belonged rightfully, if to anyone, to those who were truly superior, to the masters, to those who were strong enough to take them, and keep them, much as it was fit that the first meat at the great feast went to the greatest warrior, the greatest hero, at the long table?

"Lout! Lout!"

Even if riches did not betoken superiority, truly, there might be some point in removing them from those who thought they did, that such might thus be denied the pretext for their pretensions, that they might see themselves as they were, truly, rather like removing clothing from a woman, that she may then understand herself as what she is, among men.

"Lout, peasant!" cried the fellow.

The giant again brushed away flies.

"Lout!"

But it might be pleasant to own such things, and to give them away, thought the giant, with a lavish hand, as rings, fit for the wrist and arm, to cup companions.

Yes, thought the giant, there are reasons to want riches, many reasons.

"What are you thinking about?" asked his companion.

"Nothing," said the giant.

"You are impressed with the empire," conjectured his companion.

"Yes," said the giant.

The giant, you see, had seen much, even in his brief time on this small, mere summer world, much which had impressed him, and variously, the ships of the empire, her weapons, quite redoubtable, muchly to be feared; her riches, almost beyond his dreams; her citizenry, on the whole to be scorned, her women, many not without interest.

A shadow at his right darted toward him. In the instant of movement it had not been the most intrusive, vulgar fellow, but he who had been behind that fellow, at his shoulder, pressing in, competing for attention. It was he, the second man, rushing in, to outdo his compeer, who was suddenly lifted, croaking, eyes bulging, from the ground, his feet kicking wildly, his throat in the grasp of the giant. Instantly the tiny mob fell back. the hands of the suspended fellow pulled weakly at the hand of the giant.

"Do not kill him," said the giant's companion.

"Would you have dared to touch me?" asked the giant.

The kicking fellow, as he could, the hand on his throat like a vise, shook his head, negatively.

The giant then took two steps to the side and thrust the helpless prisoner of his grip into the stone of the wall. This was done with great force. He released the unconscious body. Hair was matted to the wall. A smear of blood on the wall, slowly placed there, traced the passage of the fellow to the stones of the street.

"Is he dead?" asked the officer of the guard.

"I did not choose to kill him," said the giant.

The head of the fellow, clearly, had the giant chosen, given his grip and his power, might have been broken against the wall, as one might have shattered an egg.

The guards looked on, in awe.

Some yards away now stood he who had been the leader of the small mob which had clung to them in the streets.

He stood there, white-faced.

"Do not kill him!" cried the companion of the giant.

The giant regarded the fellow. No, he did not think he would stand up well against the ax attack.

"No," cried the companion of the giant. *"Civilitas! Civilitas!"*

The ragged fellow turned about and fled.

The giant looked after him. He did not think the fellow could run far, or well. He thought he could be overtaken shortly, or, if one wished, pursued slowly, until he collapsed, panting, helpless, terrified, like the bark deer.

That might be amusing.

Then one could kill him.

"No, no! Do not kill him!" cried the companion of the giant. He, you see, knew the giant better than the others present. *"Civilitas!"*

But the giant did not pursue the running figure.

"What do you think would be his *wergeld*?" asked the giant of his companion, looking after the scurrying figure in the distance.

"In the empire there is no *wergeld*," said his companion.

"I do not think it would be much," said the giant.

*The concept of wergeld is one which is familiar in many societies. It is, in a sense, a man-price, and it serves, in its primitive fashion, paradoxically, on the whole, to reduce bloodshed and crime. One may not kill with impunity, you see, for one must be prepared to pay the man-price of a victim to his people, his family, his relatives. Wergeld differs from man to man, depending on such things as lineage, standing in the community and wealth. A yeoman, you see, would have a lesser wergeld than, say, a noble, one of high family, and so on. But if the noble were to slay a yeoman he would be expected to pay the* wergeld *apportioned to such a deed. The* wergeld *may be paid in coin, in animals, and so on.* Wergeld *tends not only to protect men, for they thus cannot be slain with impunity, but, even more importantly, it tends to prevent the lacerations and slaughters, sometimes devastating and well nigh interminable, disastrous to communities and families, and clans alike, which otherwise would be likely to accompany the blood feud. The matter, in theory, is done when the* wergeld *is paid. To be sure, some advantage here lies with the rich, who can best afford to pay* wergeld, *but even they, as is well known, are not likely to part lightly with their horses or sheep.*

"*Civilitas,*" said the companion of the giant, gently.

"Ah, *civilitas,*" said the giant.

*Was it not* civilitas *which made the empire truly the empire? Was this not the true gift of the empire to the galaxies, that which, when all was said and done, formed the true justification of its existence, that which was most precious in it, and of it. Did this not, this shining thing,* civilitas, *exceed the legions and the bureaucracy, the ships, the camps, the armament; did it not exceed and redeem the imperialism and the greed, the ferocity, the incandescent worlds, the exploitation and the cruelty; that is the meaning and glory of the empire,* civilitas, *had taught Brother Benjamin, who, to be sure, was no champion of the empire. Understand by this term* 'civilitas' *more than it can be said to mean, for there is more within it than can be said of it. It is one of those terms, like* 'friend' *or* 'love', *which can never be adequately defined. But understand in it, in part, at least, the unity of the highest of those hopes hinted at by words such as balance, order, proportion, harmony, law, indeed, civilization itself. It can be thought of, at least in part, as what can divide peace from war, justice from fraud, law from license, enlightenment from ignorance, civilization from barbarism. It is an ideal. It would perish.*

The giant looked about himself. The fellow who had been the leader of, or foremost in, the tiny mob which had accompanied them in the streets, had now disappeared, having beaten his rapid retreat away. His fellows, some ten or twelve others, hung back. He did not think they would further follow. One of their number, as we have noted, lay at the foot of a stone wall, unconscious. He lay beneath a crooked smear of blood, which he had painted with his own body, with the back of his head, on the surface of the wall.

The giant noticed, nearby, the woman, she in embroidered *leel,* whom he had seen earlier. She had apparently turned about and, angrily, had followed the group, for what reason he knew not.

Again their eyes met.

"Lout!" she hissed at him.

Ah, he thought, she is angry that I regarded her, at the barrier, at the guard station.

She looked about herself, contemptuously, at the fellows about her. "Cowards! *Filchen!*" she scorned them. *It has been our usual practice in this narrative to use familiar expressions for resembling life forms, or, perhaps better, life forms occupying similar ecological niches or being employed for similar purposes as life forms with which the reader may be presumed to be familiar; for example, we speak, unhesitantly, of cattle, of sheep, and such beasts, but it would be useful for the reader to understand that the animals so referred to would, in most cases, not count as the cattle, the sheep, and such with which he is more likely to be familiar. The primary justification for this practice is its utility in avoiding a distractive multiplication of nomenclatures and a prolix delineation, presumably not in the best interests of the narrative, and certainly not required for its general intelligibility, of specific and generic differences among dozen of types of creatures, many uniquely indigenous to their own world, though, to be sure, also, many of which may now be found, thanks to interstellar transportation, authorized or not, intended or unintended, understood or inadvertent, on many worlds. Occasionally we do use particular names for these creatures, particularly when there seems some point in doing so. The filch, for example, is a furtive, small, gnawing, rather rodentlike animal. We have not spoken of it as a rat, or mouse, however, because in alternate generations it is oviparous. When we do speak of rats, or mice, for example, as we feel free to do, those terms are used of animals which, on the whole, would be more biologically analogous, or at least somewhat more so, to the "rats" and "mice," and such with which the reader is presumed to be familiar. The uniformity of viable habitats, given planet-star relations, distances and such of diverse types, and the principles of convergent evolution would seem to be, in such cases, relevant considerations. In such matters, we beg the reader's indulgence.*

"*Filchen,*" she cried to the citizens about her. "*Filchen!*"

She then looked boldly at the giant.

"Barbarian!" she said.

That was the first time that that expression had been used of him, in the streets.

To be sure it was doubtless because of his appearance, the manner in which he was clad, and perhaps, too, the manner in which he carried himself, so unapologetically, so unregenerately proudly, that he had been so pursued in the streets, and so belittled.

"Let us be on our way," said the companion of the giant.

"Wait," said the giant.

Why had the woman followed the small company, he wondered.

He took a step toward the woman, not to threaten her, but merely to approach her.

She shrank back, but then stood her ground.

The tiny group about her, the fellows on which she had heaped her scorn, fled back.

It was almost as a swarm of flies might have withdrawn from the movement of a hand.

He did lift his hand, but to brush away flies.

He took another step toward her, curious.

"I am not afraid of you!" she said.

He stood still, looking at her.

Then a small, supercilious smile played about her lips, one of amusement, of contempt.

He realized that she counted upon her sex to protect her, her station, which seemed high, the guards perhaps, his companion perhaps.

Boldly she stood her ground.

"Barbarian," she hissed.

He said nothing.

She had followed the group. He wondered, why. What had motivated her? Was it hatred, was it a desire to prove to herself that she was not afraid of him, was it to revenge herself for having been made the subject, willing or not, of a man's glance, was it curiosity, was it fascination, or was it all these, perhaps, and something deeper, far deeper, which she herself could only dimly sense, but which moved her with a powerful force, one she could not resist, and which, in her heart, she did not desire to resist?

"You are a handsome fellow," she said, demeaningly. "Doubtless you turn the heads of the simple village maids."

He did not tell her that it was not unknown for there to be women in the villages not too unlike herself, women who had once been citizens of the empire, who lived in terror of the free women in the villages, and their switches and sticks.

"Lace your tunic," she said.

His broad chest was muchly bared, as he had undone much of the lacing.

He then approached her, to where she stood within his reach. She trembled, visibly, but did not withdraw.

Then she drew herself up, arrogantly. "I denounce you as an ape, and a barbarian," she said.

"You do not dare to strike me," she said.

His hand lashed out, cuffing her, sending her turning to the wall.

At the wall, half turned, she regarded him, disbelievingly, a trace of blood at her lip.

She looked wildly at the guards.

"No!" said the companion of the giant to the guards, sharply. "He is a guest of the empire!"

The giant then went to the women and pulled her out from the wall.

He stood her, trembling, before him.

"It is hot," he said.

He then, with two hands, as she cried out, and gasped, and as utterances of surprise, or protest, emanated from the guards, who were restrained by the companion of the giant, tore open, and down, to her waist, the garments of the woman.

It is thus, on some worlds, in the most genteel of markets, that slaves are exhibited, stripped merely to the hips. Usually, of course, the woman is exhibited stark naked, save perhaps for collars or bonds, that the buyers may see, fully, and with perfection, what it is that they are buying.

He then, by her wrists, holding one in each hand, forced her down, down on her knees, before him.

He looked down upon her.

Women might have some worth, he thought, as slaves.

Then he released her.

She pulled her garments up, closely about her, holding them in place.

She remained before him, fearing to rise.

"Perhaps we shall someday meet again," he said to her, "amidst the smell of smoke, I with a rope in my hand."

"You are not a gentleman," she said.

"Nor would you be a lady, naked and on a rope," he said.

"You are a barbarian!" she whispered.

"Yes," he said. "I am a barbarian."

He then turned about and left her, where she knelt, clutching her clothing about her, on the street.

In a moment the giant and his companion had come to the edge of the vast plaza, within which, in its center, more than five hundred yards away, like a jewel, ensconced in more than a dozen walls, lay the palace.

At the edge of the plaza, after the private exchange of signs and countersigns, and a brief ceremony, involving salutes and drill, escorts were exchanged, and the officer of the guard, with his men, returned the way they had come, and the giant and his companion, now in the company of a contingent of the palace guard, prepared to approach the palace.

The giant looked back up the street. The men who had followed them no longer followed, but stood there, remaining at a distance. It was not that they could not have followed onto the plaza, for they were not armed, and civilians were allowed on its delightful expanse, and there were several upon it now, but that they chose not to follow. The sport, perhaps, seemed no longer so inviting. The giant could see their companion, whom he had thrust, not gently, against the wall. He still lay crumpled at the foot of the wall, senseless, in his own blood. Rather near them, but not with them, was the woman. She was now standing, still clutching her *leel* about her. She was looking after them, after the giant, and his companion.

There was a fresh wind that, unobstructed by buildings, swept across the plaza.

"I like it better here," said the giant.

"Oh?" said his companion.

"It does not smell so much here," said the giant.

"It is the wind," said his companion.

"It does not smell so much here," said the giant, again, amused.

"No," said his companion.

Surely this must be an allusion to the efficacy of the aromatic herbs, crushed, strewn underfoot, renewed daily in this district, the emperor in residence, as we have remarked. Such muchly covered the smell of garbage, and offal, which was considerably more obtrusive elsewhere in the small city.

"Nor are the flies so bad here," said the giant.

"Ah," said his companion.

"But the woman did not smell," said the giant.

"No," said his companion.

"But it would be otherwise," speculated the giant, "if she were to be naked, and knee-deep in dung, her hair bound up high on her head, fearing the whip of overseers, cleaning stables."

"Doubtless," said his companion.

"But she could be soaked, and then scrubbed clean, and perfumed afterwards," said the giant.

"Surely," said his companion.

"I think she would soon beg the service of the hut, rather than that of the stables," said the giant.

"I do not doubt it," said his companion.

The giant looked back.

"They will not bother us further," said the companion. "It is nearly time for the afternoon dole."

"I no longer see her," said the giant.

"Forget her," said his companion.

"She was well curved," said the giant.

"Yes," said his companion.

In time the giant would breed slaves, choosing the best, from one point of view or another, for replication.

There were some fountains here and there in the plaza, and, also, here and there, some statues of gods, the old gods, revered, tutelary deities of the empire, but nothing which would afford much cover.

"Sir," said the new officer of the guard, to the companion of the giant.

"Proceed," said the companion of the giant.

The group then began to make its way across the plaza toward the palace.

*The old pantheons were complex, and diverse on the many worlds, and even within the empire, from world to world, they often varied considerably. The general policy of the empire, else-where discussed, was one of toleration, not only for the many gods in its own pantheons and their devotees, but for those of other peoples, and species, as well. The theory of the empire seemed to be muchly to the effect that, as there were many worlds, and peoples, and species, so, too, it was likely that there were many gods. To be sure, there might be more or less powerful gods, and perhaps even a most powerful god, and wars among gods, and so on. The empire did, however, occasionally, and particularly when it became hard-pressed, or alarmed, insist on the right of reassur-ing itself of the allegiance of its subjects, and the gesture, or symbol, of allegiance commonly took the form of a sacrifice, usually of a token nature, such as a flower, a sprig of laurel, a pinch of incense, such things, on an altar, often one devoted to the genius, or spirit, of the empire. It was not clear, of course, that the genius, or spirit, of the empire was a god, at all. This sacrifice was normally found acceptable, and unobjectionable, by most of the empire's subjects, spread over galaxies, except occasionally by the members of minor, deviant sects, whose unwillingness to perform the ceremony was commonly winked at.*

"It is not far now," said the companion of the giant.

The purple water of a perfumed fountain spumed upward, falling back in a shower of amethysts, forming tiny crowns as they struck the water.

*As the giant and his companion, in the company of their escort, make their way across the plaza, and before they reach the first gate, in the outer wall, it may not be amiss to apprise the reader, although confessedly in the most inadequate fashion, of something of the nature of the pantheon of the empire. In it we discover various gods, such as Orak, the king; Umba, his consort; the messenger god, Foebus; Andrak, artisan and builder of ships; Kragon, hawk-winged god of wisdom and war; and the much-coveted Dira, goddess of slave girls. In the myths she had belonged, at one time or another, to various of the gods, who won her, or to whom she was given or sold. She is usually represented as being the property of Orak, the king. She is hated by Umba, the consort of the king, and by other goddesses as well. She is commonly represented as kneeling, or dancing, or humbly serving. In representations she is often seen at the feet of other gods. She is commonly represented as collared, or chained. She serves also as a goddess of love and beauty.*

Our small company was now quite close to the main gate in the outermost wall, one of the more than twelve surrounding the palace.

Citizens fell back before the group, and many looked on, with some curiosity, or interest, having noted the barbarian. They saw only of course a fellow clad in skins, large, formidable in appearance, broad-shouldered, narrow-waisted, long-armed, large-headed, with keen eyes, and light hair, one who walked not like one from the empire, but rather as one from beyond its perimeters, one from another reality, one, curious and observant, feral and leonine, from farther, stranger, harsher worlds. We do not blame them, of course, nor hold them accountable. There was no reason then, you see, why anyone should have marked anything unusual or portentous in this particular barbarian. Surely he was no different from countless others. Even we, had we seen him then, even we, we would not have marked him, we would not have known him, we, no more than the others, would not have known who it was we saw. No one, you see, knew him then.

At the small door, in the larger outer gate, the party halted.

"It will be a moment," said the officer of the palace escort, entering the small door.

"Ho," said one of the guards.

The giant looked down, to his right, as he waited. There, to his surprise, holding her embroidered *leel* about her, that it not, as torn, fall from her, knelt the woman from the street. She was kneeling, tears in her eyes, at the thigh of the barbarian. She looked up at him, timidly, fearfully. The guards looked on, puzzled.

"Get up, woman," said the companion of the giant, irritably. "You are a citizen of the empire!"

But she did not rise. Rather, she remained as she was, clutching the *leel* about her, almost as in terror. As the giant had turned, to regard her, she was now, fully, at his feet, kneeling before him.

"I do not need the whip, to obey," she said.

The giant shrugged. The use of the whip, whether needed or not, was at the discretion of the master.

She looked to the side, not daring to meet his eyes.

He did not command her to open her robes.

"Whom shall I announce?" asked an attendant, returning with the officer of the palace escort.

This question irritated the companion of the giant.

The attendant, a herald of sorts, looked at the barbarian.

"I am Otto," he said, "chieftain of the Wolfungs."

"I," said his companion, irritatedly, "am Julian, of the Aurelianii," and then he added, with some irony, and bitter pointedness, "kin to the emperor."

"Please enter, noble sirs," said the herald, politely.

The giant and his companion then entered the first gate.

Already several cameras, monitored from within the walls, had recorded their presence, even from the time they had reached the outer edge of the plaza. This form of surveillance was continued, by relays of similar devices, visual and aural, within.

After they had entered the woman remained kneeling beside the gate, for some time.

"Begone!" finally said a guard.

She then rose, obediently, and hurried away, until, in the vicinity of one of the fountains, she stopped, and once again knelt, watching the gate.

"I have never prayed to you before, Dira," she whispered, "but I do now, for you are now my goddess and I am now your devotee. Give me your grace, dear Dira, that I may serve him well!"

## • • • CHAPTER 3 • • •

The adz is not an ax, though it bears resemblances to that device. Perhaps you are familiar with it. The large, flattish, curved blade is fixed crosswise to the handle, rather like that of a hoe, except that the instrument is not intended for use with the soil, nor is it as delicate as the hoe. A heavy, broad ringlike socket, one with the blade, contains the handle. The typical function of the device is to shape and trim wood, fashioning, for example, heavy beams and planks. It may also, of course, gouge and slice stumps, split kindling, and such. Whereas small adzes may be used by carvers, with chisels and knives and other instruments, in decorative work, as on the jambs of doors and gates, on high-seat pillars, on the figureheads and sternposts of river craft, such as ply the routes between fortified trading towns, and such, it is the larger adz that we are concerned with here. Its blade is better than a foot in length, and the handle is some four feet in length. It can be wielded efficiently only by a very strong man, or by a creature of some comparable or greater strength. It has a place in the traditions of numerous peoples, in particular, naturally, those of the forest. The ax and the adz, as the spear, and, later, the sword, are, in a sense, symbols of those peoples. Very briefly, this may be accounted for. Long ago, in the unnumbered times, long before calendars, long before even the rock markings, so long ago that one has now lost track not only of the moons, and the seasons, but the years, and the cycles, marked by the planting of a sacred oak, once every thousand years, the forest peoples were hunters and herdsmen. It was only later that they became farmers, as well. The typical settlement consisted of a cluster of huts, sometimes surrounded by a palisade, surrounded by a common grazing ground, in a clearing in the forest, the animals taken out in the morning and watched, and brought back, within the palisade, in the evening. As population increased, that of the villagers, and their animals, more land was needed, and so the forest was encroached upon. This pattern tended to be continued, and hastened, when agriculture, to be sure, of a primitive sort, was added to the economic repertoire of the peoples. One commonly cleared land for farming by burning off trees and brush, a practice in consequence of which the soil was incidentally enriched with wood ash. In some years, however, the rains would drain away the enriching minerals and the land would no longer produce its initial yields, at which time the peoples, as land was plentiful, and the forests seemed endless, would migrate, a pattern which was repeated again and again. Even in the days of mere hunting and herding, as hunters ranged further, and the commons must be larger to support more animals, the men of one village would tend to encounter those of others. These encounters were not always of a peaceful nature. Such encounters became more frequent with the development of agriculture, and the attendant regular movements, or migrations, of villagers. The village existence, with its isolation and precariousness, tended to develop both a sense of community within the village and a suspicion of strangers, and others, outside the village. It may be helpful, too, to understand that the practice of hunting was never abandoned by these peoples. Hunting, too, whether conceived of as a mere economic activity analogous to food gathering, which is not to understand, truly, the thrill of the chase, the ambush, the kill, or as a mere sport, which, too, tends to obscure, or trivialize, its darker, more profound appeals, provides training in certain skills which are not unallied to those of war, for example, the tracking, the stalking, patience, deception, pursuit, the kill, and such. One might think of war as a kind of hunt, doubtless the most dangerous, and the hunt as a kind of war, the least dangerous, the most innocent, of wars. Many times, of course, as villages grew crowded, portions of villages, only, would migrate. The village would put out a colony, so to speak. These colonies, with land and game, would flourish. Linguistic and cultural ties would tend to exist, at least latently, among these related groups. Herein, it is speculated, one finds the origin of tribes, groups of related families, or clans. Naturally one tribe, or group of tribes, so to speak, might encounter others, say, of different origins, and competition of territory and resources might ensure, with not unpredictable consequences. Those tribes which were the strongest, the fiercest, the most skilled, the least merciful, tended to be victorious in such rivalries, supplanting their foes, destroying them, driving them away, enslaving them, such things. Some of these tribes, those living near seas, or inlets, or rivers, or whose wanderings brought them to such places, and learning of the existence of different forms of folks, not all of the forests, added trading, and, of course, piracy, or raiding, to their other pursuits. Indeed, whether a vessel was a trader or a raider would often depend on the nature, and strength, of what they encountered in their farings abroad. I mention these things in order to shed more light on the nature of the forest peoples, and perhaps similar peoples. For example, the Alemanni, or, as the empire will have it, the Aatii, and the Vandals, were both forest peoples, and, because of common origins and challenges, were not too much unlike, basically, despite their terrible enmity, which had lasted for generations, until the substantial pacification, or near destruction, of the Vandals by forces of the empire. All this has to do, actually, with the adz, a particular adz which we shall encounter later, on what we shall speak of as the Meeting World. Even though the Alemanni, that nation, so to speak, and her composite tribes, such as the Drisriaks, now possessed, to some extent, weaponry, and devices, and ships, which permitted them to at least harry, if not threaten, the empire, they still retained, as some peoples, do, a sense of tradition, and certain practices, the origins of which have been lost in the mists of time, antedating even a thousand of the thousand-year-old oaks. The adz, like the ax, and the spear, and the sword, was a part of this tradition, and these practices. The particular adz we have in mind lay now in a leather case on the flagship of the fleet of Abrogastes, the Far-Grasper, king of the Drisriaks, the largest and most fierce of the tribes of the Alemanni nation. In the same compartment, near the adz, on a shallow bronze plate, and covered with a purple cloth, was a heavy, sturdy, muchly scarred, peeled stump, one which had been brought from the home world of the Alemanni.

# · · · CHAPTER 4 · · ·

"Call to the attention of the emperor," snapped Julian, turning about, angrily, in the antechamber, addressing a servitor, bearing sherbets, "that his cousin, Julian, of the Aurelianii, and Otto, first among the Wolfungs, await their audience."

"Sherbets, milords," said the servitor, placing two bowls on the marble table in the room, that between two couches. Elsewhere in the room were curule chairs.

Julian was on his feet, as he had been, after the first hour, striding the length of the room.

Otto, whom we have hitherto spoken of as the giant, who was chieftain of the Wolfungs, a minor tribe of the Vandals, sat, cross-legged, to one side, his back to the wall, facing the door.

He did not wish to sit upon the curule chairs. It was not that he could not sit upon such devices, or found them unfamiliar, or uncomfortable, for he had known such on Terennia, and on Tangara, and similar things on the ship. Indeed, he had stools, benches, and a throne, or high seat, of sorts, of crude wood, in the main village of the Wolfungs, which village contained the hut of the chieftain, his hut, larger than the other huts. The reason he did not wish to sit upon the curule chairs was because, lifting the corner of the small, silken rugs upon which they sat, he had detected a fine line in the floor which, subsequently traced, suggested an opening, marking a section of the floor through which, if released, a catch undone, a bolt drawn, the chair might descend.

"There are doubtless various panels in the room" had said Julian, irritably, "through which one might exit, if one were knowledgeable, eluding pursuers, avoiding unwanted meetings, through which guards might enter, surprising occupants, making arrests, and such. The traps beneath those chairs may even be benign, leading to stairwells from the room, or giving entry to it. Move the chairs, if you wish."

"Why are you angry?" had asked Otto.

"I do not care to be kept waiting," said Julian. He was in dress uniform, that of an ensign in the imperial navy, white, with gold braid, but, too, with three purple cords at the left shoulder, indicating the loftiness of his birth, his closeness to the imperial family itself.

"I am sorry, milord," said the servitor.

This response had infuriated Julian.

"There is nothing untoward, nor unexpected in this," said Julian.

"No, milord."

"The audience has been long arranged," said Julian.

"Yes, milord."

"You understand clearly who I am, who we are."

"I am sure the emperor will see you shortly," said the servitor.

"Convey my displeasure to the arbiter of protocol," said Julian.

The face of the servitor went white. Otto gathered that the arbiter of protocol must be a powerful man.

"Convey it," said Julian.

"I shall commend the matter to the attention of my superior," said the servitor.

"Go," said Julian.

"Yes, milord."

Julian, though one of the wealthiest men in the empire, though a member of the patricians, of the senatorial class, though kin to the imperial family itself, had, following a tradition of forebears of the Aurelianii, of service to the empire, entered the imperial navy. He had qualified for a commission, and trained, as though he might have been no more than another ambitious scion of the lower *honestori*. He was a gifted, dedicated officer. He performed his duties conscientiously. He accorded every due respect to his military superiors. Had he been unknown he would doubtless have been accounted, with little thought given to the matter, an excellent officer, and would have been innocently and deservedly popular with both subordinates and superiors alike, fair, if severe, with the former, expecting them to meet standards scarcely less exacting than those he set himself, and cooperative and dutiful in his relations with the latter. On the other hand, he was not unknown. He was of the Aurelianii. Accordingly men sought to enter his command, hoping to advance themselves in the service, and higher officers must view him with the keenest ambivalence. Though he was young and less experienced, his blood was among the highest and noblest in the empire, and his station was one to which one might not hope to attain save perhaps through royal marriage or through a special imperial appointment to the rank of patrician, doubtless conjoined with the gift of an auspicious post, or command, say, that of prefect, or treasurer, or master of the imperial police, or palace guard, or master of ships, master of the mobile forces, master of the borders, master of the horse, such things. One must treat such a subordinate with care. Perhaps, if one is politically astute, one may advance him in such a way as to advance oneself as well. And how uncertain a thing to have him in one's command, such an opportunity, yet such a danger, as well. Was it not, in a sense, like being under scrutiny, like being in the capital itself?

The servitor then withdrew from the antechamber.

"You can move the chair," had said Julian

"Then they might suspect I had discovered the door beneath the chair," had said Otto.

"They already know," said Julian.

Otto had regard him, puzzled.

"You remember the screens on the ship?" asked Julian.

"Yes," said Otto. He had eagerly learned all he could on the ship which had brought them to the summer world.

Julian had then pointed to an aperture in the wall, high, near the ceiling.

It was then that Otto had risen and gone to sit, cross-legged, to one side. It was then unlikely that he could be seen from the vantage of the aperture.

It had been shortly thereafter that the servitor had entered with sherbets, and had looked quickly about the room.

He had seen Otto in his place.

Otto did not doubt but what he had entered to ascertain his position in the room.

Shortly after they had been ushered into the room, better than two hours ago, the servitor had appeared, offering them a choice between the ices and sherbets.

"Inform the emperor we await his pleasure," had said Julian, in fury. He had been already deeply angered, from what he interpreted as the first insult, that of the outer gate, when the herald had inquired as to the identities of those he should announce. The audience had been prearranged. Was he not anticipated? Was he not recognized? Did they not know who he was? Then, what Julian took as a second insult, he had not been immediately introduced, warmly welcomed, into the presence of his kinsman, the emperor. Rather, he had been ushered into this room, to wait, as though he might be no more than some petitioner, or sycophant, some provincial magistrate, from some minor world, some ambassador from some unimportant client world, such things.

Flavored ices, not sherbets had been brought.

The ices, in their bowls of translucent quartz, perhaps from the mines of Jaria, brought then in all likelihood through the pass, or tunnel, of Aureus, had melted, now forming soft, foamlike pools of yellow and purple.

They had not been touched by either Julian or Otto.

The sherbets were now on the table, in their shallow silver bowls, with matching silver *teetos*, which is perhaps best translated as 'spoons'. They are, however, actually narrow, hollow, rodlike utensils with a small, concave, rather spatulate termination. The concave spatulate termination justifies us, I would think, in speaking of the utensil as a spoon. I should add, however, that it may also be used to draw fluids upward into the mouth, and, in this sense, can function as a straw.

Julian left the sherbets where they had been placed. He did not touch them, no more than the ices. He felt, perhaps, that the acceptance of even these trivial hospitalities might somehow seem to indicate an accommodation to his inconvenience, as though he might then seem to find it at least marginally acceptable. Otto, although he was commonly curious about many matters, did not, either, sample the ices or the sherbets. There had been openings beneath the chairs.

He recalled how the servitor, in his second visit to the room, bringing, surprisingly, unrequested, the sherbets, had looked about, and then, relievedly, marked his position. His guess had been correct then, it seemed, that he had not been visible from the aperture, not in that location.

Julian continued to pace the room.

Otto, the giant, did not betray impatience.

Yet some have lamented that greater courtesy was not shown in this matter by the imperial court, that the audience was not more promptly granted.

Otto watched a fly alight on the rim of one of the bowls of sherbet. There were flies here, too, then, even within the palace.

Then there came another fly, and another.

So there are flies in the palace, thought Otto. They were there, crawling there, like raisins, on the rim of a silver bowl, a vessel worth perhaps a rifle, even on a world where such were scarce, the possession of which could mean a magistracy. He wondered if the flies comprehended the perils of their delicious arctic? Doubtless some would become lost, perhaps even die, freezing, ensnared in the viscous trove.

Otto considered the couches about the table. On reclined on them while eating. That was something one had to learn to do, to eat in such a position. Was it so comfortable, so luxurious, so civilized, really, he wondered. They had not had such arrangements on the *Alaria,* he recalled. To be sure, worlds differ, customs differ, and one can get fewer people at a table with such an arrangement.

But Otto did not think he would care to get used to such an arrangement. It is difficult to rise quickly from such a couch. to unsheath a weapon, to defend oneself. Better the stool or bench, which could be kicked back, from which one could spring to one's feet.

Julian sat down, on one of the curule chairs.

He did not move it.

That is dangerous, my friend, thought Otto.

Perhaps it is always dangerous to sit in such chairs, on the high seats, thought Otto.

But men will sit upon them, and kill to do so. Do not all thrones rest on no more than a latch, or bolt, which might, perhaps when one expects it least, be withdrawn?

Otto's thoughts, as he waited, drifted back to the Meeting World, and a time when Julian, in virtue of complex circumstances, had been little more than his prisoner.

## · · · CHAPTER 5 · · ·

"Do not cry out, or betray emotion," had said Otto to his companion, who was at his heel, in a short, ragged tunic, much as might have been a slave. But on his body there was no sign of bondage, nor had he been branded, that the mark on his body might bespeak one subject, as much as a slave girl, to exchange, to barter, to gifting and pricing.

"I will not," said Julian.

They were flanked by Ortungs.

An Ortung ship, one which still bore the scars of the encounter with the *Alaria*, had come to orbit over Varna, which was the world to which two life rafts, or escape capsules, caught in similar gravitational geodesics, had drifted, that following their departure from the *Alaria*. In the first capsule had been a gladiator, one who had been carefully trained in the school of Pulendius on Terennia, he, and a prize won in contest, a dark-haired girl, named Janina, who need not significantly concern us, as she was slave. In the second capsule had been one man and three women. The three women were as follows, a wealthy, lovely, highly intelligent, mature woman, and two younger women, a slender, attractive blonde and an exquisitely figured, delicately and sensitively featured brunette, the sort made for chains, and surely one beautiful enough to bring a good price in almost any market. The man had been a young naval officer, an ensign in the imperial navy.

It was a muddy track they followed, as there had been a rain that morning.

The landing craft, or lighter, as one might think of it, a small vessel suitable for comings and goings, for negotiating the shallows of space, from the Ortung ship, had come down gently, not far away, in a circular, rain-soaked meadow, small, delicate animals fleeing beneath its descending shadow and heat. From it several individuals had disembarked, the broad-bladed, green, wet grass, fragrant, edged with rain, soon cutting at their ankles, muchly different from the grass about the craft, farther out oddly dried, despite the invading dampness surging back into the meadow, and close in, even yards from the twelve thrust chambers, blackened and burned. Among those disembarking were Otto and Julian. They had come from Varna. The entire matter had to do with a challenge.

"There seems no reason for your counsel," remarked Julian.

"We have not yet come to the grove," said Otto.

"I do not understand," said Julian.

"The Ortungs have borrowed certain practices from the Timbri," said Otto.

In this area, the path was, now, less muddy, and, to some extent, graveled. Clearly this was a path now, a real path, or walk, one bearing some signs of attention, no longer a simple track, such as might have been consequent on the passage of some party in single file, their numbers obscured, deliberately perhaps, by the linearity of their progression. The soles of their sandals, as they followed the path, pressed, here and there, small stones deeper into the soft soil. Tiny alkaline trickles of water, whitish, made their way, sometimes haltingly, in no more than a sudden succession of intermittent drops, backward, behind the walkers, down the slope, among the tiny, awash, dislodged stones.

*The Vandalii or Vandal nation, consisting of its five tribes, the smallest and least auspicious among them the Wolfungs, were not untypical of barbarian peoples. Such tended, almost as a matter of habit, and surely of custom, to enjoy uneasy, if not actually hostile, relations with their neighbors, wherever they might be found, which was often at hand, given the frequent movements, the periodic migrations, of such folk. These enmities tended to be long-lasting, and the hostilities involved, though intermittent, as one group might be forced to give way to another, tended to be pursued with vigor and cruelty. The surviving, successful tribes, particularly as lands, and worlds, became more scarce, tended, through culture, breeding, and tradition, through trials and raids, and the lessons of songs and deeds, to become stronger, prouder, less patient, quicker to anger, more cruel and more warlike, as the less adept, gentler, weaker, more pacifistic tribes, in accordance with the decrees of reality, recorded in the judgments of history, tended to be ruthlessly supplanted, destroyed, enslaved, made tributary, such things. In the light of such considerations, and in order that a fuller understanding of these matters may be conveyed, we mention that the Alemanni, of which the Drisriaks were a tribe, and the Ortungs a secessionist tribe, were a particularly successful people. It should also be pointed out that the Alemanni and the Vandals, another of the fiercest, and once one of the most success- ful, of such barbarous nations, were traditional, hereditary, ene- mies. The empire, of course, introduced into these scarlet equations new and terrible variables, its own existence and ambitions, new, powerful, unfamiliar weaponry, discord, bribery, intimidation, treach- ery, and such. In some generations of war with the empire the Vandals, despite some initial successes with weaponry furnished by enemies of the empire, were gradually reduced and decimated, the tribes scattered, denied significant weaponry and such. The rem- nants of the Wolfungs, for example, generations ago, had been transported to an exile world, far from familiar spacelanes. Its name was Varna. There they had been left, it seemed forgotten, though doubtless their presence was noted on some imperial records, that in case, for example, in some byway of time or politics, it might seem suitable for the empire to recollect them, and recall them, perhaps as federates, or as woodsmen, to clear worlds, or peasants, to sow and reap, to supply produce, perhaps to remote stations, or to the* limitanei, *the far-flung border troops. The Alemanni, it might be noted, on the other hand, had never had more than a series of terrible skirmishes with the empire. Always they had managed to draw back, and then wait, and then begin again their testing, their probing, their sniffing and prowling at the imperial borders. Sometimes, even, their ships had penetrated to the capitals of provincial worlds. Had the Alemanni been differently situated, in both space and time, and had they encountered the empire earlier, and under conditions comparable to those of the* Vandalii, *it seems not unlikely that their fate might have been similar. But they had not. It was only in the last generation that they had significantly appeared on the horizon of the empire.*

"You need not have come with me," said Otto to his companion, Julian. "The matter obtains between the Ortungs and the Wolfungs."

"I am curious to see how these things are resolved," said Julian.

"It will not be difficult to understand," said Otto.

In the records of the empire this world had only a number, and not a name, as many worlds. We do not know the number, nor are we sure, today, of the world, for much which might have been useful for making such determinations has been lost. The number of the world would have been, as we do know, the number of its star, followed by a numerical suffix, giving its position, counting outward from the star. The world presumably still exists, of course, on which the events took place which we are recounting. We just do not know which world it is. Possibilities have been proposed, but they remain confessedly conjectural. The world did have a name in the logs of the Alemanni, but, even so, the matter remains obscure. The Alemanni name, cumbersomely transliterated as 'Tenguthaxichai', is said to mean "Tengutha's Camp," or, perhaps, "The Camp of Tengutha," the nature of the genitive indicator being a matter of dispute among scholars. I personally favor "Tengutha's Camp" as there is some reason to believe, from other constructions, that the expression transliterated as 'ichai' in Alemanni may have meant a hidden camp, or lair. We do not know who the Tengutha in question might have been, but the name itself was common in several of the barbarian nations. We choose to avoid these various problems by referring to this world as the Meeting World, to be sure a title which might serve to designate almost any world. Meeting worlds, however, at least worlds chosen for meetings of the sort with which we are concerned, where disputes among barbarians were to be resolved, worlds rather like, in a sense, those of lonely beaches on desert islands, or those like the surface of barren skerries in the icy sea, were normally isolated, uninhabited worlds, worlds where detection and interference, you see, were unlikely.

"You did not bring weapons," said Julian.

"It was I who issued the challenge," said Otto. "It is they who will choose the weapons."

The remnant of the Wolfungs, exiled on Varna, now armed with no more than primitive weapons, and eking out their living in the forests, in the ancient manners, had been discovered by scouts of the Drisriaks, the parent tribe, or conjectured such, of the Alemanni nation. Much pleasure had it given the Drisriaks to discover their ancient enemies in such straits, in effect, disarmed and at their mercy. Many of the Wolfungs had been slaughtered, in the festivals of blood, saving, of course, the fairest of their daughters, which constitute always delicious, pleasing spoils for the conquerors. The Wolfungs had then, kneeling, denied chieftains, their heads to the dirt, humbled to the yoke of their masters, been permitted to survive, as a tributary people. This tribute was regularly collected by envoys of the Drisriaks, a tribute consisting largely of produce, amber, resin, precious woods, furs, herbs, and women. Some two years ago, however, Ortog, a prince of the Drisriaks, with followers, and ships, declared his house secessionist, and himself king of a new tribe, the Ortungs, or Ortungen. Ortog then, as he had when a prince of the Drisriaks, plied the crafts of his people, in such matters as piracy, trading, reaving where feasible within the empire, collecting tributes, and so on. It was shortly before his envoys, now in the name of the Ortungen, came to collect the tribute from the Wolfungs that the two aforementioned life rafts, or escape capsules, from a sacked and gutted, then destroyed, putative cruise ship, the *Alaria*, had beached on Varna. Ortog, who had earlier fallen into the hands of bounty hunters and traitors, and had been turned over to imperial forces at the remote station of Tinos, had been a prisoner on the *Alaria*, being transported to the Telnarian worlds, when she was overtaken by his ships and disabled.

"I hear it again," said Julian, "the clash of cymbals!"

"The Timbri," said Otto, "are fond of such instruments in their observances."

"There is singing, too," said Julian.

"Yes," said Otto.

The singing was in female voices, for such were the officiants, priestesses.

The party continued to wend its way upward, on the graveled, wet path.

Preceding Otto were two men, Hendrix and Gundlicht, of the Ortungen, men of Ortog, who had come, earlier, to the Wolfungs for the tribute. They had been surprised to learn that the Wolfungs had taken a chieftain, which they had forbidden to them, and that the tribute was refused. It had not been deemed appropriate, however, to return to the ship, arm the weaponry, and destroy the Wolfungs, and their forests, for a thousand latimeasures. The explanation for this had to do with a set of unusual circumstances.

"I hear again the cymbals," said Julian.

"Yes," said Otto.

The singing, too, could be heard, once more.

It began to rain again.

Above, in a sort of level place, through which the path led, and then, beyond it, once more ascended, toward the top of a hill, there was a thick copse.

It is a small thing we do here, thought Otto. It does not matter much. What is the life, or death, or the fates and fortunes, of a few men, or rabbits or dogs, to the world.

Gundlicht, in one hand, clutched what appeared to be a tightly rolled bundle of soiled, brocaded fabric. It was damp with rain.

"That is the grove, above," said Otto.

Again, tiny trickles of water, alkaline rivulets, flowed between the small stones, much as rivers might have flooded about boulders strewn in their path. The whitish waters stained the soles of their sandals, and, as they occasionally fought for footing, it splashed about their ankles, lashed from the grass in the meadows below. Sometimes a passing sandal dislodged a small rock, a pebble even, breaking some tiny dam, and the water rushed in its frenzied smallness down the slope. How the most fearsome of natural phenomena can be enacted on small stages, for the forces at work here, on the slope, were not so much different from those which, on grander platforms, might have awed and discomfited populations, for the smallest of winds, bending a blade of grass, is not so different, save in force and volume, from the mighty storms which uproot forests, nor the stirring of a hand in a bowl of water so different, save in its dimensions, from the vast, thunderous waves that can shake and drown continents. But even the trickles, the small drops, in their numbers, conjoined, confluent, become weighty with menace. Molecules of gas constitute both the breeze and the hurricane, as drops of water form both the gentle rain and the violent sea.

But it is hard to know, thought Otto, the turning out, of small things.

"Look," said Julian, pointing downward. Dilute, in the rivulets, mixing in with the whitish wash descending the slope, were tenuous streaks of red, serpentine in the gravel.

"Do not stop," said Hendrix.

"What is that?" asked Julian.

"It does not concern you," said Hendrix.

"It is blood," said Otto.

The gladiator had come to be raised on the shields of the Wolfungs, as their chieftain. It was he who had refused the tribute to the Ortungs, he who had issued the challenge to Ortog, king of the Ortungs.

"Aii!" said Julian, as they reached the level, as he caught sight of a dark shape, back among the shadows, suspended from a branch.

The path led through the grove.

"What is it?" asked Julian of Gundlicht, who was ahead, on the right.

"Silence, pig," said Gundlicht.

"Do not speak so to him," said Otto. "He is a free man."

"He is a Telnarian pig," said Gundlicht.

"He is a citizen of the empire," said Otto.

"So, too, as I understand it," laughed Gundlicht, "were three others in your village."

"But they were women," said Otto.

Gundlicht laughed again, knowingly.

The path was now on the level. The trees of the copse, or grove, were thick on either side. It had stopped raining now, but it was still half-dark, from the roiling clouds. There was little sound but that of the passage of the men, the tiny sounds of small stones being trod upon, the descent of drops of water from the branches of trees.

"There, another, back there, amongst the trees," said Julian.

"Keep silent," said Hendrix. "This is a holy place."

There were the tracks of a two-wheeled cart to one side. These could be easily discerned, from some damp pressed-down grass, to the left of the path, and, here and there, where a wheel had left the path, by marks in the mud.

"There is another, there," said Julian.

"You cannot see much from the path," said Gundlicht.

"Wait," said Julian.

"Do not stop," said Hendrix.

"Let him go," said Otto.

The group waited on the level, and Julian entered the grove. Otto, in a moment, followed him, and then Hendrix and Gundlicht. Otto and Julian were not prisoners. They had come because of the challenge.

"It is dark here," said Julian.

"One can see well enough," said Otto.

The creak of a rope was heard.

Julian brushed back leaves. His hand was wet. There was the smell of crushed leaves, of wet, dark branches.

There were many shadows. Rain dripped from the leaves and branches.

"What manner of place is this?" asked Julian.

There was at that moment, startling them, as they were now closer to the sound, again the clash of cymbals, and the sound of female voices, raised in song.

"It is going to clear," said Gundlicht, looking up, through the branches.

Beneath the wet, dark matting of leaves, hidden in delicate tunnels, in fragile palaces, dwelt grubs.

Julian stepped back, quickly, as a *filch,* its fur slick with rain skittered away.

"Let us return to the path," said Otto.

"Wait," said Julian.

He proceeded more deeply into the grove.

"Ai!" he cried suddenly, for in the darkness, and shadows, inadvertently coming upon it, he had literally struck against it, heavy, feeling the ribs through the fur, the fur wet. He pushed it back. It swung away, heavily. He stepped to the side, avoiding it as it returned to its place, suspended.

"What is it?" asked Julian.

"Speak softly," said Hendrix.

"Can you not see, Telnarian pig?" said Gundlicht.

"It is a dog," said Otto.

There were several other bodies, too, nearby, and an indefinite number in the grove. The dog's head was oddly pointed upward, the legs oddly dangling beside the body. The rope was about its throat.

"There is a sheep," said Otto.

"Look there," said Julian.

"That is a horse sacrifice," said Hendrix.

"And here is a pig, Telnarian pig," said Gundlicht to Julian.

The porcine creature hung upside down, holes cut in its rear shanks, through which the rope had been run.

Its throat was cut open.

In places only the dangling end of a rope swung free from a branch.

"Let us return to the path," said Hendrix.

It was at that time that they heard again the cymbals, and once more voices, those of women, raised in song.

"What is the meaning of the cymbals?" asked Julian.

"They mask other sounds," said Otto.

They turned about, and began to make their way back to the path.

"Wait," said Julian. "There, look."

"Yes," said Gundlicht.

"What is it?" asked Julian.

"Go closer," said Gundlicht.

Julian regarded the object dangling from the branch.

"Do not those of the empire perform sacrifices?" asked Otto.

"Sometimes," said Julian. "White bulls, fully grown beasts, with gilded horns and hoofs, such things."

"But it is done cleanly," said Julian.

The bronze blade, of course, bronze from immemorial tradition, moved swiftly in the sure hands of the priests, and the animal would sink to its knees or side, its head lolling, the lavers, held in the hands of neophytes, filling then with the hot blood.

"Sometimes it is not so cleanly done, in the arena," said Otto.

"Those are not sacrifices," said Julian.

"These things are done in the manner of the Timbri," said Hendrix.

"We would not do things in this way," said Gundlicht.

"I am pleased to hear it," said Julian.

"We would have hung them more properly,," said Gundlicht.

"Of course," said Julian.

"Their seeresses came to have influence over Ortog," said Gundlicht.

"It had to do with the readings, the prophecies," said Hendrix.

"I see," said Julian.

"Step carefully," said Hendrix.

Some bones, some knobs of vertebrae, and some ribs, like white branches, wet from the rain, lay among the dark, crumbled leaves. To one side there was a skull.

"The ropes break, in time," said Gundlicht.

The eyes of a *filch*, beady and bright, observed them, peering up from beneath leaves, where it had taken refuge.

In the grove there was no sound of birds. They were not now active, because of the rain.

The *filch* drew back, quickly, under the leaves.

Such a creature, though an omnivore, and surely not averse to scavenging, would profit little from the grisly trove introduced into its environment. There are temporal limits imposed on viable scavenging for mammalian and mammalianlike creatures. By the time portions of such weights might fall naturally to the leaves, the laws of chemistry would have had their say, producing cadaverine alkaloids. The taste of these is aversive to such creatures, apparently experienced as repelling and abhorrent. Those of their ancestors, or of generative life forms, for whom the taste was acceptable, or even reinforcive, presumably died, poisoned. We leave it to others to ponder on the interplay of that which is found marvelous in the living of it and healthfulness, and that which is found inhibiting, diminishing and depressing in the living of it, and disease and death.

The party then returned to the path, where a number of Ortungen, from the ship, had been awaiting them.

Shortly thereafter the sun came out.

On the ascent, having resumed it, they noted more blood, dark in the gravel. It had washed down, with the water, from above. To be sure, there was not much of it.

They continued to ply their way toward the top of the path.

Birds sang.

These creatures were again, now, active in the grove below.

They, unlike the *filchen,* fluttering about, pecking, alighting, had no difficulty in reaching the weights prior to the formation of natural toxins.

To be sure, the weights were not always without some profit even to the tiny *filchen,* as bits of matter might fall to the leaves, dropped by birds, perhaps lost in their small disputes, or even worms, or maggots, gorged, bright and swollen, like pearls.

It was hot now.

Otto shaded his eyes.

Water steamed from the flat surfaces of rocks to the side.

In a few minutes they had reached the top of the path.

Several bodies lay there, some in the mud, near a cart, others on the cart. Much ropage was wrapped about these bodies. It seemed the bodies were otherwise naked. Their ankles had been crossed and bound. To the crossed, bound ankles of each was attached a length of rope, some ten feet in length. The throat of each was cut, a gash going back, deep into the neck. The eyes of some of these bodies was still open, quite widely.

"Come along," said Hendrix.

The path had, at its height, debouched into a wide, circular area, and near the center of this area there was a small platform, something like a yard high, and, near the platform, was an altarlike structure, of flat stones. Above this structure there reared two vertical posts, one planted on each side of it, with a heavy crosspost lashed in place, high, between the two vertical posts.

Two Ortungs, from within the clearing, were making their way rather in the direction of the group with which we have been concerned, but actually toward the vicinity of the cart. They dragged a body behind them, which Julian, looking back, saw them turn about, and then leave near the cart, with others.

There were several individuals near the center of the clearing, some on the platform, some about it, others about the altar.

"That is our king, Ortog, on the platform," said Hendrix, "the tallest, he helmed in gold."

Otto said nothing.

He had met the magnificent Ortog before, on the *Alaria*, on a measure of sand. Ortog had not known the stadium blade. It had not been a good match. The gladiator had declined to administer a death blow. Shortly thereafter the *Alaria*, had come under attack by pursuing Ortung ships.

From where they were, several yards away, they saw two of the Ortungs drag a roped man toward the altar.

About the altar were several women in long, white gowns. Some of these held sistrums and cymbals.

The man did not protest.

The sistrums began to jangle.

Cymbals were poised.

Ortungs threw a rope, attached to the man's bound ankles, over the crossbar. The music became more agitated as he was drawn upward, by his ankles, until he hung, head down, over the altar. A curved object lay, flattish, to the right, on the altar. This object, as would be clearly observed shortly, was a large, bronze, sicklelike knife. One of the white-gowned women, she who seemed first among them, threw over her head the hood of her gown, covering her head, as is customary in such a rite. Four other women now crowded close about the suspended figure. They seized the roped body, to hold it in place. Two others brought forth a large bronze vessel, rather like a shallow caldron. It had three clawlike feet. It was carried by two circular rings, or handles, which, when released, hung down, beside the vessel. This low caldronlike vessel, on its clawlike feet, they placed on the altar. The head, as it hung downward, was almost within it, and much of the hair was actually within it, and could not be seen for its sides.

"Ortog was betrayed some months ago," said Hendrix. "He was captured by bounty hunters, with the aid of traitors. He was taken to Tinos, an outpost of the empire, and delivered there to his enemies."

"Such as this dog!" said Gundlicht, striking Julian, who drew back, angrily.

"Desist," said Otto.

"He is only a half-naked thrall, in rags," said Gundlicht, puzzled.

"He is a free man, and with me," said Otto.

"You would defend a dog of the empire?" asked Gundlicht.

"He is free. He is with me." said Otto.

"Ortog," said Hendrix, "was rescued, while being conveyed to Telnaria."

"Yes," said Otto.

Otto did not mention that there had been no intention of conveying Ortog as far as Telnaria.

"Do you know who those pigs are?" asked Hendrix of Otto, turning, indicating the bodies, in the mud, and on the cart, behind them some yards, to their left.

"No," said Otto.

"Do you know who that is?" asked Hendrix, turning back toward the altar, indicating the rope-swathed figure dangling head down over the altar.

"No," said Otto.

Then, in the midst of a din of cymbals, the white-gowned, hooded woman, who seemed chief among the others, who was a priestess, of the rites of the Timbri, her head now covered in the folds of her hood, drew back, by the hair, with her left hand, the man's head, while with her right hand she lifted from the surface of the altar, where it lay near one of the three clawlike feet of the caldron, the large, bronze, sicklelike blade.

There was a climactic clash of cymbals.

"It is done," said Hendrix.

"It takes some time for them to die," said Gundlicht.

Once more Otto and Julian heard female voices raised in song, as they had earlier, on the trail, and in the grove.

The officiant had now uncovered her head.

"So who are these men?" asked Otto, looking back.

"Ortog was given into the hands of bounty hunters, by traitors, and even those he thought his brothers," said Hendrix.

"And they were hunted down?" asked Otto.

"To the last man," said Hendrix.

"I see," said Otto.

"And he," said Hendrix, indicating the body dangling over the altar, and the bronze vessel, "was the leader of the bounty hunters."

"He died well," said Otto.

"And he was only a brigand, not even of a people," said Hendrix.

Otto shrugged.

"I am proud of him," said Hendrix.

In a time two men removed the caldronlike vessel from the altar, that which had been brought to it by two women. They carried it to the side, where the two women were waiting. The women removed the lid from a large bronze vat, on a heavy wooden sledge, which would be drawn by chains. Into this vat the men emptied the contents of the caldronlike vessel, after which the women replaced the lid. The two men returned the caldronlike vessel to the vicinity of the altar. The two women in white came then to stand beside it. Other men were lowering the body from the framework at the altar. It was dragged past the group with which we have been concerned. The bloodied hair left streaks on the turf behind it.

"I did not know the Ortungs practiced the rites of the Timbri," said Otto.

"It is the influence of the priestess, Huta, of the Timbri," said Hendrix, with distaste. "She it is who with her tricks, and the readings, convinced Ortog that he should be king and not prince, who put it into his head that he should found his own tribe."

"But you, and Gundlicht, like Ortog, were Drisriak," said Otto. "How is it that you followed him?"

"We took rings from him," said Hendrix. "We would die for him, he is our lord."

Loyalties among the barbarian peoples, it might be mentioned, are seldom simple. Seldom, unlike those of more civilized groups, are their loyalties to abstractions, such as institutions or states. Loyalties tend rather to be based on blood and debt, and are owed, in the final analysis, more to leaders, and, derivatively, to lines or families, than anything else. Indeed, it is out of these basic forms of primitive allegiance that the tribal forms tend to emerge. Even in the tribal matrix the primary loyalty is customarily viewed as being owed to one's lord, the giver of shelter, the provider of loaves.

There was a sudden howl of misery coming from behind the altar, and a twisting, struggling figure, but one almost totally covered with rope, was dragged into view.

"Ortog! Ortog!" it cried. "Have mercy on me! Do not hurt me! Do not do this to me! We have played together as children! We have stood back-to-back, as men! Have mercy! Mercy!"

Ortog raised his hand, to the women, and the cymbals began to clash.

The mouth of the man continued to move, crying out. Tears streamed down his face. But he could not be heard, because of the sound of the cymbals.

He was thrown across the altar, and, by the trailing rope on his ankles, hoisted by two men into position, the rope being then fastened in such a way as to suspend him, his head and throat at the convenience of the officiant.

Otto inclined his head to Hendrix, who spoke to him, his lips close to the giant's ear.

"That is Andrax, leader of the conspirators," said Hendrix. "He has been saved for last, and had been permitted, by intent to watch the fate of his predecessors."

Otto nodded.

The mouth of the suspended man continued to move, frantically, wildly, but it was not clear if sound were being emitted, and was simply not audible because of the din, or if no sound were being emitted, perhaps because the vocal cords had failed him, and there was nothing remaining, then, but the frenzied, terror-stricken, wild movements of a contorted visage.

Four women came to hold him steady, which they could do only with difficulty. Two other women brought the caldronlike vessel, which had been earlier emptied into the vat on the rude sledge, from the side of the altar and placed it on the altar, as they had before. The women holding the man, as he was taller, pulled his head up and back, and then released it, so that it was then partly within the rim of the vessel. The priestess, once again, with two hands, drew over her head the hood of her gown.

There was a fiery climactic clash of cymbals.

The figure then squirmed, twisting on the rope. No longer was there any question of its capacity to utter sound.

"He is not dying well," said Hendrix.

"You are not proud of him," said Otto.

"No," said Hendrix, "in spite of the fact that he is of the people."

"He is not of the people," said Gundlicht. "He is a traitor."

"True," said Hendrix.

"Are you not all traitors?" asked Otto.

"We have followed Ortog, who is our lord," said Hendrix.

"We are of the people, still," said Gundlicht, "of the Alemanni."

"But not of the Drisriaks," said Otto.

"No," said Hendrix, "not of the Drisriaks."

"You do not approve of the rites of the Timbri," speculated Otto.

"No," said Hendrix, "but we abide the will of Ortog, our lord."

"And what would you prefer?" asked Otto.

"The old ways," said Hendrix, shrugging. "The adz and the block."

The officiant had now thrown back the hood of her gown. She had high cheekbones. Her hair was long, and dark.

"That is Huta, the priestess," said Otto.

"Yes," said Hendrix.

Once again, then, were the voices of the women, saving that of the high priestess, raised in song.

"It is over now," said Hendrix.

"It is hot," said Gundlicht.

"It will be good for visibility," said Hendrix.

"Yes," said Gundlicht.

The tall figure on the platform, that in the golden helm, turned to regard the group with which we have been concerned. A man beside him lifted his hand.

"We may approach," said Hendrix. "Ortog, prince of the Drisriaks, king of the Ortungen, will see you now."

"I do not see Gerune, the sister of Ortog, on the platform," said Otto.

Hendrix stiffened.

"She is with the women, in the tents," said Gundlicht.

"Remain in the background," said Otto to Julian, "lest Ortog recognize you, from the *Alaria*."

Julian nodded.

It was unlikely, however, that anyone who had been on the *Alaria* would have recognized in the barefoot, ragged fellow at the heel of Otto, chieftain of the Wolfungs, the impeccably groomed young officer, in full dress uniform, with purple cords at the left shoulder, of the *Alaria*. Surely he could be no more than the meanest of servants and was perhaps even a field slave, fit for a collar and kennel at night, and shackles during the day.

"Come along," said Hendrix. "Ortog will see you now."

## • • • CHAPTER 6 • • •

How strange it seemed to her that he should appear there, there, in the threshold of the library, of her office, he so massive, so watchful, so unexpectedly there, there in the court complex on Terennia, and that she had not inquired as to what he might wish for she knew without asking what he wanted and would have and that she was that for which he had come and could he know that beneath the judicial gown, so voluminous and grand, so somber and stately, there were only wisps of silk which she had purchased in a shop of the *Alaria* and had scarcely dared to wear and now how could it be that that was all she wore beneath the somber vesture of the court, that must be wrong, and she had leapt to her feet and fled toward the wall which had disappeared before her, and she found herself on wild, stony slopes, in the moonlight, that could not be right, for there was no such terrain in the vicinity of the courts, but there she was, and she saw him behind her, standing where the wall should be, and then she fled in terror, running from him, over those wild, stony slopes, a stunted tree here or there, with long, dark branches reaching out to snatch at her gown, billowing behind her, a patch of brush here and there, which could tear at her flesh, scratching it in a thousand places, making it bloody, which could be smelled by wolves, and she running lost her footwear, first the half boot on her left foot, and then that from her right, why was she not wearing stockings, and was running, stumbling, gasping, looking behind her, was he behind her still, surely he was gone now, she was frantic, her feet were bare, bruised and cut now on the stones, and she ran, the long dark garmenture of the court flying behind her, and then she stopped.

No, he was behind her still, not feet away!

Again she ran and the gown melted from her and she was clad in naught but the bits of silk from the *Alaria* and fleeing thusly before him.

Were they the only two living things in this wild, frantic, windswept moonlit world?

No, for she could hear somewhere, somewhere behind her, and behind him, the thunder of the movements of large numbers of horses, and the songs of thousands of men.

She could see behind her now, far back, the lights of a thousand fires, some great encampment.

Where were the ships of the empire, the legions come to protect her?

She turned again wildly to flee but had hardly hurried thence a step when about her body, like a whisper of much portent, there descended and tightened, then so terribly tight, she could not hope to slip it, a rope of dark, braided leather, pinning her arms to her sides, cutting back into her flesh, and at the slightest release of its tension she fell forward, heavily onto her left shoulder, and then he was crouching near her, she dared not look at him, and he moved her, turning her, not gently, to her belly and she lay there then, prone on the stones. While the rope, that snake of braided leather, was still on her she felt her ankles seized in massive hands and crossed, and then, quickly, with a narrow thong and three tight loops, bound, tightly, making it impossible for her to rise to her feet.

The braided rope was then removed from her body, and she sensed him standing beside her, looking down at her, thinking whatever thoughts he chose, coiling the rope.

He then again crouched beside her and her hands were taken up, behind the back of her head, and then, the palms of her hands, facing the back of her head, tied together there, with her long, dark

hair. This was done in such a way that even had she torn the hair
from her head, her wrists would have still been securely fastened
to one another. Another loop of her hair, about her throat, secured
her hands in place, where they were, behind the back of her head,
this, too, done in such a way that even if the hair were torn from
her head, the loop would remain in place, like a neck cord. She
then lay quietly thusly secured. She felt the flat of a knife, cold
thrust betwixt her flesh and the silk she wore, and then turned and
moved, the back of the blade against her flesh, like a fine line.
Then, in a moment, she heard the knife snapped back into its
sheath. He stood. She trembled. His booted foot turned her, to her
back. She lay at his feet, the bits of silk beneath her. He then
reached down and with a cry of delight, of triumph, of exultation,
lifted her over his head, her head and feet down, her body bent like
a bow, lifted her upward, high, exultant, toward the moon. Then
he placed her on her knees on the stones, and looked at her, and
then turned away. She struggled frantically, on her knees. She
almost fell. She saw gleaming eyes to the side, those of beasts.
Her flanks and thighs and calves had in her flight been cut by the
brush and thorns. He turned about. Could he have known that she
would in another instant have screamed piteously, begging for him
to return to her side, to come back for her? In the moonlight surely
he could not sense the trembling of her lip. She thought to kneel
straightly, proudly, defiantly, before him, but then she knelt down a
little, as she did not wish to be beaten. But she did not lower her
head to where she could not see his eyes, should he approach, for
in them she hoped to read her fate. He considered her. She tried to
kneel a little straighter, not more proudly, nor more insolently, but
more attractively, a little more beautifully, a bit more interestingly.
Surely she might at least make an interesting gift, if only for some
loyal subordinate. But he must not give her away! He must keep
her! She would do anything to be kept. Did he not know she had
seen him in a thousand dreams, thusly stalwart, thusly armed,
thusly imperious, thusly commanding, thusly uncompromising? He
came again toward her, over the stones, and took from her ankles
the thong, that she might stand. She lifted her chin, timidly,
beggingly, that he might tie his rope about her neck, that forming
then a tether to lead her, and then, you see, she would have no
choice but to follow him, tethered in that fashion, helpless,
vulnerable, at his mercy, no more then than a lovely, curved beast,
who might somehow prove of interest to someone, hopefully to
someone, hopefully, indeed, desperately she wished, to him, but

about his lips there was only the tiniest of smiles. Did he know the bonds that already held her, stronger than stout chains, those of what she needed and craved, those of her condition, and nature, those of what she was, in the most secret recesses of her heart?

Please, tether me, she though.

You must give me no choice!

Tether me!

Will you not grant me even that, a simple tether? Will you not throw even such a tiny sop to my pride?

He turned and began to walk rapidly away, toward the campfires in the distance.

She staggered to her feet.

She heard a growl to her left.

It frightened her, terribly.

She felt the hot breath of a beast on her calf. She could see its shaggy form, silverish, in the moonlight.

Had she been able to free and lower her hands she might have touched it.

With a cry of shame, and delight, and fear, she hurried after the retreating figure, leaving behind her her old life.

In a moment it seemed she found herself in a brightly lit tent, one resplendent with golden hangings. A fitter was measuring her for chains, and then, as she sat, her ankles were shackled. Her captor observed this. She was then knelt. The bonds of her hair were slashed away, freeing her wrists, She sobbed that her hair was thusly cut, so callously, so casually. Her captor had observed this, unmoved. He had not objected. She could not then be a high girl, to be so treated. She knelt, holding her hands out, as the fitter indicated, before her. She watched him, as he watched her small wrists being fitted with manacles. He then carried her to the side of the tent, where other women lay, or knelt, or reclined. He threw her among the women, the other women, she now only one more among them, and perhaps not even so much as they. He fastened a chain, run from a heavy stake driven in the ground, a stake from which other chains, too, ran, to the chain which linked her ankle shackles.

With the bonds on her, kneeling there, with the other women, she suddenly realized that now, at last, finally, here, in this place, all choices had indeed been removed from her. No longer were choices hers. She was now, irrevocably, what she was, whether she wished it or not.

She trembled in terror, understanding what she now was, and that there was no going back.

It was what she was, and would remain.

Her fate, and destiny, like that of the other women in the tent, were now inalterable.

There was no going back.

"I am owned?" she said.

The fitter laughed.

"Yes," said her captor, he who caught her in the moonlight, he who had brought her here, putting her with the others.

She knew herself now a different sort of being than ever she had been before, save in her heart.

But now it was real, and public, as much as being a pig or dog.

She felt terribly helpless, and vulnerable and frightened.

He saw that she knew now what she was, simply, and that she knew herself his, just as simply, and he smiled, and she saw that he found in this some satisfaction.

She, kneeling, lifted her hands to him. "Brand me," she said. "Collar me. Whip me!" And it seemed to her that there were stripes upon her back, which impressed her bondage upon her, and a mark, upon her thigh, which would be recognized throughout galaxies by magistrates and merchants, and on her fair throat, light, closely fitting, gleaming, locked, a collar.

"I would have a name, Master!" she wept.

"You have not yet earned a name," he told her, and then turned about, and left.

She moved a bit after him, her hands extended to him, but, in a moment, was held up, short, and could move no further, could not follow him, because of the chain.

She felt herself then being stirred, being poked with a stick.

She lay on a thin, narrow, straw-filled pallet. It was covered with canvas. It lay directly on the floor.

She pulled the small blanket more closely about her.

She had not heard the key in the lock.

"Brand me," she whispered. "Collar me."

But then, beneath the cover, her fingers felt her left thigh. There was a mark there. And then her fingers went to her throat. She felt a chain there, leading up to a heavy collar, which she vaguely recollected had been put on her, over the house collar. The heavier collar fastened her to a ring in the wall, in the cell.

Again she drifted back, toward the tent with golden hangings, "Whip me," she said.

"Do you wish to be whipped?" asked a voice, from some-where, seemingly intrusive, alien, far off.

"No, no!" she said, quickly. It seemed she could recall the whip, or a whip, from somewhere. "No, please, do not whip me!" she whimpered, turning, squirming, pulling the blanket up about her. It seemed she remembered the whip, or some whip, from somewhere, someplace. "I will do whatever you want," she said, in a small voice, frightened. "Please do not whip me."

There was laughter, from somewhere.

The laughter of a man.

"Please give me a name," she moaned.

"You have a name, a house name," said a voice. "It is 'Flora'."

She then felt the blanket drawn away from her, and she pulled her legs up tightly, and lifted her head, looking up, and saw one of the keepers, a stick in one hand. There was a tiny lamp in the corridor, outside the bars.

"Come, Flora," said he, "the day begins."

Yes, thought the girl. I am here, truly. And I need not beg the whip, for I have been whipped, at least once, for instructional purposes. I hope they do not do it again. I am eager to obey them. I will do my best to please them. And I am branded. The tiny slave rose is there, high, on the left thigh, just under the hip. It is tiny, but it is clear. There is no mistaking it. And I do wear a collar, though a house collar, beneath a holding collar, keeping me to the wall.

She then went to her knees at the side of the pallet and put her head down to the floor, rendering obeisance to the keeper. He crouched near her and she, her head still down, felt the key fitted in the holding collar lock, and the holding collar, with a sound of chain, was removed from her, and dropped to the side. The keeper then again stood. She then kissed his feet, softly, tenderly, as she had been taught.

"Are you ready for your lessons, Flora?" he asked.

"Yes, Master," she said.

"Kneel up," he said.

She straightened her body, and knelt in one of the positions she had been taught.

"You have come along well, Flora," he said. "It is hard to believe that you are from Terennia."

She was silent, not knowing if it were permitted to respond.

"You are incredibly beautiful," he said.

"Sometimes," he said, "those from worlds like Terennia, where they have been starved, and denied, turn out best, becoming the most feminine, the softest, the most eager, the most vulnerable, the most piteously needful, the most passionate, the most uninhibited, the most helpless and shameless, and beautiful, of all. Yet it all, in the end, depends on the female."

He put the stick beside her cheek, and she moved her cheek a little, against it, looking up at him.

"You understand that Terennia is now behind you, forever, do you not, my pretty little slut?"

"Yes, Master," she said.

He regarded her.

"You are beautiful enough to be sold to a high family on a pleasure planet," he said.

"And as your training progresses, you will become more beautiful, and more helpless, and more needful," he said. "You do not know, little bitch, so ignorant and simple, and naive, as you now kneel before me, how helpless you will become, how much at the mercy of men, and your needs."

"You are not a man," he said.

"No, Master," she said.

"What may be asked of you?"

"Anything."

"What is expected of you?"

"Everything," she said.

"Is it your intention to be hot, devoted and dutiful?" he asked.

"Yes," she said.

"Are you to be obedient?"

"Yes," she said.

"What is to be the nature of your obedience?" he asked.

"Instantaneous and total," she said.

"What is your hope?" he asked.

"To be found pleasing," she said.

"What is your intention?" he asked.

"To be pleasing."

"Subject to what qualifications or reservations?"

"Subject to no qualifications or reservations," she said.

"None?" he asked.

"None whatsoever," she said.

"You are then to be fully, and totally, pleasing?"

"Yes, Master."

Again he examined her.

"In time, Flora," said he, "so feminine, so soft, so yielding, so helplessly passionate, you will become a piteous, begging dream of pleasure for a man, a meaningless slut, of course, and one despised and scorned, but one for whom planets might be bartered."

She did not respond, as she did not know if it were permitted.

"You may follow me from the cell," he said.

He then left the cell, and she, on her hands and knees, followed him, for she had not been given permission to rise. In the hall she waited behind other girls, in a line, also on all fours, who had been released earlier from their cells. In time she, with the others, those who had been earlier released, and those who were subsequently released, followed the man with the stick, who was one of their keepers, in the house of the connoisseur, their heads down, not permitted to lift them, from the corridor of cells, one of several in the house, to the waste pits and washing bowls, and thence to the feeding troughs, and thence to the training rooms.

She was eager to learn all she could.

She could not believe what she had learned already, things of which once she had not even dreamed.

And small, homely tasks, too, were taught her, things she might once have regarded as beneath her, but which were quite appropriate for her now, given what she now was, and seemly surely, in any event, for one such as she, for one of her disposition, with such small, delicate hands.

Too, she was becoming aware in herself of rising tides of passion, and needfulness.

Already she had begun to suspect what men might do to her, and how much at their mercy she was.

She hoped that they would take pity on her, and be kind to her, if only because she was so helpless, and so needful, so desperately needful, and only a slave.

# ▪ ▪ ▪ CHAPTER 7 ▪ ▪ ▪

"It is a fine tent," said Otto.

"We may die within it," said Julian.

In the tent were many of the high men of the Ortungs. Among them, too, other than ranking tribesmen, the aristocracy of the Ortungs, or Ortungen, were *comites*, retainers, of various nations, peoples and species. Clerks, too, were present, for the recording of documents, the witnessing of proceedings, the signing of names, and such. There was a cleared place in the center of the tent. In this cleared space, on the dirt floor, strewn with rushes, stood Otto, his arms folded. Behind him, and to his left, closer than he would have cared, more prominently visible than he might have wished, stood Julian. He had intended to remain in the background, but he had been thrust forward, contemptuously, following a brief sign from Hendrix to the guards. Hendrix thought it useful, and pertinent, that the nature, and lowliness, of the companion of Otto, a young fellow barefoot and in rags, and a mere citizen of the empire, one with no people, with no tribal entitlements or rights, surely no more than a mere thrall, be evident. In this way Hendrix made clear to Ortog, and the others, that Otto, although he might be chieftain of the Wolfungs, was much alone. Was he not hapless, unaccompanied by high men? Where were his princely trappings, where his *comites*, his retinue? How poor, or few, or weak, or cowardly, were the Wolfungs! There was the reputed chieftain of the Wolfungs, with no uniformed, gift-bearing servitors or stern, calm men-at-arms, with gleaming blades and shields of polished silver, only a ragged fellow with him, barefoot and dirty, the sort who might tend pigs for his masters by day and be penned with them, chained, by night. Even one who was of the despised empire! Otto, of course, had not wanted Astubux, or Axel, or others of the Wolfungs, their high men, to come to the Meeting World. What had to be done there was his to do alone, if it could be done at all. Rather their place was with the tribe. If he failed it must be they who must try to sustain and profit the people, the Wolfungs, either by submitting to the conditions of the Alemanni, accommodating them with tribute, or, if this was impossible, leading the people again into the forests, trying to conceal themselves therein, fleeing once more, as times before, from the Alemanni, whether Ortungs or Drisriaks. Julian, the young man, had requested permission to accompany Otto, and to this request Otto had acceded. Julian had had his reasons for desiring to accompany Otto, and Otto had had his reasons for acceding to his request.

"The slaves are lovely," said Otto, looking to his right, to the side of the dais, which was a few feet before him. There, kneeling, were three blond slaves. They were women taken from the *Alaria*, and Otto, when on the ship, had seen them, here and there, in the lounge, and elsewhere, though, to be sure, not as they now were. Once, after the attack, and boarding, of the ship, though Otto had not seen them at this later time, they had been chained at the side of the stage in the ship's auditorium, the auditorium then being used by the Ortungs as a command center.

"They are beautiful, and well curved," said Otto.

"Yes," said Julian.

There was no difficulty in making these determinations. The women did not now, you see, in spoiled, supercilious regal splendor, wear their exorbitantly expensive robes, and their fine silks and jewels, as they had when Otto had seen them earlier, in the lounge and elsewhere. Rather, they wore now, as had been exactly the case when they had been put at the side of the stage on the *Alaria* as he had not seen them earlier, only chains.

"They are display slaves," said Julian.

"But doubtless they are often put to other uses, too," said Otto.

"Doubtless," said Julian.

Otto regarded the women.

Perhaps once, even in chains, they might have dared to meet his gaze, or even responded with stiffening, resentment or defiance, such naive resistances, but now, even though they had doubtless been only recently familiarized with their new condition, they looked away, not daring to meet his eyes, or surely not without permission. How different they were from what they had been before, and how little time had elapsed! They were obviously highly intelligent. They had learned a great deal in a very short time. Already their bodies had lost much of the stiffness, the tension, the defensiveness, of the free woman. Their expressions, their attitudes, were entirely different.

Otto continued to regard them.

Before they had been far above him, scarcely deigning to notice him, save, perhaps, as one might notice a magnificent animal, paying him a coin perhaps, that he might attend upon them in the privacy of their compartments, but they were not far above him now, as they were slaves, and he a chieftain.

There was now in them a needfulness, a beauty and vulnerability.

They were quite different from what they had been before.

Slavery produces a remarkable transformation in a woman.

He considered them, appraisingly, appreciatively, pondering on their value.

In most markets, he speculated, it would have been considerable.

They knelt, suitably, in appropriate positions.

Perhaps they were not unaware of his scrutiny. Perhaps, they had, too, secretly, a furtive glance here and there, considered him. It is hard for a slave not to do such things, not to wonder at what it might be, to be in the arms of a given master, his to do with as he pleases, to be subject to his whip, as they are fully, thrillingly, aware of their own vulnerability, that they can be purchased, and owned, that they must obey, and, with all their zeal, strive to please.

How beautiful they had become.

What truly strong man does not desire to own a woman?

Knowing themselves under his scrutiny, and knowing themselves slaves, they trembled.

What truly feminine woman does not desire her master, wherever he may be?

One of the blond slaves stole a glance at Otto.

But Otto's face, at that instant, had been dark with anger. He had, at that moment, recalled another woman, you see, a dark-haired woman, slim and exquisite, one who had once been an officer of a court, on Terennia, too, one whose mother, a judge, had sentenced him to the arena.

And he had later trusted her, that lovely, exquisite creature, but she had betrayed his trust.

How he despised her!

In what utter contempt did he hold her!

How he hated her!

The blond slave quickly, alarmed, lowered her head.

She did not wish to be thrown to dogs.

The exquisite young dark-haired woman, who had been the officer of the court, had come eventually into his power. Her thigh now bore a mark, one which would be recognized throughout the galaxies. He had had it put on her, with a hot iron. In the village of the chieftain on Varna she now served, his claiming disk on a cord, knotted about her neck. He had kept her, for his amusement, and for low tasks. He had not even seen fit to give her a name. He had never even deigned to put her to slave use.

Let her moan at night, naked in her cage, ignored, neglected, putting her hands through the bars, pleading for his touch, for the humble solace of a slave.

How he despised, and hated, and desired, her!

"The Ortungs are rich," said Otto, looking about himself.

"Surely less so than the Drisriaks," said Julian.

"Note the treasures, the chests open, they fearing not one coin will vanish," said Otto.

"They are careless, or naive," said Julian.

"It is called honor," said Otto.

"Perhaps," said Julian.

"Ortog is rich," said Otto.

"He is ostentatious," said Julian.

Otto had been raised in the tiny *festung* of Sim Giadini. That is near the heights of Barrionuevo, on the world of Tangara.

The contents of one of the smallest of the several coffers scattered about, with rolls of rich cloth and such, among which the high men, and others, stood, would have surely sufficed to pay the tithes of his village to the *festung* of Sim Giadini for a thousand years.

One of the kneeling women, glimpsing Julian, suddenly gasped, lifting her small hands, the wrists chained, to her face. But, a slave, she dared not speak. Too, his eyes warned her to silence. Then, tears in her eyes, she blushed scarlet, that he should see her so. And was he, too, now a thrall, a slave, subject to the huge, blue-eyed, blond-haired brute with him? Had he, one of his station, of the empire, come to this, no more than a ragged slave or servitor, at the shoulder of a barbarian?

Otto, too, had noted her response, and, seeing his eyes upon her, as well as those of Julian, she put her head down, with the tiniest sound of chain, that from the collar on her neck.

Hendrix, too, had noted her response, but made little of it, supposing it to register little more than her dismay at seeing Julian, one presumably such as she herself once was, one of the empire, but one here, in this place, as herself, in a position of unimportance and lowliness, and of service, if not of actual bondage.

Ortog, king of the Ortungs, prince of the Drisriaks, on the dais, standing, was in converse with others about him. He had not, as yet, acknowledged the presence of Otto and Julian.

Hendrix was amused at the response of the female slave. Did she think that men of the empire would rescue her? Let her then behold one, the barefoot fellow in rags behind the bold Wolfung. Let him hope that he might be spared to tend flocks for his masters. Let her compare, she on her knees, a man of the empire with his betters, setting him against, to his disadvantage, true men, the Ortungs, and their allies, mighty men, muscular and keen-eyed, clad in glossy furs, with golden rings and jeweled weapons.

And even if the men of the empire should come, in a thousa
ships, with their bombs, and rays, and flaming cannons, lingering
technologies from other ages, did she think, truly, given what she
now was, and what had been done with her, that she would be
rescued, and restored to wealth and dignity? No, her value was now
quite other than it had been. Indeed, it was now, for the first time,
real, in a quite practical sense, for a price could be set on it. On
thousands of worlds within the empire, and beyond it, you see,
slavery was wholly legal. On these worlds, it was not only
accepted, but acclaimed and prized. Indeed, on many of them, it
had been specifically instituted as a remedy, or partial remedy, for
serious social problems, such as the conservation of resources, the
protection of the environment, and the control and management of
the population, with respect not only to such mechanics as size and
distribution, but with respect to subtler considerations, such as the
diversity and quality of the gene pool. Others found it, or one of its
many equivalents, a natural ingredient in a stable, orderly society,
one in which various parts were harmoniously interrelated, in such
a way as to produce a healthy whole. Others saw in it a recognition
of, and a civilized refinement of, and enhancement of, the order of
nature. Other societies, of course, thought little of it, no more than
of the air they breathed or the soft rains which grew their crops. It
was part of the way things were, like the earth and the wind. They
did not think to question these things, or how they might have
come to be, no more than an erect posture, a prehensile append-
age, binocular vision. Such things, their ways, if they stopped to
reflect on such matters, seemed more rational to them than a myth
of sameness, which no one believed, coupled paradoxically with
an ideal of success, betraying the myth itself, challenging everyone, in a chaos of competitions, pitting individual against individual, group against group, to stake their future and self-esteem on
obtaining a prize which, in the nature of things, almost no one
could win.

Ortog now, still standing on the dais, turned to regard Otto,
chieftain of the Wolfungs.

He recalled him well.

The last time he had seem him, or looked upon him closely, had
been on the *Alaria*, in a small makeshift arena, an illuminated
patch of sand in one of the holds, amidst tiered benches.

Another of the blond women, kneeling at the side of the dais,
not she who had blushed and lowered her head, looked at Julian.
Their eyes met. Her lip curled slightly. In her eyes there was

im. She scorned him, for his lowliness, for his rags. vere far above him, were far more than he. But rayed, as though inadvertently, to the steel collar on its chain, running to the stout ring, to which other chains, too, were fixed. As though idly, he viewed the light, lovely, but inflexible, unslippable rings encircling her small wrists. Then his glance wandered, but obviously so, to the shackles clasping her slim, fair ankles. Then, at his leisure, he surveyed her enchained beauty. She tried to hold herself straight beneath such a gaze but then her lip trembled, and in her eyes, where insolence had reigned before, there now flickered understanding, and fear. For all his filth, and rags, he was a free man, or seemed so, and was at least a man, where she was naught but female and slave. She knew she could be put upon a slave block and sold. She knew she could be sent to him, even one such as he, even though he might be a mere thrall, on her hands and knees, carrying to him, in her teeth, delicately, so as not to mark it, a whip.

She looked down, and away.

"Otto, chieftain of the Wolfungs," announced Hendrix, addressing himself to Ortog, who stood on the dais.

"And Julian, of the empire," said Otto.

"And Julian, a worthless dog, of the empire," added Hendrix.

"Who is free," said Otto.

The blond woman who had earlier looked with disdain upon Julian shuddered. He was free!

"Who is free, a free worthless dog of the empire," added Hendrix.

She did not raise her head. Hendrix's insult to Julian, or to Otto, or both, was immaterial to the realities involved, realities as obdurate, and incontrovertible, as the collar on her neck, and the chains on her limbs. She was a thousand times lower than Julian, a thousand times lower than he, even were he a worthless dog, for he was free and she was slave.

"I am Ortog, king of the Ortungs, prince of the Drisriaks," said Ortog.

He made no reference to their former meeting, or to the business which had occurred on the *Alaria*.

Otto nodded, his arms folded upon his mighty chest.

"Send for Gerune, princess of the Drisriaks," said Ortog, king of the Ortungs, prince of the Drisriaks, sitting himself on the royal stool, on the log dais, floored with planks, it at one end of the spacious, slopingly turreted tent, handing his golden helm to a shieldsman.

"She is shamed, she would not come, milord," said a free woman. She was standing back, in her long dress, it was brown, to one side.

In the hand of Gundlicht was the small, closely rolled bundle of soiled, brocaded cloth, that which he had brought with him, from the ship. He had received it in the hut of Otto, chieftain of the Wolfungs.

"Her presence is awaited," said Ortog.

"She is indisposed," said the woman.

"Bring her," said Ortog.

There was a sound of delight from one of the three women chained to the side of the dais.

Ortog glanced in their direction.

The women looked down, and were silent, frightened.

Such excuses would not serve them, you see, for they were owned, and must be ready, at any moment, to render any service, or pleasure, no matter how exquisite or intimate, that the master might desire. He does not wait upon their convenience, or pleasure. It is they who must wait, zealously, upon his. Instant obedience is the least of what is expected of a slave. They knew, of course, the common sisterhood which they shared with free women, who they now recognized as being in nature, if not in law, as much slave as they. The resentment of the slave for the free woman, eluding her slavery, and pretending it did not exist, and their fear and hatred of them, are not so much unlike, really, the seemingly irrational hatred, and intense concealed envy, which free women feel for slaves. The thought that Gerune, princess of the Drisriaks, princess of the Ortungs, was to be summoned to the tent, before the assembly, pleased them considerably. Too, in the pens and kennels, and at their work, they had heard the delicious rumors, which one scarcely dared whisper, as to how the lofty Gerune had been paraded through the corridors of the *Alaria*, bound, and gagged, and on a rope, as naked as a slave. Some fellow, it seemed, had thus managed to make his way publicly, but unsuspected, seemingly merely conducting a prisoner to her place of incarceration or enslavement, to an obscure, neglected area where escape capsules had been stored. In the ship, in the march through the corridors, she had been seen by literally hundreds of jeering, lustful Ortungs, as exposed to their gaze, their crude banter and raillery, as any stripped captive or slave. Naturally this considerably please the slaves.

"Gerune, princess of the Drisriaks, princess of the Ortungs," called a herald, from a side entrance to the tent.

There, in the threshold of that smaller entrance, her long, thick, braided blond hair, in two plaits, falling behind her, even to the back of her knees, slimly erect, splendid in rich, barbaric garments, angrily, obviously not pleased at all, two warriors behind her, stood Gerune.

Otto regarded her. She was as beautiful as he remembered her.

Julian, too, regarded her. He had seen her briefly before, in a corridor of the *Alaria*, in the vicinity of some locks, in one of which an escape capsule had been positioned.

She was quite as beautiful as he, too, remembered her.

"Greetings, my brother, milord," said Gerune.

"Greetings, noble sister," said Ortog.

Gerune's eyes briefly met those of Otto, chieftain of the Wolfungs, and then she looked away. In this brief exchange of looks each had seen, in the eyes of the other, the recollection of a relationship, an intimacy which had once obtained betwixt them, that of captor and captive, that it was at his hands that she, though a princess of the Drisriaks and Ortungs, had been, as might have been any woman, stripped and bound.

Her eyes and those of Julian, too, met. She could not be blamed, surely, if, in the first instant, she did not recognized the handsome young officer from the *Alaria* in the ragged servitor in attendance on the Wolfung chieftain, for he had been but briefly glimpsed in the corridor outside the locks. But then, after a moment, she recollected him quite well, even in his present appearance. She blushed. And the certainty of her recollection was doubtless abetted, at least, and made far more embarrassing, by the openness of the way he looked upon her, with a maleness, and relish, he did not feign to conceal. Reddened she then further. He, though of the empire, had seen her at the feet of the chieftain, then a mere gladiator clad in Ortung armor, near the lock.

There was a small stir in the tent.

The slaves, with a tiny sound of chains, looked too, toward Gerune. Once she, too, had been as helplessly in the hands of a man as they now were, irremediably and institutionally.

But Gerune was free.

She did not deign to so much as glance at the slaves.

She is indeed beautiful, thought Julian.

Gerune looked away from him.

"Approach, noble and beloved sister," said Ortog.

Many barbarians, you see, and those of many civilized worlds, and of many groups, political or otherwise, wish to view their women, though not necessarily those of others, in certain fashions, fashions to which the real woman, the natural woman, in all her delicacy, complexity and depth, is largely irrelevant.

Ortog indicated a place at his side where she might stand.

To this place Gerune, holding her long skirts closely about her, began to make her way.

There was, from somewhere in the tent, to the right, as one would face the dais, back among the men, a tiny ripple of laughter but, as Ortog looked up, angrily, it was quickly suppressed.

In her approach to her place Gerune, at the laughter, had stopped. Then she had resumed her journey.

She had now ascended the dais, and was at the side of Ortog.

"I am not well, milord," she said to Ortog. "I would be excused."

"Bring a stool for the princess," said Ortog.

One was brought, and upon it the princess, reluctantly, took her seat.

It was quiet in the tent.

"Let the proceedings being," said Ortog.

A clerk came forward, who held a set of three waxed tablets, tied together at the top by string. On such tablets matters may be scraped away, put in other form, rearranged, and such, later to be copied in a proper hand on parchment, to which Ortog might put his sign.

"The purpose of this court is to dispel scandalous rumors, uncomplimentary to the house of Ortog," said the clerk.

There was some laughter from among those of the assembly. There were doubtless several there who had witnessed, though unknowingly at the time, the discomfiture of the princess, Gerune.

"Or to establish their veracity," said Ortog.

There was a murmur of assent to this among the men present.

Gerune looked up, startled.

"It is charged," said the clerk, "that the body of the princess Gerune was, on the fourth day of the *codung* before last, publicly bared on the ship *Alaria*, as brazenly as that of an ordinary market slave."

"That is false!" cried Gerune, leaping to her feet.

One of the blond slaves looked at her, with amusement, but kept her hands down, on her spread thighs.

On most worlds in the galaxies pleasure slaves kneel with their knees spread, as this is a beautiful position and serves, too, to remind them that they are slaves. It also increases a sense of vulnerability in the woman, and is psychologically arousing. In some women this simple position, kneeling, and thusly, is all that is required for the conquest of frigidity.

"No," said Otto, his arms remaining folded upon his mighty chest. "It is true."

"Do you, Gerune, noble princess, recognize this man?" inquired the clerk, indicating Otto.

"No!" she cried.

"That is strange, Princess," said Otto, "for I recall you well."

"Fool," she cried. "Do you not know the danger in which you stand!"

"Shall I describe her to you, intimately?" Otto asked Ortog.

"Beast!" wept Gerune.

"That will not be necessary," said Ortog.

"Permit me to be excused, milord!" said Gerune.

"No," said Ortog.

"I have a grievous headache!" she wept.

"Sit down," said he, "woman."

The blond slaves laughed.

"Lash them," said Ortog.

The lash fell amongst the former citizenesses of the empire.

The slaves cried out with misery.

Men laughed.

"Enough," said Ortog, not even glancing at the chastised slaves.

The leather blade desisted then in its admonitory rebuke.

The slaves then, in misery, weeping, gasping, shuddering, remained crouched down, keeping their heads to the earthen floor, making themselves small in their chains.

There was more laughter, that of mighty masters.

Julian was momentarily embarrassed for the women.

But perhaps they now understood better that they were only slaves.

Gerune had resumed her seat.

Her face was set, angrily.

She had been furious at the slaves, who had laughed at her discomfiture, laughing at her, clearly, as though she might be naught but another woman, a woman being put in her place by strong men, a woman no different, ultimately, than they. But, even more, she resented the fashion in which she had been treated by her brother, that she was to resume her seat, that she was to remain in the tent, that she was, despite her wishes, to await the outcome of the proceedings. Also, she was alarmed, for she had taken for granted that the court was so arranged that the charge against her, on her word, and on the expected denial of the chieftain of the Wolfungs, who surely was not mad, would be dismissed. But it seemed her word was not being taken as sufficient and, to her amazement, the Wolfung seemed determined to acknowledge his role in the alleged events of the fourth day of a recent *codung*. She might be a princess, but she was, when all was said and done, only a woman. She, like the slaves, and other women, were ultimately at the mercy of men. This thought, now brought home to her, more clearly than it had ever been before, save, of course, for a particular set of events on the *Alaria*, disturbed her, and, on some deep level, thrilled her. She was also apprehensive because she now realized that she did not understand, clearly, what was going on about her, or how she figured in these matters. There seemed to be political currents about her, deep, obscure currents which eluded her.

"The princess," said the clerk, "denies the allegations involved in the charge."

"Yes," said Gerune, firmly.

There was some laughter from the assembly. The slaves, their backs striped, kept their heads down.

"Is he who putatively subjected the princess to this outrage present?" inquired the clerk.

"There was no outrage. They are all lies. It is only a story," said the princess.

"I am he," said Otto.

There was a response in the assembly to this claim, one of satisfaction.

The slaves dared to raise their heads, to look with awe upon Otto, one who had dared to treat a princess as though she might be no more than they, only a slave.

"Two matters, it seems, must be clarified," said the clerk. "First, we must have assurance that this outrage was committed, and secondly, that he who so boldly claims this deed for his own is he who has that right."

"Who amongst you," called Ortog to the assembly, "has witnessed the matter of the charge?"

"None has witnessed it, as you can see, milord," said Gerune.

"It is my understanding, milord," said a man, "that we may speak openly and freely."

"Such was the custom in the courts of the Drisriaks," said Ortog, "and so, too, it is in the court of the Ortungs. It is thus among all the Alemanni."

"Hundreds witnessed the parade of one whom they took to be a captive or slave," said the fellow, a tall fellow in a long cloak, with a ring of gold on his upper left arm.

"But it was not I!" cried the princess. "It must have been another, not I!"

"More than seventy yeomen have been marshaled outside," said the man, "who are prepared to supply evidence in the matter, either positive or negative. Too, we have brought together the officer and his men who recovered the woman in question, in the corridors of the *Alaria*, the woman who, at that time, insisted vociferously and determinedly upon her identity as the princess Gerune."

"Dismiss this matter, my brother," begged Gerune.

"Bring in some of these men, and the officer and his men, those who recovered she who claimed to be the princess," said Ortog.

"Please!" protested Gerune.

Several men were introduced into the tent, including those who had recovered the woman in question.

"Hold your head up," said Ortog to his sister.

Tears in her eyes, clutching her robes about her, she did so.

"Examine her closely," said Ortog to the men. "Make no mistake in this matter."

Surely, thought Gerune, they will have been instructed to deny such a damaging identification.

"Forgive me, milord," said a man, "but it is she."

"Yes, milord," said another, "it is she."

"No!" cried Gerune.

"I am sorry, milady," said a man.

To her misery the men, and the officer and his men, as well, several of whom regarded her with great closeness, clearly intent on responsibly discharging their duty to the court, were unanimous, however regrettably so, in their testimony.

Gerune paled, and then reddened, under this examination. She felt almost as though she might have been a slave. To be sure, there were many differences. For example, she was not naked, nor was she handled, nor her mouth forced open, that the quality and condition of her small, fine teeth be ascertained.

"It is she, undoubtedly, milord," said the last of several witnesses.

Gerune even remembered some of these men from the trek through the corridors, the jeering tones, the bestial leers, the approving looks, the gestures indicating what she might expect, if she had fallen into their hands, rather than into those of another.

"Be it accepted then," said Ortog, "that it was done onto the princess Gerune, on the *Alaria*, on the fourth day of the *codung* before last, substantially as was specified in the charge."

"Have you no feelings for me, my brother?" asked Gerune.

"I must seek truth, and do justice," said Ortog. "I am king."

"How you have reduced my value," said Gerune. "I joined with you for love, fleeing with you and others the hall of our father."

"You joined with me, that you would be the highest woman in the Ortungs," said Ortog.

"Of what value am I now," she asked. "How will you arrange my marriage? How will you mate me now to the advantage of the Ortungs?"

"Such matters are no longer of importance," said Ortog. "And you have already contributed to the advantage of the Ortungs."

"How so, milord?" she asked. "I do not understand."

"Proceed," said Ortog to the clerk.

"Milord!" protested Gerune.

"Is he who stands now before you, milady," asked the clerk, "he who on the fourth day of the *codung* before last removed, or caused to be removed, your regal habiliments and placed you in bonds more suitable to a slave than a princess?"

Gerune was silent.

"Thence, and thusly, marching you, exhibited, through the corridors of the ship *Alaria*?"

"No," said Gerune.

There was a stir of surprise in the assembly. Otto, too, regarded her with surprise.

"Surely you desire some terrible vengeance, dear sister," said Ortog.

"It was not he," murmured Gerune, her head down.

"I do not understand," said Ortog.

"She is a woman," said his shieldsman, who held the golden helmet. "She has felt the ropes."

"Strange," said Ortog.

Gerune lifted her head a little. Briefly she met the eyes of Otto, who was puzzled. She looked away from him. She then met the eyes of Julian, who, too, was puzzled. She then again lowered her head.

"I can prove the matter," said Otto.

Gerune stiffened.

"I did as it is thought with the princess," said Otto, "as it was congenial to my plan for escape from the ship and, as she was a woman, as it pleased me. Her royal garments, too, in accord with my plan, and as it pleased me, and that she might understand herself and her relationship to me better, I put on a slave, one whom I had won in contest."

Gerune looked up, angrily.

Ortog's face flushed with fury. There was a cry of rage from the assembly.

The chained slaves stole glances at one another. How pleased they were! How they hated Gerune!

"These garments were on the slave when we made good our escape from the *Alaria*," said Otto. "I kept them." He pointed to the soiled bundle in the hand of Gundlicht. "Those are the garments," said Otto. "Let them be examined, and identified. I returned them to your envoy on Varna."

Women of the princess were called forth and they, with others, confirmed that the garments were those of the princess, which she had had upon her on the fourth day of the *codung* before last. Some of these women had even sewn the garments themselves, and others had adorned the princess with them on the day in question. The jewelry, too, by certain merchants, and craftsmen, was identified, some even by their marks.

"The court accepts," said Ortog, "that he before us now, he who claims the deeds involved in these matters, is fully and lawfully entitled to do so, that they are, as he claims, his."

There was a response of satisfaction from the assembly.

"You are a fool," said Gerune to Otto.

His eyes flashed for a moment, and Gerune, in spite of her position and power, and the men about her, shrank back. She could scarcely dare conjecture what it might be to be alone with such a man, and at his mercy.

"You are Otto, who claims to be the chieftain of the Wolfungs," said Ortog.

"I am Otto, chieftain of the Wolfungs," said Otto.

"They have no chieftains," said Ortog.

"I have been lifted on the shields," said Otto.

"We have forbidden the Wolfungs chieftains," said Ortog. "Surely you know this. The Wolfungs, of the Vandals, are a tribe tributary to their betters, first the Drisriaks, now the Ortungs, and are permitted to exist only upon their sufferance."

"Do the Drisriaks know you come for the tribute of the Wolfungs?" asked Otto.

"As it is explained to me, you refused the tribute," said Ortog.

"Yes, they did, milord," said Hendrix.

"Yes, milord," said Gundlicht.

"You returned, empty-handed, from Varna, bringing no grain, no pelts, no women."

"Yes, milord," said Hendrix.

"Yes, milord," said Gundlicht.

"They had no grain, no pelts?" asked Ortog.

"They had such things," said Hendrix.

"And no satisfactory women?" inquired Ortog.

"They had some beauties," said Gundlicht.

"But they are not now in our collars?"

"No, milord," said Gundlicht.

"The tribute was refused?" said Ortog.

"Yes, milord," said Gundlicht.

"Is this true?" Ortog asked Otto.

"Yes," said Otto.

"Why?" asked Ortog.

"The Wolfungs are no longer a tributary tribe to the Drisriaks, or the Ortungs," said Otto.

"And why is that?" asked Ortog.

Otto shrugged. "I have been lifted upon the shields," he said.

"You are well aware, I trust," said Ortog, "that our ships could burn away your forests, and destroy the Wolfungs, once and for all."

"Some might escape," said Otto.

"We could destroy your world," said Ortog.

"Who are the Ortungs?" asked Otto.

"We are Alemanni," said Ortog.

"You are not a true tribe," said Otto. "You have no recognition, no legitimacy. It is only that you have broken away from the Drisriaks."

"We have ships, and cannon!" cried Ortog.

"So, too, have bands of brigands," said Otto.

"You are bold," said Ortog.

Otto was silent.

"We could destroy Varna," said Ortog.

"But that would not expunge the insult," said Otto.

"No," mused Ortog, "that would not expunge the insult."

He looked at Gerune, who looked away.

"You would be, I conjecture," said Otto, "more than a band of brigands."

Men cried out, angrily. Some stepped forward, blades half drawn, from the side. Ortog motioned them back. Otto had not moved, but continued to stand, his arms folded across his chest, before Ortog, seated on the dais.

"Antiquity, and custom, do not, in themselves, bestow legitimacy," said Ortog.

"But may be taken as the tokens thereof," said Otto.

"The most ancient, and honorable, of tribes must have had beginnings," said Ortog, "though these beginnings may not have been understood at the time."

"Doubtless," said Otto. "And I doubt not, as well, that at the foot of every dynasty, at the founding of every tribe, though we many not remember him, though his name may be lost, there was once a brigand, or soldier, or seeker of fortune, or pirate."

"Lying dog!" cried a man.

"Do you object?" asked Ortog.

"No," said Otto.

"I see you as such a man," said Ortog.

Otto shrugged.

"We carry legitimacy in our holsters, in our scabbards," said Ortog.

"It is true that in the end," said Otto, "there is only the weight of the rock, the point of the stick, the blade of the knife."

Ortog looked down at the soiled clothing, the garments, the jewelry, and such, which had been identified as that of the princess. These things lay across his knees.

"But I have been lifted on the shields," said Otto

"I, too, have been lifted on the shields," said Ortog, looking up, angrily.

"But only by renegades," said Otto.

"Slay him!" cried a man.

"Hold," said Ortog.

"Legitimacy, in the normal course of things, is an accretion," said Otto, "bestowed in a moment of forgetfulness, a gift of time, taken for granted thereafter."

Ortog did not speak.

"But sometimes history may be hurried on a little," said Otto.

"Speak clearly," said Ortog.

"I come before you," said Otto, "bearing a priceless gift, one I do not think you will care to refuse, the free and uncoerced recognition of the Ortungen as a tribe of the Alemanni nation."

Ortog looked closely at Otto.

"I bring you legitimacy, or the supposition thereof, as though wrapped in a cloth of gold."

"That could be weighty, milord," said the clerk. "The Wolfungs are a traditional and unquestioned tribe of the Vandal peoples."

"It is for such a purpose," asked Ortog, skeptically, "to benefit the Ortungen, that you have entered into the ritual of the challenge?"

"Not at all," said Otto. "The Wolfungs are muchly at the mercy of the Ortungen, as hitherto of the Drisriaks. I would change that. It is for that reason that I have issued the challenge. You, or your champion, must meet me in combat. If you, or your champion, are victorious, I shall be slain, the Wolfungs will have no chieftain, which is what you have wished, and things will be as before. If, on the other hand, I am victorious, you will abandon all claims upon the lives and goods of the Wolfungs."

"You have done grievous insult onto my sister, the princess Gerune," said Ortog.

"Accept then the challenge," said Otto.

"I could have you slain now," said Ortog.

"But only as a brigand might order a killing," said Otto.

"It is the challenge of one chieftain to another, milord," said the clerk.

"Such things have not been done for a thousand years," said Ortog.

"I have issued the challenge," said Otto.

"Such challenges can only be between chieftains of tribes," said the clerk to Ortog. "He is chieftain of the Wolfungs, of the Vandals. He has seen fit to accord you this challenge. Seize this opportunity, milord. It is a rare one. In accepting it, you are acknowledged chieftain of the Ortungs, and the Ortungs a tribe, that in the eyes not only of the Wolfungen, an acknowledged tribe of the Vandals, but in those of all the Vandal peoples, and of a hundred other peoples, as well.''

"Does milord hesitate?" asked Ortog's shieldsman.

"What is your origin, your true people?" asked Ortog of Otto.

"I do not know," said Otto. "I was raised in the *festung* village of Sim Giadini. It is on Tangara."

"You are only a peasant," said Ortog. "How could I, a chieftain, in honor and propriety, accept a challenge from one such as you?"

"I have been lifted upon the shields," said Otto.

"He has the look of an Otung," said one of the men from the side.

Ortog was silent. He had, himself, long ago, on the *Alaria*, vouchsafed a similar speculation.

Julian looked closely at the first fellow who had spoken, and then at Ortog.

The Otungs, or Otungen, were the largest, and fiercest, tribe of the Vandal peoples.

"No matter, milord," said the clerk. "He has been lifted upon the shields. Accept the challenge."

"Do not hesitate, milord!" called a man from the fellows to the left of the dais.

"Such a thing would consolidate the people, milord," said the clerk.

"Your sister," said Otto, "is well curved, and would bring a high price upon a slave block."

Men cried out with rage.

"Beware," said Ortog.

Otto shrugged. "She is only a woman," he said.

"You permitted yourself to be captured," said Ortog, angrily, to Gerune.

"I could not help it, milord," said Gerune. "I was overpowered."

"I see," snarled Ortog.

"I am a woman," said Gerune.

"Only a woman," snarled Ortog.

"I am a princess!" she said.

"And you were taken as easily as any woman. You could have been made a slave."

"I am a princess!" she cried.

"Only a woman," snarled Ortog.

"And that becomes clearer," said Otto, "if her regal robes were to be again removed."

"Beware, Wolfung!" said Ortog.

"Accept the challenge!" urged the clerk.

"Accept the challenge!" said the shieldsman.

"As I have issued the challenge," said Otto, "you may, as is the custom of our two peoples, choose the weapons."

Ortog looked down at the garments, the jewelry, and such, of the princess Gerune, which had been removed from her on the *Alaria*, and returned to Hendrix and Gundlicht on Varna, some days ago. These various items still lay across his knees.

"You have shamed me, and the Ortungs," said Ortog to Gerune.

"I am sorry, milord," said Gerune, tears in her eyes.

"You may, of course," said Otto, "choose a champion."

"I have a mind," said Ortog to Gerune, "to keep you in the tents from now on, to conceal you from the eyes of those you shamed."

Gerune looked at him, stricken.

"You would have less freedom than a slave girl," said Ortog.

"Please, no, milord," wept Gerune.

"And it would be fitting to force you to wear these soiled rags, which have been put upon the body of a slave girl, until they stink and rot, and fall off your body," he said, "as a badge of your shame."

"It would be better," said Otto, "to have her keep her body washed and perfumed, and clad as that of a slave, as such a garmenture is enhancing to the beauty of a woman."

Gerune looked at him, startled. Perhaps she had never realized that men might speculate as to what she, or, indeed, other women, might look like, clad as slaves.

She wrung her hands, then, wildly, in misery, and looked down, at just that time, at the three slaves to her left, kneeling there, chained in their place. There were all regarding her. Then they looked away, frightened, crying out, for Gerune, in hysterical helplessness, in rage, in fury, that they should dare look upon her, and as though they might share some smug, common sisterhood with her, they only slaves, leapt to her feet and, sobbing, seized a whip, from a keeper, and threw herself down, amongst them, sobbing wildly, striking wildly, hysterically, about. At a sign from Ortog the keeper wrenched the whip away from Gerune. Ortog then, as she stood there to the left, on the rush-strewn earthen floor, below the dais, amongst the cowering, beaten slaves, she half bent over, weeping helplessly, indicated that she should resume her seat.

She turned suddenly, defiantly, and fled toward the side entrance of the tent but her way, there, was blocked by two warriors, those who had conducted her to the tent.

She turned about, and then ascended, again, to the surface of the dais, resuming her seat.

There was laughter from among the men.

The free women in the tent, some of them her own women, looked down.

Even their lofty mistress, to such men, Ortungs, and others, was only a woman.

"I have issued the challenge," said Otto.

Ortog angrily seized up the jewelry and robes from where they lay, across his knees, and then held them before himself for a moment, and then, wadding them together, hurled them angrily to his left, to the floor, to the foot of the dais.

"Take those things," said Ortog to a frightened free woman.

She hurried to gather up the items.

"Put them among the stores from which we clothe slaves for our pleasure," said Ortog.

"The robes, too, milord?" asked the woman, from her knees. She was not more than a yard or two from Otto.

"But first, of course," said Ortog, "they must be cut into revealing rags."

"Yes, milord!" said the women.

In a moment she had gathered together the jewelry, the bracelets, the necklaces, the chains and such, and the robes, and hurried from the tent.

"That was not necessary, milord," said Gerune.

"You have shamed me, and the Ortungs," said Ortog.

"The challenge has been issued," Otto said.

"Accept it, milord," said the clerk.

"Accept it, milord," said the shieldsman, with the golden helmet.

"You," said Ortog, paying no attention to the others about him, "you, step forward."

He was pointing at Julian.

Julian, reluctantly, stepped forward, from where he had been standing, rather behind the left shoulder of Otto.

"I see you have with you," said Ortog to Otto, "a lowly, and despicable thrall."

"He is, of course," said Otto, "a free man, of the empire."

"Step forward," said Ortog to Julian.

Julian took another step forward.

"I think we have met before," said Ortog.

"Yes," said Julian.

"You are an officer in the imperial navy," said Ortog, "but, I take it, no ordinary officer. I saw you on the *Alaria*, and noted your place of honor, and the deference accorded to you."

"Who is he, milord?" inquired his shieldsman.

"As you see," said Ortog, "a worthless dog, clad in rags."

"Milord?" said the clerk.

"He has some relation to the imperial family," said Ortog. "I am sure of it."

Men gasped. Some even stepped back, so dreaded and awesome seemed the mysterious empire. It was one thing to mock and scorn the empire, but they were only too well aware of its power. Seldom would they stand against its ships. It would not have occurred to them to meet it in force. Its history, its deeds, its terrors, its terribleness, loomed large in their imagination and fears. One of the most potent defenses of the empire was its simple presence, so extensive and subtle, looming so mightily in titanic legend.

"Rope him, like a pig, and put him on his knees," said Ortog.

Julian was rudely seized and bound, and thrown on his knees before Ortog.

Men breathed easier.

"You were, when last I saw you, as I recall, leveling a pistol at me, on an imperial ship," said Ortog to Julian.

"Unfortunately," said Julian, "I did not receive an opportunity to fire."

It was at that time that the ship had been first struck by the pursuing Ortung fleet.

"I think you will bring an excellent ransom," said Ortog.

Otto had not attempted to interfere with Julian's discomfiture.

He did not care to be diverted from his purpose.

"The challenge has been issued," Otto reminded Ortog.

"That is true, milord," said the clerk to Ortog.

"On our camp world," said Ortog to Julian, "you will tend pigs, but, as you are of high birth, your chains will be of gold."

"On what world do you think it would be appropriate for your sister to be sold as a slave girl?" asked Otto.

Ortog regarded him, irritably.

"Her particular form of beauty might bring a higher or lower price on certain worlds," speculated Otto.

This was true. Certain worlds preferred blondes, and certain worlds redheads, and so on. The princess Gerune was, as we have noted, blond. This tended to be a popular hair color on many worlds, for slaves.

"Take him away," said Ortog, pointing to Julian. "It will take some time to arrange for his ransom."

Julian was dragged to his feet, and rudely conducted, stumbling, from the tent.

"Secure recognition for us," said a man, pleading, from the side.

"Such a recognition, by tribal custom, must carry weight even with your father, Abrogastes," said a man.

"Accept the challenge," urged the clerk.

"Accept the challenge," urged the shieldsman, he with the golden helmet in his grasp.

"Accept the challenge," pressed others.

Ortog regarded Otto, evenly. "The challenge, of course," he said, "is accepted."


## · · · CHAPTER 8 · · ·


The blade of the adz, the larger adz, one of the sort with which we are concerned here, is better than a foot in length. The handle, in which the blade is fixed, socketed, crosswise, is some four feet, or approximately so, in length. It can be wielded efficiently only by a very strong man, or a creature of some comparable, or greater, strength. This instrument has a place in the traditions of numerous peoples, in particular, as one would suppose, those of the forests. Indeed, the adz, as the ax and the spear, and, later, the sword, is, in a sense, a symbol of such peoples.

The particular adz we have in mind is now enclosed in a leather case. In the same compartment in which we find the adz, on a shallow bronze plate, and covered with a purple cloth, was a heavy, sturdy, muchly scarred, peeled stump, indeed, one which had been brought, some time ago, from the home world of the Alemanni peoples.

We beg the indulgence of the reader, in reminding him of these things.

It may also be recalled, though it is not recounted in this manuscript, that some days ago, while Hendrix and Gundlicht were entertained in the hut of Otto, chieftain of the Wolfungs, one of their radios, that of the Ortungs, was surreptitiously used to broadcast a message to an imperial fleet, supposed to be in the quadrant, presumably having come in response to distress calls from the *Alaria,* which vessel had been destroyed after the Ortungs had taken their leave of her.

One of the risks of transmitting such a message, of course, is that one does not know who or what may hear it.

This message had, in fact, been overheard.

The vessels, however, did not turn toward Varna, which was speculated to be its source.

Their objective was other than Varna.

They themselves traveled in radio silence.


## ▪ ▪ ▪ CHAPTER 9 ▪ ▪ ▪


"I have been sent to you, and have been commanded to address you as 'Milord'," she said.

The two warriors, behind her, withdrew from the threshold of the waiting tent, closing the flap behind her.

She was enveloped in a dark cloak and hood, and her head was down. She spoke softly.

Otto could barely hear her.

He approached her and brushed back the hood, and she raised her head.

"Gerune!" he cried.

"Yes," she said, angrily.

"It is the princess," said Julian. His limbs were confined in chains of gold.

"You stink of swine," she said to him, angrily.

Julian had been permitted to come to the tent of Otto, that he might there, on the morrow, render him service, that in the manner of the second. Otto had brought none other with him, that by his own will.

"Why have you been brought to the tent?" asked Julian.

Gerune looked at him, in fury.

Then she lifted her chin, disdainfully, as Otto undid the string at the throat of the cloak and, gently, parted it, and lifted it back.

Gerune was quite beautiful.

About her neck, on a string, was a tiny key.

"Do not dare to look upon me!" Gerune hissed to Julian.

But his eyes marveled at her loveliness, relishing it in the full, exciting glory of masculine passion.

Gerune could not resist, had she been so minded, the lifting away of the dark cloak.

Otto put the cloak over his arm, and turned her about. Her tiny wrists were confined behind her body, in the delicate, tasteful, but efficient, inflexible cuffs of a female slave.

Doubtless it was to these devices that the tiny key at her throat, on its string, answered.

"It seems your brother thinks highly of you," said Otto.

"I have shamed the Ortungs," she said.

"It is for that that you have been sent here, on this night," said Otto.

"Yes," she said. "It is my punishment. I am to serve you, as might a female slave. Then, suitably chastened, after the morrow's combat, I am to be sequestered, put from public view, and, though free, will be less free even than a female slave."

"It is unfortunate," said Julian. "You would make an excellent female slave."

"Dog!" she cried.

"You are a woman," said Julian. "You would learn quickly enough, under the whip."

She viewed him with fury.

"Naked dog!" she snarled.

Julian was not naked but his tunic had been muchly torn away, considerably baring the young aristocrat's form. This had amused the herders in whose keeping he had been placed.

"Naked, chained dog," she snarled.

His wrists were before his body, confined in golden manacles. His ankles were shackled, in shackles of gold, these joined by a short chain, that, too of gold.

"Free your wrists," said he, "female."

She looked away.

"Your necklace is fetching," he said.

She tossed her head, causing the tiny key on its string to dance at her throat.

"And your ensemble," said he, "is stunning, doubtless the latest fashion for barbarian princesses—being displayed in imperial markets."

"For the evening," said Gerune to Otto, "I am yours. Do with me as you wish."

"Is it true?" said Otto.

"Yes," she said.

Then she added, "Yes, milord."

Otto reached for the key on its string. It was looped, and tied, rather closely about her neck, that she could not slip it. Fear entered briefly into her eyes. She drew back a bit from his hand, as it was near her beauty.

He lowered his hand.

"Perhaps you should cry out," suggested Julian.

She looked at him, in fury.

"But then your cries would doubtless be disregarded by those outside," he said.

"Yes, they would be," she said.

"And then perhaps," suggested he, "as you are subdued, and vanquished, your soft cries, your moans of helpless ecstasy, suitable for a slave girl, might be reported to your brother."

She paled.

"Forgive me, milady," said Otto. And he reached to the string about her neck and took it with two hands, gently. He then broke it.

She looked at him, startled.

She had not expected to be freed.

To be sure, the hands of slave girls are often freed, that they may the better serve.

But he had not simply jerked the string loose, taking it in one hand, snapping it free, peremptorily, against the back of her neck. He had freed her of the string carefully, but surely.

He turned her about and as she trembled, his hands so near her, inserted the tiny key in the locks.

In a moment she rubbed her wrists, her hands freed.

"Milord?" she inquired.

He tossed the cuffs to one side, with the key.

"Garb yourself," said he.

She took the cloak and drew it, closely, wonderingly, about her.

"I do not understand," she said.

He regarded her.

"Milord," she added.

"You are a free woman, and a princess," he said. "You will be treated with honor."

She looked at him, wonderingly.

He pointed to a corner of the tent, where some blankets were strewn on the ground. "There will be your place, milady," he said. "I advise you this night to be essentially silent and unobtrusive, for you are beautiful, and we are but men."

"Yes, milord," she whispered.

She then went to the place which Otto had indicated and knelt there. She made certain the cloak covered her, save for her throat and head, which were bared.

"Perhaps you should not kneel," said Otto. This posture, in a woman, can enflame a man.

"Yes, milord," she smiled.

She then half knelt, half sat. Julian had often seen women in that posture in slave markets, chained by an ankle against a wall. She pulled the cloak up, about her throat. Then she looked down, demurely. A shapely ankle, with it small foot, peeped out from beneath the cloak, and then, as though self-consciously, with a superior smile at Julian, she drew it back, removing it from sight beneath the cloak.

"She knows what she is doing," complained Julian, "the vixen."

"How can it be?" asked Otto. "She is a free woman."

"She is a woman," said Julian.

Too, it must be remembered that once, some time ago, on the *Alaria*, the princess Gerune had felt bonds. The symbolism of such things, the psychological suggestions associated with them, their reverberant emotional impact, so inexplicable, seemingly ancient and mystical, the memories they recall, the truths at which they hint, are things no woman ever forgets.

That evening food was brought to the tent.

"Do not eat it," said Julian to Otto.

"She is in the tent," said Otto. "I do not think it will have been tampered with."

They could not know, outside, for example, whether or not Gerune would be permitted to eat.

"They do not need to drug you, or poison you," said Gerune.

"Why?" asked Otto.

"They are not of the empire," said Gerune.

"Bitch," said Julian.

"Dog!" she exclaimed, angrily.

She lay at the side of the tent, on the blankets, her weight partly on her right elbow, the cloak up about her. You could not see her well, because of the darkness.

"You will eat first, bitch," said Julian.

Gerune looked away.

"I must eat, to keep up my strength," said Otto.

He had not been fed in two days.

"It will not matter," said Gerune.

"Why do you say that?" asked Otto.

"Because you will lose," said Gerune.

"How do you know that?" demanded Julian.

"You have no chance," she said, bitterly.

"The weapons are unfamiliar, the chosen champion presumed invincible?" inquired Otto.

"No," she said.

"I do not understand," said Otto.

"I will partake of the food," said Gerune.

"You will indeed," Julian assured her.

She looked up at him, angrily.

Otto lit a small lamp in the tent and hung it on the forward pole.

"Perhaps you should remove your cloak," said Julian. "The bodies of slave girls are exquisite in this sort of light."

"Dog of the empire," she hissed.

"Are you hungry?" inquired Julian.

"Yes," she said.

"Then, eat," said Julian.

He took a chunk of bread from the broad trencher on which it had been brought, and threw it to the blankets before Gerune.

"You throw me food as though I were a female slave!" she said.

"And a slave would be grateful for as much," said Julian.

"You are only a despicable thrall of the Wolfung!" she said.

"I am a free man of the empire," said Julian.

"And I am a princess of the Ortungen!" she said.

"Would you prefer, Princess, to crawl to me, and take food in your mouth, from my hand, like the bitch you are, or as the slave you should be?"

She looked down, trembling.

It is common for slaves to be fed in such a fashion. They are, of course, being slaves, lower than bitches.

She reached for the chunk of bread.

"Wait, Princess," said Otto.

He retrieved the piece of bread and handed it to her.

"Thank you, milord," she said.

"She is not a slave, she is free," said Otto to Julian.

Julian watched carefully while Gerune finished the bread. He then, from the trencher, brought her samples of the food there, and, carefully, watched her eat each bit.

Gerune looked up, angrily, at Julian.

"We will wait some time," said Julian. "The effect may be delayed, and they may have an antidote for the princess."

"Dog," said the princess.

"She may have developed, over time, through graduated doses, an immunity to certain poisons," said Julian.

Certain rulers, and high men, had done this.

"I do not imbibe poisons," said the princess.

The technique was dangerous, however, sometimes resulting in the sickness and death of the subject, and was also on the whole of little protective value, in virtue of the variety of toxins available to the potential assassin. A cabinet of antidotes, depending on the symptoms manifested, was generally preferred. Too, of course, in royal households, the acquisition of foods and their preparation tended to be carefully supervised. A number of such households, too, utilized the time-honored practice of skilled food tasters. These, contrary to popular belief, were normally free persons, and were often trained chemists, physicians, and such. Their senses, particularly those of taste and smell, were both acute and highly trained. The services of such men, who were sometimes court physicians, as well, were valued far above those of animals and slaves. Sometimes, too, particularly within the empire, samples of certain foods, prior to being served, were literally subjected to chemical analysis. But even so, many were the emperors who had died at the table. It is interesting to add, in this respect, that little attention, on the whole, was paid, or needed to be paid, to such matters in barbarian courts. In the barbarian court there tended to be a unified *ethos*, an ordered oneness, an organic wholeness, a tribality, a community. There one was commonly environed with individuals known to one, with one's comrades in arms, one's brothers, so to speak. One had a history in common with them. It was quite different from the situation in civilization where one had about oneself not a community, not a band of brothers, but a world of milling, swarming strangers, an aggregate of self-seeking, often hostile, competitive units, innocent of honor and tradition, many of which might have something to gain, and little to fear, from shifts in power. Too, in the barbarian situation there was commonly at hand no maze of nameless streets, no anonymous crowds, so to speak, in which one might immediately lose oneself, seeking escape or refuge. In a barbarian community reprisals tended to be swift and sure. Their hunters were efficient and relentless. The barbarian community tends to be organic, with a structured hierarchy, its parts, each essential and celebrated, in harmony with one another. It knows that there is a jungle, but it keeps it at bay; it does not invite it within. It is joyous to feast with one's companions. It is dangerous to eat with strangers.

"They can kill us now, if they want," said Otto. He picked a piece of meat from the trencher and, holding it in both hands, began to tear at it with his teeth. They had not been permitted utensils.

"You see, dog of the empire," said Gerune, later, "the food is acceptable."

"But poorly prepared," said Julian. "If you were mine, you would be taught to prepare food properly."

"I, cook?" asked Gerune.

"It would figure among several of your other duties," said Julian.

"Such as?" she asked.

"Surely you can guess," he said.

"Dog, dog!" she cried.

"It seems," said Otto, "that the food has not been tampered with."

"It would not be necessary to do so," she said.

"Why?" he asked.

"You will see in the morning," she said, "milord."

"You do not care to speak further of this matter?" asked Otto.

"Beware the priestess Huta," said Gerune.

"She of the Timbri?" said Otto.

"Yes, milord," she said.

"What has she to do with the Ortungs?" asked Otto.

"She has come to have much influence over my brother," said Gerune.

"Do you approve of this?" asked Otto.

"No, milord," said Gerune.

"In what way does she figure in the affairs of the morrow?" asked Julian.

"You wear chains," she said, scornfully.

"Would that you were truly a female slave," said Julian. "You might then be tortured. You would then speak."

She drew back form him, shuddering, clutching the cloak more closely about her.

"Speak further," said Otto.

"What is to be done," she said, "is worthy only of the empire, not of my people."

"You do not care for it?" asked Otto.

"No, milord," she said.

"Will you not speak further?" asked Otto.

"I may not, milord," she said.

"Speak!" cried Julian.

"No, naked thrall," she hissed.

"You require a taste of the whip, Princess," said Julian.

"Dog!" she hissed.

"I will lock your wrist behind you, in slave cuffs," said Julian, "and make you writhe, and cry out, like a slave girl!"

"You would not dare!" she cried.

He took a menacing step toward her, extending his chained hands toward her.

"No," said Otto, sternly.

Julian arrested his advance, angrily.

"Would that you were my slave," he said. "You would learn quickly enough your fate!"

She shrank back before him, even to the wall of the tent.

"No," said Otto. "She is free."

Julian turned away, angrily.

"Let us retire," said Otto. He lifted the globe on the lamp. He blew out the tiny flame.

"Milord," she said, late that night.

"Yes," said Otto.

"Do you want a woman, milord?" she asked.

"You are free," he said.

"You are not to survive the morrow," she said.

"You are free," he said.

"Yes, milord," she said.

# • • • **CHAPTER 10** • • •

"Let the auspices be taken," called Ortog, from a dais.

This dais was outside, open to the sun and air, but it, and the area for viewers, and the field of the challenge itself, were within a large, oval, temporary enclosure, some seven to eight feet high, wall-like, formed of braced poles and yellow silk. This silk billowed in the wind. If one listened carefully one could hear it. Occasionally a bird's cry, too, could be heard, from somewhere beyond the enclosure. It was traditional that challenges be met in the open air, and on a natural surface, such as earth or grass. To be sure, they sometimes took place on a small island, in a river, or on a bleak skerry, offshore, or even, interestingly enough, in a stream itself, commonly one dividing warring territories.

"As the king wishes," said Huta, of the Timbri, in her white gown.

Her cheekbones were high, her eyes bright, her hair as dark as the night of sunless Sheol.

"Let the truthful, consecrated blood, sacred to the ten thousand gods of Timbri, be brought," she called.

Two women, perhaps acolytes, or novices, escorted two men who brought forth, and placed a few feet before the dais, on a surface of linked boards, supported by two trestles, a large, sealed container.

"That will be blood from the sacrifices," said Julian, whispering to Otto.

They stood rather alone, a bit before, and to one side, of the dais.

On the dais, but clearly isolated there, stood Gerune. None regarded her. None would stand near her. She had, last night, been taken to the tent of the Wolfung. She had spent the night there. She had been put there, as much at his mercy, as much to be used as he might wish, as any slave girl. Not even her own women would now look upon her. She wore, however, having been carefully dressed therein, within the women's tents, that she might appear resplendent upon the dais, adding glory to the day, intricately worked, regal, barbaric garments, these garments, too, with gold and jewels, muchly bedecked.

The two men who had set the container on the surface of linked boards now withdrew.

The two acolytes removed its lid.

Otto looked about himself.

There were many within the enclosure, much as there had been within the great tent, and many were the same individuals, warriors, soldiers, ambassadors, traders, guests, free men, free women.

On the dais, with Ortog, were his shieldsman, and the clerk, and other high men.

Hendrix and Gundlicht were to one side, to the right of the dais as one might face it.

A priestess brought forth a large wooden pole, and plunged it into the container, and began to stir the liquid within it.

She lifted it and blood, fresh and bright, dripped back into the container.

Men cried out with awe.

"How can it be fresh?" asked Otto. "Surely now it must be caked and hard."

"It is done with chemicals," said Julian, irritably.

"What are chemicals?" asked Otto.

"Substances," said Julian, "iron, salt, a thousand things."

Otto was silent.

He had been raised in a *festung* village. There were many things he did not understand.

"We are so helpless!" Julian said suddenly, angrily. He pulled a little at the golden manacles confining his wrists.

Some men regarded him, and then looked away.

Gerune turned, too, and looked at him, but then lifted her head, loftily, in misery, and looked away.

"I wonder if Ortog has tried to contact an imperial fleet with respect to your ransom," said Otto.

"Do not concern yourself with me," said Julian.

"He will doubtless wait a time," said Otto. "It will be done through intermediaries. He will not wish to reveal his own position."

"Consider your own peril, my friend," said Julian.

"I wonder if your message, from Varna, was heard," said Otto.

"It would seem not," said Julian.

"Surely an imperial fleet would be in the quadrant," said Otto.

"One does not know," said Julian.

"The *Alaria* surely had time to transmit distress signals, calls for help," said Otto.

"We are far from the scene of the *Alaria*'s misfortune," said Julian.

"You transmitted a message from Varna," said Otto.

"It seems it was not heard," said Julian.

"Bring a plain piece of cloth," said Huta to a priestess, "a simple piece of cloth, one no different from any other."

A cloth was fetched.

Surely there seemed nothing unusual about it.

"Would you care to inspect this cloth, milord?" inquired Huta of Ortog.

"No, milady," said Ortog.

Huta held the cloth by its corners, and turned about, displaying it to the crowd. It was some two-foot square.

"I should like to inspect it," said Otto.

"You would detect nothing unusual in it," said Julian.

"There are many slaves present," said Otto.

This was true, and there was a purpose for it. Earlier, in the great tent, there had been, near the dais, rather at its foot, to the right, as one would face it, chained in place, only three slaves, three only, blond display slaves, women who had been taken from the *Alaria*, women who had been, in a former reality, one now quite abrogated and superseded, citizenesses of the empire. But there were now several slaves present, perhaps between forty and fifty, many kneeling, their wrists chained behind, or before, their bodies, in the first row of the viewers, the men standing behind them.

"Yes," said Julian. "And one of the most beautiful is on the dais."

"She is free," Otto reminded Julian.

"She is a beautiful slut," said Julian, admiring Gerune.

She looked down at him, and then glanced away, quickly.

"Yes," said Otto.

"Do you not think she would make an excellent slave?" asked Julian.

"Yes," said Otto. "I think she would make an excellent slave."

"You note," said Julian, "that her former garments, and jewelry, are about."

"Yes," said Otto.

And, indeed, it was to display such things that so many slaves were present.

On each of the slaves present there was some shred, or particle, of what had been the regal garments of Gerune on the *Alaria*.

Those garments had been cut, and torn, to pieces, until they were now little more than scarves and ribbons.

At the foot of the dais, rather to its left, chained there much as they had been in the great tent, one might again notice the three blond display slaves, spoken of upon occasion earlier, the former citizenesses of the empire, taken from the *Alaria*. Their adornments, such as they were, may be taken as typical of those of the slaves present. One wore, knotted about her left ankle, much as though it might be a slave anklet, such things, metal and locked, used in some locales to identify slaves, a shred of cloth, cut from the garments which Gerune had worn on the *Alaria*. Another had such a strip of cloth thrust loosely, and then looped there, about her collar. The third had such a piece of cloth knotted about her upper left arm. These three, too, among them, shared the jewelry which had been worn by Gerune, bracelets, after the placement of which their manacles had been replaced, and several necklaces, thrown over their heads, the hair then taken back and lifted up, thence to be replaced attractively, arranged and smoothed, over the strings and chains. The hair of the women had not been cut since their capture. Long hair tends to be favored in slave girls, as it is attractive and there is much that can be done with it, both cosmetically and in the performance of their more intimate tasks. It may also serve, upon occasion, as a bond. Cutting the hair short, or shaving the head, is normally a punishment. To be sure, much depends on the tasks to which the girl is set. Long hair is less practical, for example, if she is to be put to the cleaning of stables. The length, style, arrangement and such of a slave's hair, is, as one would expect, a function of the will of the master. She must wear it as it pleases him, and may make no changes without his permission. It is so, of course, in effect, with the grooming of any animal.

"How shamed must be Gerune, to see her garments, her jewelries, thus displayed on the bodies of mere slaves," said Otto.

"Yes," said Julian, approvingly.

"Do you not feel sorry for her?" asked Otto.

"As she is a free woman, and I am a free man, in a sense, of course," said Julian. "But if she were a slave, then I would not feel sorry for her."

"No," said Otto. "One would not feel sorry for her then."

"Then she herself would be only a slave," said Julian.

"Yes," said Otto.

"Behold, milord," called Huta. "I dip within the consecrated blood, the blood of truth, the plain cloth, innocent of all design and preparation, and call upon the ten thousand gods of Timbri, if it be their will, to vouchsafe us a sign."

She thrust her white-clad arms, to the elbows, into the container of blood, plunging the cloth into the liquid. then she straightened up, her sleeves scarlet with blood, but holding the cloth beneath the surface of the blood, it now stirred about her submerged wrists.

"Vouchsafe us a sign, O gods of the Timbri!" she cried.

Then she drew the cloth from the liquid and held it up, first to the dais, then turning, showing it to the crowd on all sides. Men cried out with awe. Women screamed.

"Aiii!" cried Otto.

The cloth bore upon its surface, outlined in blood, the sign of the Ortungs.

"The auspices have been taken," announced Huta.

"Come forward," Ortog called to Otto, who stepped before the dais, followed by Julian.

The priestess Huta handed the cloth, it bearing the sign of the Ortungs, to another priestess, who folded it carefully, and carried it away.

"You are Otto, claiming to be chieftain of the Wolfungs," said Ortog.

"I am Otto, chieftain of the Wolfungs," said Otto.

"Let him be chieftain," whispered the clerk to Ortog. "He must be chieftain, for the matter to be proper."

"I salute you," said Ortog, lifting his hand, "chieftain of the Wolfungs."

"I am chieftain of the Wolfungs," Otto said.

"Salute me," said Ortog.

"I salute you," said Otto, lifting his hand, "Ortog, prince of the Drisriaks."

"And king of the Ortungs," said Ortog.

"And king of the Ortungs," said Otto.

There was then much cheering in the enclosure, the raising of weapons, the clashing of them. Pistols, too, and rifles, were fired into the air. It seemed even, far off, that there was, too, the sound of gunfire.

"We do not need your recognition to be what we are, a sovereign tribe of the Alemanni peoples, the Ortungs," said Ortog.

"In any event," said Otto, "you have it."

"Long live the Ortungs!" cried an ambassador.

"Long live the Ortungs!" cried others.

"You have what you wanted," said Otto. "Now I would have

what I want, that the predations of the Ortungs against the Wolfungs cease.''

'' 'Predations'?'' asked Ortog.

"The Wolfungs are tributary to the Ortungs," said the clerk.

"That the Ortungs renounce all claim to the Wolfungs as tributaries," said Otto.

"But we are fond of the Wolfungs," said Ortog, grinning.

"Especially of their women," called a man from the side.

There was laughter.

"This matter rests," said Otto, "as I understand it, on the outcome of the challenge."

"Agreed," said Ortog.

"It is you who will meet me?" inquired Otto.

"No," said Ortog.

"You will choose weapons, then, and a champion, as is your right," said Otto.

Once before Ortog and Otto had met in combat. It had occurred on a square of sand, in a small arena, one improvised in a section of the *Alaria*'s gigantic hold. Otto was then a gladiator, being groomed by Pulendius, master of the school of Pulendius, and his trainers, for matches in major arenas.

The experience was not one which Ortog was eager to repeat, nor was it one which he could, in justice, have been expected to repeat.

Ortog was a king, not a pit killer. It was no dishonor for an unarmed, naked man to decline to enter the lair of a vi-cat. Even Abrogastes, his father, lord of the Drisriaks, fierce and terrible, would not be expected to accept such an invitation. Such a thing would not be courage, but insanity.

Too, there were some risks to which a king, if only in virtue of his responsibilities, should not subject himself.

"The arrangements will be explained to you by my advisor and confidante, Huta, of the Timbri," said Ortog.

There was laughter.

"What is one, and what is many?" inquired Huta.

"I do not understand," said Otto.

"Are the stars many?" asked Huta.

"Yes," said Otto.

"But they are all stars, are they not?" asked Huta.

"Yes," said Otto.

"Thus they are also one," said Huta.

"I do not understand," said Otto.

"Is the principle of individuation, of oneness, one of form or matter?" she asked.

"I do not understand," said Otto.

"Many can be one, and one can be many," she said.

"I do not understand her speech," said Otto. "Perhaps she is very wise."

"Or mad, or clever," said Julian.

"Bring forth, milord, the champion," said Huta.

"Bring forth the champion," said Ortog.

From back, from among the men, a large, simple, slow-moving fellow, blond and blue-eyed, was led forth by the arm. He was very large, and broad-shouldered, but soft, and carried no weapons. His eyes were glazed. He did not seem clearly aware of what was about him.

"He is drunk, or drugged," said Julian.

"Choose another champion," said Otto.

"Behold, the champion!" said Ortog, and gestured, again, to the side.

Another such fellow, seemingly identical to the first, was led forth.

"They are the same," said Otto, puzzled.

"Twins," said Julian.

"Bring forth the champion!" called Ortog, again.

Another such fellow was conducted forth.

"I am to fight three?" asked Otto.

But again, and again, the call for the champion was issued. Then, at the end, as the crowd stood quiet, uneasy, there were brought before the dais ten such fellows, seemingly somnolent, narcotized. Men supported some of them.

"It is called cloning," said Julian. "It is a process whereby genetic identicals may be produced."

"There is the champion," said Huta, pointing to the ten men before the dais.

"That is ten champions," said Julian.

"It is one," said Huta. "They are one!"

"Ten!" said Julian.

"Were you given permission to speak, thrall?" asked Huta. "Let his tongue be cut out!" she cried to Ortog.

"No," said Ortog.

"They do not seem to be fighters," said Otto.

"They are not," said Ortog.

"They are drunk, or sick," speculated Otto.

"Drunk, or drugged," said Julian.

"They will not be quick," said Otto.

"They do not need to be," said Ortog.

"Surely I am to fight them all, at the same time?" said Otto.

"You will meet them one at a time," said Ortog.

"I do not understand," said Otto.

"Do you not fear he will win, milord?" inquired the clerk.

"No," smiled Ortog.

"Does milord intend to surrender so lightly his rights to the property and women of the Wolfungs?" asked Ortog's shieldsman.

"Not at all," said Ortog.

"The king of the Ortungs is generous," said Otto. "But I beg his indulgence, and request that he put before me a true fighter, a suitable champion, if he wishes, his finest warrior."

"I am he," said Ortog. "How else is it that I have rings to give?"

"Then meet me," said Otto, puzzled.

"No," said Ortog.

"I do not wish to slay drunken, or drugged, men," said Otto.

"Why have these champions been drugged?" asked Julian.

"That the champion be not too much aware of what is occurring," said Ortog.

"I do not understand," said Otto.

"Bring forth the device," said Ortog.

"Do not do this thing, my brother!" cried out Gerune.

"Be silent, shamed woman," he snarled.

"She spoke without permission," said Julian.

"She is free," said Otto.

"If she were roped at my feet, as a slave," said Julian, "she would not have dared to speak."

"No," said Otto, "but then things would be quite different."

"Yes," said Julian.

"Bring forth the device!" called Ortog.

The apparatus was brought forth.

Far off, it seemed there sounded a cry, perhaps that of a bird. The wind snapped the yellow silk which, with its poles, formed the wall of the enclosure.

"Hold his arms!" cautioned Ortog.

Four men seized Otto, and held him fast. Two others restrained Julian.

Huta's laugh rang out merrily in the enclosure.

It appeared at first a complicated device, but it was not really so. Two chairs, facing one another, with a heavy metal backing behind the head of each, were linked together beneath a small tablelike platform, on which, on an adjustable stand, its base fixed in the platform, was something which looked like a horizontal pipe, or tube. Feeding into this tube, vertically, entering it at the center, rather at the breech at the center of the horizontal tube, was another tube.

"Put them in the chairs," said Ortog.

There was a murmur of anger from the men about.

Otto shook away those who would hold him and sat in one of the chairs. There were caliperlike grippers attached to the heavy metal backing, behind the head. He placed his head, unbidden, between these calipers, or pincers. They did not restrain his head, but merely positioned it. One could leave them only by moving forward, or downward, not to the side. Their purpose was to prevent any reflexive movements to the side.

"No!" cried Julian.

"Silence, thrall," said Huta.

The first of the large, soft, somnolent individuals was placed in the seat opposite Otto.

"The charge," said Huta, "is entered into the vertical tube, at this point. The tube is precisely made, as are the charges. The drop is a fair one, insofar as such things can be tooled, to the thousandths of an inch. There is, in so far as can be assured, exactly the same chance that the charge will fall to the left as to the right, exactly the same chance that it will enter the barrel to the left as the barrel to the right."

"I understand," said Otto.

"Do you wish to be tied in the chair?" asked a man.

"No," said Otto.

"You can reach the trigger?" asked a man.

"Yes," said Otto.

"If you do not wish to participate, you have lost the challenge," said another man.

"Abandon the challenge," urged Julian.

"I do not," said Otto.

"It is too late to abandon the challenge," said Ortog.

"The Ortungen are without honor!" cried Julian.

"Your ransom is doubled!" said Ortog.

"Do not interfere, my friend," said Otto, "if you would again see your worlds."

The pipe was being adjusted now.

The man opposite Otto was tied in the chair, not because he was unwilling to take that place, as he had little understanding of what was transpiring, but rather in order to hold him in position.

"Do you understand what they are doing?" Julian asked Otto.

"Yes," said Otto.

"Your skills, such as they may be, and if you retain any, are herewith neutralized, completely," said Ortog. "The outcome is a matter of chance."

"Of probabilities," said Julian, angrily.

"He does not need to cooperate," said Ortog. "If he wishes, he may leave the chair, and be quickly, mercifully, put to death."

"There is one chance in two that you will die on the first firing," said Julian. "The chance of escaping the first firing is one in two; the chance of escaping two firings in a row is one in four; the chance of escaping three firings in a row is one in eight; of four, one in sixteen; of five, one in thirty-two; of six, one in sixty-four; of seven, one in one hundred and twenty-eight; of eight, one in two hundred and fifty-six; of nine, one in five hundred and twelve; of ten, one in one thousand and twenty-four."

"I am ready," said Otto.

"You cannot even count so high, my friend," said Julian, despairing.

"I know what a thousand is," said Otto. "I think I know. It is a great many."

"You could have put him against dwarfs, or women!" raged Julian.

"Like the leaves of a tree, like the stones on a beach," said Otto.

Let those who are familiar with mathematics congratulate themselves on their knowledge of a simple number, such as a thousand, but let them, too, aside from marks on paper, and procedures of counting, and such, see if they can visualize that number, say, a thousand leaves or a thousand stones. Are they visualizing a thousand, truly, or nine hundred and fifty, or a thousand and ten?

"Dwarfs are amusing," said Ortog. "And one would surely not wish to waste women in such a manner. They have much more pleasant uses."

"Milord!" cried Huta, in horror.

Her priestesses and acolytes gasped, too, some placing their hands to their breasts. They exchanged wild glances. Such women are vowed to chastity.

"It is a high number, surely," said Otto.

There was one trigger for the apparatus. It was mounted on a small, movable box, which we may refer to as the trigger box, or housing. This box rested on the table. From it, an insulated cord ran to the base of the stand.

"Forgive me, Lady Huta," said Ortog.

The pipe was adjusted on the stand. It was arranged in such a way as to be level with, and focused toward, the center of Otto's forehead. The barrel of the pipe, its muzzle, was somewhat lower on the fellow across from Otto. It was centered there just above the bridge of the nose. This was because Otto was the taller man. The muzzle, on each side, was about four inches from the faces of the men.

"Place a charge," said Huta.

One of the men who had been assisting the priestesses removed a spheroid from a box and dropped it into the vertical tube.

"You may fire first," said Ortog.

"Is there any advantage in firing first?" asked Otto.

"None," said Ortog. "The trigger fires the device. One does not know where the charge is."

"Let him fire first then," said Otto.

"Wait, milord!" called Hendrix, from the side. "This is not the way of the Drisriaks, nor should it be the way of the Ortungs."

"This is not a matter of steel, of a duel in which glory may be sought, a cutting with knives, the thrust of the blade, the sort of thing of which songs are made!" cried another man.

"It has been decided," said Ortog.

"It is a mockery of honor!" cried another.

"All has been arranged," said Ortog, angrily.

Overhead, but muchly unnoticed, there was a flight of birds, hurrying to the west.

"I will be the champion of the Ortungs!" called Hendrix.

"And you would die!" said Ortog. He himself, on the *Alaria*, had once crossed blades with the seated blond giant. He had not cared to do so again.

"I am swift," called Gundlicht, stepping forward, "Let me fight him, in the ways of honor."

"Yes!" called others.

"Me!" called another.

"No, I!" cried another.

"He would kill any of you," screamed Ortog.

"How can it be?" cried a man.

"Can you not see the breeding, and the blood, in him?" inquired Ortog.

"Let the match begin!" called Huta.

"He is an Otung!" called Ortog.

Otto did not move.

The men were stilled for an instant.

"Of royal blood!" cried Ortog.

"I am a peasant, from the *festung* village of Sim Giadini," said Otto.

Julian regarded Otto wildly.

"I am sure of it!" said Ortog.

"They are a race of warriors, the fiercest of the Vandal peoples!" said a man.

"They were destroyed by the empire!" said another.

"The Alemanni are the greatest of all the peoples!" cried a man.

"Yes, yes!" shouted others.

Julian's mind raced.

These cries, and the stirring of the crowd, its murmuring, and unease, tended to obscure even the sounds of the wind at the yellow silk.

"Let the match begin!" called out Huta.

"Yes," said Ortog. "Let the match begin!"

"No, milord," begged his shieldsman.

"It has been arranged by the priestess Hutar," said Ortog.

"Please, milord!" begged a man.

"It has been decided," said Ortog.

"Milord!" protested another.

"Who is king of the Ortungs?" asked Ortog.

"Ortog is king of the Ortungs," said a man.

"Let the match begin," said Ortog.

"Let the match begin," said men.

"Press the trigger!" said Huta.

Her words were addressed to the man fastened in the seat opposite Otto.

"The trigger! The trigger!" cried Huta.

"Here, this," said one of the men who had been assisting the priestesses. He took the trigger housing, on its cord, running to the stand, and put it in the hands of the fellow opposite Otto.

"Wait," said another man, he who had also been assisting the priestesses. He thrust up, and back, the head of the man opposite Otto, indeed, he held his head in place by the hair, pulling it back, that it would be properly positioned within the caliperlike grips attached to the shielding at the back of the seat.

"Press the trigger," said the first man.

"Trigger?" asked the lethargic form in the chair across from the chieftain of the Wolfungs.

"This, this," said the first man.

"I am the champion?" asked the man across from Otto.

"Yes, you and the others, they are all the champion," said the man who had literally thrust the trigger housing into the fellow's hands.

"It is glorious to be the champion," said the lethargic creature, slowly.

"Yes, yes!" said the man near him.

"I am glorious?" asked the lethargic form.

"Yes! Press the trigger!" said the man.

A second flight of birds passed overhead, hurrying like the first, to the west.

The finger of the fellow opposite Otto slowly moved toward the trigger, or switch, and rested upon it.

"Press it!" said the man nearest him.

There was a sudden flash of fire and light, and a cry of horror from men, and screams from slave girls, and the fellow who had been standing behind the shielding of the fellow across from Otto, holding the fellow's head up, and back, by the hair, now held, dangling from his hand by the hair, half of a head, the eyes opened wildly, no longer seemingly dazed. There was a slick matting, smoking, of blood and flesh and brains smeared upon, and dripping from, the shielding across from Otto. Blood pumped up, like an underground spring, through the throat, and spilled out, over the remains of the lower jaw.

Gerune screamed and threw her hands before her face. Slave girls wept, and put down their heads, shuddering, sickened. Some retched onto the grass. Many, those who could do so, buried their face in their chained hands. The three display slaves turned away, sick, moaning in horror, in their chains.

"Get rid of that!" screamed Huta, pointing to the most of a body, still fastened opposite Otto.

"Bring the champion!" called Ortog, shaken.

The remainder of the man who had been fastened opposite Otto was freed from its place and dragged to one side.

Another man, another of the original ten, the champion, or champions, if you like, was dragged toward the chair.

"No!" he cried. It was the sight of what was before him, I suppose, the spattering, the stew, of blood and flesh, the cast-aside part of a head, the bleeding, still-convulsing body of the other, that had shocked him into some sort of soberness, or awareness.

He was wrestled into this place, and bound there, bodily, save for his arms.

"No!" he cried.

Another charge was placed in the device.

"No, no!" he cried.

"Press the trigger or die!" cried Ortog.

The fellow's hand, shaking, reached toward the trigger.

But his hand did not reach the trigger box, for Otto had swept it toward himself.

He then rose from the chair, to the consternation of all.

"What are you doing?" cried Huta.

Otto's hand was on the adjustable stand, that which provided the mount, the support, for the barrel. He tore this stand, in a rending of metal, from the platform.

"Sit down! Take your place!" cried the fellow who had placed the spheroidal charge, it now dormant, like an unexploded bomb, within the apparatus.

"Do so!" cried the other, his fellow.

"The challenge has been met, and I am victorious," announced Otto.

"No, no!" cried Ortog.

Otto then set the device against himself, one barrel at his own chest, the other, opposite, trained on the breast of Ortog, who rose from his chair, turning white.

Swords leapt from sheaths, weapons, with small, swift sounds, darted from holsters.

"Kill him, kill him!" screamed Huta.

"No, no!" cried Ortog, thrusting aside his chair, backing away a step.

Otto's finger was on the trigger of the device. It was there tightly, the tiniest particle of energy away from activating it. The smallest reflex, the slightest jerk, as of a blow striking him, the lash or thrust of a blade, the impact of a projectile, even the breath of a ray, would fire the device.

"Has the challenge not been met?" inquired Otto. "Am I not victorious?

The opposing barrels of the device, torn from the tablelike platform, were aligned, the rear barrel to the chest of Otto, the forward barrel to toward the dais, and the breast of Ortog.

Ortog's shieldsman inched toward his lord.

"Do not move!" cried Otto, fiercely.

"Go back," said Ortog, softly. The flash leaves the barrel with almost the speed of light.

The shieldsman returned to his place.

Ortog seemed much alone now on the dais.

His high men had drawn away from him. Gerune now was closest to him.

At the foot of the dais, on its left, looking outward, even the display slaves drew away, to the extent they could, huddling down, terrified. Their chains were taut against the common ring.

Otto was ringed with weapons.

He paid them no attention.

"Well, milord," said Otto. "Who has won the challenge?"

Ortog drew himself up.

He was king.

"The tribute of the Wolfungs is as nothing," said the clerk.

"You can buy their women, or others, doubtless better, in a thousand markets," said his shieldsman.

"The Wolfung has won, milord," called Hendrix.

"The challenge has been met, and survived, milord!" called Gundlicht.

"The Ortungs are now a recognized tribe," said his shieldsman, urgently.

"That is what we want," said the clerk.

"Give him the liberty of the Wolfungs, as a gift," pressed his shieldsman.

"I have won their liberty," said Otto.

"I await your answer, milord," said Otto.

"The challenge has been met," said Ortog.

There was a cheer from the men present.

"No, no!" cried Huta.

"You are victorious," said Ortog.

Otto lowered the device.

Weapons were sheathed.

"No, no, milord!" cried Huta.

"Be silent, woman," said Julian.

"Chained thrall!" screamed Huta. She tried to strike Julian but he caught her wrists, and she struggled, briefly, futilely, helplessly.

The other priestesses, and acolytes, cried out with dismay.

"Respect the sacred person of the priestess!" cried Ortog.

"She is only a woman," said Julian.

The priestess cried out in fury.

There were cries of protest, too, from her fellow priestesses, and the acolytes.

"Unhand her," demanded Ortog.

Julian then flung her hands down, contemptuously, away from him. She staggered back.

There seemed cries, too, somehow, those of men, from some distance to the east.

"I hear something," said a man.

"I, too," said another.

"Press the trigger, Wolfung," said Ortog to Otto.

"As milord wishes," said Otto.

"Yes, I hear it!" cried a man.

Some of the kneeling slave girls raised their heads in alarm, looking about themselves. The three display slaves looked about themselves, trying to place the sound.

"It is coming from the east," said a man.

Otto pressed the trigger on the trigger housing, held in his hand. Almost instantly there burst from the forward barrel, that which had been trained on the breast of Ortog, it now held downward to Otto's right, a flash of fire. It tore open the turf. A hole now gaped there, better than six inches in width, and indeterminately deep. It smoked. Grass was charred at the edges.

Ortog turned white.

Men shuddered.

"Now you may kill him, milord!" cried Huta.

"Be silent, woman!" cried men.

"No!" she cried. "No!"

"Listen!" cried a man.

"I am priestess of the Timbri!" cried Huta.

"Be silent!" cried a man.

"Listen, listen!" cried another.

Ortog raised his head, listening.

At that moment, suddenly, almost noiselessly, over the curtain, or wall, of yellow silk to the right, to the east, there appeared the dark, circular shape of a hoverer. It was not more than a yard above the silk. Leaning over the gunwales of the ship were riflemen. Rifle fire ripped downward, tearing into the throng. Then there was another such ship, and more fire. Men tried to run. Circular holes appeared suddenly, black-rimmed, and spreading, in the yellow wall. Armed men were seen on the other side. Slave girls screamed. Some leapt up and fell, tangled in their chains. Men cried out. Men pushed against one another, and buffeted one another. Many fell, stumbling over others. Otto seized Julian and flung him to the ground. Fire from the ground swept upward. More of the small, circular ships passed over the enclosure. Gerune huddled on the dais, her robes over her head. Wood splintered, burning, about her. Julian freed himself of Otto's grasp and, half hobbling, half crawling, fighting his chains, made his way to the dais. "How dare you touch me!" cried Gerune. But Julian had drawn her, forcibly, from the dais, and behind it, where he thrust her beneath its timbers. The three display slaves, too, had taken refuge there, and huddled helplessly there, in the smoke and fire. Others, too, slave and free, had fled beneath it. Men fled to the west, but some there reeled and fell, plunging backward, their chests smoking. Ortog stood on the dais, a pistol in his hand. He fired upward. None of the ships returned his fire. "There is another!" cried a man in misery. More fire was exchanged. Otto hurried to the dais and joined Julian. "It is lost!" said Otto. Men fired upward. More of the shallow, circular ships passed over the enclosure. "Where is he who holds the key to your chains?" demanded Otto. Julian looked about himself, wildly. "I do not know," said Julian, pulling at the chains. "There!" cried Julian. "There!" He pointed to a body near the front of the dais, that of one of Ortog's yeoman. Otto crawled to the body and drew it under the dais, and tore away the wallet at its belt. In moments he had freed Julian of his bonds. "We must flee," said Otto.

"I will not leave without her," said Julian, indicating Gerune. She looked at him, wildly.

"You love me!" cried Gerune.

"You can judge of that when you are whipped," exclaimed Julian, angrily.

"Dog!" she wept.

"We must flee!" said Otto, seizing Julian by the arm.

"It is no use," said a man. "We are surrounded."

On the surface of the flaming, blackened, splintered dais, Ortog stood, alone, cursing, firing his pistol into the air, at the ships. He had not been fired upon. No one had returned his fire. Then, cursing, he flung his empty pistol from him.

Already, in the enclosure, men were standing, their hands lifted, their weapons cast aside.

Some of the slaves, who were out in the enclosure, knelt, lifting their chained wrists imploringly, beseechingly, to the ships. Then they put their heads down to the ground. Others, whose wrists were fastened behind them, already knelt with their heads to the ground, weeping, hoping to be spared, rendering obeisance to they knew not whom.

"Slaves, out," called one of the surrendering men, his hands raised.

The slaves who had taken refuge under the dais, with the exception of the three display slaves, who were chained in place, crept out, and went to the center of the enclosure, to kneel there, with the others. The three display slaves emerged from beneath the dais, and knelt there, as they had before. Their chains would permit them no more.

Ortog stood on the surface of the dais, alone.

Otto and Julian emerged from beneath the dais.

Otto went toward the center of the enclosure. He did not raise his hands, but he was unarmed, and he stood in full view of the ships. It was obvious that he did not intend to offer any resistance. "Do not raise your arms," said Otto to Julian. "We are not as the others, and I want them to understand that."

And so resistance was ended within the enclosure. There were slaves there, and priestesses, and acolytes, and many men, traders and others. Most of the men, with the exception of Ortog, and Otto, and Julian, stood with their arms raised.

They were vulnerable to the ships.

Too, they were clearly surrounded. They could see armed warriors about, many of them even within the remains of the enclosure, the tattered, burned yellow silk here and there fluttering from shattered, awry poles, like flags.

Then a ship, moving very slowly, appeared above the remains of the wall of silk. It approached the center of the enclosure, and then stopped there, and remained in place, some twenty feet in the air. A man stood at the bow, with his hands on the gunwales of the small vessel.

"It is Abrogastes," said a man, "lord of the Drisriaks."

## ▪ ▪ ▪ CHAPTER 11 ▪ ▪ ▪

"Aii!" cried men, drawing back,

The sound is difficult to describe, but it is one that, once heard, is not to be soon forgotten.

It is too swift to be a tearing sound.

But, too, it is not like the descending ease of a curved blade, little more than a momentary whisper, the stroke delivered from behind, dividing the vertebrae, opening the neck, then arrested, with the small, sharp sound of touching wood.

It is much more crude than that.

It is more analogous to the blow of an ax, held in two hands, delivered downward, striking crosswise into a felled log, except that it lacks that ring, the resonance of men making their marks on the world, shaping wood to their ends. It is more like the sudden chopping through a different material, through, say, a twisted vine, and thence further vegetable matter, the sound not altogether unlike that of splitting a gourd or melon, the blow then stopped, muffled, the sound not clean or sharp, by the weighty, rude, scarred surface of the base. The muffling of the sound has to do with the damping effect, the insulation, so to speak, provided by the intervening material, that between the instrument and the base. There is little splintering, too, or what there is, better, tends to be obscured, the intervening material providing shielding from the bursting chips and needles of wood that would attend, say, the blow of an ax into wood. Too, of course, the base tends to be washed with fluid, after each stroke, suddenly, plentifully, and this causes many of the small particles of wood, drenched, to run down the sides of the base. The wielder of the instrument, wearing a large, leather workman's apron, stands before his work. In this fashion, the blood, for the most part, of which there is a great quantity, and which tends to leave the body with considerable force, sometimes to a distance of several feet, reaches him. Indeed, one cannot stand before the object of attention without being drenched with it. Indeed, sometimes the operator, or workman, if you prefer, is even temporarily blinded by it, and must wipe it from his eyes with the back of a forearm. This orientation, that before, or behind, if one wished, the object of attention, has to do with the manner in which the blade is fixed on the haft, or handle. If it were an ax, for example, the operator, or workman, so to speak, would merely have to stand to one side or the other, each operator, or workman, in such a business, having his preferred side, some preferring the left, others the right. One normally stands before the object of attention, of course, rather than behind it, because this orientation provides a much better access to it. The blow may be more accurately, and surely, delivered. The sound, it might be mentioned, is also conditioned by the fact that the blade is, purposefully, not ground as closely as that of an ax. It is, by intent, duller. The whole matter then has a certain roughness about it. One dares not speak of terribleness, or brutality here, for fear of injecting value judgments into the narrative. My purpose is not to praise or blame, but to recount, simply to relate, what happened. There is a conjecture that the adz is used, incidentally, imperfect implement as it might seem for such a purpose, precisely because it, unlike the ax, is not a weapon. Indeed, its deliberate dullness may be intended to emphasize that fact. To die by a weapon, you see, is regarded among certain warrior peoples as a very desirable end. Indeed, there is a thought among many of them that it is not only honorable, but glorious, to so perish, and that those who do so perish are beloved by the gods of war, such as Kragon, and are thence made welcome in a thousand halls and worlds beyond the stars, where they may feast and fight to their heart's content, until the end of time, until the stars grow cold, and the halls themselves, like the stars, grow dim and vanish. But there is no honor, you see, in dying by the adz. It is shameful to die so. It is not a weapon. It is a tool. Indeed, it is not even wielded by a warrior, but rather, and intentionally, by a workman. And how then, if one should perish so, so shamefully, so disgracefully, could one hope to enter into the far halls? Would one not find at the entrance the spear of Kragon barring one's way? Perhaps, at best, one might hope to glimpse the lights of such halls from afar, set among distant snowy hills, looking up from one's labors, those of the lowliest of villeins, in the darkness.

Abrogastes, on the throne, on the dais, in the same tent in which Ortog had held his court earlier, made a sign with his hand.

Women cried out with misery, recoiling.

Yes, it is a terrible thing to die so.

In a moment, Abrogastes made another sign.

It is not a sound that is easy to forget.

"Those!" said Abrogastes. "Bring them forward!"

Nine men were brought forward, the large, simple, blond-haired, blue-eyed men who had figured in the challenge, that pertaining to the status of the Wolfungs.

Abrogastes regarded them, curiously.

"They are much the same," he said.

"They are one, milord!" called the priestess Huta, from the side.

"You set ten men on one?" Abrogastes asked Ortog, who, bound, and in the charge of two Drisriaks, stood below the dais.

"One at a time," said Ortog.

"In some machine, one at a time, which might kill either champion, regardless of courage or skill?"

Ortog was silent.

These things and their rationale, of course, had been explained to Abrogastes.

"And how will that improve the bloodlines?" asked Abrogastes.

Ortog looked away.

"And how can such a thing please the gods?" asked Abrogastes.

Ortog did not respond.

"Were there such a thing as the Ortungs," said Abrogastes, "they would be shamed."

"We are shamed, my father," said Ortog.

"It dishonors our traditions, it mocks the ceremony of war, it shames the ritual of challenge."

"It permits the gods to decide," said Ortog.

"Do not slander the gods," said Abrogastes. "Do not put upon them the business of men. They wait upon men, to see what they will do. Men must be brave, and glorious, first, to win the favor of the gods. The friendship of the gods is not easily earned. It is a hard thing, and requires much effort."

"I think there are no gods," said Ortog.

"Blasphemy, milord!" cried Huta. She stood out a bit, in her white robes, with the bloodstained sleeves, from her fellow priestesses and acolytes.

"These are the champion?" asked Abrogastes of Huta.

"Yes," said Huta.

"And they are one?"

"Yes!"

"But one died in the device, did he not?" inquired Abrogastes.

"Yes, milord," said Huta.

"So one is dead, is he not?" inquired Abrogastes.

"Yes, milord," said Huta.

"And they are one?" asked Abrogastes.

"Yes, milord," said Huta.

"Then they are all dead," said Abrogastes.

"Milord?" asked Huta.

"Kill it," said Abrogastes, indicating the nine men before him. Each then, who might have been a sturdy yeoman, patiently tilling his land, who might have hunted, and skated on frozen rivers, and climbed snowy mountains, and warmed himself at night with bowls of soup, cooked by a loving wife, was taken to the block where the workman, with one or more blows of the great adz, attended to his labors.

"Your champion is dead," said Abrogastes to Ortog.

"Yes," cried Huta. "The champion of the Ortungs is dead! Long live the Drisriaks!"

Hendrix and Gundlicht, in their bonds, turned angry glances upon the priestess.

"Long live Abrogastes! Long live the Drisriaks!" cried Huta.

"Why did you yourself not meet the challenge?" asked Abrogastes of Ortog.

"The Wolfung would have killed me," said Ortog.

"Then choose another," said Abrogastes.

"I know none whom he could not kill," said Ortog, angrily.

"The challenge then should have been surrendered, in honor," said Abrogastes.

Ortog shrugged.

"He can kill you?" asked Abrogastes of Ortog, regarding Otto narrowly.

"Yes," said Ortog.

"How is that?" asked Abrogastes.

"He is an Otung, and has been trained in arenas," said Ortog.

"Is that true?" asked Abrogastes.

"I am a peasant," said Otto, standing, unbound, Julian slightly behind him, "from the *festung* village of Sim Giadini, on Tangara. It is true that I have fought for the pleasure of populaces."

"Many times?" asked Abrogastes.

"Yes, milord," said Otto.

"He is chieftain, too, of the Wolfungs!" cried Huta.

"Yes," said Otto.

"The Wolfungs are tributary to the Drisriaks," said Abrogastes.

"No," said Otto.

There was laughter from many Drisriak warriors.

"You won the challenge," said Abrogastes.

"Yes, milord," said Otto.

"But it was meaningless, unnecessary," said Abrogastes, "for the Ortungs do not exist."

"I have recognized them," said Otto, quietly.

There were gasps of surprise from those present.

Ortog, Gundlicht, Hendrix, Ortog's shieldsman, his clerk, others in the hall, turned wildly, elatedly, toward Otto.

"Do not speak so!" whispered Julian, startled.

"It is so spoken," said Otto, folding his arms upon his mighty chest.

"The Ortungs, as of today, no longer exist," said Abrogastes.

Otto shrugged.

"How is that, my father?" inquired Ortog.

"They have been destroyed, their camps, their fleet," said Abrogastes.

Ortungs looked upon one another with dismay.

"Surely some have escaped!" cried Ortog.

"Perhaps, some, fugitives, *filchen,* fleeing for their lives."

Gerune, who, unbound, in the full regalia in which she had witnessed the matter of the challenge, and its resolution, was sitting on the dais, on a chair, to the left of her father, put her face in her hands and wept.

"The Ortungs are no more," said Abrogastes. "They are as grass, cast to the winds."

Gerune's body shook with sobs.

"Faithless daughter," said Abrogastes.

"Long live Abrogastes! Long live the Drisriaks!" called Huta.

"Traitorous son," snarled Abrogastes.

"To the block with him!" called a man.

"To the block with the traitorous princess, too!" called a man.

Gerune looked up, in terror.

"Yes!" cried Huta.

"Both betrayed the Drisriaks!" cried a man.

"Yes, yes!" said Huta.

"To the block with them both!" cried men.

"No, no, Father!" wept Gerune, falling to her knees before her father. His arm swept her to the side, and she then half knelt, half lay, by her chair, looking wildly about her.

"To the block with them both, and all the Ortungs!" cried men.

"Yes!" cried Huta.

"Some Ortungs have sworn me allegiance," said Abrogastes. "I have given rings to some."

Ortog looked up, suddenly, at his father. Other Ortungs, too, suddenly, wildly, regarded him.

"The fault, it seems, was not theirs," said Abrogastes. "They were misled."

"Who here was misled?" asked Abrogastes.

"I," cried a man.

"I," cried another.

"And I, too," cried others.

"Were you weak and foolish?" asked Abrogastes.

"Yes," they cried.

"Take them to the block," said Abrogastes.

"No, mercy!" cried men.

But again, and then again, and then again the brawny, leather-aproned workman raised the mighty implement, the long-handled, heavy adz.

Even some of the Drisriaks turned away.

The heavy blade, by now, you see, was muchly dulled.

Abrogastes looked about himself, at his men, at Ortog, at Gerune, the shieldsman, the clerk, Hendrix and Gundlicht, merchants, ambassadors, warriors, Otto, Julian, Huta, the priestesses and acolytes, huddled to one side, and others.

The eyes of Abrogastes glistened.

The ground ran with blood. Some of the reeds, which had covered the earth within the tent, were soaked with blood. Parts of some, crushed and broken, drifted in shallow currents. Here and there, streams of blood, increased by new contributions, ran among the feet of those standing. Here and there, too, stood pools of blood. Many present, in the vicinity of the block, were spattered with it. Much of the earth within the tent was now no more than churned mud. Blood filled even the depressions of footprints. Body after body, and the parts thereof, were drawn, or thrown, outside. The cries of scavenging birds could be heard. They had come, many of them, from the grove, that on the approach to the place of the sacrifices. Too, like leaves, swarming and rustling, crept keen-sensed *filchen*, come from acres about, many, too, from the grove, gathering excitedly, as at a dump of offal.

"You, forward!" said Abrogastes. He pointed at one of the few Ortungs left.

The fellow, his arms pinioned behind him, was pushed forward.

"Will you serve me?" asked Abrogastes.

"Yes," said the man.

"Take him to the block," said Abrogastes.

"Kill me with a weapon," he begged, "that I may die well, that I may perish honorably!"

Abrogastes lifted his hand.

"That I may be permitted to go to the halls of the gods!" begged the man.

Abrogastes made a sign with his hand.

It took the adz, even with its weight and leverage, three strokes to complete its work.

"It was a hard one, a tough one," said a man.

"Yes," said another man.

"But it is the tool, too," said a man. "Its edge is flattened."

"Yes," said another man.

The head of the implement, and the handle, to a foot below the blade, were thick with the slime of flesh and tissue.

The workman wiped his broad face, and spit to the side. He squinted. He blinked, again and again. His eyes stung with sweat. It ran, too, down his face and neck, profusely, and his chest, and his arms and legs. His body was slick with sweat and blood.

Abrogastes looked about.

Men shrank back.

"Those women," said Abrogastes, "put them forward."

"They are my maidens!" said Gerune. "Take pity on them!"

Ten women were pushed forward.

"Those, too," said Abrogastes.

Ten older women, too, of diverse births and station, attendants also on the princess, one of whom had carried away the jewelry and garments of Gerune from the council tent earlier, at the command of Ortog, were thrust forward.

"Remove their clothing," said Abrogastes.

"Father!" protested Gerune.

"Of those, too," said Abrogastes.

"Please, no, Father!" begged Gerune.

Then the two groups of women stood in the tent, in the scarlet mud, in accordance with the words of Abrogastes, lord of the Drisriaks.

"I am thinking of making these women slaves, all of them," said Abrogastes to Huta, priestess of the Timbri.

"No, milord!" cried the women. "Please, no, milord!"

They fell to their knees in the dark mud, moaning, weeping, and crying out, some extending their hands to Abrogastes for mercy.

"What think you, milady?" asked Abrogastes of Huta. "Do you think these women might be suitable for slaves?"

He indicated the two groups of women, the maidens and the older women.

"Eminently so, milord," said Huta.

"I think you are right," said Abrogastes.

"One can see that they are slaves," said Huta.

"Take them to the ships, and make them slaves," said Abrogastes.

"Excellent, milord," called Huta.

The two groups of women, weeping, were dragged to their feet and hurried from the tent.

"They are not slaves!" said Gerune.

"They will be, by nightfall," said Abrogastes.

Huta laughed.

In the council tent, there were, incidentally, no female slaves. Those, including the three blond display slaves we have referred to earlier, had all been gathered together, outside, and taken, bound hand and foot, in the small ships, the hoverers and floaters, to the larger shuttlers, some distance away, which would communicate with the corsairs, or lionships, in orbit. By now, unbound and stripped, each was in her tiered kennel, the gate's bars thrust shut, and locked in place.

"He!" said Abrogastes. "Bring him forward!"

The clerk was thrust forward. His hands were bound behind his back, with cord.

"Are you Ortung?" inquired Abrogastes.

"No, milord," said the clerk.

"Are you Telnarian?"

"No, milord."

"You can read and write," said Abrogastes.

"Yes, milord," said the clerk.

"Have you taken fee with Ortog?"

"Yes, milord," said the clerk.

"Have you served him well?"

"I have done my best to serve him well," said the clerk.

"What are your feelings toward the treacherous prince of the Drisriaks?" asked Abrogastes.

"My feelings, milord?" asked the clerk.

"You hate him, and have served him only out of fear, and have been secretly revolted by his treachery," suggested Abrogastes.

"I am sorry, milord," said the clerk. "I cannot in truth give you the answer you desire."

"Have you received rings from him?"

"One such as I does not receive rings, milord," said the clerk.

"You are his friend?"

"My station is not such that I might be his friend," said the clerk.

"Yet you have served him well?"

"I have always endeavored to do so, milord," said the clerk.

"Free him," said Abrogastes.

The clerk, to his wonder, was freed.

"As you served the Ortungs," said Abrogastes, "so you will now serve the Drisriaks."

"Yes, milord," said the clerk.

Abrogastes then turned his attention to Ortog.

"I would be reconciled with my father," said Ortog.

Abrogastes then regarded the shieldsman, bound to one side. "You are shieldsman to Ortog, prince of the Drisriaks?" asked Abrogastes.

"To Ortog, prince of the Drisriaks," said the shieldsman, "and, too, king of the Ortungen!"

Men gasped.

"What is the duty of a shieldsman?" inquired Abrogastes.

"To place the life of his lord above his own," said the shieldsman.

"A shieldsman should then die before his lord," said Abrogastes.

"Yes, milord," said the man.

"Take him to the block," said Abrogastes.

"Hold!" cried the man.

Abrogastes lifted his hand.

"Let it be by the ax, or the blade of some weapon," said the man.

"Lord!" cried Hendrix, suddenly, angrily, from where he stood, bound, amid Drisriak warriors. "Reflect! Show mercy to your son! These things are not his fault, though he may have been weak. If you seek blame here look no further than the wicked Huta, priestess of the Timbri!"

"No!" cried Huta, alarmed.

"Your son fell beneath her baneful influence," said Hendrix. "It was to her readings, her prophecies, and wiles and tricks, that Ortog succumbed. It was she who led him astray!"

"No," said Ortog, "I would break, in any event, from the Drisriaks."

"Were you unlike him in your youth, milord?" called Gundlicht, he, too, bound, near Hendrix.

"I am king of the Drisriaks," said Abrogastes.

"And what if you had not been?" asked Gundlicht.

"But he has lost," said Abrogastes.

"It is Huta who is to blame!" called Hendrix.

"It is true she enflamed his ambition, and led him on," said Gundlicht.

"Is this true, Lady Huta?" inquired Abrogastes.

"Certainly not, milord!" said Huta. "I am priestess of the Timbri, the humble and obedient servant of the ten thousand gods of the Timbri. I, and my sisters, are holy women, sworn to chastity, sacred virgins all. We have no interest in the affairs of the world! We have no interests in material goods!"

"And what of power?" asked Abrogastes.

"We have, of course, no interest in such things," said Huta.

"I am not fond of the rites of the Timbri," said Abrogastes.

Otto recalled the sacrifices, those on the plateau above the grove.

"Forgive me, milord," said Huta. "But it is not the place of their priestesses to question the observances and appointments of the ten thousand gods. It is ours only to humbly do their will."

"I have heard there were signs," said Abrogastes. "Is that true?" he asked Ortog.

Ortog shrugged in his bonds.

"Yes," said Huta suddenly, elatedly, "we can prove our teachings, and our truth, by signs!"

"It seems the signs were false," said Abrogastes.

"Perhaps the priestesses of the Timbri may prove to be of use to you, milord," said Huta.

"But the signs were false," said Abrogastes.

"They are never false," said Huta.

"But did they not favor the Ortungs?" asked Abrogastes.

"Once, perhaps," said Huta.

"Not long ago?" asked Abrogastes.

"Might they not have been misread?" called one of the older priestesses.

"Perhaps," said Huta, apprehensively.

"It is sometimes difficult to read the signs, milord," called one of the priestesses.

"The matter can be dark and difficult," said another.

"But," cried Huta, "might it not be that the will of the gods has changed?"

"Yes!" cried a priestess.

"Yes!" said another.

"Can it be that the will of the gods has changed?" asked Huta.

"It is possible," cried a priestess.

"Yes!" averred another.

"Let us take again the auspices," said one of the priestesses.

Hendrix laughed, bitterly.

Abrogastes lifted his hand, for silence.

"Bring a plain piece of cloth, a simple piece of cloth, one no different from any other," said Huta.

"I will bring one," said one of the priestesses. It was she who had, earlier, outside, fetched another cloth, that which, after having been soaked in blood, had borne upon its surface, as though emblazoned there, the sign of the Ortungs.

In moments the priestess, under guard, had returned to the tent, bearing with her a roll of cloth, tied closed with a string.

She gave this cloth into the hands of Huta, and retired to her place.

Huta undid the string and unrolled the cloth, which, like the other, was some two-foot square.

She turned about, solemnly, displaying the cloth to those in the tent.

Then she faced Abrogastes.

"Would you care to inspect the cloth, milord?" asked Huta of Abrogastes.

"Use another cloth," suggested Hendrix.

"It would not do," said Huta, patiently, "as it would not have been blessed on the world of the Timbri."

"Milord?" she asked Abrogastes.

"I do not need to examine the cloth," said Abrogastes.

"Let the auspices be taken!" called a priestess.

"Let the auspices be taken," repeated the priestesses, and the acolytes.

"Milord!" protested Hendrix.

But Abrogastes lifted his hand, and there was silence.

Huta knelt down in the tent, at the edge of a depression, one of those pools in the tent, smelling, and thick, half blood, half mud.

"Let the blood be consecrated!" called the priestess who had brought the cloth.

"It is consecrated!" said the priestesses.

"It is consecrated," said the acolytes.

"Let it be the blood of truth," called the priestess who had brought the cloth.

"It is now the blood of truth," said Huta.

"It is the blood of truth," said the priestesses.

"It is the blood of truth," called the acolytes.

"Behold, milord," called Huta, looking up at Abrogastes. "I press down within the consecrated blood, the blood of truth, this plain cloth, innocent of all design and preparation, and call upon the ten thousand gods of the Timbri, if it be their will, to vouchsafe us a sign."

The cloth was pressed down, into the liquid, into the thickness of the half-clotted blood, in the mud.

"Vouchsafe us a sign, O gods of the Timbri!" called Huta.

She then lifted up the cloth, and then stood, displaying it. The Drisriak warriors in the tent cried out in awe.

The cloth bore upon its surface, brightly, as though emblazoned there, the sign of the Drisriaks.

"You see, milord?" called Huta.

"There can be no mistaking so obvious a sign, milord," called the priestess who had fetched the cloth.

"Its meaning is incontrovertible!" called another.

Ortog seemed shaken.

Men looked at one another, wildly.

"The gods look upon you with favor, milord," said Huta to Abrogastes.

"Glory to the Drisriaks!" cried a man. This cry was taken up, too, by many others. Even the merchants and ambassadors present, uneasy, fearful, bound and under guard, joined in this cry.

"I am much impressed," said Abrogastes.

"It is nothing, milord," said Huta.

"I did not know you had such power," said Abrogastes.

"The power comes not from us, milord, but from our gods," said Huta.

"It seems," said Abrogastes, "that your gods tend to favor those with the heaviest armaments."

"Milord?" asked Huta.

"But I congratulate you on having planned well, on having prepared for various contingencies."

"I do not understand you, milord," said Huta, uneasily.

"What is it that you wish?" asked Abrogastes.

"We ask nothing for ourselves, milord," said Huta.

"It is seldom that a king encounters such restraint," said Abrogastes. "Surely you would have something?"

"Perhaps that we might prove to be of some use to you, milord," said Huta.

"How so," asked he.

"The Drisriaks would be invincible, were they allied with the gods of the Timbri," said Huta.

"Ah," said Abrogastes.

"Secure victory," said Huta. "Ally yourself with our gods, milord."

"And how could this alliance be brought about?" asked Abrogastes.

"Through the offices of the priestesses of the Timbri," said Huta.

"That would be a most inestimable gift, indeed," said Abrogastes.

Huta bowed her head, modestly.

"And what would you ask for this priceless favor?" inquired Abrogastes.

"We ask nothing, as we have no concern with the affairs of the world, nor with material possessions."

"You would ask nothing?"

"The generosity of Abrogastes, lord of the Drisriaks, is, of course, well known," said Huta.

"What is it that is most prized by you?" asked Abrogastes. "What is it that you most desire?"

"Surely milord knows," said Huta.

"What?" asked he.

"We are holy women, sacred virgins," said Huta.

"Yes?" said Abrogastes.

"What we most desire is that we serve our gods well, and then, when all is done, join them."

"You have served your gods well," said Abrogastes.

"Milord?" said Huta.

"Go to join them," he said.

"Milord!" cried Huta.

Blades leapt forth from sheaths, and at a sign from Abrogastes, Drisriak warriors seized the priestesses, and began, seizing their hair and putting them to their knees, to put them to the sword.

There was screaming.

Ambassadors, merchants, and others drew back.

"Spare those two," said Abrogastes, pointing to the two young acolytes.

Then, after bloody moments, screams, seizing, plunging bodies, reddened blades, only Huta herself, and the two acolytes, were left.

Huta, on her knees before the dais, the hand of a warrior in her hair, tightly knotted there, looked up, wildly, in terror, at Abrogastes, lord of the Drisriaks.

"The gods of the Alemanni, of the Drisriaks," said Abrogastes, "are not the gods of the Timbri."

"Mercy, milord!" cried Huta.

Abrogastes lifted his hand.

"No, no, milord!" wept Huta.

Abrogastes motioned that the warrior who held the priestess should release her.

The priestess looked wildly about her.

"My gods are false gods!" she cried.

The two young acolytes, one on her knees, the other on all fours, looked at her, wildly.

"They are false gods!" cried Huta.

"And why have you done what you have done?" asked Abrogastes.

"I wanted power!" she cried.

"It is not appropriate that women have power," said Abrogastes.

"No, milord!" said Huta. "Forgive me, milord!"

"When women have power, they abuse it," said Abrogastes.

"Yes, milord!" wept Huta.

"Thus they should not have power," said Abrogastes.

"No, milord!" cried Huta.

"How did you bring out the sign of the Drisriaks on the cloth?" asked Abrogastes.

"It has to do with washes, and stains, and reactions," wept Huta. "The blood interacts with chemicals in a prepared pattern, that causing the pattern to emerge."

"You had such cloths prepared for various contingencies," said Abrogastes.

"Yes, milord," said Huta.

"And the other matters, the sayings, the readings, the prophecies, such things."

"They are false, milord," she said. "One relies on vagueness, on research, on inquiries, on the hopes of those who attend one, on sensitivity to the responses of the interrogator, to his movements, to his expressions of attention, any number of things."

"They are all false things," said Abrogastes.

"Yes, milord," said Huta. "They, and other such things, are familiar to conjurors, mountebanks, tellers of fortune, and such throughout the galaxies."

Abrogastes made again to raise his hand.

"No, no, milord!" cried Huta. She put her hands to the collar of her robes.

Abrogastes regarded her.

Swiftly Huta tore her robes down about her shoulders.

The two acolytes regarded her with horror.

Then, with a wild look at Abrogastes, Huta tore down her robes, until they lay back, upon her calves, as she knelt.

"No!" cried the acolytes.

"Strip yourselves, little fools," said Huta, "if you would live. The game is done! These are men!"

"The game?" cried one of the acolytes.

"Yes," snapped Huta.

"But the gods!" cried the second of the acolytes.

"They are false!" said Huta.

"We must die for our faith," said one of the acolytes.

"The faith is false," said Huta. "It is an infantile fabrication."

The acolytes wept, looking about themselves.

"Die, if you will," said Huta.

"It is not true?" wept one.

"No," said Huta.

The second acolyte seemed paralyzed with misery and fear.

"Consider your bodies!" said Huta. "They are made for men. Strip!"

The first acolyte, with numb fingers, kneeling, drew away her robes.

"See!" said Huta. "That is what you are, a woman! Understand it!"

The second acolyte then, suddenly, forcibly, fighting with closures, divested herself of her robes.

"Yes, yes!" said Huta. "Kneel well! Good! See? See? You are not a man! You are quite different from a man! You are a woman! Understand it! Accept it! Rejoice in it! You are precious! Men will pay much for you!"

The acolytes exchanged terrified glances.

Then one, suddenly, made a wild, tiny, helpless sound, one it seemed of misery, and yet, one, too, of elation, and utter irrepressible relief, and joy. "The fighting is done!" she sobbed. "It is done, finished!"

"Yes! Yes!" wept the other, thankfully.

"Take them away, make them slaves," said Abrogastes.

The two young women lifted their wrists willingly, even eagerly, to the cords that bound them. Then, each, her wrists bound before her, and on a tether formed from the binding on her wrists, was conducted from the tent.

Huta then, in the midst of her discarded robes, knelt before Abrogastes.

She looked up at him.

"And what of you?" asked Abrogastes.

"I beg mercy, milord," she wept.

"Kill her, milord!" cried a man.

"Let her die the death of a thousand tortures!" cried another.

"Yes!" cried another.

"Please, no, milord!" begged Huta.

"What shall be done with her?" inquired Abrogastes.

"Slay her!" cried men.

"I beg to be looked upon, as a man looks upon a woman," she said.

"Is that not a fair request from a woman?" asked Abrogastes.

"Not from such as she!" cried a man.

"Please, milord," begged Huta.

"You are not without interest," he said.

"Find me pleasing," she begged.

"I would as soon cut your throat as look at you," he said, in anger.

"Please, no, milord," she said.

"Yet your body is luscious," he said.

"Let it please you, milord," she begged.

"You look well, stripped," he said, musingly.

"Thank you, milord," she said.

"I wonder what you would bring in a market," said Abrogastes.

"Please do not think of me so," she wept.

"Perhaps you would like for your beauty to purchase your life," said Abrogastes.

"Yes, yes!" she said.

"Perhaps it might," he said, "at least for a brief time."

"You are generous, milord!" she cried with joy.

"Your life, perhaps for a brief time," he said, "—but not your freedom."

"Milord?" said Huta. "Oh! No, no, milord!"

"If you wish," said Abrogastes, "you may declare yourself a slave."

"But I would then be no more than a dog or pig!" she cried.

"You would be less," said Abrogastes.

"Please, no, milord!" she cried.

Abrogastes raised his hand, and the warrior nearest Huta took her hair in his hand, and pulled her head back.

A knife went to her throat.

"No, no!" said Huta, frantically, shaking her head.

The warrior released Huta and stepped back, that at a sign from Abrogastes.

"I declare myself a slave," said Huta. "I am a slave."

There were sounds of satisfaction from the men about, for little love was lost for the former priestess of the Timbri, no more now than any other woman in bondage.

"You are now subject to claim," said Abrogastes.

"Yes, milord," she said.

"I claim you," said Abrogastes.

"Yes, milord," she said.

"Whose are you?" he asked.

"Yours, milord," she said.

"Your name is 'Huta,'" he said.

"Yes, milord," she said.

"Bring a collar for this slave," said Abrogastes, "a heavy one."

Such a collar was brought and placed on the slave. It was of heavy iron, a half inch thick and some two and a half inches in height. It fitted closely. It was fastened with a hasp and staple, and stout padlock, the lock in front, dangling.

Huta winced.

"Crawl to my son, Ortog," said Abrogastes, "and kiss his feet."

Huta obeyed, and then she lifted her head, to look up at him, fearfully.

Ortog did not look down upon her.

"What do you think of my new slave?" asked Abrogastes.

Ortog then looked down at Huta, and then, again, lifted his head, and looked away.

"Surely you could find better in any market," he said.

"Here, girl," said Abrogastes, snapping his fingers. "Lie here, at the side of my chair, on the dais."

Huta crept to the surface of the dais, and, frightened, lay down, near the right, front leg of the chair of Abrogastes.

"Look up at me," said Abrogastes.

"Yes, milord," said Huta.

"When women have power, they abuse it," said Abrogastes.

"Yes, milord," said Huta.

"Thus they should not have power," said Abrogastes.

"No, milord," said Huta.

"Do you have power now?" asked Abrogastes.

"No, milord," she said.

"Are you absolutely powerless?" asked Abrogastes.

"Yes, milord!" she said.

He looked down upon her.

"Yes, Master," she said.

Abrogastes then turned his attention again to the shieldsman who had been standing to one side.

Unnoticed, Huta, naked and collared, lying at the side of the chair of Abrogastes, no more than a slave, and Gerune, a princess, sitting on his left, on her chair, her back straight, in her regalia, exchanged glances. In Gerune's eyes there was a strange mixture of emotions, hatred, contempt, pity, and many others, and among them, another emotion, a strange one, one she fought to deny and suppress, that, it seemed, could it be possible, of envy. But Huta turned her eyes away quickly, perhaps failing to note the hint of envy, or perhaps more than a hint, in the countenance of Gerune, fearing as she did to look into the eyes of a free woman. Slaves can be much beaten for such things. Too, it was with strange emotions that Huta lay in her place, in shame, in misery, in fear. But she was aware of other feelings, too, feelings which she tried desperately to force from her mind, an incredible exhilaration and relief of sorts, a sense, paradoxically, of total liberation. Each inch of her, too, seemed alive. Had she been so much as touched, anywhere, she would have cried out helplessly. But, too, of course, she was conscious, very conscious, of the weighty collar on her neck. It had been put on her, and she could not remove it, no more than could have any other slave girl. She squirmed a little, and then lay fearfully still, frightened that someone might have seen her. It was not necessary for her to wear such a heavy, uncomfortable collar. A lighter one would do quite as well. But she knew that such matters were not up to her.

She looked up, a little, and saw a man's eyes upon her. Then she put down her head, trembling.

How he had dared to look upon her!

Did he think she was a slave?

But, of course, now, she was a slave!

Suddenly she feared men.

She knew she belonged to them, and must serve them.

She considered, suddenly, with momentary alarm, that she, now a slave, would be branded. She did not think that Abrogastes would put the mark on her with his own hand. That would be too much an honor for her. No, doubtless some common fellow, skilled in such matters, one used to the handling of irons and women, would do the job, doubtless she only one in a lot of several. She hoped the mark would be pretty. In any event it would be on her. And its meaning would be recognized throughout the galaxies.

She lifted her head, again, and saw that another fellow, too, had his eyes upon her, as she lay, like a dog, at the side of her master's chair.

Never before had she been looked at in that fashion!

She knew she must now respond to men, uninhibitedly and totally, in the fullness of her long-suppressed female passion, for inertness and frigidity were no longer permitted her. She must now learn to obey and feel. If necessary the lash would instruct her in such matters.

Another man's eyes were upon her, too.

And she was not yet even marked!

She hoped the brand would not hurt too much. After a little while, she told herself, it would not hurt.

But the mark would still be upon her, even then, that mark whose meaning was recognized throughout the galaxies.

It was with strange feelings, mixed and tumultuous, that she lay at the side of her master's chair.

A warrior hurried to the side of Abrogastes and spoke to him, confidentially. Abrogastes nodded, impassively.

These things were noted by Julian.

But then the attention of all was focused on Abrogastes, who addressed himself to the shieldsman.

"Will you serve me?" asked Abrogastes.

"No, milord," said the shieldsman.

"Go to the block," said Abrogastes.

"You would deny me even death by the blade," said the shieldsman.

"Yes," said Abrogastes.

The shieldsman then shook away the warriors who would have held his arms and went to the block, and knelt before it, putting down his head.

The workman grasped again the handle of the mighty adz.

"Hold," said Abrogastes.

The workman lowered the adz.

"Would you enter the halls of Kragon?" inquired Abrogastes.

"Yes, milord!" said the shieldsman.

"A blade might be used," said Abrogastes.

"Milord!" said the shieldsman.

"But on one condition," said Abrogastes.

"Milord?" asked the man.

"Forswear your lord," said Abrogastes.

"Never!" said the shieldsman.

"You would be a villein until the end of time, laboring in the darkness, rather than forswear your lord?" inquired Abrogastes.

"Yes, milord," said the shieldsman.

"I release you!" cried Ortog.

"No, milord," said the shieldsman.

"Free him," said Abrogastes. "I have need of such a shieldsman."

The shieldsman was freed of his bonds and he stood, unsteadily, his eyes wild.

He went to kneel before Ortog.

"I forswear you," said Ortog. "You are no more my shieldsman." Tears ran down the face of Ortog.

"Milord!" wept the shieldsman.

Then he rose up to go before the dais and knelt before Abrogastes.

"I am your man," he said.

"You are my man," said Abrogastes.

Abrogastes then turned to regard Ortog.

"How is it that you can inspire such loyalty in a man?" asked Abrogastes.

"Surely it is no different from what your men feel for you," said Ortog.

"Such loyalty might well be learned by a son," said Abrogastes.

"It might have been better taught by a father!" cried Hendrix, from the side.

"No!" said Ortog. Then he turned, again, to face Abrogastes. "I am too much like you, to follow you," said Ortog.

"You left the Drisriaks," said Abrogastes.

"In such ways tribes begin," said Ortog.

"But you have lost," said Abrogastes.

"Yes," said Ortog, "I have lost."

"And there are costs to be paid, penalties to be exacted," said Abrogastes.

"I am ready," said Ortog.

"You are a traitor to the Alemanni, to the Drisriaks," said Abrogastes.

Ortog did not respond.

"You should have been your own champion, or have chosen another, fairly," said Abrogastes.

Ortog looked at the slave, lying at the side of the chair of Abrogastes, but then looked away.

She did not meet his eyes.

"He can kill you?" asked Abrogastes, indicating Otto, who stood back, Julian a little behind him.

"Yes," said Ortog, angrily.

"I would see what a traitor can do," said Abrogastes.

"Wolfung!" he cried, rising up from the chair, and pointing to Otto.

"Milord?" asked Otto.

"You will fight," said Abrogastes.

"Am I *invited* to do so?" asked Otto.

"Yes," said Abrogastes.

"It will be my pleasure to accept," said Otto.

"He is no executioner!" cried Julian to Abrogastes.

"Be silent," said Otto.

Julian, startled, stepped back.

"Let the king of the Ortungs choose his weapon," said Otto.

"The prince of the Drisriaks may choose his weapon," said Abrogastes.

"Free me," said Ortog.

His bonds were severed.

"I choose the ax," said Ortog.

"You may choose the ax, or some comparable weapon, one neither clearly superior to nor inferior to the ax," said Abrogastes to Otto.

"This," said Otto, striding angrily to the workman and tearing from his startled grasp the bloody adz, "is my weapon!" He brandished it, angrily.

"That is not a weapon!" cried Abrogastes.

"I have chosen it as my weapon," said Otto, "and the challenge has begun!"

"It is a weapon, so chosen, milord!" said the spared clerk to Abrogastes.

Abrogastes turned an angry glance upon him, and the clerk put down his head.

"He is right, milord," said a man.

"You are a clever rogue, Wolfung," said Abrogastes, resuming his seat.

"It is a weapon!" cried a man.

"Those who perished by the adz feast now in the halls of Kragon!" said another.

The Drisriak warriors lifted their hands, and weapons, and cheered.

Abrogastes looked about himself, scowling.

"It is so, milord!" cried men, joyfully.

"It seems only fair, milord," said Otto, "that if you would permit your son to perish by a weapon, for you did not know what he or I might choose, then, so, too, you should be willing to permit his followers to have similarly perished."

"Yes, milord!" cried men, eagerly.

"I have chosen the adz," said Otto. "Is it a weapon, milord?"

Abrogastes looked at Ortog, narrowly.

"It seems, my father," said Ortog, "that you bear me love still."

"Yes," said Abrogastes. "It is a weapon."

Men cheered.

An ax was brought and placed in the hands of Ortog.

"I am grateful to you, Wolfung," said Ortog.

"It is controversial," said Abrogastes, angrily, "the matter of weapons and such."

"Some claim, milord," said the clerk, "that only those who die in battle are worthy of the halls of Kragon."

"Others, milord," said a man, "that only those who die with a weapon in their grasp."

"And in such things, milord," said a man, "it is said that it is only warriors who may enter the halls of the gods."

"Perhaps they will need their clerks," said the clerk.

There was laughter.

"And what of women, Father," asked Gerune, suddenly. "Have they no place in the halls of the gods?"

"Doubtless some serve there," said a man.

There was laughter.

"But they cannot earn their way there?" asked Gerune.

"No," said a man. "Those who are there are selected to be there, as choiceless as women purchased at a market, to serve as cupbearers and slaves."

"I see," said Gerune.

"Perhaps the gods have no concern with us," said Abrogastes.

"Perhaps there are no gods," said Ortog, bitterly.

"What think you, Wolfung?" asked Abrogastes. "Are there gods?"

"I do not know, milord," said Otto.

"What think you, little Huta?" asked Abrogastes, looking downward, to his right.

"I do not know, Master," she said, frightened. "I am only a slave."

"It is a suitable answer," said Abrogastes. "Do not cover yourself," he said.

"Yes, Master," she said.

"Much is obscure," said the clerk.

"The adherents of Floon claim to know the answers to all," said a man.

Floon was a gentle, itinerant teacher, a humble salamanderlike creature, from a largely aqueous world, who had preached peace and love, and such things. He had died in an electric chair, or, perhaps better, a burning rack. Already the first wars in his name had been waged.

"They are fools," said another man.

"They grow stronger," said another man.

"Let us consider the suns, and rocks, and iron, and ships, and the blades of weapons, and gold!" said Abrogastes.

"Yes!" said men.

And then he looked down at Huta, to his right, "And the bodies of women!" he added.

Huta looked down, frightened.

Gerune stiffened.

"Yes!" said men.

"They are real," said Abrogastes.

"Yes, yes!" said men.

"Fight!" said Abrogastes to Ortog and Otto.

"When have I obeyed you, Father?" asked Ortog.

Then he turned to Otto. "I salute you, Wolfung," he said, "for the honor you have shown me, undeserving though I have been, and for the respect you have shown my people, the Ortungs, unworthy though we may have been." Then he struck down at the stump with the ax, half burying the blade in the stump. Then he turned to Otto. "Strike," he said. "I am ready."

But Otto lifted the adz and with a mighty blow drove the head of the adz deeply into the stump, to the very socket of the weapon. Men cried out with wonder, seeing the force of such a blow.

Hendrix and Gundlicht cried out with joy.

Ortog turned to Abrogastes. "I bid recognition for the Ortungs, my father," he said. "Let the Ortungs be. I would be reconciled with you."

"Come to my arms," said Abrogastes, rising.

Ortog, tears in his eyes, advanced to his father, his arms open.

He stepped to the height of the dais.

Huta screamed.

Ortog fell back, stumbling from the dais.

Abrogastes, on the height of the dais, his eyes terrible, looked down upon his son, now fallen to the earth.

In the hand of Abrogastes, gripped there, was a bloody knife.

"Do you think I am so easily cheated?" asked Abrogastes of those within the tent.

"My brother!" cried Gerune, and fled from the dais, to kneel beside Ortog.

"He was your son!" cried a man.

"I have many sons," said Abrogastes.

"He wanted reconciliation!" said another.

"Now we are reconciled," said Abrogastes, wiping his weapon on his thigh, then sheathing it.

"A blade was used," said a man.

"Even now Ortog enters the halls of Kragon," said another.

"It is for the best," said another.

"Perhaps we will meet again, each in the beauty of our youth, in the halls of Kragon, my son," said Abrogastes. "And we may then dispute these matters properly."

"And afterwards," said a man, "lift cups together, feasting in joy."

"Who will win?" asked a man.

"I will win," said Abrogastes.

"To whom in the hall will go the hero's portion?" asked another man.

"It will be mine," said Abrogastes.

Gerune knelt beside Ortog, weeping.

"Thus perishes a traitor," said Abrogastes.

"Remove him," said Abrogastes.

"Bring spears," said a man. "Lash a cloak between them."

"Release those two," said Abrogastes, pointing to Hendrix and Gundlicht.

"Take your lord to the grove," said Abrogastes.

"Yes, milord," said Hendrix and Gundlicht.

"I would precede them, with a candle, if I may, milord," said the clerk.

"He was not your lord," said Abrogastes.

"You are devoted to him?" said Abrogastes.

"Then precede him, as you will," said Abrogastes.

"I would follow them, if I may, milord," said the shieldsman.

"Why?" asked Abrogastes.

"He was my lord," said the shieldsman.

"Do so," said Abrogastes.

"Thank you, milord," said the shieldsman.

It was now late in the day, and it was half dark in the tent.

In a short time the simple bier, of two spears, with a cloak lashed between them, was prepared.

Ortog was placed upon the bier.

Otto threw his own cloak over the body.

The bier was lifted to the shoulders of Hendrix and Gundlicht. It was then carried from the tent. Preceding the bier was the clerk, who carried a lighted candle. Following it, some paces behind, his sword upon his shoulder, was the shieldsman. Gerune was left behind, kneeling where she had been, sobbing, before the dais.

Abrogastes, who had resumed his seat during the preparation of the bier, had now again risen.

"Stand up," said Abrogastes to Huta.

"Yes, Master," she said. "Oh!" she said, as her wrists were lashed together, tightly, behind her back.

"Prepare the ships," said Abrogastes to a man.

"Yes, milord," he said.

Then, from the dais, he looked down on Gerune.

"We are not yet done here," said Abrogastes. "There is one more to deal with, the traitress, Gerune."

Gerune looked up, frightened.

"Take her to the block," said Abrogastes.

"She is your daughter!" cried a man.

"I have many daughters," said Abrogastes.

"Please, no, Father!" cried Gerune.

But she was dragged by a warrior to the stump. There she was placed on her knees and a warrior, crouching beside her, tied her hands behind her back. The workman worked the ax and adz free from the stump. Gerune's head, by the hair, was drawn forward, and down. She whimpered. The workman seized the adz and lifted it.

"No," cried Julian. "No!"

"Silence," said Otto.

Julian stepped back, uncertain, confused.

"It seems a simple end for her, milord," said Otto. "Is it not quick, and honorable?"

"How speak you, Wolfung?" asked Abrogastes.

Abrogastes made a sign to the workman, and he lowered the adz, and stood back.

Gerune could lift her head only a little from the block, held there by the hair as she was.

She looked to Otto, and then to her father.

"She is only a female," said Otto. "And it is said that she was marched naked, bound, through the corridors of an imperial ship, the *Alaria,* thus muchly shaming the Drisriaks."

"Yes?" said Abrogastes.

"Surely then some other end might be more appropriate for her," said Otto.

"Something more terrible and shameful?" asked Abrogastes.

"Yes," said Otto.

"Something suitable for a traitress?"

"Yes," said Otto.

"Remove her clothing and throw her to the mud," said Abrogastes.

"Please, no, Father!" cried Gerune.

But it was done, as Abrogastes had commanded.

Gerune then lay in the mud, stripped, her hands still tied behind her back.

"Traitress!" said Abrogastes.

"Forgive me!" wept Gerune.

"For treachery there is no forgiveness!" said Abrogastes.

"Mercy!" she wept.

"There is none for a traitress," said Abrogastes.

"You cannot treat me in this fashion!" cried Gerune. "I am a princess!"

"Lie in the mud, traitorous princess, as naked and bound as a slave!" said Abrogastes.

"No, no!" cried Gerune.

"And when I pronounce my next words," said Abrogastes, "you will no longer be a princess!"

"Please, no, Father!" wept Gerune.

"You are no longer a princess," he said.

She sobbed, no longer a princess.

"What think you, Huta?" asked Abrogastes.

"I am only a slave, Master!" said Huta.

"Do not forget it," said Abrogastes.

"No, Master!" said Huta.

"I am your daughter!" cried Gerune.

"When I pronounce my next words," said Abrogastes, "you will no longer be my daughter."

"No," she cried, "no!"

"You are no longer my daughter," said Abrogastes.

She sobbed, disowned, forsworn.

Men cried out with approbation.

"Do not treat me thusly!" she wept. "If I am no longer a princess or your daughter, show me at least the respect that is my due as a free woman!"

"Prepare!" said Abrogastes.

"No, Father!" she cried.

"Traitress," he said.

"Please, no, Father!" she cried.

"When I speak my next words," said Abrogastes, "you will no longer be a free woman."

"No, no!" she cried.

"You are a slave," he said.

She sobbed wildly, lying bound in the mud, a slave.

Drisriaks cheered.

Surely it was suitable punishment for one who had once been a traitorous princess.

"She is subject to claimancy," said Abrogastes.

Men drew back, looking upon the slave with contempt.

"Who wants her?" asked Abrogastes.

Men regarded her with disgust.

"None wants her?" asked Abrogastes.

No one spoke.

"Surely her body is not without some interest," said Abrogastes. "And I speculate that she would bring a reasonable price in a market."

Doubtless these things were true, for the slave was quite beautiful, but yet none spoke.

"Would she not look well under the whip?" asked Abrogastes. Then he looked at Huta. Huta quickly lowered her head.

Men laughed.

"I think, milord," said a man, "that we do not find her of interest."

"The adz!" cried a man.

"The adz!" cried another.

"Send her to the block!" cried another.

A warrior appeared in the entrance of the tent, the front entrance, behind the Drisriaks, the merchants, the warriors, Otto, Julian, and others. He made a sign to Abrogastes.

Abrogastes lifted his hand, for silence.

"There is little time," he said. "We are going to the ships."
Julian and Otto exchanged glances.

Those in the tent who were merchants and ambassadors, and artisans, craftsmen, and such, who had been at the court of Ortog began to tremble.

Abrogastes waved his hand toward them.

"Go your ways," said he.

"Thank you, milord!" they cried and, freed, hurriedly, undetained, unobstructed, left the tent.

"Let the signal for the return to the ships be sounded," said Abrogastes.

A warrior quickly left the tent.

"Take this slave," said Abrogastes, indicating Huta, "and see that she is placed, well bound and helpless, in my hoverer."

"Yes, milord," said a warrior, and seized Huta by the upper left arm, and conducted her rudely, in her collar, with her hands tied behind her back, from the tent.

"Wolfung," said Abrogastes.

"Milord?" asked Otto.

"We will come soon for the tribute," said Abrogastes.

"I think you will not find it, milord," said Otto.

"We shall see," said Abrogastes.

"Kill him, now, while you may," urged a man.

"He may not," said Otto, "for I am come here for a challenge, in which matter I have been successful."

"I shall not detain you," said Abrogastes.

Otto nodded.

"Beware in the future, Wolfung," said Abrogastes.

"And may you beware as well, milord," said Otto.

"He has the audacity of an Otung!" cried a man.

"See that the tribute is ready, when it is called for," said Abrogastes.

"Do not delay, milord," said a man. "Time is short. Cut off the head of the slave."

"Cut off her head!" cried others.

"No!" cried Julian, loudly, stepping out from behind Otto.

"'No'?" inquired Abrogastes.

"I will take her," said Julian.

"You, a thrall?" asked Abrogastes. "A thrall can own nothing."

"I am not a thrall, milord," said Julian, firmly.

Abrogastes looked to Otto.

"He is a free man," said Otto.

"I am a citizen of the empire," said Julian.

"Kill him!" said a man, drawing his knife.

"You are here in some ambassadorial capacity?" inquired Abrogastes.

"No, milord," said Julian.

"And how have you been employed here?" inquired Abrogastes.

"I have been tending pigs, milord," said Julian.

This announcement was greeted with laughter from the Drisriaks.

"It is fitting," said a man, "that those of the empire, whom we see fit to spare, should tend our pigs."

There was more laughter."

"You are filthy, and barefoot, and in rags," said Abrogastes.

Julian went to kneel in the mud, next to the distraught Gerune. He lifted her head in his hands. He looked into her eyes, which were bright with terror, and tears.

"You are well curved," he said.

"Dog!" she wept.

"Do you want to die?" he asked.

"What does it matter?" she asked.

"You are right," said Julian. "You are only a slave. What does it matter?"

She regarded him, startled.

"You are right," he said. "It does not matter."

Tears sprang anew to her eyes.

"Put the slut at the block!" said a man.

The slave looked wildly about.

"Do you want to die?" Julian asked her.

"No," she said.

"Speak more clearly," said Julian.

"I do not want to die," she said.

"Speak more clearly," he said, angrily.

"I do not want to die—*Master*," she said.

"Ah," said men.

"It seems the slut learns quickly," said a man.

"They all do," said another.

Julian then stood up, and stepped back from the slave. "Kneel," he said.

The slave, bound, struggled to her knees.

"Excellent," said men.

"You are well curved," said Julian.

"Thank you, Master," she said.

There was laughter.

"Here," said Julian, pointing to his feet.

"Go, stupid slave, to his feet, and kiss them," said a man.

The slave, on her knees, moved to Julian, and put down her head, to his feet.

"Aii!" said men.

She then straightened up, and regarded Julian with awe.

"I will take her," he said.

"Give her to him," men urged Abrogastes. "Let her belong to a tender of pigs!"

"She is yours," said Abrogastes.

"Thank you, milord," said Julian.

The slave collapsed to the mud near the feet of Julian.

"I thought I knew her," said Abrogastes. "I thought that she would require a strong and unflinching master. I see that any master will do."

"As you say, milord," said Julian.

Outside now there was a piercing whistle. It was the signal for returning to the ships.

"You," said Julian, pointing to the fellow who had, when he had learned that Julian was of the empire, drawn his knife. "Give me your knife," said Julian.

The man looked at Abrogastes.

"Do it," said Abrogastes.

Julian took the knife and then crouched beside the slave.

"Master?" she asked.

"You are Gerune," he said, naming her.

"Yes, Master," she said.

He reached to her hair.

"What are you going to do, Master?" she asked.

"You have long, fine hair," he said.

It was blond hair, in two long, thick braids, which, had she stood, would have fallen to the back of her knees. It had never been cut.

"Master?" she asked.

"A slave," he said, "does not need such long, fine hair."

"Master?" she asked.

"Oh!" she wept, for he, gathering the hair together, in handfuls, cut it from her, close to the head.

Then he stood up, and returned the knife to the warrior, who sheathed it.

Gerune wept.

"Such hair," said Julian, "was more fit for a princess than a slave."

She put down her head, sobbing.

"You are now more fit for lowly tasks," said Julian.

"Yes, Master," she wept.

Abrogastes stepped from the dais.

Abrogastes made a sign to the workman, he who had wielded the adz, and to two warriors.

"Remove the block and tray," he said.

"Yes, milord," they said.

The whistle sounded once more outside.

Abrogastes looked about himself. He looked back to the dais. He regarded the trampled, muddied earth. He regarded the pools of blood, the broken reeds, the footprints. He recalled the vengeances, the slaughters and enslavements of the afternoon. He regarded the workman, his leather apron, and his arms, drenched with blood. He looked back to where Ortog had fallen. He looked down, at the bound slave.

He then looked at this men.

"It is good!" he said.

He then, followed by his men, left the tent.

Otto followed the others out.

Julian, too, a moment later, left the tent. He carried a bound slave.

"She is unconscious," said Otto, considering the slave in Julian's arm, her head back.

"It is just as well," said Julian.

"She should give you much pleasure at the foot of the couch," said Otto, regarding the slave.

"I will see to it," said Julian.

The hoverer of Abrogastes was not far away, only some yards from the tent.

*Filchen* scurried about, disturbed. Birds rose into the air, like protesting leaves in the wind. But, in a few moments, the birds descended again. And soon the *filchen*, too, wary, their tiny ears upright, their small, round eyes bright, creeping back, returned to their feeding.

Julian looked up at the sky.

"I think it would be well to conceal ourselves," said Otto, "until we know the nature of the new arrivals."

"The woods?" said Julian.

"Yes," said Otto.

They were now quite near the hoverer of Abrogastes.

Already the lord of the Drisriaks was within the hoverer, his hands on the gunwales.

"The tent, milord?" a man asked of Abrogastes.

"Burn it," said Abrogastes.

A torch was lit.

"We have found golden chains!" said one of the Drisriaks to Abrogastes.

These would have been found, presumably, near the place of the challenge.

"We have no time to concern ourselves with such things," said Abrogastes.

The man threw the chains over his shoulder, and hurried to a hoverer.

A moment later the hoverer of Abrogastes rose from the turf.

The slave, her body buffeted by wind and pelted with dust, stirred in Julian's arms, but she did not recover consciousness.

Otto and Julian watched the departure of the hoverer of Abrogastes.

Within the hoverer, Otto surmised, though he could not make this determination, given the distance of the ship, the height of the gunwales, the armoring of the hull and such, would be a bound slave. Doubtless she would be, too, bound to metal rings, fixed in the plating of the hoverer's deck. In any event that is a common way in which captives and slaves are secured in such a vessel. The arrangement not only keeps them fixed in place, which is fitting and desirable, but can, under certain circumstances, such as abrupt maneuvers, serve also to keep them literally within the vessel. She might be, as well, gagged, in order that, in the event of engagements or violent actions, of one sort of another, her responses would be less distractive.

Otto and Julian, the latter carrying the unconscious slave, made their way from the crowded area outside the tent, from the hurrying men, the assemblage of small ships.

They returned to the trail, which would lead downward, past the grove.

They paused on the height to look into the distance, to the meadow where the ship of Hendrix and Gundlicht had landed, that ship which had brought them to this world. It was a shambles of blackened steel.

Behind them the tent was ablaze.

Once again there was a piercing blast from the whistle.

On the trail downward, they met two men, the shieldsman and

the clerk, who were hurrying upward, that they might reach the hoverers before they departed. The clerk averted his eyes as they passed. The shieldsman, for a moment, just for a moment, met the eyes of Otto, and then he, too, hurried past.

"Let us go to the woods edging the meadow," said Otto.

"Good," said Julian.

That portion of the woods, because of the destroyed ship, would not be likely to draw fire.

In a short while, on the way downward, they came to a grove. Otto paused on the trail at that place.

Then he continued on, followed by Julian.

A quarter of an hour later they had crossed the meadow, and entered the woods.

It was dusk now.

One could still see a glow, and, in places, flames, from the height of the plateau.

Hoverers, like dots, some in formation, rose from the plateau, and then moved eastward.

Smoke, a darkness against a darkness, billowed upward.

"We are safe now," said Julian.

They stood at the edge of the trees, looking upward, toward the trail, the grove, the height of the plateau.

Behind them they had placed Gerune on the leaves.

With a vine they had lashed together her ankles and, with the same vine, extended from her ankles, fastened her to a tree.

She was still unconscious.

"But we are stranded on this world," said Otto.

"I do not think so," said Julian.

"Oh?" said Otto.

"No, my friend," said Julian. "I do not think so. Rest now, if you wish, and I will watch."

There was a tiny whimper behind them, and they turned about. Gerune moved a little in the darkness. One could hear the crinkling of the leaves.

"She is recovering consciousness," said Otto.

"Oh, oh," moaned Gerune. Then she cried, "Oh!" and there was the sound of her ankles pulling suddenly against the vine which fastened her to the tree.

"Be silent," said Julian, going to crouch near the slave.

She slid forward on the leaves, that she might sit upright.

She looked at Julian.

He took her head in his hands, holding her helplessly, and pressed his lips fiercely upon hers.

She uttered tiny sounds of protest but they were muffled in the uncompromising ferocity of his kiss.

Julian drew back.

She looked at him, reproachfully.

"Do you not know how exciting you are?" he asked. "Have you never been kissed before, as a slave? No, of course, doubtless not."

Few women, other than slaves, can guess what is the passion of a male.

Few women, other than slaves, have any conception of the heights, the aggressions, the sheer power of uninhibited male passion.

Once again he took her head firmly in his hands and pressed his lips against her.

"Oh," she said, suddenly, softly.

Then suddenly she understood herself as what she was, a woman, the complement to this passion, its other, and her entire body seemed bathed in need and flame, and she squirmed in her bonds, his, and he drew back a little and she whimpered, protestingly, and thrust her head forward, pressing her lips timidly, fervently, to his, and then Julian took her by the shoulders and threw her from him, to her side, on the leaves, where she lay, her eyes wide.

"Perhaps, later," he said, "there will be time for a slave."

She lay there quietly then, helpless, spurned, discarded until wanted.

She tried to understand herself and her feelings, her desires, her needs. She feared she might be going mad. Why had no one told her of these things? Were they so dangerous, really? Were they such dreadful secrets? She knew herself now, and this frightened her, terribly, a woman, and slave.

She moaned a little, in her bonds.

"Be silent," said Julian.

She sobbed, softly.

"Sleep," he said to her.

She closed her eyes, and shuddered, and lost consciousness.

"You, too, should rest," said Julian to Otto.

"I am weary," said Otto, and lay down.

It was toward midnight when Julian gently shook Otto awake.

"What is it?" said Otto, quickly.

"Look," said Julian, standing, and pointing upward, to the west. "A light in the sky."

"What is it?" asked Otto, standing, looking to where Julian had pointed.

"Wait," said Julian, eagerly.

"There," he said, after a time.

Overhead there was a set of lights, and a mighty shape moved among the clouds, a shape designed to enter and negotiate atmospheres, as well as traverse the depths of space.

"What is it?" asked Otto.

"It is an imperial cruiser," said Julian.

"There are other lights, too," said Otto, looking upward.

"It is an imperial fleet!" said Julian.

## · · · CHAPTER 12 · · ·

Standing at the edge of the woods Julian and Otto watched the lights, approaching across the meadow.

Some men were approaching, on foot.

"They saw you," said Otto.

"Yes," said Julian.

An hour before, as a patrol craft had scouted the meadow, at an altitude of some thousand feet or so, Julian, waiting, having emerged from cover, caught in the beam of one of its searchlights, had lifted his arms, signaling the craft. He must have seemed small, and white, there below, signaling. The craft had blinked its lights twice, and then moved on.

"They have seen us," had said Julian, elatedly, returning to the wood.

Now some men were approaching, carrying flashlights. They had dismounted from a hoverer, left on the other side of the meadow.

"Excellent!" said Julian.

"Be careful, do not be precipitate," said Otto.

"Have no fear, my friend," said Julian.

He withdrew a few feet into the darkness of the woods.

"Oh!" cried Gerune, awakened by a blow, from the side of Julian's foot.

He bent down and untied the vine from the tree, that by means of which Gerune's ankles had been secured to it. This left the other end of the vine, that which bound her ankles together, as it was.

He then carried her, bound hand and foot, to the edge of the trees. There he put her down, on her knees.

"See the approaching lights?" he asked.

"Yes," she said.

"Men approach," said Julian.

Gerune squirmed a little, helpless in her bonds.

"Those will surely be men from the empire, men from an imperial fleet."

She looked at him, wildly.

"Do you wish to run away?" he asked.

"I am bound hand and foot!" she said.

"There is no escape for you," said Julian. "And when you are branded there will be no doubt of it."

"You are not going to put me under the iron!" she said.

"You are a slave," said Julian. "Of course you will be branded."

She shuddered.

The lights were closer now, rather in the vicinity of the shambles of the destroyed ship, coming across the meadow, now about one hundred yards away.

"Listen to me," said Julian, "and listen carefully."

She looked up at him, piteous, bound.

"It is my recommendation," said Julian, "that, if you wish to live, and not be tortured, and then nailed to a gate in some provincial town, that you conceal your antecedents."

"It is wise counsel, slave girl," said Otto. "Attend your master."

"Remember," said Julian, looking down at his bound slave, "you are no longer a princess. You are no longer the daughter of Abrogastes. You are no longer even a free woman. You are a slave. As a slave you have a name only by my will, that of your master. Too, as a slave, you are no longer of the Alemanni, or the Drisriaks or the Ortungs. You are tribeless. You no longer have a people. You have only masters. You are an animal, as much as a pig or goat. You are owned. You are property. You are a slave, and only a slave."

Her eyes were wide.

"Do you understand?" asked Julian.

"Yes!" she said.

"Kiss my feet," snarled Julian.

Swiftly she put down her head to his feet, kissing them.

"Lick them!" said Julian, watching the lights approach.

"Yes, Master, yes, Master!" she sobbed.

"Lift your head!" said Julian.

She looked up, tears in her eyes.

"We are now going to untie your ankles," he said. "You will doubtless be ordered out first. You will go quickly, and be obedient."

"Yes, Master," she said.

Julian freed her ankles, and then helped her to her feet. She stood, unsteadily, behind Julian and Otto.

The lights, now, stopped.

Julian, his hands raised, emerged from the woods.

He was instantly caught in the beams of several of the lights.

"Who are you?" called a man.

"Julian, of the Aurelianii," said Julian, proudly, "ensign in the imperial navy."

"Of the Aurelianii!" said a man.

"Can it be truly he?" asked another.

"Hold!" said a voice behind the lights. "We do not know it is he." A light flashed past Julian, toward Otto and Gerune. They half closed their eyes against the blaze. "Who is with you?"

"Two," said Julian, "Otto, a barbarian auxiliary, and a female slave."

"Send the slave forth," said the voice.

"You will show them what you are, a slave," said Julian.

Gerune moaned.

"You will hurry forth," said Julian, and kneel, head to the turf."

"Send forth the slave," said the voice.

"Go," said Julian.

Gerune, her hands bound behind her, hurried forward, and, when she reached the men, knelt, her body bent forward, her head down, to the turf.

Flashlights played upon her body.

"A pretty one," said a man.

The voice of command, from behind the lights, said, "Check her bonds."

Her hands were pulled up a little, behind her, and inspected.

"She is well tied," said a man.

"Put her on a leash," said the voice of command.

A leash was snapped about her throat.

She trembled, her head still down. It was the first time, doubtless, she had worn a slave leash. To be sure, on the *Alaria*, some time ago, she had been marched through corridors on a rope, and that is much the same thing.

"Come closer, sir," said the voice behind the lights to Julian.

Julian advanced.

"Hold!" said the voice behind the lights.

Julian stopped.

"Is it you, can it be you?" asked the voice from behind the lights.

"Yes," said Julian, "it is I."

"It is he, he!" said a man.

"Yes!" said another.

"Sir!" suddenly cried the voice from behind the lights. He stepped forward.

Julian saluted him, for his rank was higher than his own.

The man returned the salute, sharply. "Forgive us, Excellency!" he said. "We could not be sure."

"I am afraid I am not in uniform, and that I smell of pigs," said Julian.

"Bring the hoverer," said the officer, speaking into his radio. "And inform the fleet that we have found his excellency."

The hoverer came slowly over the grass, and alit, some yards from the party.

"With your permission we will stow this for you, and secure it properly," said the officer, indicating Gerune.

"Certainly," said Julian.

"Stand up," said one of the men to Gerune.

She stood up, on her leash.

"Aii," said the officer, examining her with the flashlight.

"She is lovely," said one of the men.

"Stand straighter," said Julian to Gerune.

She stood more beautifully, lifting her chin.

"Oh, yes!" said a man.

Gerune cast a frightened glance at Julian.

"She is a beauty," said the officer. "Where did you pick her up?"

"Here," said Julian.

"She looks Drisriak," said the officer.

"Perhaps," said Julian. "But when I picked her up she was only a slave."

"Who are you, girl?" asked the officer.

"I am only a slave, Master," she said.

"And a low slave, it seems," said the officer.

"Yes, Master," she said.

"Perhaps a scullery slave," said the officer.

"Oh?" said Julian.

"That can be told from the hair," said the officer to Julian. "See how it is cropped short?"

"Yes," said Julian.

"I envy these barbarians their women," said the officer, "that they can use beauties like this even for mere scullery slaves."

"They have an eye for women," said Julian.

"And they get the most out of them," said the officer.

"True," said Julian.

"Some of their slaves are former ladies of the empire," said the officer.

"Commonly," said Julian.

"Doubtless they serve well," said the officer.

"Yes," said Julian.

"I have known ladies of the empire," said the officer, "whom I would not have minded owning as slaves."

"Perhaps you could buy them back, and keep them as slaves," said Julian.

"An interesting thought," said the officer.

"And how then would they serve you?" asked Julian.

"With perfection," said the officer.

"Excellent," said Julian.

The officer played his flashlight, again, upon Gerune. He illuminated her left flank.

She straightened, frightened.

"She is not yet branded," said the officer.

"That will be attended to, shortly," said Julian.

Gerune shuddered.

"See that this cargo is stowed, and well secured," said the officer to a man.

"Yes, sir," he said.

Gerune was led away on her leash.

"This is my friend, Otto, an auxiliary," said Julian, indicating Otto.

"Such troops have their uses, I am sure," said the officer, bowing.

"May I invite you aboard?" asked the officer.

"It is my pleasure," said Julian.

"We are only a few moments from a shuttler," he said.

"You received my message?" asked Julian.

"A message was received, with your call signal, purportedly from Varna," said the officer.

"It was authentic," said Julian.

"But it was broadcast on a band commonly utilized by barbarians," said the officer.

"It was an Ortung radio, with a fixed frequency," said Julian.

"We suspected a trap," said the officer.

"But you took precautions?" said Julian.

"Surely," said the officer.

"The Drisriaks," said Otto, "doubtless also took the message for an Ortung communication. It brought both the Drisriaks and the imperial fleet to this sector."

"Drisriaks have been hunting Ortungs," said Julian.

"And it seems they found them, in the vicinity of 738.2," said the officer. "The Ortungs were decimated. There was much debris."

"How came you to this world?" asked Otto.

"It was en route to Varna," said the officer, "and when we detected the traces of barbarian ships, we chose to investigate."

"Both Drisriaks and Ortungs were here," said Otto.

"Abrogastes himself was here, only hours ago," said Julian.

The officer whistled.

"You will doubtless attempt to pick up his trail and deal with the Drisriak fleet."

"There is little chance of overtaking lionships," said the officer.

"You will do your best," said Julian, angrily.

"Yes, sir," said the captain.

It might be noted that, even at that time, the empire had many enemies, some of them technologically sophisticated, some of them even within her own borders.

"It will not now be necessary to proceed to Varna," said the officer.

"I will need a ship," said Julian.

"To return to Telnaria?" said the officer.

"Eventually," said Julian, "but first we must return to Varna."

"Excellency?"

"There are arrangements to be made there," said Julian, looking at Otto, "and, too, we may wish to pick up some cargo."

"Yes," said Otto.

"I am sure the admiral will put as many ships at your disposal as you wish, your excellency," said the officer.

"A single corvette will do," said Julian.

"Doubtless accompanied by a convoy of destroyers," said the officer.

"A corvette will do," said Julian.

"As your excellency wishes."

The officer turned about then and went toward the hoverer, some yards away. Gerune had already been placed on board.

Otto and Julian remained for a few moments in the meadow.

Julian looked up to the sky, to the east.

"Abrogastes presents a great danger to the empire," said Julian.

"He is lord of the Drisriaks," said Otto, "and they are the largest and most dangerous tribe of the Alemanni nation."

There were eleven tribes in the Alemanni nation.

"I fear," said Julian, "that he may bring together a league of barbarian peoples, the Alemanni, and others."

"It would not be easy," said Otto. "There is much rivalry, much envy, much suspicion and jealousy among such peoples."

Long had the empire exploited such matters.

"Surely the empire can defeat mere barbarians," said Otto.

"It is not the same empire that it once was," said Julian.

"It has thousands of ships, it can destroy worlds," said Otto.

"There are hundreds of such peoples," said Julian.

"The empire has nothing to fear," said Otto. "It is eternal."

"Once there was no empire," said Julian.

"I cannot conceive of a reality without the empire," said Otto.

"Its loss would mean the downfall of civilization," said Julian.

"There is nothing to fear," said Otto.

"Abrogastes is your enemy, as well," said Julian.

"Yes," said Otto.

"I will urge that the Wolfungs be supplied with a weapon," said Julian, "one capable of destroying a ship in orbit."

"We would be muchly grateful," said Otto.

"You desire to serve the empire?" asked Julian.

"It must be preserved," said Otto.

"We have many enemies," said Julian.

"True," said Otto.

"Abrogastes is our greatest enemy," said Julian. "I fear him most of all."

"Why?" asked Otto.

"It is not that he now has so much power," said Julian, "or so many ships, or even that the Alemanni is a populous nation, but other things, frightening, terrible things."

"What?" asked Otto, puzzled.

"He is like a shark," said Julian, "who can detect a drop of blood in the water, an erratic movement."

"I do not understand," said Otto.

"He can smell corruption where others can sense only soundness," said Julian. "He can see weakness where others see only strength."

"Ah," said Otto.

"He is a statesman, a warlord," said Julian.

"Of course," said Otto.

"He has vision. He can think new realities. He can ponder new orders, new ways of life. He has ambition, he has patience. He is ruthless."

"But he is weak now," said Otto.

"Yes, he is weak now," said Julian.

"So there is nothing to fear," said Otto.

"At least Ortog is dead," said Julian.

"No," said Otto.

"'No'?" said Julian, startled.

"Did you not see the point of entry of the knife?" asked Otto. "It was below and to the side of the heart."

Julian regarded Otto, closely.

"We study such things in the school of Pulendius," said Otto. "It behooves the gladiator to have some sense of anatomy."

"That is why you threw your cloak over him!" said Julian.

"Yes," said Otto, "that if he should give some sign of life it might be less likely to be detected."

"And that is why the clerk averted his eyes, and the shieldsman, on the trail, cast you such a look?"

"Doubtless," said Otto.

"Ortog lives?"

"The wound was grievous, he may by now be dead," said Otto.

"Did Abrogastes know how he struck him?"

"I would surmise so,'" said Otto.

"Why did he not kill him?" asked Julian.

"I do not know," said Otto.

"He was prepared to have you fight him," said Julian.

"He may have known that I had once spared Ortog on the *Alaria*," said Otto.

"How could he know that?"

"I do not know," said Otto. "Perhaps from witnesses, men or women from the *Alaria* who were embonded by the Ortungs, and then later acquired, with other loot, by Drisriaks."

"But it was important for him to punish treachery, and see justice done," said Julian.

"It seems it was well punished," said Julian. "The Ortungs were decimated, and Ortog, at best, is left grievously wounded, stranded, on a remote world."

"He was prepared to have his daughter beheaded," said Julian.

"But she was not beheaded, was she?" said Otto.

"No," said Julian.

"But instead she was reduced to slavery," said Otto.

"A most horrifying and grievous punishment for her," said Julian.

"But one surely eminently suitable, considering her crime," said Otto.

"Certainly," said Julian.

"But, besides," said Otto, "she is a slave."

Julian looked up at Otto.

"She may not understand it yet," said Otto, "but she is a man's slave. One can tell it from her body, her expressions, her movements. She will never be fully happy until she is a man's slave."

"Did Abrogastes know that?" asked Julian.

"I think it possible," said Otto. "Besides, is it so different, being a mating pawn, or being bought and sold in markets. Is it not much the same thing?"

"Yes," said Julian.

"At least in markets," said Otto, "the bidding, and its meaning, and such, is clear."

"Yes," said Julian.

"And would you kill your own son?" asked Otto.

"No," said Julian.

"I think that Abrogastes might," said Otto.

"But this time he did not," said Julian.

"No," said Otto. "This time he did not."

"Do you think that Huta is a slave?" asked Julian.

"She looks well in a collar," said Otto.

"Do you think she is a slave?"

"She will need a strong hand, and a taste of the whip," said Otto.

"But do you think she is a slave?"

"Certainly," said Otto.

"It seems that many women are slaves," said Julian.

"Yes," said Otto.

"Do you think that all women should be slaves?" asked Julian.

"Yes," said Otto.

"I think you are right," said Julian.

"Gentlemen," said the officer, from the deck of the hoverer, "I have informed the shuttler of our imminent departure."

Otto and Julian shortly thereafter boarded the hoverer.

It was, like most such ships, circular, and open, rather like a metallic coracle.

This particular vessel was some twenty feet in diameter. Its hull was armored. The crew of such a vessel normally consists of two men, and these were the two who had remained with the vessel when it had been left across the meadow, but there were now seven men on board, not counting Otto and Julian. The officer, and his four companions, figured more in the category of soldiers, or, perhaps better, marines, than crew.

"We will soon be at the shuttle," said the officer.

Julian went to the side of the vessel, just within the bulwarks. He lifted aside a piece of canvas.

There, beneath it, on the metal plating of the deck of the hoverer, lay Gerune, who looked up at him, seeing him bending over her, and the black sky, and stars, above him. Her wrists were now before her body, held closely together there, locked in slave cuffs; a chain ran from the linkage of the cuffs through a metal ring, to her ankles; there, at the ankles, the chain joined another linkage, that linking her shackles.

"How did you like wearing a slave leash?" asked Julian.

"I must go where it bids me," she said.

He continued to look upon her.

"It is fitting that it was on me, for I am a slave," she said.

"This is the first time you have worn slave chains, is it not?" inquired Julian.

"Yes," she said.

He continued to regard her.

"Yes, Master," she said.

"How do you like them?" he asked.

"I may not object," she said, "for I am a slave."

"How do you like them?" he asked.

She put her head to one side.

"It is fitting that they are upon me," she said, "for I am a slave."

"The cargo is stowed, and secured, to your satisfaction, I trust," said the officer.

"Yes," said Julian.

The arrangement would not only keep the cargo in place, and helpless, but would serve, as well, to keep it within the vessel, even in events such as steep climbs and perilous bankings, even inversions.

"I hope you do not mind that we put a canvas over her," said the officer, "but my men have been a long time without women."

Gerune trembled, looking toward the men.

She began to suspect what it might be to be a slave, and she knew herself a slave.

There was a tiny sound of chain on the metal plating, and against the ring, as she, frightened, drew her wrists in, more closely to her body.

"I understand," said Julian.

He lifted the corner of the canvas, to throw it again over the slave.

"Please, wait, Master," she whispered.

He crouched down, beside her, the corner of the canvas in his right hand.

"You are not really going to have me branded, are you, Master?" she asked.

"Yes," he said.

"But I was a princess," she said.

"Barbarian princesses, and women who were once barbarian princesses, are not unknown in imperial markets," he said.

"I was the daughter of Abrogastes," she said.

"You are now no more than a slave, and you will be branded," said Julian.

"But how can you have such a thing done?" she asked. "It is not civilized."

"On the contrary," said Julian, "it is preeminently civilized. Indeed, it is a feature of a civilized society. Its efficiency is unquestioned. Surely you can understand that it is useful and appropriate, for legal and other purposes, to identify properties."

She looked away.

"The highest civilizations," said Julian, "have always held slaves."

"And doubtless there has always been some means of appropriately identifying them?"

"Yes."

"I will be branded then," she said.

"Yes," he said.

"I beg you to relent," she said.

"No," he said.

"You are going to do with me exactly as you please, aren't you?" she said.

"Yes," he said.

"Even to the iron?"

"Yes," he said.

"Your excellency," pressed the officer.

"Look forward to your branding," said Julian.

Gerune looked up at him, wildly.

He prepared to throw the cover over her.

"You are my master, aren't you?" she said.

"Yes," he said.

Then his visage was blotted out, and the dimly lit bulwarks, lit by the instrument lights, and the black sky, and the bright stars.

She then lay there, on the metal plating, beneath the canvas.

"I, Gerune, am going to be branded," she said softly to herself. That seemed to her for a moment incomprehensible, that Gerune should wear a brand. But then she realized that there was nothing untoward or surprising in that. 'Gerune' was, after all, only a slave name. In one sense, then, she was no longer Gerune, certainly not the Gerune she had once been. In another, of course, she was Gerune, because that was the name that her master had decided to give her. In this second sense, then, there was surely nothing surprising about an iron being heated for her, as for countless others.

She shuddered.

There was a tiny sound of chain. She heard men laugh, but she could not see them.

She lay there very quietly then, fearing to move.

She supposed it would not do to tell her master, or others, that she had been thrilled to be on a leash, that it excited her to wear slave chains.

What ancient, strange message, what profound message, did these things speak to her?

She lay there then, not moving, knowing herself naked, and a slave, under a canvas, at the mercy of men.

"Belt in," she heard the officer say.

Shortly thereafter the hoverer rose into the air.

She lay there, beneath the canvas, astounded, not at the motion of the vessel, but at herself.

"Yes," she whispered to herself, softly, "yes!"

She feared to be branded, of course. It would not do to deny that. But, too, now that she was a slave, now that that was what she was, she wanted it done.

Indeed, she had often wondered, from the time of puberty on, what it would be, to be branded.

Her emotions were complex, for, mixed with her fear, you see, there were many other emotions, as well, those of curiosity, of anticipation, of tremulous excitement, of literal elation, even, I suppose it should be admitted, of eagerness.

Oh, she would protest, or cry, or such, particularly if such things were expected of her.

But, between ourselves, she could not wait for the mark.

"How terrible I am!" she thought, delightedly, squirming just a little, but hopefully not so much that her movement could be detected beneath the canvas.

But there was no laughter.

The men, it seemed, were not then concerned with her.

Their minds were on other things.

She had been forgotten.

But she was then suddenly terrified. She could be bought and sold. What if her master simply decided to rid himself of her in some way?

She knew she was passionate.

Her skin was like flame.

Now she must try to be sufficiently beautiful, sufficiently obedient, sufficiently zealous.

"I will try to please you, my master," she said. "I will try desperately to please you, with all that I am and have! Please keep me, Master. Please keep me!"

In a few moments the hoverer had alit near the shuttler. She was aware, then, even through the canvas, through the tiny interstices of thick weaving, of the lights.

She could hear men moving about, within the hoverer, and outside, shouting, calling out.

"I ask nothing of you, my master," she said softly, to herself, "but it is my hope that you will sometimes show me a little kindness."

## · · · **CHAPTER 13** · · ·

"A drink, sir?" inquired the stewardess.

Tuvo Ausonius looked up at her, instantly noticing that the top button on the high collar of her jacket was undone.

"Sir?" she inquired.

Surely she must realize what was wrong?

It was warm in the cabin. The air conditioning was laboring, and enjoying little success. The gases were weak, the system less than tight. The motor itself could be heard. It had required two manual restarts in the past hour. Surely the procurement office could obtain parts for such devices, and services for them. Citizens were entitled, surely, to at least such minimal consideration. But it was not easy to obtain parts, or even the necessary gases, these days.

It was different, not even so long ago.

And communications were difficult, sometimes impossible.

Certain worlds had been out of touch for months, for example, Tinos, far off in the eighty-third imperial provincial sector.

It was not necessary, surely, for her to lean forward in that fashion.

"No," said Tuvo Ausonius.

The stewardess turned away.

"You are out of uniform," said Ausonius, after her.

She turned back, surprised, to face him.

"The upper part of your neck can be seen," he said. "It is bare."

She lifted her fingers to her throat.

"Button your collar," he said.

She looked at him.

"Sir?" she asked, puzzled.

"Button it," he said.

"It is very warm, sir," she said.

Ausonius was irritated with this reply, that she should attempt to so mitigate her lapse, that she should attempt to excuse her provocative disarray, seizing upon so obvious a pretext as the temperature in the cabin.

"That is no excuse," he said.

"Are you an inspector?" she asked, frightened.

"I am a civil servant," he said, modestly, dryly, leaving the nature of his duties menacingly obscure.

He had boarded at Miton. That is not one of the original Telnarian worlds, but it does lie within the first provincial quadrant. More than a million functionaries on ten thousand worlds would have gladly changed places with Tuvo Ausonius, to have a post so close to the heart of the empire.

"Ah," she said, relieved.

The line was a private one.

"But one not without some importance," he said.

Private lines, of course, were licensed by the empire, and dependent on the empire for their routes.

There were also, incidentally, many imperial lines. The empire regarded it in its own best interest to maintain her own systems of communication and transportation, public as well as military.

The stewardess turned white.

Tuvo Ausonius conjectured that she was of the *humiliori*.

"I am afraid I shall have to report you," he said.

"No!" she said, quickly. "Please, no!"

Some other passengers looked in their direction.

Tuvo Ausonius, from her alarm, conjectured, to his satisfaction, that she was indeed of the *humiliori*. To be sure, that was almost certain from her position on the vessel.

Tuvo Ausonius drew out a notebook and pen.

"What is your name, and employment number," he asked.

She fumbled with the top closure of the collar.

Ausonius regarded her.

Then, in a moment, the collar was fully fastened, the final closure pulling it up tightly under her chin.

She looked at Ausonius, pathetically.

"Please," she said.

"Shall I call for the superintendent?" he asked.

"No," she said. "No!"

"Sesella," she said. "Sesella Gardener." She then gave him the number he had requested.

She looked down at him. He now had a hold over her. It was as though he had her on a chain.

"May I speak to you privately?" she asked, urgently.

"Certainly," smiled Tuvo Ausonius.

He followed her to a small area on the ship, in the nature of a tiny galley, which was closed off by opaque curtains from the main cabin.

In the galley she turned to face him, tears in her eyes.

He regarded her.

She wore the uniform of the line, the dark jacket and trousers, and the tight-fitting cap which kept her hair hidden. The uniform was supposedly designed to be appropriate for sames, a uniform that might with equal felicity, or, better, lack of it, conceal sexual differences. Supposedly it was designed to hide bodies. But Tuvo Ausonius's lip curled. How he despised the line! How disgusting it was, really. There could be no doubt that the pretense of concealment was rankly hypocritical. The cabin attendant was clearly female. That could be told from the curves within the garment. Too, her face had the sweet delicacy of that of a female. Indeed, even her lips suggested the slightest tincture of lipstick. Surely she had not dared to apply cosmetics!

She looked up at him, pathetically.

"Do not report me," she begged.

He regarded her, impassively.

"Please, do not!" she said.

He took his thumb and, to her horror, wiped it heavily across her lips. He looked down at the reddish stain on his thumb, with disgust. She had indeed been wearing lipstick, though perhaps the slightest hint of it. Yet there was no mistaking the smudge now, running from her smeared lips, to the left side of her chin. She looked up at him with misery. He held his hand out and she hurried to seize a tissue, and wipe it clean. Then she tried to cleanse her own lips and chin of the mark.

"What a profligate, wicked creature you are," he said.

"Please, please," she said.

His expression was impassive.

"Do not report me," she begged. "I will do anything."

She drew away the cap she wore, and let her hair, which was darkly lovely, fall about her shoulders.

"Wicked creature!" said Tuvo Ausonius.

"Please," she begged.

"Perhaps you would look well on your knees," he said.

She looked at him, wildly. Surely he was not such a man. He had not taken her by force, and put a chain on her.

"No!" she whispered.

He was surely not the sort of man before whom a woman kneels, and knows she must obey.

"How can you want that? How can you ask that? You are of Miton!"

"I only said, 'Perhaps,' " he said.

"But you are a same," she said, "superior to nature, above sexuality, beyond such things, a noble, tender, sensitive, caring nonman, the truest of men!"

"It was merely an observation," he said.

"No, no," she whispered.

He regarded her, impassively.

She fell to her knees, before him.

"I am at your mercy," she said. "I will do anything."

"I will give you my address, on the summer world," said Tuvo Ausonius. "I shall be there for a few days."

He turned back to look at her. She was still on her knees. She held the bit of paper in her hand, with the address written on it, in a careful, precise script.

"I will take that drink now," he said.

"Yes, sir," she said.

"There will be no charge," said Tuvo Ausonius.

"No, sir," she said.

"And wipe your face," he said.

"Yes, sir," she said.

Tuvo Ausonius then returned to his seat. He gave his attention, for a time, to his notebooks, but then, after a little while, looked out the porthole, at the blackness of the night, and the brightness of the stars.

He saw his face reflected in the glass, and then returned his attention to the interior of the cabin.

He flicked on the viewer fixed in the back of the seat in front of him, but there was nothing there to interest him, and he turned it off.

Tuvo Ausonius was an executive in the finance division of the first provincial quadrant, and was posted on Miton. He was a level-four civil servant. There were several imperial employees under his supervision. He was also, of course, as were most imperial civil servants, of the *honestori*. Indeed, to the disgust of Tuvo Ausonius, appointments in the civil service, above the second level, carried the *honestori* status with them, whether the employee's antecedents warranted it or not. More importantly, Tuvo

Ausonius was of the minor patricians, being related in the 103rd
degree to the original Ausonii. He was as yet unmarried, having to
date successfully resisted various pressures brought to bear upon
him both privately by superiors and publicly by directives of the
imperial administration. The numbers of the imperial aristocracy,
over the past several generations, doubtless for several reasons,
and doubtless all quite understandable and acceptable, had tended
to decline. This was, however, a source of concern to the senate
and to the imperial administration. Ausonius was not clear on why
he had been called to the summer world, and not the capital world,
particularly at this time in the fiscal year. He feared it might have
to do with appearing before a mating board, perhaps one appointed
by the empress mother, he and hundreds of others, in their turn,
expected to explain their prolonged bachelor status. It is not that
Tuvo Ausonius had never been involved in such matters. Indeed,
that fact would surely constitute his best defense against the
challenges of such a board. Once, credentials having been examined on both sides, careful, mutual, detailed inquiries completed,
and even pictorials exchanged, arrangements, to the weariness and
disgust of Tuvo Ausonius, had been finalized. The fortunate young
woman, for she was far beneath him, being related only in the
105th degree to the Auresii, was a court officer on Terennia, a
position which she had occupied in virtue of the influence of her
mother, a judge in a small city in the northern hemisphere of that
world. Also lending her assistance to the arrangements was another
significant personage of the same city, its mayor. Matters had
proceeded quite far. The prospective bride had even, reportedly,
embarked for Miton, from Terennia, on an imperial cruise ship, the
*Alaria*. The *Alaria*, however, had never appeared in orbit about
Miton. Its fate was obscure. It was speculated that an explosion on
board had damaged the ship irreparably, or that, perhaps, due to
detector malfunctions, it had encountered a meteoric rain of such
an extent that evasive maneuvers were ineffective and of such force
that the shields and hull had crumbled beneath the impacts. As the
reader knows, the fate of the *Alaria* was other than as these
conjectures would have it. Its fate, of course, in general terms, had
been clear to the imperial ships which had responded to her distress
calls, but, until later, it was not understood, even on certain high
levels, precisely what had occurred. It had not been thought
necessary, in the interests of retaining public confidence, to inform
the public that the loss of the *Alaria* might be explained in terms
other than those of accidents, for example, that its loss might be

attributable to the activities of unwelcome intruders. In any event, Tribonius Auresius, for that was the unlikely name of the prospective bride, had not arrived on Miton. This eventuality was greeted with some relief by Tuvo Ausonius, but also, interestingly, with some irritation, as he had invested a great deal of time in inquiries and a not inconsiderable expense in negotiations. Tribonius Auresius was, of course, a masculine name, though its bearer was anything but masculine, as she later learned. That name had been bestowed upon her by her mother, doubtless in the interests of assisting her daughter to remain true to the upper-class *ethos* of Terennia, which was, we note, not unlike that of Miton. Indeed, Miton, for just such reasons, was one of the worlds on which the judge, and her colleague, the mayor, both of whom hoped to considerably improve their fortunes through the young woman's marriage, conducted their matrimonial and economic searches. The daughter, as it might be recalled, from an earlier account, was less than enthusiastic about the prospect of voyaging to Miton and becoming the bride of Tuvo Ausonius. She had already despised him, and had resolved to make his life miserable, even to the extent of ridiculing him in public and squandering his resources. To be sure, given an assemblage of circumstances, she, doubtless fortunately for Tuvo Ausonius, never received the opportunity to put these plans into effect. Due to the same assemblage of circumstances, she was no longer of either interest or value in the marriage market, though, to be sure, she might have figured in, and would quite possibly have been found of some interest or value in, markets of other sorts.

"Your drink, sir," said the stewardess.

"Thank you," said Tuvo Ausonius.

The stewardess looked at him, frightened.

"Seven in the evening, on the first day after debarkation," said Tuvo Ausonius.

That would give him time to make the necessary arrangements.

"Yes, sir," she whispered.

"It will begin then," he said.

" 'Begin'?" she asked.

"Yes," he said.

"Also," he added, "you will come suitably prepared, suitably garbed, perfumed, adorned, made-up, you understand."

"Yes, sir," she said.

# · · · CHAPTER 14 · · ·

There were many rich hangings in the hall, which were noted by Otto as he followed Julian, and the servitor, past guards, toward large doors, rather in the distance, rather more than fifty yards away, hung with purple velvet, leading to what he took would be an audience chamber, that of the emperor himself.

"We have waited long enough!" snapped Julian to the servitor.

"I am sorry, your excellency," said the servitor.

There were vessels of gold and silver, too, on pedestals, here and there, in the hall.

They would make rich loot, thought Otto. To be sure, the loot of most interest to him was that of soft flesh, the sort which could be purchased in many markets throughout the galaxy. The empire was rich in such loot. Barbarian ships, usually few in number, and stealthy, sometimes struck well within the provincial quadrants, to secure it. Some raids had taken place even within the worlds of Telnaria itself.

What terror they had struck, even to the heart of the empire!

Many women of the empire awakened, frightened, in the night, hearing the smallest of sounds.

"Your audience must be brief," said the servitor, "as the emperor fatigues easily."

"It will be brief," said Julian, angrily.

Otto noted a bronze, representing Orak, the king of the gods, in the Telnarian pantheon. Orak was standing, looking outward, a great spear grasped in his right hand, its butt on the ground. At his feet, beside him, facing in the same direction, kneeling naked, collared and in chains, her head lifted, as though she might have just been addressed, was an image of Dira, the goddess of slave girls.

Many slave girls, he knew, prayed to Dira, that she might help them to be more pleasing to their masters.

To be sure, she could not always hear their prayers for sometimes she must be attending to her own masters.

Often she was busy, bearing wine and such.

Too, more than once she had been punished by Orak or others, even she, for having failed on some occasion to be fully pleasing.

Even the fair back of Dira, it seems, had felt the lash.

Sometimes the fault was for having interceded for an unworthy slave girl.

It is little wonder she had her devotees.

"Stop here," said the servitor.

At the purple-hung doorway there was a detection device, through which, slowly, Julian, Otto, and the servitor passed. Apparently its operator, at the desk console, screened from those at the device, did not detect anything calling for attention. No alarm, incidentally, would sound if there were some difficulty, for that might alert the individual, or individuals, at the device. Any difficulty would be registered by a silent, visual signal, read by the concealed operator. A variety of expedients, depending on the device, might then be activated, ranging from destructive beams to the sudden descent, traplike, of plastic cages.

Otto brushed away a fly, back, away from his head.

"Enter," said the servitor.

The two great doors, with the purple hangings, swung back, and Otto saw, before him, at the end of a long carpet, on a dais, in a great room, four individuals on tall, solemn thrones.

"The empress mother," whispered Julian, "the emperor, and the two sisters of the emperor."

There were several other individuals, as well, within the chamber, which was lofty, and lit from windows high in its dome, through which light, in shafts, swarming with dust, fell. Otto's attention was first, however, taken by the figures on the dais.

"Julian, your cousin, your majesty," said the servitor, "and guest, one Ottonius, an auxiliary."

"Have you brought me a toy?" asked the boy on the throne.

"No," said Julian, angrily. He then addressed himself to the empress mother. "We have been waiting long," he said.

The servitor gasped, as did several others in the room.

"There is no toy?" asked the boy, turning on the throne, looking at one of the men near the foot of the dais.

"Your majesty," said the man, drawing from his dark robes a small globe, filled with numerous, tiny, brightly colored particles. "See?" He turned the globe about, and the particles within it changed their position, seeming to float and swirl, and fall about, in a thousand manners.

"Give it to me!" said the boy, and, in an instant, it was within his grasp.

"You see, your cousin Julian loves you," said the darkly clad man. "He brought you a toy."

"No!" said the boy. "It is from you! It is from you, Iaachus!"

"You are right, your majesty," said Julian, angrily. "It is from your dear Iaachus. I did not bring you a toy."

"You should have brought him a toy," said the empress mother, a stern, short, dour woman, with a wrinkled face, oddly contrasting with the stiff richness of her robes. "You know he is fond of toys."

The emperor's sisters exchanged amused glances.

The empress mother's throne was just slightly behind that of the emperor, on the emperor's right.

"Pretty!" said the emperor, turning the small globe about in his hands.

The emperor, Otto guessed, was some fifteen or sixteen years of age.

He had a sallow complexion, and there was something at the side of his mouth, which seemed to be saliva.

"I have come here on imperial business," said Julian, addressing himself to the empress mother, "a business which, I believe, has been made clear to you in advance."

Otto looked about the room. There were some well-armed guards in the room, but most of those present seemed to be civilians, of great wealth and station. This he conjectured from their garments and adornments. None of their apparel, of course, matched the richness and ornateness of that of those on the dais, that of the empress mother, that of the emperor, that of his two sisters. The women looked spoiled and pampered. The men looked bored and weak. He did not think the women would know how to give a man pleasure, but he supposed they could be taught, if necessary, with the whip. He was much surprised at the appearance of the men, that they should be counted among, as he supposed they were, the aristocracy of the empire. How different they were from the aristocracy of the barbarians, powerful men, hungry men, covetous, lustful, jealous, possessive, greedy, ruthless, ambitious, warlike, inured to hardships, accustomed to danger, eager for gain, zealous for adventure. I see now, thought Otto, how it is that men such as these need their armies and navies, others to do their fighting for them. Some, he thought, could not even lift the two-handed sword which, in the hands of a strong man, with two blows, could cut a horse in two, or the war ax which might with five blows shatter foot-thick timbers and the bar behind. The only man, other than the guards, who seemed to command attention, and awareness, was the darkly clad figure called Iaachus. His intelligence, Otto conjectured, would be extremely high. His influence, Otto suspected, would be considerable.

"Yes," said the empress mother, "your request has been considered."

The name of the empress mother was Atalana.

"Favorably, I trust," said Julian.

The emperor continued to play with the toy, fascinated by the continually shifting variegations of its interior.

The name of the emperor was Aesilesius.

"Pretty, pretty," said the emperor.

"Yes," said the empress mother.

"I am awaiting your decision," said Julian.

Otto, standing behind Julian, his arms folded, considered the women in the room. He found them, pale as they were, of much greater interest than the men. Many were doubtless wives of senators, for most here would surely be of the senatorial class, but his attention was drawn more to the younger women. Some might be daughters of others in the room, but several, he supposed, would have some other function, such as that of serving as attendants to, or companions to, the empress mother, and the sisters of the emperor. They would be, in a sense, I suppose, to have recourse to a familiar expression, ladies-in-waiting. The eyes of some of these rested upon him. It was seldom, he supposed, that they had seen one here who was so far removed from their own class and kind. But he sensed, too, in the eyes of several of them, he was regarded with more than mere, or idle, curiosity. Perhaps they were curious to know what it might be like, to be in the arms of such a man, pressed helplessly to him, knowing that they would be used to quench, if only for a time, a passion greater than any they had ever known. Perhaps they wondered what it would be like to stand before him, in his tent, awaiting his pleasure, and then being commanded to divest themselves, completely, of those impediments to his assessment. Perhaps they wondered what it would be like to be examined by such a man, frankly, intimately, turned about, and posed, considered. Perhaps they wondered what it might be like to belong to such a man. Some of the women in the room wore simple, long gowns, white and woolen. They were sleeveless gowns. The feet of these women were bare. They, he did not doubt, though they wore no obvious sign of bondage, were slaves. He saw the parted lips of some, as they gazed upon him. Another, surreptitiously, thrust a bit to one side the strap on her gown, that at the left shoulder. It was the signal of a female in heat. He was familiar with it from the house of Pulendius. They were doubtless starved for the touch of masters. He did not doubt that beneath their simple gowns, commonly on the left thigh, beneath the hip, there would be a brand. He then let his eye rove to the two sisters of the emperor. Both were older than the emperor, who had perhaps been born late in the mother's life. One was perhaps twenty-five and the other twenty-three. The older one was taller, and blond. Her throne was the farthest to the left, as one looked toward the dais. The younger sister was shorter and dark-haired. Her throne was just to the right of her sister's throne, as one would look toward the dais. The name of the older sister was Viviana. The name of the younger sister was Alacida.

"There are matters within your proposal which call for further clarification," said the empress mother to Julian.

The sisters of the emperor seemed little concerned, as did the emperor, busy with the small chromatic globe, with the affairs of state.

The two young women, Otto noted, were regarding him, from within the layered walls, the high, rigid defenses, of those stiff, heavy, brocaded robes of state. He wondered if anything stirred, hot like blood or soft and warm like woman's flesh, within those high, elaborate fortresses of fabric and gold. He wondered what they might look like, barefoot, in long, sleeveless, white woolen gowns, or less.

"The matter is quite simple," said Julian. "I am requesting a commission, in the rank of captain, for Ottonius, my colleague, that he may recruit *comitates*, a company, drawn from various worlds, to function in an auxiliary capacity."

"There are many units in the *auxilia*, already, your majesty," said a man.

The *auxilia* were largely formed of barbarians, almost always from the same tribal groups. Later barbarians, of diverse tribes, would figure in the regular forces, as well.

"Why, dear Julian," inquired the empress mother, "do we need yet another unit of such?"

"Since the senate and people of Telnaria," said Julian, acidly, "have seen fit to extend the citizenship, unearned, gratuitously, to so many worlds, recruitment has dwindled, deplorably, to a trickle. Men of the empire refuse to touch steel, preferring gold, or even free bread and amusements."

Citizenship in the empire, and its associated benefits, it might be remarked, were at one time, rare and muchly coveted. One route to citizenship was service in the armed forces, a route of which countless men of ambition and intelligence availed themselves. A citizenship earned is, of course, a citizenship respected and prized. When citizenship is regarded as something that is due one, on the basis of having been born, or such, the state suffers. Soon blocks of votes are being sold, in effect, to the highest bidder. Once again, I merely observe this, refraining from comment.

"The winds of what men prize have changed," said Iaachus.

"Soon," said Julian, "the armed forces will consist of barbarians!"

"They are hungry," laughed a man. "They will work cheap."

"Why should we weary ourselves with martial labors, when there are others who will serve us well, and cheaply."

"Beware," cried Julian, turning, pointing upward, back, "there are wolves among the stars!"

"Set wolves to fight wolves," said a man.

"But they must be wolves as fierce, as terrible, as those who prowl even now at our borders!" said Julian.

"The empire has nothing to fear," said a man.

"The empire is eternal," said another.

"Our technology, our weapons, our ships will protect us," said another.

"And what will you do when the barbarians, too, have such technologies, such weapons, such ships?" asked Julian. "Abrogastes, of the Alemanni, of the Drisriaks, already has lionships, which are the equal of our destroyers, and even faster."

"I have never heard of Abrogastes," said a man.

"Let us hope that you never do," said Julian.

"Pretty," said the emperor, looking into the small globe.

The empress mother rose from her throne and, with a cloth, wiped the side of the boy's face, removing the saliva that ran there. She then resumed her place.

"May I speak, your majesty?" inquired Iaachus.

"Surely," said the empress mother.

"In what way, beloved Julian, noble scion of the Aurelianii, that family in whose debt we all so consciously and gratefully stand, would the commissioning of this colleague of yours, this Ottonius, serve the empire?"

"Am I requested to supply a justification," asked Julian, "for what I am entitled to, as the smallest of favors, of considerations, given my lineage and my station?"

"Of course not," said Iaachus. "Forgive me."

"It is only a captaincy," said another man. "It might have been granted without an audience."

"I want the audience," said Julian. "I want it clearly understood that the empire is not secure, that it is in grave danger, or will soon be in grave danger."

"Revenues decrease," said a man. "Planets grow less arable. It is hard to collect taxes. Men flee. Men leave their occupations."

"The bindings will stabilize matters," said a man. "They will guarantee the security of the tax base."

"I am most regrettably forced to my proposal," said Julian. "I, more than any, fear barbarians in the service of the empire. I, more than you, understand them. I realize the danger they pose. But these risks must be accepted. There is no choice. Civilization, *civilitas* itself, is at stake. Patriotism, civic duty, allegiance, are no longer mighty forces in the empire."

"Nonsense!" cried a man.

"In what unit have you served?" asked Julian.

The man stepped back, and looked downward.

"He is only one man," said a man, indicating Otto.

"It is the beginning," said Julian. "It is a new concept. In the past the *auxilia* have been almost always recruited from particular tribes, allowed to settle within the borders of the empire, as *federates,* their land granted primarily in exchange for recruitments. These tended to be uniform units, keeping their own tribal structure and leadership. Their allegiance, in the last analysis, was to their own groups."

"Surely there have been mutinies," said a man.

"I envision," said Julian, "barbarian mercenaries, drawn from various worlds, recruited on the basis not of tribal membership but of qualities and skills, however terrible and merciless these may be, men owing their allegiance not to tribes and tribal leaders, but to their own captains."

"Who will be dependent upon our commissions, and pay," said a man.

"Yes," said Julian.

"Landless men, pure fighters, with no worlds," said a man.

"Dependent on the empire," said Julian.

"Warriors," said a man, shuddering.

"Yes!" said Julian.

"Mercenary warriors," said another.

"Yes, yes!" said Julian.

"What think you, noble Iaachus?" inquired the empress mother.

"An interesting, but dangerous, idea," said Iaachus.

"It is too dangerous," said the empress mother.

"There are no viable alternatives," said Julian.

"Surely the assessment of he of the Aurelianii is overly pessimistic," said a man.

"Not at all," said Julian, angrily.

"The empire has always had its problems," said a man.

"What think you, noble Iaachus?" asked the empress mother.

"I respect the views of Julian, whom we all dearly love," said Iaachus, "even though I am sometimes pained to disagree with them."

"Yes?" asked the empress mother.

"But I fear that the empire, or certain distant, unimportant parts of it, may now indeed be in some slight danger."

"But there is nothing for us to fear?" asked the empress mother.

"No, of course not, your majesty, not here, nor in Telnaria itself."

"Give us your counsel," said the empress mother.

"We might begin slowly," said Iaachus, "and then, if things did not seem auspicious, withhold support, simply abandon the project."

"These men could go where we want, be sent to the points of greatest danger!" said Julian.

"They might prove a most useful arm in the service of the empire," said Iaachus.

"I am not convinced of the value, or necessity, of such a thing," said the empress mother.

"No decision need be reached at this instant, of course," said Iaachus.

"Pretty, pretty!" said the emperor, lifting up the globe.

"Yes," said the empress mother. "It is very pretty."

"Your friend is barbarian?" said a man.

"I think so," said Julian.

"And what are his qualifications for such a captaincy?" asked the man.

"Assess them," said Julian, angrily.

"Camarius," said the man.

"Sir?" said one of the guards.

The man pointed at Otto and Camarius rushed upon Otto who seized his descending arm, twisting it, and kicking the man from him, but not releasing the arm, jerking it from the socket and the man cried out with horror and pain and then Otto, with an inhuman noise, at once a snarl and a cry of rage, for he was an impatient and easily angered man, jerked him by the injured arm to him as he screamed, and threw him, face upward, down, upon his knee, thrusting down, in fury, to break his back across that living fulcrum.

"No!" cried Julian. "No!"

The guard's eyes were bulging and wild, one arm lifted helplessly, the other useless at his side.

"*Civilitas!*" screamed Julian.

Otto rose up, throwing the guard from him, angrily, to the carpet. The guard rose to his feet, half crouching, and hurried away, whimpering.

Otto's eyes were terrible to behold.

"*Civilitas,*" said Julian, soothingly.

Otto then regarded the man who had ordered the soldier to approach him, but the man stepped back. The hands of guards were on their weapons.

"It is all right," said Julian. "It is over now." Then he faced the man who had ordered the soldier forward. "Have you further questions?" he asked.

"No," said the man.

The assemblage in the court was stunned, and silent. Otto stood there, in a narrow shaft of light, it sparkling with dust, descendant from one of the high windows in the dome. All eyes were upon him. Even the emperor regarded him.

"The decision of the emperor will be conveyed to you," said Iaachus to Julian. "I will do my best to press for a favorable response."

Otto angrily looked about himself, from face to face.

He looked into the face of the men, and into the faces of the women. These latter seemed to draw back, some lifting their hands to their bosom.

The eyes of the slave girls were wild.

Had Otto so much as snapped his fingers they would have hurried to him, to kneel.

He regarded the sisters of the emperor, blond Viviana, and dark-haired Alacida.

They seemed startled.

He had no doubt that now something stirred, and profoundly, beneath those robes.

They looked wildly away, flushing scarlet.

He conjectured, in his anger, in his fury, what they might look like, kneeling naked, on ropes.

They too could learn, like any other woman, to respond instantly to the snapping of a man's fingers.

"I am afraid of him," said the empress mother.

"There is nothing to be afraid of," said Julian.

"Oh, oh!" suddenly cried the emperor, putting his head down, holding the colored globe close to him, as though to protect it, and striking about with his free arm.

"What is it?" cried a man.

"It is a fly," said a man.

"Guards!" said the empress mother, she, too, leaping up from her throne, to rush to the emperor.

The emperor burst into tears.

"What is wrong?" asked Otto.

"The emperor fears insects," said Julian, irritably.

Two guards were about the imperial throne, trying to drive away the insect.

"It is all right," said the empress mother, holding the boy to her.

"The audience is at an end," suggested Iaachus.

"Yes, yes!" said the empress mother. "There, there, darling," she crooned.

The older of the emperor's two sisters, Viviana, the blonde, regarded the emperor with ill-disguised contempt. The younger, Alacida, dark-haired, looked upon him with embarrassment, and pity.

"The audience is concluded," said Iaachus.

Men and women began to take their leave.

"I will do my best to further the success of your business," Iaachus said to Julian.

"My thanks, Counselor," said Julian. "Your majesties," said Julian, to the dais.

Julian and Otto watched the men and women leaving the room.

The slave girls had hung back, looking at Otto.

"Go!" snapped Iaachus to them and they turned about and hurried from the room.

The two sisters of the emperor, too, it seems, had dallied. But then, seeing Otto's eyes upon them, they lifted their heads and took their leave.

"I wonder what they would look like, in collars, curled in the furs," said Otto.

"They are of the highest class of patricians, the senatorial class," said Julian.

"I wonder what they would look like," said Otto.

"What do you think?" asked Julian.

"I think they would look well," said Otto.

"So do I," said Julian.

The emperor, clinging to his globe, was hurried from the audience chamber, in the keeping of the empress mother, followed by ladies-in-waiting, and guards.

"The emperor has not yet lost interest in his toy," said Otto.

"It will doubtless continue to fascinate him for a long time," said Julian.

"He is simple?" asked Otto.

"He is feebleminded," said Julian.

"Who rules?" asked Otto.

"Iaachus," said Julian, wearily.

"Who is Iaachus?" asked Otto.

"He is the arbiter of protocol," said Julian.

"Do you trust him?" asked Otto.

"No," said Julian.


# ▪ ▪ ▪ **CHAPTER 15** ▪ ▪ ▪


It was a light knock, a timid knock.

Tuvo Ausonius looked up from his columns.

The knock was repeated, a timid, light knock, but rapid now, pressing, urgent, as though someone might fear to remain outside in the ill-lit street.

Tuvo Ausonius gathered his papers together, arranged them, and inserted them in one of the pockets of a leather portfolio, which he then buckled shut.

Again the tiny frightened knock sounded, pleadingly.

Tuvo Ausonius rose from the table in the sparsely furnished room.

He went to the door.

He slid back a viewer and ascertained the frightened eyes of a woman, her face muchly concealed in a dark hood.

The woman was admitted, and, behind her, after looking about, outside, Tuvo Ausonius shut the door, thrusting home two bolts, then locking them in place.

In the room there was now an aroma of perfume, strong, heady. The woman thrust back her hood, revealing her loose, dark hair. She looked about, frightened.

"Is this the place?" she asked, disbelievingly.

The room was quite simple, quite plain, and almost bare of furnishings. There was, however, a table, a simple, worn, scratched table, once darkly varnished, with one dark, wooden chair. On the table lay Ausonius's portfolio. There was also a heavy dresser to one side, and a heavy, massive bed, anchored to the floor. At the foot of this bed, though it could not be seen from where the woman and Tuvo Ausonius stood, there was a heavy metal ring, fixed in the floor. There were two windows, rather high, one in the same wall as the door, and the other across from it. The height of the windows was to prevent individuals peering into the room. There were no coverings for the floor, save a small throw rug, ragged and grimy, near the table. There were no hangings, or pictures, at the walls. They were unadorned, and cracked and chipped. In numerous places paint had peeled from the plaster. There was much peeling and cracking in the ceiling, as well, and several brownish circles, like rings, were overhead, where water had soaked through. There were run marks, too, of water at the walls, some from the ceiling and windows, some from tiny crevices high in the walls, stains which wended their way downward to the floor.

"Yes," said Tuvo Ausonius.

"This is your room?" she asked.

"For now," said Tuvo Ausonius.

"It is dark," she said.

Given the nature of the room, its smallness, its lack of furnishings, its need of repair and paint, the limitations of its tiny windows, even in the daylight it would have been, at best, dingy.

"I will turn up the lamp," he said.

He went to the wall and rotated a dial which increased the illumination of the single swivel light in the ceiling. By means of a small wheel he then adjusted the beam of the swivel light so that it fell on the woman, illuminating her, rather as though she stood in a spotlight.

She blinked a little, and stood there, in the light, clutching the cloak about her.

"I was afraid in the streets," she said. "I had difficulty finding this place. I did not dare come in a conveyance. Men called out to me from the darkness.''

There was a tiny jangle from within the cloak.

This sound intrigued Tuvo Ausonius.

"Perhaps they smelled your perfume,'' suggested Tuvo Ausonius.

"What sort of woman did they think I was?'' she asked.

"Perhaps you can guess,'' he said.

"Do you like it?'' asked the stewardess.

"It is appropriate for you,'' he said, "though perhaps it might be more obvious.''

"I am wearing it for you,'' she said. "I hoped you would be pleased.''

"I think it will do nicely,'' he said.

"Where are your things?'' she asked, looking about.

"Do not concern yourself with them,'' he said.

He noted that her hair was lustrous. It had doubtless been washed, treated, brushed, combed, such things.

"Have you no light supper prepared?'' she asked.

"I see that your feet are bare,'' he said.

"I thought you expected such things,'' she said.

He put his hands to the borders of her dark cloak, closely clutched about her.

She lifted her eyes to his, pleading.

"You are here,'' he reminded her. "Surely you do not wish to be reported to the line.''

"You cannot do these things to me!'' she said.

"Oh?'' he asked.

"I am a same!'' she said.

"We shall see,'' he said.

"It was only a minor violation of the regulations,'' she said, "and the ship was terribly uncomfortable.''

"Such an infraction is surely sufficient for dismissal,'' he said. "And what, too, of your intolerable discourtesy, your flagrant insolence, your provocative impropriety?''

"You cannot say such things!'' she said.

"Surely I shall,'' said Tuvo Ausonius, "for they are all true.''

"I will do whatever you want,'' she said.

"Let us see what we have here,'' he said. He then parted the dark robe.

Surely it was the stewardess as none others had ever seen her.

Then he dropped the dark cloak to the floor, behind her.

"Stand straighter,'' he said.

Her dark hair was lustrous, as it fell, glistening, behind her, about her shoulders. About her throat, twice twined, were beads, and a necklace of threaded, tiny coins. The lovely sweetness of her upper body was haltered high, snugly, in scarlet silk. The sheen of her beauty descended then, with perfection, to a narrow waist, sweetly slender, which was encircled closely with a tight black, cloth cord, that sustaining the two overlapping sheets, front and back, skirtlike, of scarlet silk. Beneath this silk could be sensed the rounded joy of her belly and the flare of a love cradle that might have driven men mad.

"Loosen the belt a little," said Tuvo Ausonius.

She did so, and the rounded sweetness of her belly was then more than hinted at, and the scarlet silk then was low on her hips, held there only by the sweetness of their flare.

"Kneel!" said Tuvo Ausonius.

Immediately the stewardess knelt before him, in the pool of light.

Tuvo Ausonius then suddenly felt sensations, and feelings, which he had never felt before.

He sought to rid himself of these feelings.

They were not in his plans.

She was incredibly beautiful, kneeling before him.

There were several loose bracelets on her right wrist, and an armlet on her upper left arm.

They might appear to be of gold, but would not be so, no more than such things affected by street women, or coin slaves.

It was the jangle of these bracelets which Tuvo Ausonius had heard before, shortly after she had entered the room, that delicate sound which had earlier intrigued him.

She smoothed the silk a little.

There was, again, the tiniest sound from the bracelets.

Yes, it was an intriguing sound.

The silk, as she now knelt, was between her thighs, thus contrasting with their milky white softness, and, of course, that they might be bared to him.

She knelt back, her hands on her thighs, the bracelets on her right wrist, the armlet on her upper left arm.

Tuvo Ausonius was not insensitive to her charms.

"You lack only the brand and collar," he muttered to himself.

She looked up at him, her eyes half closed against the light.

"It is nothing," he said.

"I forget your name," he said.

"Sesella," she said. "Sesella Gardener."

"Do you think you are a same?" he said, angrily.

"No," she said. "I do not think I am a same, truly. I have never thought, really, not for years, that I was a same."

He glared down at her, unwilling to see her, but yet unable, it seemed, to remove his eyes from her.

He had realized what a woman could be.

He must remain strong, he must remember his purpose.

"Stand up," he said.

She complied.

"No," he said, angrily. "I do not think you are a same."

The only good women, he reminded himself, forcibly, were sames.

How small she was, compared to him, and her shoulders, so small, so soft, so white, so exciting.

Suddenly, to his anger, he realized that she must have some inkling of the effect she had on him.

"I had a hard time finding this place," she said. "It is not in one of the better districts."

"I suppose not," he said.

"It is a poorly lit area," she said.

"Perhaps," he said.

"It is a shabby district," she said.

He did not tell her what sort of district it was.

Fitting for you, he thought.

She looked about, at the room, at the floor, the walls.

She did not seem overly pleased.

She looked up, toward the ceiling, toward the peeled paint, the irregularly concentric brownish rings.

Her eyes were half closed, against the glare of the swivel light.

"It is fortunate it is not raining," she said. "It seems the ceiling leaks."

"Perhaps it has been repaired," he said.

"It is a very high ceiling," she said.

"This is a summer world," said Tuvo Ausonius. "The rooms are often so constructed, that they may be cooler, the warmer air rising upward."

"Of course," she said, blinking, looking down.

"You do not seem pleased with the room," he said.

"It was not what I expected," she said, lightly.

Yes, she sensed her power.

He could change that, quickly enough.

"I think it will do very nicely," he said.

This remark seemed to alarm her somewhat. Certainly it would remind her that she was here, and as he wished.

Yes, it will do very nicely, for what I have in mind, he thought.

"What do you think of the table?" he asked, pointing to it.

She regarded its worn, darkly varnished surface. "You are not going to put me on it, are you?" she asked, uneasily.

Now she was surely less certain of her power.

"Certainly not," he said, as though he found the very thought distasteful.

Still it was surely a charming thought, pleasing himself with her on such a surface.

He almost regretted that he was a same.

Now she was again surer of her power.

He noted this with satisfaction.

"You did not bring anything to eat or drink," she said.

"Do not concern yourself with such matters," he said.

She looked at the bed. "Do you want me to get in bed?" she asked.

"No," he said.

"'No'?" she asked.

"No," he said.

"I do not understand," she said. "What am I to do?"

"Go to the foot of the bed, and stand there, and await further instructions," he said.

"There is a ring here, in the floor," she said.

Tuvo Ausonius went to the heavy, dark dresser against one wall and, with a sound of sliding wood, opened the top drawer. He reached within the drawer. There was a sound of heavy links of chain, moving on the wood. He drew out a sturdy, common "Y" chain, of some two feet in length, with its three rings at its terminations, each now open.

He placed the "Y" chain on the foot of the bed. He also picked up the throw rug and then placed it on the floor, at the foot of the bed, near the ring.

She looked down at it.

In this way, he conjectured, she might be more comfortable.

"You will now," he said, "remove your clothing, completely, even your necklaces, your bracelets, and such."

"Very well," she said.

"Why have you turned your back to me?" she asked.

He did not respond to her.

How could she ask such a foolish question? How could he look upon her? How could he dare to look upon her? Why would he even care to look upon her? Did she not know he was above such things, that he was a same?

She put her hands to the back of her neck, to remove her necklaces. She smiled to herself. She enjoyed removing her garments. She wished to strip herself, and bare her beauty, to reveal it in all its marvelous loveliness to a male, that it might find in that its meaning and birthright, and, too, that she might, to her joy, understand something of how precious she was to men, what a treasure she was to them, what a wondrously perfect and desirable creature she was. She knew that men fought and killed for women such as she. She knew that they sought women such as she, and, ruthlessly, in markets, bought and sold them.

She laid the necklaces on the foot of the bed.

"No one knows I am here," she said.

She thought he might wish reassurance on this matter.

"It doesn't matter," he said.

"Oh," she said.

She slipped the armlet from her upper left arm and put it on the bed. Then she removed the bracelets, and placed them there, as well, with the armlet and necklaces. Tuvo Ausonius, his back turned, heard the bracelets, moving against one another, being placed on the bed. She reached behind her back, to the closures on the halter.

"You are not looking at me," she said.

"No," said Tuvo Ausonius.

She placed the halter on the bed.

She reached to the narrow, black, cloth cord, now low on her hips, that sustaining the skirtlike sheets of scarlet silk. As it now was on her, so low, so provocative, so exciting, so responsive to her slightest movements, she might even have been a dancer, or tavern slave.

She hesitated.

She turned about, so that her back would be to him, if he should turn, if he should suddenly wish to see her.

Let her beauty be to him as a revelation.

She untied the cloth cord and gathered together the two sheets of flowing, sheer silk.

These things she then put behind her on the bed.

"I am naked," she whispered.

"What?" he asked.

"I am naked," she said.

"Absolutely?" he asked.

"Yes," she said.

"Kneel down, on the rug, at the foot of the bed," he said.

"I have done so," she said.

"Can you reach the chain on the foot of the bed?" he asked.

"Yes," she said.

"It is a "Y" chain," he said. "It has three terminations, each with a ring, now opened. Before you, fixed in the floor, you see a large, heavy ring. Chain yourself to it. This will be done in the following manner. The ring at the bottom of the "Y" is to be closed, and locked, about it. The two rings at the terminations of the arms of the "Y" are to be closed, and locked, about your wrists, snugly. Do you understand?"

"Yes," she said.

Tuvo Ausonius listened carefully.

He heard three clicks, first, one click, and then, a little later, one after the other, two more clicks.

"Are you chained helplessly?" he asked.

He heard her pull against the chains. Did he detect some fear in her movements?

"Yes," she said.

He did not doubt but what this was true, as she would doubtless expect him to check the closures on the three rings, satisfying himself that they were all locked, and that the wrist rings were suitably snug, even tight, upon her wrists.

"May I speak?" she asked.

It interested him that she would request permission to speak. But he supposed that when a woman finds herself as she was, that she might naturally be apprehensive, as to whether or not she may speak. What if it were not desired, at such a time, to hear her speak?

"Certainly," said Tuvo Ausonius.

"I have wondered—" she said.

"Yes?" he said.

"Earlier you suggested that my perfume might be more obvious," she said.

"It is quite acceptable," he said. "And it will do very nicely."

"I wondered what you meant," she said.

"Only that another perfume might have been even more appropriate for you."

"I do not understand," she said.

"That of whore, or slave," he said.

"Oh," she said. But her response did not seem angered, or protestive.

"I wonder what it might be like to wear such perfumes," she said.

"Perhaps you will one day learn," he said.

"Do not jest," she said.

Tuvo Ausonius was silent.

"But how such things must excite and arouse a woman," she said. "How helpless they must make her!"

"I am sure that your perfume might count as such," said Tuvo Ausonius.

She made a tiny, helpless noise. There was a tiny rustle of chain.

"You are not going to do these things to me, and then still report me to the line, are you?" she asked, frightened.

"Of course not," said Tuvo Ausonius.

"Thank you," she said.

Besides, thought Tuvo Ausonius, that would not be at all necessary, not now.

She pulled at the chains.

"I am helpless," she said.

"Yes," said Tuvo Ausonius.

"This is the first time a man has put me in his power," she said.

"It will not be the last," said Tuvo Ausonius.

"You are going to keep me as mistress?" she asked.

"Scarcely," said Tuvo Ausonius.

"What are you doing?" she asked.

Tuvo Ausonius, being careful not to look at the woman at the foot of the bed, gathered up the articles on the bed, the necklaces, the bracelets, the silk, and such.

"Why do you not look at me?" she said.

He put the articles on the floor, near the table, rather as though they might have been removed there. He then drew back the bedclothes, and rumpled them, in such a way that they appeared to have been naturally displaced, but in such a way, too, that she could not reach them from where she was chained, at the foot of that massive bed, anchored to the floor.

"What are you doing?" she asked, again, pulling at the chains.

"Move back," he said to her, his eyes on the floor.

She moved back a bit, as she could, until, in a tiny bit, she came to the end of the chain.

She was now off the small rug.

Being careful, again, not to look at her, he drew away the small rug and put it back where it had once been, near the table. It was now not far from the discarded adornments and garments, either. Indeed, might someone not have stood on the rug, while removing the adornments and garments, and slipped them to the floor, there, in that place?

Too, he had decided that one such as she did not need the comfort even of the tiny rug.

The chains and the floor were suitable for her.

"Look at me!" she cried. "Look at me!"

But of course Tuvo Ausonius did not do so.

He did look about the dingy, shabby room. He was rather well satisfied with it. It seemed a suitable room for punishing a woman such as she.

He placed a tiny object, metal, on the top of the dresser.

"What are you doing?" she asked.

He did not bother to respond to her.

He retrieved his portfolio from the surface of the darkly varnished table.

He turned away.

"What are you doing?" she asked. "Where are you going?" she asked. "Wait!" she called.

He paused by the door.

"I am naked, and chained!" she said. "I am helpless! I can reach nothing! Where is the key!"

"It is on the top of the dresser," he said.

It would be immediately obvious, in that place, to anyone who might enter the room.

"I cannot reach it!" she said.

"No," he said. "You cannot."

"Look at me!" she begged.

"No," he said.

"Release me!" she said.

"You will be released, at least of those particular impediments," he said, "by the proper authorities."

" 'Authorities'?" she said.

"In the morning," he said. "You see I, in order to effect an economy, in order to save the empire money, a predilection appropriate enough in the case of a conscientious official, am in the habit of renting inexpensive quarters. You can imagine my dismay in the morning when I arrive to take occupancy and find the room occupied, as it is."

"I do not understand," she moaned.

"One of your customers, it seems, left you as you are."

" 'Customers,' " she said, startled.

"What was your name, again?" he asked. "It has slipped my mind."

"Sesella," she said. "Sesella Gardener!"

"Doubtless the first thing the authorities will request to see is your license."

"I do not understand," she said.

"On this world," he said, "it is against the law to practice prostitution without a license."

"I am not a prostitute!" she said.

"But only now have you been caught," he said.

"I am not a prostitute!" she said.

"How long has it been going on?" he asked.

"I am not a prostitute!" she cried.

"And the penalties for such are not light," he said.

"What are they?" she said.

"In the future," he said, "you need not concern yourself about your perfumes. They will be decided for you, or you must submit them for approval to others."

"No," she cried. "No!"

But Tuvo Ausonius had left, closing the door behind him.

## ▪ ▪ ▪ CHAPTER 16 ▪ ▪ ▪

"Please," she said, hurrying forward, and kneeling.

It was dawn, outside the summer palace. Otto and Julian had spent the night in the palace.

"I will do my best to further your business," Iaachus had assured Julian, once again, even as they had left the inner gate, but moment, ago.

"Do you think he will do so?" had asked Otto.

"I do not know," had said Julian. "It is hard to read Iaachus."

"I think he fears you," said Otto.

"Why?" asked Julian.

"Your blood, your lineage, your station," said Otto.

"Perhaps," said Julian.

It was scarcely light when Julian and Otto left the palace, now no longer in the company of guards, though, doubtless, they would be watched, as they took their way across the great plaza, in the center of which rose the domes and spires of the palace.

In an inner courtyard, as they had made their way across the damp flagstones, Julian had pointed upward, to a window, and then to another. They were dark now.

"Those are the quarters of the princess Viviana," he said, "and those of the princess Alacida."

A slave girl, carrying a two-handled vessel of water, knelt down, on the damp stones, and put her head down.

It was hard even to detect the color of her hair in the light.

She lifted her head, after they had passed, to look after them.

"Did you see the curtain move, in the window of the princess Viviana, and a shadow in that of the princess Alacida?" asked Julian.

"Yes," said Otto.

"It seems they are watching," said Julian.

"What for?" asked Otto.

"Who knows?" said Julian.

Otto had speculated, idly, how such windows might be reached, perhaps from the roof.

It might be a coup, he thought, to steal a princess.

He wondered if Viviana, or Alacida, or both, would make a good slave girl.

Shortly thereafter they were outside the palace.

They had seen a small figure in the vicinity of one of the fountains rise up, when they had exited the palace. The figure was scarcely detectable in the light, and had almost been lost against the marble of the fountain.

Doubtless it was no more than some pathetic vagrant.

"See?" asked Julian.

"Yes," had said Otto.

"Beware," had said Julian.

"I see it," had said Otto.

It had hurried forward.

Now it knelt before them, some yards from the outer gate.

"I have been waiting for you, all night," she said. "They would not let me wait by the gate, close to it, like a dog, as I wished. They would not let me."

"Surely we know you," said Julian.

"Yes," said Otto, looking down on the figure.

"Who are you?" asked Julian.

"One who became yesterday a devotee of Dira," she said.

"The goddess of slave girls," said Julian.

"Yes," said Otto.

"Who are you?" demanded Julian.

"Renata Alerina Gina Ameliana," she said.

"Of the Amelianii?" said Julian.

"Yes," she said.

This, then, was no pathetic vagrant, despite how small she seemed, how piteous, how pleading, how humble, kneeling there before them in the half darkness, on the damp stones, clutching about herself some shreds of embroidered *leel*, doubtless once fine stuff, but torn now, ripped from the collar downward, and damp and soiled, from the night spent in the open, spent waiting, on the stones of the plaza.

"You are a lady," said Julian.

"As much as I may be now," she said.

"You are rich," he said.

"There is wealth in my family," she said. "But such things are meaningless to me now."

"Your family are gold merchants," said Julian. He did not say this approvingly. Like many of the high aristocracy he had a contempt for business and trade.

"Since yesterday iron and leather mean more to me," she said.

"I do not understand," said Julian.

"I have looked into the eyes of a master," she said. "And now I know that I can only be happy in obedience, and in selfless love and service."

"I do not understand," said Julian.

"I now know that I can only be fully happy as a total slave." Julian looked down at her.

"I have learned myself," she said. "I have looked into the eyes of a master. I am now a devotee of Dira."

She then put her head down, to the feet of Otto, and kissed them.

"I would be yours," she said.

"Do you understand what you are saying?" asked Julian.

She lifted her eyes to those of Otto.

Would he permit her to straighten her body, to kneel upright before him?

He did so.

"You do not understand what you are doing," said Julian to the kneeling figure.

"Shall I open my robes?" she asked Otto.

"No," said Otto.

"The collar," said Julian, angrily, "is for thieves, debtors, criminals, barbarians."

"No," she said.

"It is for low women," he said.

"No," she said. "It is for women."

"It is for those women who are unfortunate enough to find themselves put in it."

"No," she said.

"Women live in terror of the collar!"

"I do not," she said.

"It is for those women who deserve it," he said, "those for whom it is appropriate!"

"And for what woman is it not appropriate?" she asked.

"You beg the collar?" asked Julian.

"Yes," she said, looking up at Otto. "I beg the collar!"

"Have you considered," asked Otto, "what it might be, to be done with as masters please, to be bought and sold?"

"Yes," she said.

"You are crying," said Julian to her.

"Do you think you would have but one master?" asked Otto.

"I would expect, over time," she said, "to have many masters. I would try to serve them well."

"Doubtless, at times," said Otto, "you would regret your decision, and find yourself terrified."

"Yes," she said, "and I would know myself helpless."

This was she, or course, whom we had met the preceding day, she of the embroidered *leel*, who, having angered Otto, had been cuffed, who had had the *leel* torn down, to her hips, who had been forced, her hands held, to kneel down before him, as though she, though a fashionably dressed free woman, might be no more than a slave.

"You would belong to him?" asked Julian.

"Yes," she said.

"Perhaps I would use you to breed slaves," said Otto.

"Then that would be the will of my master," she said.

"Perhaps I could try you out, and see how you are," said Otto.

"I am untrained!" she said.

"You seem intelligent," said Otto. "Perhaps you could learn."

"I would apply myself with the greatest diligence!" she said.

Otto turned away from her and he, and Julian, walked a few paces, toward the edge of the plaza.

Behind them they heard a sob, and, turning, they saw the small figure, forlorn, behind them, still kneeling.

"If you wish," said Otto, "you may follow me."

With a cry of joy she sprang to her feet and, clutching the torn *leel* about her, hurried after them.

"Perhaps, on the way," said Otto, "we might pass a slaver's house."

"There are some," said Julian. "Papers could be prepared, the proper signatures affixed, and such."

Julian turned to the woman, who was following them, a few paces behind, to the left.

"You understand," he said, "that once such a thing is done, it is done?"

"Yes," she said.

"You could even be purchased to serve in your own house," he said, "and would be there then no more than any other slave."

"Yes," she whispered.

"I think the whole thing, though impeccably legal, is best handled quickly and quietly," said Julian.

"Yes," said Otto. "I think that that would be best for her."

"You are concerned with her?"

"Certainly," said Otto. "She is a free woman."

"But later?"

"Then such things would not matter," said Otto. "Then she would be only a slave."

They continued on their way.

"What are your plans?" asked Otto.

"I am going to return to one of my family's villas," said Julian, "and there await word with respect to your commission."

"The matter is being deliberated?" asked Otto.

"I suppose so," said Julian.

"When will we hear?" asked Otto.

"I do not know when, of if, we will hear," said Julian.

"You have enemies in the palace?" asked Otto.

"It would seem so," said Julian.

"Iaachus?" asked Otto.

"Perhaps," said Julian.

"The royal family?" asked Otto.

"I think that is quite likely," said Julian.

"They fear you?"

"I think so," said Julian.

"Are their fears justified?" asked Otto.

Julian turned about, and addressed the woman at their heels. "Lag back," he said.

She slowed her pace until there were several feet between her and the pair she followed.

"Yes," said Julian, irritably, to Otto.

Otto then turned about, and motioned that the woman should join them. When she did so, Otto put her before them, and they followed her, one on each side, she in the place of honor, a free woman.

"I do not think I should be here, before you," she whispered.

"You are a free woman," said Otto. "It is the place of honor. Precede us."

"You might even remember, afterwards, if you care to," said Julian, "how you were once such that you preceded free men."

"I do not know where to go, where to turn," she said.

"I will direct you," said Julian.

She turned about.

They continued on their way. They kept to better streets. Afterward they could return to the port, more conveniently, through a poorer district.

"Turn right, here," said Julian.

## • • • CHAPTER 17 • • •

"Send the slave, Flora, forward," said the connoisseur.

The girl, whose house name was Flora, hurried forward, to kneel on the tiles before the connoisseur, her head down, to the tiles, the palms of her hands upon them, performing obeisance.

Following her forward were two leather-clad men, one on each side of her, who took their station on each side of her, and a little to the back. These were the keeper, or warder, of her corridor, and one of the trainers, to whose lot she had been assigned.

The connoisseur looked from the papers, attached to the clip-board he held, to the girl, and then back to the board.

"She has been whipped only three times," said the connoisseur.

"Yes," said the trainer, "the instructional whipping, once when I felt she did not obey quickly enough, only two strokes, and once because it pleased me to do so."

The girl, her head down, trembled.

She could see, as she knelt, out of the corner of her eye, the coil of the trainer's whip.

"That is really only twice," said the connoisseur. "The two strokes is only an admonition, the sort of thing that might be done at any time, for any reason."

"Then twice," said the trainer.

"You have been whipped very little, Flora," said the connoisseur.

"I have tried to be pleasing, Master," she said.

"Kneel up, Flora," said the connoisseur, "your back arched, your hands behind the back of your head."

"She is a sleek little thing," said the connoisseur.

"A pretty little piece of livestock," said a man beside the connoisseur, a dealer.

"You have done well, Emon," said the connoisseur.

The keeper inclined his head, accepting the compliment.

The diet and exercise of such stock is, of course, carefully supervised.

"I see by the papers, Rigg," said the connoisseur, "that she has been trained, within the limitations of the brief time at our disposal, to give the most intimate and satisfying of slave pleasures to a master."

"Yes," said the trainer.

"You may place your hands on your thighs, Flora," said the connoisseur. "She applied herself, in learning such lessons?" asked the connoisseur.

"Zealously," said Rigg, the trainer.

"Little Flora apparently realizes that it is well for her to learn such things," said the connoisseur.

Rigg laughed.

"Adeptness in such skills can considerably improve the quality of a girl's life," said the connoisseur, "elevating her price, quite possibly enabling her to obtain a richer, better master, lighter tasks, and such."

"Certainly," said Ambon, the dealer.

"But I think," said Rigg, "that there is another reason, as well, that she applied herself so eagerly to her lessons."

"The whip?" asked the connoisseur.

"Other than that, too," said Rigg.

"What?" asked the connoisseur.

"Speak," said Rigg to the girl.

"That I am a slave, Master," she said.

"As are the other women in this house," said the connoisseur.

"Yes, Master," she said.

"Completely," he said, "as yourself."

"Yes, Master," she said.

In a sense she had known this for a long time, of course, even before becoming a slave.

"We have raised your value, Flora," said the connoisseur.

"Thank you, Master," said the girl.

"Many men could not now afford you," said the connoisseur. "You may even find it tempting, in some markets, to obtain a master, to conceal your skills."

"Yes, Master," she said.

"But I would not permit my seller to know that," he said.

"No, Master," she said, shuddering.

"And such matters will be public, on your papers," said the connoisseur.

"Yes, Master," she said.

"I would recommend perfect honesty, in all respects and matters," said the connoisseur.

"Yes, Master," she said.

A slave girl must be completely truthful, and totally honest. She is not a free woman.

"You have come far, in a short time, little Flora," said the connoisseur, "but remember that your training, and such, is really quite limited, only a matter of a few days, indeed, that, in a sense, it has only begun."

"Yes, Master."

"You must struggle to continue to learn, and grow," he said.

"Yes, Master," she said.

"I see," said the connoisseur, returning to the clipboard, "that she has done well in cosmetics, perfumes, adornments and such."

"Yes," said Rigg.

"In slave dance?" asked the connoisseur.

"There was no time," said Rigg.

"But surely you have taught her at least some of the movements, which are useful in giving intimate pleasures to masters?"

"Of course," said Rigg.

"Sewing, cooking, cleaning, such things?"

"Only some elementary knowledge in such matters," said Rigg.

"Many men want a complete slave, Flora," said the connoisseur, "one who can serve them in all ways and things. Many men, for example, will expect you to keep their quarters in perfection."

"I know little of such things, Master," said the girl.

"Perhaps you can compensate for such inadequacies, or distract the master from too keen an awareness of such things, by the excellence of your services in the furs."

"It will be my hope to do so, Master," she said.

"While striving to improve your expertise in such homely skills," he said.

"Yes, Master," she said.

"Many men want everything from a woman," he said, "*everything*."

"Yes, Master," she said.

"But, as you are a pleasure slave, I would give my greatest attention to my services in the furs."

"Yes, Master," she said, gratefully.

"As I recall, from my own cursory examination, when she was brought to this house, her body is responsive," said the connoisseur.

"We have confirmed that," said Rigg. "It is responsive, uncontrollably so."

"She will then be much at the mercy of masters," said the connoisseur.

"Helplessly so," said Rigg.

The girl put down her head.

"And yet she is still a virgin," said the connoisseur, wonderingly.

The girl blushed, wholly.

"A virgin?" asked Ambon, the dealer.

"Yes," said the connoisseur. "It is seldom, Flora," he said, "that a girl, and certainly a slave, with flanks such as yours, is a virgin."

"My master," she said, "is not pleased with me, and has seen fit, after my embonding, to ignore me, and treat me with great coldness."

"I will make you an offer for her!" said the dealer, suddenly.

Terror transfigured the girl's features.

To be sure, she could be bought and sold with the same facility as a pig.

"Alas," said the connoisseur, "we do not own her, but she is merely being boarded here, for a time, to be trained."

"You could pretend that she was stolen, even that you were raided," said the dealer.

"We are an honest house," said the connoisseur.

"Ah," smiled the dealer, and leaned back in his chair.

"Master," asked the girl, pleadingly, "may I speak?"

All eyes went to her. Even Emon and Rigg seemed surprised that she had spoken. To be sure, it was merely to request permission to speak, which permission may be granted or not, as the master sees fit.

The connoisseur looked at her, interested. "Certainly," he said.

The fact that he had said "certainly" must not, however, be taken to mean that such permissions are always readily forthcoming. Indeed, sometimes a girl is not permitted to speak for hours, sometimes for days. Sometimes, even in the furs, she must serve, with all her attentiveness, her skills and zeal, in silence.

"I still belong to the same master, do I not?" she asked.

"I do not know," said the connoisseur. "I do not know who your master is. I only know who has signed you over to us, and to whom, upon the receipt of an appropriate signature, we will return you."

"I may have been sold, while I am here, in school?" she said.

"That is quite possible," said the connoisseur. "Indeed, it is often the case that training of this sort is given to a girl to increase her value, because the master intends to put her up for sale, hoping to make a profit on her."

She groaned.

"I do not know who my master is then," she said.

"No," said the connoisseur. "But doubtless you will soon learn."

"You do not know who my master is?" she said.

"No," said the connoisseur. "I know little more than the place to which we are to deliver you."

"May I beg to know the place?" she asked.

"You will learn it in time," he said.

"Please, please, Master," she begged, weeping.

The connoisseur looked to the dealer, and to Emon and Rigg, and then shrugged. "Very well," he said. He read off to her an address, and a world.

"But I do not know that place, or world!" she cried.

"Doubtless you will come to know it, at least for a time," said the connoisseur, "for it is there that you will be delivered to your master."

The pretty slave regarded the connoisseur, agonized. She put her hand, timidly, to the metal collar on her neck, a rather simple, plain collar, the collar of the house. It was all she wore, other than her brand.

"It is there," said the connoisseur, "that you will kneel before your master, and present the flower to him, as you have been taught, the slave flower."

"You will offer it to him humbly," said Emon.

"And it will be his to pluck," said Rigg.

"Masters!" cried the girl.

"Take her away," said the connoisseur, signing one of the sheets on the clipboard.

She was pulled to her feet, and turned about.

She looked back over her shoulder, in misery and fear.

"Master!" she wept.

"You will be shipped this morning," said the connoisseur.

She was conducted, weeping, from the room.

The connoisseur turned over a page from those on the clipboard.

"Next," he said.


# ▪ ▪ ▪ CHAPTER 18 ▪ ▪ ▪


"I am innocent!" she cried. "I am innocent!"

"Is she covered?" asked Tuvo Ausonius, alarmed, keeping his back turned to her.

"Yes," said the officer.

Tuvo Ausonius turned about to see the girl, struggling, swathed in buckled canvas, from her thighs to her throat, forced down on her knees, on the street, outside the small apartment, with its door opening onto the street.

"You have the complaint?" asked Tuvo Ausonius.

"Yes," said one of the officers.

"He!" cried the girl, squirming in the canvas, turning to face Tuvo Ausonius. "It was he, he! He was here!"

A small crowd had gathered.

"I only arrived from Miton this morning," said Tuvo Ausonius. "I am of the *honestori*."

"Yes, sir," said the officer.

"I believe the complaint is in order."

"It is," said the officer.

"I did not neglect to sign it, did I?" inquired Tuvo Ausonius.

"No, sir," said the officer. "It is signed."

"You have the warrant?" asked Tuvo Ausonius.

"Yes, and endorsed," said the officer.

"Then everything is in order?"

"Yes," said the officer.

"Down on your knees, bitch!" said the other officer, forcing the girl back down on her knees.

"This has been quite distressing," said Tuvo Ausonius.

"The apologies of the city," said the officer.

"What is going on?" asked a man, joining the small throng.

"A prostitute, unlicensed," said the officer to the man. "We caught her."

"I am not a prostitute!" cried the girl.

The officer near her buckled a leash on her neck.

She looked up at him, wildly, leashed.

"I did not realize that this was a prostitution district," said Tuvo Ausonius. "This is all very embarrassing."

"Concern yourself no longer, sir," said the officer. "The matter is done now."

"I need not appear anywhere to testify?" asked Tuvo Ausonius.

"No, sir," said the officer. "The matter is clear, and the complaint is sufficient."

"I am not a prostitute!" cried the girl.

"How do you know she is a prostitute?" asked a man.

"Smell her!" laughed another.

"There are these, too," said the officer. He held up, bunched in his hand, evidence, some jewelry, a scarlet halter, two rectangles of provocative scarlet silk, such things.

There was laughter from the men about.

"She claims to be a Sesella Gardener, a stewardess, from Wings Between Worlds," said the officer in whose keeping was the leash.

"I am!" cried the girl.

"Doubtless she is," said a man.

"But not for long!" said another.

The girl looked at the speaker, frightened.

Men laughed.

"Don't you make enough money with Wings Between Worlds?" asked a man.

"It seems she wished to supplement her income," chuckled a fellow.

"You should have bought a license, dearie," said one of the women in the throng, in golden sandals, with a gown of purple silk.

"The city is particular about such matters," said another woman.

"Too particular," said another.

"It serves you right," said another woman.

"We have to pay, and so should you, dearie," said another.

"The nerve of the cheating little bitch," said another.

"Now you will get what you deserve," said another.

"Good, good!" said another woman.

"Cheat, cheat!" hissed another.

"I am not a prostitute," she wept.

"How was she caught?" asked a man.

"This gentleman," said the officer, "came to assume occupancy of the apartment and found her here, apparently having made unauthorized use of the premises. Apparently her last customer had left her stark naked, chained to a slave ring."

"That seems appropriate," laughed a man.

There was laughter.

"I am not a prostitute!" protested the girl, tears in her eyes.

"Certainly you must be a poor one," said one of the women.

"She does not even have a license," said another.

"Apparently she was not sufficiently concerned to be fully pleasing to her customer," said the officer.

"If you're going to be picky, and uppity, you'd better have a license, dearie," said a woman.

"I speculate," laughed a man, "that she will soon be such that she will be zealously concerned to be fully pleasing to men."

"To any man," laughed another.

"Yes," laughed another.

The girl wept, and raised her eyes, pleadingly, to Tuvo Ausonius.

"Tell them the truth!" she begged.

"I have never seen you before in my life, young lady," said Tuvo Ausonius.

"Tell them the truth!" she wept.

"I have," said Tuvo Ausonius.

"He is lying!" she cried.

"Silence, prostitute bitch!" said the officer who had her in custody.

He shortened the leash, meaningfully.

"She should think up a better story," said a man. "One can see by the fellow's garb that he is a same."

"Poor fellow," said another man.

"He would not know what to do with a woman," said another.

There was a ripple of laughter in the throng.

This sort of talk irritated Tuvo Ausonius. He was proud of being a same, of course. Still, they did not always command the respect due to them on account of their superior virtue. Indeed, some people even regarded them as pathetic fools. That was sometimes a bit irritating. But, more importantly, Tuvo Ausonius was no longer quite as confident in his sameness as he had been before yesterday evening. What if it were not best to be a same? What if there were two sexes, quite different, really? He had not forgotten how she had looked at his feet, in scarlet silk. That is not the sort of thing that it is easy to forget. Sometimes Tuvo Ausonius had wondered what it might be, not to be a same, but a man. But then he had dismissed such thoughts as beneath him, and grossly improper. But that was before he had seen her at his feet, in scarlet silk. Such a woman, and perhaps others, would not be easy to forget.

"Be quiet," said a fellow. "He is of the *honestori*."

Tuvo Ausonius supposed that such a woman might make an acceptable domestic servant.

Certainly some sames kept such servants, who lived in. They would have to be suitably garbed, of course, in same wear. And, of course, he would not have to so much as lay a hand on one. He knew certain sames who kept such servants. Actually, as everyone knew, they were purchased slaves, as free women on Miton, sames, at least those who were well-to-do, did not perform domestic labors. Such were beneath them. Tuvo Ausonius had sometimes wondered what went on in such domiciles, when the doors were closed, and the shades drawn. Doubtless nothing. But still one wondered. And he, if he were to keep such a servant, so to speak, would surely not have to lay a hand on her.

Then he put such terrible thoughts from his mind, for he was a same.

Perhaps it had been a mistake to have permitted himself to look upon her at his feet, in scarlet silk.

Then he reminded himself, again, sternly, that he was a same.

The top button on her jacket had been undone, lasciviously baring her neck.

That neck was now muchly more bared, and wore a leash.

She had leaned toward him, as he had occupied his seat in the vessel.

Now she wore brief canvas, buckled tightly upon her beauty.

She had removed her head covering in the tiny galley, revealing her hair. Now it was loose, abundant, distraught, marvelous about her shoulders, over her leash, and it might be considered by anyone, as much as though she were a slave.

How right it was that she should be so served!

What a wicked woman she was!

How richly such as she merited punishment!

He was pleased to have arranged it.

The officer who held her leash drew it taut. She looked up at him, frightened. She tried to draw back.

It was at this moment that three figures, coming down the street, came to the edge of the throng. This group, or at least two personages of it, were sufficiently unusual or imposing, at least for the district, that the crowd, rather naturally, those who were aware of them, parted, that they might pass. One wore the uniform of an officer in the imperial navy; the other was a blond, blue-eyed giant of a man, clad in skins; the third figure was unimportant as she was a stripped, branded slave. Her hair had been cut short, apparently carelessly and brutally, and her wrists were bound together, behind her back.

"Way, way, please," said the officer.

"Make way!" said the officer of the city, seeing the naval officer.

"Make way!" said the other officer, as well, he who held the girl's leash.

"Thank you, my friends," said the naval officer.

He had removed the purple cords from his left shoulder, in order to attract less attention, in order to remain, in effect, incognito in the streets. Purple was, of course, the color of the patricians, and the three cords would have marked him, for those who understood such things, as being of the highest of ranks, of the highest of bloods, as high as that of the imperial house itself.

"Oh!" said the slave, who was pressing closely behind the officer and the fellow clad in skins, as they made their way through the small crowd.

The officer, and the fellow clad in skins, turned about.

"I was touched! I was touched!" said the slave. She tried to pull her hands apart, but they were tied well, behind her back.

The fellow clad in skins surveyed the crowd behind the slave. Some men stepped back, not meeting his eyes.

"You!" said the blue-eyed giant. "Was it you who touched the slave?"

"No!" said a man.

"You?" he inquired of another.

"No, not I," said the fellow addressed.

"Do not be angry, fellow," said one of the officers of the city.

"You cannot expect to take her through the streets with bared flanks and not have her touched," said a man.

"Not a beauty like that," said another.

The slave straightened at this, startled, suddenly elated. How pleased she was that she had been found appealing. Surely such a gratification had never been hers as a free woman, to have been so openly, so candidly, commented upon.

But still, surely, they had had no right to touch her as they had. She was not theirs!

"I am not angry," said the blue-eyed giant.

"She is attractive," pointed out another man.

"Is she yours?" asked a man.

"Yes," said the giant.

"Yes," said the slave. "It is to him that I belong! I am his!"

Men regarded her, surprised.

"It was he, Master!" said the slave, indicating a fellow in the crowd. "He it was! I am sure of it!"

"Was it you?" asked the giant.

"You have her in the streets, slave naked," said one of the officers of the city. "You are pressing through a crowd. You could not expect anything other, surely, if there are men here."

Some of the men looked at Tuvo Ausonius, in amusement. Tuvo Ausonius reddened in anger.

"Was it you?" asked the giant, repeating his question to the fellow who had been indicated by the slave.

"Yes," said the fellow. "It was I."

"Yes, yes, it was he!" said the slave. "Now you will suffer!" she said to him.

"Go to him," said the giant.

"Master?" she asked.

"Now," said the giant.

She went to stand near the fellow.

The giant waved his hand toward her.

"Master!" protested the slave.

"My thanks!" said the fellow.

He took her firmly by the arm.

"Oh!" cried the slave.

In a few moments, at another gesture from the giant, the fellow desisted, and the slave, permitted to leave his vicinity, hurried to her master and, scarlet, and trembling, wide-eyed, knelt against his leg, pressing herself against it.

"Oh, Master," she moaned.

As she knelt she was no more than a yard or two from, and on the same level as, the prisoner, Sesella Gardener, the stewardess, kneeling, buckled in canvas and leashed, in the keeping of one of the officers of the city.

"Next time," said the giant to the man, "request my permission. I think you will find that I am inclined to be generous."

"My apologies!" said the man.

"Surely you must complete what he has begun!" begged the slave of her master.

"What is her name?" asked a man.

"I have not yet named her," said the giant. "She does not yet have a name."

"Will you name her?" asked a man.

"I do not know," said the giant. "I have not yet decided."

She looked up at her master, frightened.

Some slaves are kept without names, of course, but normally they are given a name, by the master's will, as a dog might be, that they may be conveniently summoned and referred to.

And even such a name is often precious to a slave, even though it is only a slave name.

"She seems new to her condition," said a man.

"It has been a matter of less than an hour," said the naval officer.

"Doubtless she will learn quickly," said a man.

"That is my expectation," said the naval officer.

"She had better!" said a man.

"Yes," said another.

There was laughter.

"Master!" begged the slave.

"Slave, slave!" hissed Sesella Gardener. "How disgusting you are!"

The slave looked at her, wonderingly. "Are we not sisters?" she asked. "Pity me!"

"I am a free woman," said Sesella Gardener. "You are only a slut of a slave!"

"Master," whimpered the slave, looking up at the giant, "what you permitted him to do to me!"

"You are a slave," said the giant.

"I have strange feelings," she said, kneeling at his thigh, looking up at him, tears in her eyes. "I have never had these feelings before. I am uncomfortable. I do not know what to do!"

There was laughter.

She squirmed on the stones.

"I am helpless," she said. "I am at the mercy of men. I beg kindness!"

"We must be on our way," said the naval officer.

"You will complete what he began, will you not, Master?" begged the slave. "I beg to be touched! I beg it! I will do anything!"

"You must do anything, in any event," said the giant.

"Yes, Master," she moaned.

"I am so helpless," she wept. "I am so helpless!"

"What a slut she is!" cried Sesella Gardener.

"You, too, will learn such helplessness," the officer holding her leash assured her.

"No, no!" said Sesella Gardener.

"Ah, but yes, my pretty little prostitute," said the man holding her leash.

"No, no!" said Sesella Gardener. "And I am not a prostitute! I am not a prostitute!

"Oh!" she wept, in pain.

"Your denials grow tedious," said the man.

He stood to her left, the leash in his left hand, looping up to her throat. Her head was up, held there, painfully. His right hand was still anchored in her hair. It was twisted tightly about his fist. She did not dare to move.

"Oh!" she said, again.

The slave regarded her, agonized.

"Oh!" cried the prisoner.

"No, no!" cried the slave. "Do not hurt her!"

Men looked at her.

"Please do not hurt her," said the slave, in a small voice.

"Is it yours to interfere?" asked the giant.

"No, Master," she said.

"Did you request permission to speak?" asked the giant.

"No, Master," she whispered.

"Stand," said the giant.

She rose unsteadily to her feet.

He then held her by the hair and cuffed her, twice, once with the flat of his right hand, a stinging blow that left her face red, and then a backhand blow, lashing, with the back of his right hand.

She then sank, again, to her knees.

There she looked across to Sesella Gardener, whose head was still held tightly by the officer's hand in her hair.

"I need nothing and want nothing from a stinking slave," said Sesella Gardener, between clenched teeth, not daring to move her head, even a quarter of an inch.

"Yes, Mistress," groaned the slave.

"You must learn," said the giant, "that is not yours to interfere in the doings of men."

"Yes, Master," she said.

The officer of the city removed his hand from Sesella Gardener's hair.

"When it is convenient," said the giant, "you will receive your first whipping."

"Yes, Master," said the slave.

"For, obviously, you have much to learn."

"Yes, Master," she said.

Sesella Gardener now shook her head, tossing her long, lustrous hair about, arranging it as she could, by these movements.

Tuvo Ausonius noticed this. She is vain, he thought, as vain as a slave girl.

"It is time to leave," said the naval officer.

"Please, Master," begged the slave. "May I speak?"

"Yes," said the giant.

"I was concerned for her," said the slave.

"It is permissible to be concerned, and to be kind," said the giant. "It is not always permissible to speak. And it is not permissible to interfere."

"Then, ultimately, I am totally powerless!" she wept.

"Yes," he said.

"Am I truly to be whipped?"

"Yes."

"I shall try to be more pleasing."

"That would be wise on your part," he said.

"Master!"

"Yes?"

"I am needful."

"That is common in a slave girl."

"Will you touch me, sometimes?"

"Perhaps if you beg prettily enough," he said.

"I shall! I shall!" she said.

"Slut!" said Sesella Gardener, kneeling, leashed, tossing her lovely hair about her shoulders with a movement of her head.

Tuvo Ausonius wondered what it might be to own Sesella Gardener, to truly own her, fully, as a master owns a slave girl.

He put such thoughts from him.

The naval officer then turned about.

The giant looked down at the slave, at his feet, and then he lifted his eyes, and surveyed the throng. Then he looked down, again, at the slave.

"No, Master," she breathed. "Please, no!"

"You have my permission," he said to the throng. He then turned about, to follow the naval officer.

The slave scrambled to her feet, following him.

"Oh!" cried the slave. "Oh!"

Men laughed.

"Oh!" she cried.

But she did not dare now to object, nor to show resentment, nor to even concern herself with the ascertainment of the identity of those to whose attentions she found herself subject, those whose interest, as she now understood, was only too naturally and comprehensibly stirred by one such as she. She had learned that a woman such as she, a slave in the streets, unless put under some particular protection, must expect such things.

Clearly her master had begun her instruction.

But had it not begun even with the searing of the iron?

Beyond the crowd, the assemblage of which had been parted by their passage, she turned to look back. There, at the end of the corridor opened in the throng, small, much alone, kneeling, on the leash, she saw Sesella Gardener.

"Slut! Slut!" cried Sesella Gardener to her. And then Sesella Gardener spat downward, on the stones.

The slave then turned about, to hurry after her master. How wrong she had been, she realized, to have implicitly put herself on a level with a free woman, daring to speak of her as though she might be a sister, daring to speak on her behalf, before men, as though she, too, might be free.

She must learn her place, and all that it might mean, that she was a slave.

"Get on your feet, my pretty little prostitute," said he who held the leash of Sesella Gardener.

She looked up, in mute protest.

He shook the leash.

She rose to her feet.

She blushed. She had seen slaves respond to a similar signal.

"You claim," said the officer in charge, he who had been in closest converse with Tuvo Ausonius, "that you are not a prostitute."

"Yes!" she said.

He lifted up the silk and jewelry.

There was general laughter.

"Too bad, dearie," called one of the women in the crowd.

"We paid for our licenses!" called another.

"Too bad you didn't!" called another.

"Now you'll get what you deserve!" said another.

"Slave bitch!" called another.

"No, no!" cried Sesella Gardener.

"You do not care for slaves, do you?" asked the officer who held her leash.

"They are sluts, sluts!" said Sesella Gardener.

"It is time to return to headquarters," said the officer who had been in closest converse with Tuvo Ausonius.

"Come along," said the officer who had the dark-haired beauty in custody, giving a tug on the leash.

She looked at him, wildly.

"You have an appointment to keep," said a man.

"Yes," called one of the women, "with a hot iron!"

Sesella Gardener spun to face Tuvo Ausonius.

"You have done this to me!" she cried.

"I do not know what you are talking about," said Tuvo Ausonius.

"Do not let him know where I will be sold!" she cried to the officers of the city.

"I have not the least interest in such matters," said Tuvo Ausonius.

She was then led away.

She tried to hold back for a moment, but then the leash was taut.

She also felt a sudden, sharp blow, below the small of the back, delivered with the flat of a man's hand, one of the throng, which sped her quickly forward.

There was laughter.

She looked back over her shoulder once, at Tuvo Ausonius, and was then out of sight.

"Where are such women sold?" Tuvo Ausonius inquired of a bystander.

He was told.

## · · · CHAPTER 19 · · ·

"You summoned me, your majesty?" said Iaachus, arbiter of protocol.

Atalana, empress mother, lifted her eyes from the cup of stimulant, a small bowl of steaming *kemac*. She put it back, with two hands, on the small table which was across her lap on the canopied bed-of-state.

Iaachus surveyed, briefly, the women in attendance on the empress mother. Most were young, all were highborn. He was not impervious to the charms of women, but he was more attentive to the charms of power. He saw women largely in terms of their political applications, which tended on the whole to be somewhat different from those of men. Too, women, both slave and free, like wealth, tended to be perquisites which accompanied power.

"You have considered the matters concerning which I have recently spoken to you?" she asked.

"Yes," said Iaachus.

He glanced about, somewhat uneasily, at the women in attendance.

"Concerning the emperor's birthday," said Atalana.

"Ah," said Iaachus. "Of course."

"Will you please draw the drapery a little, Elena," said the empress mother. "There is too much glare in the room."

"Yes, your majesty," said the woman addressed, a pretty young patrician with brown hair and gray eyes, of the senatorial class, who, smiling knowingly, hurried to the drapery.

In a softer light the harsh lines of the empress mother's pale, drawn, severe countenance would be softened.

"Are you amused at something, my dear?" asked the empress mother.

"No, your majesty," said the woman, quickly.

"The glare hurts my eyes," said the empress mother.

"Yes, your majesty," said the young woman.

It was the manner of Iaachus to take note of such small exchanges.

Some of the other ladies in attendance exchanged glances.

The empress mother lifted the cup of *kemac* again from the table on the bed and, inhaling its fragrance momentarily, once again put it to her lips.

"Perhaps a play panoply of armor, and weapons, suitably blunted," said Iaachus.

"He is an emperor of peace," said Atalana.

"Perhaps a game of draughts?"

"He finds such things frustrating," said Atalana.

"Perhaps a pony?" suggested Iaachus.

"Too dangerous," said the empress mother.

Once again the lady Elena smiled. Surely she was very confident of her position in the palace, in the service of the empress mother.

The empress mother regarded her, over the cup of *kemac*.

The woman looked down, smiling, standing with others of her station, some on each side of the bed.

"He will be sixteen," said Iaachus.

"Yes?" said the empress mother.

"Nothing," said Iaachus.

She finished the tiny cup of *kemac*, and replaced it on the small table.

"What?" asked Atalana.

"It was only a thought," he said.

She waved her hand and one of her ladies in attendance removed the table. Another adjusted the covers about her frame, and another, the lady Elena, the cushions behind her back and head.

"I thought, perhaps," said Iaachus, "as he will be sixteen—perhaps a slave girl."

The lady Elena stifled a laugh.

Immediately the empress mother turned to regard her.

The lady Elena, casting her eyes down, moved back, quickly, from the side of the bed.

The other ladies in attendance, almost immediately, moved away from her.

The lady Elena found herself, though in the room with fellows, much alone.

"And perhaps you, Elena," snapped the empress mother, "will be that slave girl!"

The women in attendance gasped.

"Yes, your majesty," whispered the girl, terrified.

She looked wildly at Iaachus, the arbiter of protocol, who met her gaze impassively.

Women such as she, she knew, might disappear one night from the palace. A reason could always be found. Who would know if she showed up on a chain, in a market, on some distant world? Too, who would care, or what would it matter, for she would then be of no account. She would then be only another marked-thigh girl.

"Leave us!" said the empress mother.

Only too willingly did the ladies in attendance scurry from the room, taking care only to separate themselves from the lady Elena.

"Your experiment was interesting," said the empress mother.

"A trivial business," said Iaachus. "I expect she will serve you most dutifully from now on."

"Would you like to add her to your women, Iaachus?" asked Atalana.

"At my country villa?" said Iaachus.

"Of course," she smiled.

"I shall give the matter thought," he said. "You would not mind if I did not keep her, but merely used her for a gift, or gratuity, or sent her off to be sold somewhere?"

"Of course not," said Atalana. "Such matters would be entirely up to you."

"As to the emperor's birthday," he smiled.

"He will receive the usual thousand gifts, from a selected thousand worlds," she said.

"Together with the usual tributes and taxes."

"Of course," she said.

"Are we alone?" she asked.

Iaachus looked about the room, and opened the nearest doors. The ladies in attendance had withdrawn to other quarters. Iaachus speculated that it would not be likely that any were now conversing with, or embroidering or sewing near, the lady Elena.

"Yes, your majesty," said Iaachus.

"I do not know whom I can trust," she said, plaintively.

"You have billions of loyal subjects, of thousands of species," said Iaachus.

"Are the frontiers secure?" she asked.

"Yes," he said.

"I fear he of the Aurelianii," she said.

"The ambition of the Aurelianii is well known," said Iaachus.

"I fear they have designs upon the throne," said Atalana.

"That is possible," said Iaachus.

"What of his plan to enlist barbarians, in the mobile forces?" she asked.

"I think it would not be judicious to oppose it," said Iaachus.

"You would then grant the barbarian beast an imperial captaincy, to form a company?" said Atalana.

"It is one thing for a commission to be authorized, granted, drawn up and such things," said Iaachus. "It is another for it to become effective."

"I do not understand," she said.

"Many things might occur," said Iaachus. "For example, it might be received too late."

"You have a plan?" she asked.

"Yes," he said.

"But what of he of the Aurelianii?"

"He figures most prominently in my plans," said Iaachus. "The barbarian is incidental."

"Have you taken steps to put your plan into effect?" she asked.

"Yes," he said.

"You may kiss my hand," she said.

Iaachus did this, with suitable deference. He then withdrew from the royal bedchamber, that chamber in which the empress mother, at her leisure, before the heat of the day, was accustomed to informally receive envoys, petitioners and such.

As he left he heard her ring for the return of her highborn attendants.

Slave girls were not in immediate attendance on the empress mother.

In the corridors, passing amongst priceless hangings, pictures and such, as guards lifted weapons in salute, he wondered what the lady Elena, who was surely both young and beautiful, and doubtless slave juicy, might look like chained in the basement of his villa. He thought that might be an excellent start for her, teaching her what she was, before he had her marked. To be sure, perhaps he should have her marked first, that she might then understand, from the very beginning, what she was. Yes he thought, I will do that. That will save me a good deal of time.

In this, as it turned out, he was correct.

# ▪ ▪ ▪ CHAPTER 20 ▪ ▪ ▪

"Have you been kept waiting, Flora?" asked Emon.

"We are dreadfully sorry," said Rigg, "but we were unexpectedly busy."

Flora, naked in her cell, chained by the wrists to a ring, kept her head down.

"We had to process a girl," said Emon. "The papers, prints, measurements, everything."

"She was a beauty," said Rigg, crouching down and unlocking the slave cuffs which held Flora's small wrists in their clasp.

"Was she more beautiful than you, that is what you are wondering, isn't it?" asked Emon.

"No, Master," said Flora.

Flora had heard the woman cry out, doubtless as she was marked.

"Stand up," said Rigg, rising to his own feet.

Flora stood up.

"I am to be shipped?" she asked.

"Yes," he said.

"As I was informed?" she asked.

"Yes," said Rigg. "You know the address and the world."

"But who will be there?" she moaned, as Rigg took her arm in his grasp.

"You will be there," said Rigg, conducting her from the cell.

"And your master," said Emon, closing the cell door behind them.

"May I speak?" she asked.

"Yes," said Rigg.

"Have I been sold to a new master?" she begged, as she was being led along the hall.

"It is possible," said Rigg.

"We do not really know," said Emon.

"You will learn soon enough," said Rigg.

They stopped a moment.

The heavy door to a processing room was open.

A cleaned iron, among others, hung on the wall, together with chains and collars. The brazier, as she could see, was still hot. There was a table in the room, on which was a miscellany of objects, papers and writing materials, pads, sponges, measuring tapes, and such things. This table was large enough and sturdy enough to support a considerable amount of weight. Flora remembered what that table had felt like, its rough texture, on her back, and belly.

To one side there was a pile of discarded clothing, what appeared to be *leel*.

On the floor, near the brazier, doubtless where a woman had been knelt, there was a considerable amount of shorn hair.

Rigg closed the door.

"Was she, Master?" asked Flora.

"What?" asked Emon.

"More beautiful than I?" asked Flora.

"You are both quite beautiful," said Rigg. "It is only that your beauties are quite different."

"You would both be held for late in a sale," said Emon.

"But is she more beautiful than I?" begged Flora.

"I do not think so," said Rigg.

"No," said Emon.

"What is her master like?" asked Flora.

"Be pleased that you do not belong to such a man," said Rigg.

"You would be in no doubt as to your slavery in his hands," said Emon.

"My master, or he who was my master," she said, "is such a man."

She remembered him, with indescribable emotions. He was the sort of man before whom she could scarcely muster the strength to stand. How often she had dreamed of him! How often she had desired to serve him selflessly, to touch him timidly, to love him in any way she could. He was the sort of man before whom a woman is at best a pleading, abject slave. He was imperious, powerful, uncompromising, the sort of man who will do precisely what he wishes with a woman, and from whom he will get exactly what he wants, and more. He was the sort of man before whom a woman, even when free, feels an almost overwhelming impulse to kneel and perform obeisance. She wanted to kneel before him, to belong to him, to be governed, to be broken, to be crushed in his arms, to be mercilessly ravished, to be put to his purposes, to obey, to find herself helpless, to know herself wholly a woman. He was to her many things, power, nature and master.

"Here is the box," said Rigg, indicating a small, sturdy metal box, with bolts and locks.

"It is so small," she said.

"Get in," said Rigg.

She crouched down and crept into the box. The door closed behind her. She turned about, quickly, frightened, as bolts were thrust into place. She pressed her hands against the metal door from the inside, and peered through the tiny, rectangular, thickset grille, at eye level, as she now knelt. She heard the key turn in locks. The key itself was taped to the top of the box. There was a slot at the bottom of the box, now bolted shut, through which a shallow pan might be slipped.

"Please!" she begged, as Rigg prepared to affix the shipping label to the box.

She strove to read the label which he, briefly, showed to her. It was hard to read, through the grille. There was the address and the world on the label, which were as she had been informed, and the name of the shipping house, of course, with its address, and its world. The shipping charge was reasonable, and calculated by weight, as she was cargo. The contents were slave, female, house name "Flora," brown hair, brown eyes, one hundred and ten pounds in weight. As one could see then, the freight charge in her case would be comparatively slight.

"The van is here," said a man.

Rigg affixed the shipping label to the outside of the door.

"Wait," said Emon.

A wire was twisted about, through two staples, one on the door of the container and the other on its body, in such a way that the door was tied shut with the wire. Two small, red, disklike blocks of wax were then placed on each side of the wire, about its twisted closure, the ends of the wire then protruding below the disklike blocks, spreading, something like an inch on each side. These tiny plates of wax were then, with a match, heated and fused together. Thus the door could not be opened without breaking this closure. Emon then, with a small hinged tool, rather like a pair of pliers, pressed together, firmly, the sides of the still-warm, soft, platelike closure, formed from the two fused red disks. He then removed the tool. The blocks were now better shaped and fused, and on each side of the small, platelike closure there was now an imprint.

"That is the virgin seal," said Rigg.

"Yes, Master," said the girl.

"It will protect you on the ship," said Emon.

"Yes, Master," she said.

"Do not forget the slave flower," said Rigg.

"No, Master," said the girl.

"Farewell," said Emon.

"Farewell," said Rigg.

"Farewell, Masters," said the girl.

In a moment two handlers had entered the house and, lifting and tilting the container, placed it on a dolly.

Within, the freight, terrified, wept.

## ・・・ CHAPTER 21 ・・・

"Mercy! Mercy!" cried Tuvo Ausonius.

He was forced down to his knees before the curule chair.

The black, metal holding rod, used for controlling and guiding, was snapped into its adjustable sockets, on the mounts fixed on the floor before the chair. There were other such paired mounts, to receive other such bars, elsewhere in the dank, dimly lit chamber, one several levels beneath the commissioner's quarters.

Tuvo Ausonius knew where he was, as he had not been blindfolded. His arrest had been effected quite openly, the officers arriving during daylight hours with the rod and cuffs, and conducting him quite publicly through the streets.

The rod was behind the small of his back, and his arms had been brought forward about it; his hands, in the cuffs, were rather at his sides; held closely there by the arrangement of cuffs and chain. The rod could not slip from its position as two small, looped chains, attached to the rod, one on each side of the body, were snapped about his arms, just above the elbow.

The two officers who had placed Tuvo Ausonius on his knees now stepped back.

Tuvo Ausonius was naked, save that a rag had been twisted about his loins, perhaps that his modesty as a same might be respected.

Ausonius winced as a bright light, set somewhere above, illuminated him.

The curule chair, at the moment, was empty.

Ausonius, his eyes half closed, shut against the glare, tried to look to the guards. He could do so only with difficulty, as they were rather behind him, on each side. He could read nothing in their expressions or carriage, save perhaps that they would do with him what they were told.

A door opened and an officer of the city entered.

"Mercy!" cried Tuvo Ausonius.

The officer, who carried some papers, regarded him.

"I am innocent!" said Tuvo Ausonius.

"Of what?" asked the officer.

"I do not know," said Tuvo Ausonius. "Why am I here? With what have I been charged?"

The officer, looking down upon him, did not choose to respond.

"There has been some mistake," cried Tuvo Ausonius. "I am Tuvo Ausonius, of Miton, an honest citizen, a patrician, a level-four civil servant in the government of his majesty, the emperor!"

"My record is impeccable," said Tuvo Ausonius.

"I am a patrician," he said.

"I am innocent!" he said.

"You will be heard, of course," said the officer. "His lordship himself will hear your case."

"His lordship?" asked Tuvo Ausonius.

At this point a tall, darkly clad figure appeared in the doorway.

Tuvo Ausonius pressed back against the metal bar fixed in its sockets.

"Your lordship," said the officer, deferentially.

The darkly clad figure nodded and approached, taking the papers from the officer. "Thank you, Commissioner," said the darkly clad figure.

This appellation startled Tuvo Ausonius.

The darkly clad figure took his place on the curule chair, and leafed through the papers.

"I am innocent, your lordship," said Tuvo Ausonius.

"You may leave, Commissioner," said the darkly clad figure.

"Yes, your lordship," said the officer, and withdrew.

The darkly clad figure was masked.

"Tuvo Ausonius, civil servant, fourth level, Miton, a same world, finance division, first imperial quadrant, member of the *honestori*, even of the minor patricians—" said the masked figure, looking through the papers.

"Of the Ausonii," said Ausonius, "in the 103rd degree!"

"That is quite impressive," said the masked figure.

"An excellent dossier," said the masked figure.

"Yes, your lordship!" said Tuvo Ausonius.

"On the whole," said the masked figure.

"Your lordship?" asked Tuvo Ausonius

"There does seem the matter of mating," said the masked figure. "You are aware of the encouragements of the imperial government in these respects? You are aware of the empress mother's concern in such matters?"

"Oh!" cried Tuvo Ausonius, relievedly. "Certainly! Do not fear! I searched avidly for a spouse! A marriage was arranged, indeed, with an inferior, but technically suitable member of the patricians, one from the acceptable world of Terennia, one whose descent fell, even if only barely, within the guidelines for my station, a Tribonius Auresius!"

The masked figure raised his eyes from the papers.

"That is a woman, of course!" said Ausonius. "Sames often give their female children masculine or neutral names, in order to help them better attain in their psychology and behavior the goals and ideals of sameness."

"But you are not mated," said the masked figure.

"Alas, no!" cried Tuvo Ausonius. "Perhaps you have heard of the *Alaria*?"

"Yes," said the masked figure.

"It was lost!" moaned Tuvo Ausonius.

"Several ships have been lost," said the figure.

"There was doubtless a malfunction, or a meteor storm," said Tuvo Ausonius.

"Doubtless," said the masked figure.

"My proposed bride was on board the *Alaria*," said Tuvo Ausonius, in a choked voice.

"But you have not made other arrangements?"

"I was at a loss, I was heartbroken," said Tuvo Ausonius. "You can understand."

"I think so," said the masked figure.

"But now, after this time, of course," said Tuvo Ausonius, "I am more than willing to mate. Does the board have a candidate in mind? I would be eager to comply, whoever it might be. I am a good citizen."

"Your citizenship is commendable," said the masked figure. "Do you think this business has to do with a mating board?"

"Does it not?" asked Tuvo Ausonius, apprehensively.

"The empire does not practice coercion," said the masked figure. "The empire is the very condition of freedom, as you know."

"Certainly," said Tuvo Ausonius.

"Very few individuals, statistically, are arraigned before mating boards," said the masked figure, "and little more is necessary, in most cases, than presenting some evidence, reasons, arguments, or such, pertinent to the matter. You have done far more than is expected by such boards, having actually gone to the lengths of arranging a marriage, and such. You would be instantly, and without question, exonerated. Too, the empire can surely respect your sense of loss, your feelings."

"Then this matter is not in connection with a mating board?" asked Tuvo Ausonius.

"Certainly not," said the masked figure.

"Why do you think you were brought to this world?" asked the masked figure.

"I do not know," said Tuvo Ausonius.

"The empire has had its eye on you for a long time," said the masked figure.

"Oh?" said Tuvo Ausonius, uneasily.

"Your record appeared outstanding," said the masked figure.

"Your lordship?"

"You were summoned here to be commended, to be honored for your devotion to the empire, to be rewarded and promoted."

"Your lordship!"

"But in examining your accounts, preparatory to clearances for the award," continued the figure, "a number of unusual, subtle, serious discrepancies appeared."

"Impossible!" cried Tuvo Ausonius.

"There are special formulas, not generally publicized, for detecting such discrepancies," said the figure.

"My work is outstandingly accurate," said Tuvo Ausonius.

"Perhaps it contained some inadvertent errors?"

"Perhaps," said Tuvo Ausonius. "But I find that hard to believe."

"So does the examining board," said the figure. "The errors are of such a nature, such a frequency, such a proportion, that it is impossible that they can be the result of inadvertence. They demonstrate, incontrovertibly, to the board, evidence of extensive, profound, shameless peculation."

"I do not understand," said Tuvo Ausonius. He suddenly seemed very much aware of the cuffs on his wrists, how hard the cement was beneath his knees.

"Perhaps you have enemies?" suggested the figure.

"But who, for what purpose?" cried Ausonius.

"In light of your record, and your imposing lineage, I have been reluctant to process the matter," said the masked figure.

"I am innocent!" said Tuvo Ausonius.

"I have even thought, on the basis of your record and such, before these matters came to my attention," said the masked figure, "that there might be a place for you in the service of the palace itself, perhaps at the tenth level, as a special agent, a confidential agent, to be sure, charged with the conduct of delicate affairs."

"I will do anything!" said Tuvo Ausonius.

"In such an event, I was considering turning over to you those records, and such, which constitute the putative evidence of those alleged, say, misdemeanors, that you might do with it what you wish."

"Your lordship!" said Tuvo Ausonius.

"It would be tragic, indeed, if an innocent man were to be sent to a mining planet, there to serve out whatever portion he might manage of a fifty-year sentence of hard labor."

"I am innocent!" cried Ausonius.

"I believe you," said the masked figure.

"Thank you, your lordship!"

"But there is another more serious matter," said the masked figure, regretfully.

"Your lordship?" asked Tuvo Ausonius, frightened.

"And that is why you are clad as you are, and on your knees, and chained," said the masked figure.

"I do not understand," said Tuvo Ausonius, pulling at his restraints.

"Commissioner!" called the masked figure.

The officer returned to the room.

"You, Tuvo Ausonius, of Miton," said the masked figure, reading from the papers, "are charged with attempting the chastity of a free woman, one Sesella Gardener, of Miton, and engaging in activities with the object in view of having a free woman, this same Sesella Gardener, reduced to the condition of animal and slave."

"No! No!" cried Tuvo Ausonius.

"Bring forth the witness," said the masked figure.

Sesella Gardener entered, angrily, righteously, followed by two officers.

She was clad in gray, bulky, disguising same garb, boots, coveralls, and stiff, high-collared cloak, her hair, even, concealed beneath a dark, gray cap.

The top button on the coveralls, and the top closure on the stiff cloak, designed to conceal her upper body, were fastened shut.

Tuvo Ausonius, kneeling there on the cement, constrained, regarded her with misery and fear, but, too, oddly, with disappointment.

How different she was before, thought Tuvo Ausonius, that startling beauty of some two weeks ago.

It was not altogether impossible, however, even now, to recognize something of that wondrous vision of desirability, so small, so luscious, so deliciously curved, even in the gray, almost-shapeless vengeful thing which stood to the right of the masked figure's chair. Tuvo Ausonius now had a better sense of such things.

"Is this he?" asked the masked figure.

"It is he!" cried Sesella Gardener, pointing at the kneeling Tuvo Ausonius.

"No!" said Tuvo Ausonius.

This encounter was quite ironic in its way, and certainly unexpected, for it was this very night that Tuvo Ausonius had expected her to be put up for sale, at the commissioner's auction. Indeed, he had thought that he might even, as he had nothing better to do that evening, attend the auction. He did not intend to make a bid, of course. That would not be appropriate for a same. On the other hand, he had considered his resources carefully, if only as a matter of idle speculation. Such women, he supposed, might prove useful, for example, for domestic tasks, for housework, shopping, cooking, such things.

"Is it true that this man attempted your chastity, that of a same?" asked the masked figure.

"I expected him to!" said Sesella Gardener.

"I never laid a hand on her!" cried Tuvo Ausonius. "I mean I was not even in the city the night one of her clients, it seems, left her chained at the foot of the bed!"

"We have verified that he was in the city, and that he had rented the room," said the commissioner.

"The morning prior to the alleged incident?"

"Yes," said the commissioner. "We have the disembarkation reports, the passenger lists, the rental agency's records, such things."

"It was he who had me disrobe, and put me at the foot of the piece of furniture, and made it such that I could not depart!" said Sesella Gardener.

"It was he who chained you naked at the foot of the bed?" said the commissioner.

"Yes!" said Sesella Gardener, reddening.

"She disrobed voluntarily!" said Tuvo Ausonius. "And she put herself in the relevant impediments."

"Is that true?" asked the masked figure.

"He commanded me to do so," she said, angrily.

"And you obeyed?"

"Yes."

"Although a putatively free woman?"

"Yes," she said, uncertainly.

"Interesting," said the masked figure.

"I had no choice," she said. "He was going to report me to the company."

"For what?" asked the masked figure.

"For disarray," she said, "even for insubordination, discourtesy, lies, lies!"

"She was in disarray on the vessel, and she leaned over me, and she removed her cap, making her hair naked in front of me, in one of the ship's galleys," said Tuvo Ausonius.

"I was afraid," she said. "I did not want to be reported. I did not want to lose my position!"

"You say that you expected him to attempt your chastity?" asked the masked figure.

"Yes," she said.

"And yet you went to the room?"

"Yes," she said.

"Did he attempt your chastity?"

"No," she said.

"The first charge then, Commissioner, must be dismissed," said the masked figure.

"It now is," said the commissioner, making a notation.

"Why did you say that?" asked the masked figure.

"I expected him to!" she said.

"Perhaps you wanted him to," said the masked figure.

"No!" she cried.

"But, Tuvo Ausonius," said the masked figure sternly, "that leaves the most serious charge in place, that you acted in such a way as to have in view the enslavement of a free woman, this very Sesella Gardener."

"Yes!" cried Sesella Gardener.

"No!" cried Tuvo Ausonius.

"You left her chained in a room," said the masked figure.

"No!" said Tuvo Ausonius.

"Some of the fingerprints on the manacles were his?" asked the masked figure.

"Yes," said the commissioner.

Tuvo Ausonius's prints had been taken shortly after he had been brought to the commissioner's headquarters.

Apparently they had matched some of the prints, at least, on the manacles.

Tuvo Ausonius put down his head in misery.

Sesella Gardener cried out with pleasure, clapping her hands.

"Surely you must have understood that the authorities, to whom you reported the incident, would take her for a woman of pleasure, and one unlicensed, thus subject to impounding, and reduction to slavery."

Tuvo Ausonius looked up, agonized, and then, again, lowered his head.

"I find you guilty," said the masked figure.

"Yes!" cried Sesella Gardener, in triumph.

She looked at Tuvo Ausonius.

"That is where you belong, down there on your knees, you chained, stripped, filthy *filch*!" she cried.

Tuvo Ausonius looked up, angrily.

"The plaintiff may strike the defendant," said the masked figure.

Sesella Gardener rushed to Tuvo Ausonius.

"You are nothing now, patrician *filch*!" she exclaimed.

She struck his face, repeatedly, with her small hand, back and forth.

"*Filch*, pig, dog!" she cried.

"That is enough," said the masked figure.

Sesella Gardener, distraught, furious, oddly enough with tears in her eyes, backed away from Tuvo Ausonius.

"Punishments, in normal cases of this sort," said the masked figure, "might be expected to be severe, considering the gravity of the offense, conspiring to reduce a rightfully free woman to the indignities and shame of bondage, so hateful to her, but this is obviously not such a case."

Tuvo Ausonius looked up.

"Free him," said the masked figure. "And take her into custody." The two officers behind Tuvo Ausonius bent to free him of the bar and cuffs. Sesella Gardener cried out in protest, as she was seized by the other two officers who had accompanied her into the chamber. Tuvo Ausonius, bewildered, rose unsteadily to his feet. "Remove her clothing, completely," said the masked figure. "And bring a bar and cuffs suitable for her, and put her in the sockets to my left."

In a moment Sesella Gardener's beauty was wholly bared, as much as it had been at the foot of the bed in the shabby room, as much as it had been in her small cell in the building for the past two weeks, to the pleasure of the guards, until, to her amazement, same garb was brought for her, and she was informed of the arrest of Tuvo Ausonius. It has been but a moment's work for the indictment to be drafted. Shortly thereafter she had been brought down to the chamber, to testify. She now knelt, wide-eyed and bewildered, the prisoner of a bar and cuffs, suitable for her smaller frame, fastened in a pair of raised sockets, adjusted as to height, to the left of the masked figure.

"You say," the masked figure asked Tuvo Ausonius, "that this female person was in disarray, and that she bared her hair to you on some ship?"

"Yes," said Tuvo Ausonius, "and she knelt before me on the ship."

"He suggested that I do so!" said the prisoner.

"And you knelt?"

"Yes," she said, petulantly.

"You look well on your knees," said the masked figure.

THE CAPTAIN • 215

She pulled at the cuffs, but this moved the linking chain across her waist, tightly, and she stopped, instantly, realizing to her apprehension, and yet excitement, that this might accentuate her beauty, with what consequences she dared not speculate.

"You originally declared in the indictment," said the masked figure to the kneeling girl, "that this esteemed citizen of the empire attempted your chastity."

"Yes," she said.

"You lied?"

"Yes," she said.

"Why?"

"I was angry! I wanted to involve him in difficulties! Consider what he did to me, how he made me act!"

"For such an act you could be sent to a penal colony," said the masked figure.

"If he had been a man he would have attempted my chastity!" she said.

"And doubtless would have removed it from you?"

"Yes," she said, angrily.

"I am not a barbarian," said Tuvo Ausonius.

"When a woman is clad as you reportedly were, all men are barbarians," said the masked figure.

She looked up at him, angrily.

"You cannot thrust a torch into straw and not expect it to catch fire," said the masked figure.

"He did nothing!" she said.

"He is a same," said the masked figure.

"I changed my testimony!" she said. "I only said that I expected him to attempt my chastity, and that is true!"

"Such an expectation is irrelevant to the charge," said the masked figure.

"The charge was dismissed," said the commissioner.

"Yes," said the masked figure.

"Why have you put me on my knees, and taken away my clothes, and chained me?" she asked.

"Is perjury not sufficient?" asked the masked figure.

She pulled at the cuffs, and then, again, stopped, instantly.

"It is a crime, is it not," she asked, "to attempt to unlawfully reduce a rightfully free woman to bondage!"

"Yes," said the masked figure.

"I am such a woman!" she cried.

"Scarcely," said the masked figure.

"But you found him guilty," she said.

"Of having in view your subjection to bondage, certainly," said the masked figure.

"Why then am I chained as I am?"

"You are a free woman," said the masked figure, "but not a rightfully free woman."

"I do not understand," she said, almost in a whisper, backing against the bar.

"I think you understand very well," said the masked figure. "There are many counts against you, earlier and later, among them that you came as you did to his room, that you were clad, adorned and perfumed as a prostitute or less, that you obeyed, and so on."

"I do not understand any of this," she said.

"Your lordship," said Tuvo Ausonius. "May I have a garment?"

"Certainly," said the masked figure. He raised a hand in the direction of the commissioner, and the commissioner nodded to one of the two officers who had entered with Sesella Gardener. The officer immediately left the room.

"It is all madness, and all a mad combination of coincidences and circumstances," said Sesella Gardener, wildly.

"You were scouted by sames, and by private agents, and agents of the line," said the masked figure. "It was known that you chafed under the restraints of sameness. Your tendency to leave the top button of your uniform undone was noted, even under less exacting circumstances, your tendency to lean near to male passengers, your habit of neglecting the full complement of undergarments appropriate to a female same, thus permitting your lineaments to be conjectured, even your habit of touching your lips with the hint of cosmetics. It was not difficult to conjecture the closely guarded secrets of your innermost nature."

"It is all coincidence!" she wept. "How unfortunate I am! The flight was not my regular flight. I was transferred to it at the last minute. Even the ships were changed, one substituted, one of many, whose climate machinery was laboring and, as yet, unrepaired. And why was I assigned to the executive compartment? I should not qualify for such an assignment for years! Why did that man have to be one of my passengers?"

"An incredible assemblage of circumstances," admitted the masked figure.

The officer who had left the room now returned with a long cloak, with which, gratefully, Tuvo Ausonius covered himself.

He then, clad in the voluminous folds, looked down at Sesella Gardener, to his right, but to the left of the chair of the masked figure.

"I could not have been expected not to have noticed, and not to have taken offense, at her slovenly disregard for the etiquette of appearance and her forward, provocative behavior," pointed out Tuvo Ausonius.

"Certainly not," said the masked figure.

"Perhaps another might not have reported her," said Tuvo Ausonius.

"Perhaps not," admitted the masked figure.

"But certainly I would," he said.

"Most probably," agreed the masked figure.

"What is to be done with me?" begged Sesella Gardener.

"I am considering transmitting you to a penal colony," said the masked figure. "The charge would be unlicensed prostitution."

She looked up at him, in misery.

"You see the justice of the charge, surely," said the masked figure. "First, you are a free woman, and not a slave. Thus, the applicable category in your case if not that of slave, say, bondgirl or thrall, but that of prostitute. Secondly, you went to the room in order to exchange, or sell, your favors, in this case for exemption from disciplinary action."

"I had another reason, as well," she said, her head down.

"I am sure you did," he said.

She looked up.

"How do you feel about your chains?" he asked.

"They hold me well," she said.

"What do they tell you?" he asked.

"That I must do as I am told," she said.

"You are familiar with the usual punishment for unlicensed prostitution, aren't you?" asked the masked figure.

"Yes, your lordship."

"What is it?"

"Reduction to slavery," she said.

"But in your case," he said, "I am prepared to be lenient, and have you sent to a penal colony."

"The minimum sentence to such a place is twenty years," she said.

"Yes," he said.

"What does one do there?" she asked.

"The guards find applications for female prisoners," said the masked figure.

"The charge would be unlicensed prostitution?"

"Yes," he said.

"Such a sentence, with all due respect, your lordship," she said, "would be mistaken."

"How so?" he asked.

"I am not a prostitute," she said.

"What are you?" he asked.

"I am a slave girl," she said.

Tuvo Ausonius gasped.

"You are not branded, you are a free woman," said the masked figure.

"In my heart, your lordship, I know that I am a slave girl," she said. "I have known it for years."

"Interesting," said the masked figure.

"Disgusting slave!" cried Tuvo Ausonius.

"I beg your indulgence, and forgiveness, your lordship," she said, "for my debasement, my degradation and weakness. But there are such women, and I am one of them. I do not think that there is any longer any point in denying it. I want to be owned and mastered, to have no choice but to obey. I want to love and to serve, selflessly, unstintingly, with all that I am and can be."

"Surely you are terrified at the thought of becoming a female slave," said the masked figure.

"It is what I am," she said. "Beyond that I do not know what to think. I sense that it is my true freedom. I do not think I could be happy in any other life."

"Your thinking must be corrected," said Tuvo Ausonius.

"To agree with yours?" she asked. "I have spent my life with such thoughts. They are gray, meaningless and empty."

"Terrible, terrible!" said Tuvo Ausonius.

"Some women want to know that they are alive, really," she said. "They desire real experiences, strong experiences."

"What of tenderness and sensitivity," said the masked figure, amused.

"Such things," she said, "are surely very precious, and doubtless a girl muchly treasures them, but they are meaningful only when set against a background of power and mastery."

"Degraded slut!" cried Tuvo Ausonius.

She looked at him, angrily. "I do not apologize for what I am!" she said.

"You would choose the brand, as opposed to a mere twenty years in a penal colony?" asked the masked figure.

"Yes," she said.

"Why?"

"I am a slave."

"I think I shall send you to a penal colony," said the masked figure.

"Please do not!" she said.

"I can do what I wish," he said.

"Yes," she said, putting her head down, trembling, "the power is yours."

"What do you think I should do, Tuvo Ausonius?" asked the masked figure.

"It matters not to me, of course, your lordship," said Tuvo Ausonius.

"She is well curved," said the masked figure.

"I am a same," said Tuvo Ausonius, "we do not notice such things."

"The penal colony is, of course, by far, the lesser punishment," said the masked figure.

"The lighter punishment might be appropriate for a different woman, a higher woman," said Tuvo Ausonius, "but consider this one, what she is, her debased nature, the utter worthlessness of her."

"True," said the masked figure.

"Too, as a free woman she would be priceless, of course, but she would actually have no value," said Tuvo Ausonius. "As a slave, she would presumably be worth at least something. For example, she could be bought and sold."

"True," said the masked figure.

The masked figure turned to Sesella Gardener, the stewardess, from the line Wings Between Worlds.

"You understand," he said to her, "that as a slave, you might come into the keeping of anyone. For example, you might be sold, and you would then belong, wholly, to whoever bought you."

"Yes," she said.

"You might even come into the keeping of our esteemed Tuvo Ausonius," he said.

"Oh, no!" she cried. "Please, no! Do not jest, your lordship! Do not even hint at such things!"

"It is surely a possibility," he said.

She struggled helplessly, futilely, but she could not even rise to her feet, as she was held.

"You are to be herewith, on numerous grounds, and particularly prominent among them those of fittingness, with my next words," said the masked figure, "pronounced slave."

She looked up at him, trembling.

"You are a slave," he said.

"Take her away," said the masked figure. "See that she is branded before nightfall."

The slave's guiding rod was freed from the sockets and she was pulled to her feet.

"Trust that you come into the keeping of a good master," said the masked figure.

She was thrust from the room.

She looked back, once, wildly, over her shoulder at Tuvo Ausonius.

"She came to your room, did she not?" asked the masked figure.

"Yes," said Tuvo Ausonius.

"One wonders why," said the masked figure.

"Yes," said Tuvo Ausonius. "It is all very strange."

"She mentioned that there was another reason, other than her concern with her position with the company, and such."

"As I recall, she did," said Tuvo Ausonius.

"I wonder what it might have been," said the masked figure.

"I have no idea," said Tuvo Ausonius.

"Some women have needs," said the masked figure, "a complex spectrum of needs."

"Perhaps some low, terrible women," said Tuvo Ausonius.

"Such as slaves?"

"Perhaps," said Tuvo Ausonius.

"She is now a slave," said the masked figure.

"Appropriately so," said Tuvo Ausonius.

"I think she may have found you attractive," said the masked figure.

"Surely not," said Tuvo Ausonius.

"You are not a bad-looking fellow," said the masked figure.

"She hates me," said Tuvo Ausonius.

"That might make it interesting then, to own her," said the masked figure.

Tuvo Ausonius regarded the masked figure, startled.

"Surely you found her attractive?" said the masked figure.

"I am a same." said Tuvo Ausonius. "Such matters are of no interest to us."

The masked figure turned to the commissioner, and the two officers who had remained in the chamber. "Thank you, gentlemen," he said.

They bowed and withdrew.

"Tuvo Ausonius," said the masked figure.

"Yes, your lordship," said Tuvo Ausonius.

"I am confident that you are innocent of peculation, and such, but the evidence is surely serious. I fear you have enemies."

"I do not know who they could be," said Tuvo Ausonius.

"I, too, have enemies," said the masked figure.

"You, your lordship?" said Tuvo Ausonius.

"Unfortunately, yes," said the masked figures. "In these days intrigue, ambition and malice abound."

"I am innocent," said Tuvo Ausonius.

"I think that you are likely to fare very badly if you do not obtain a friend, a protector, in a high place, someone of importance, someone with considerable influence."

"Alas, I know no one!" said Tuvo Ausonius.

"At some risk to myself, I could be such a one," said the masked figure.

"Your lordship!" exclaimed Tuvo Ausonius.

"But there is a serious difficulty."

"Your lordship?"

"I admire your insight and courage, your insight in detecting that the former Sesella Gardener was rightfully, and naturally, a female slave, and your courage, despite the risks involved, in attempting to see justice done, to bring about her fitting reduction to embondment, thus bringing to an end her pretensions as a free woman."

"It is nothing, your lordship," said Tuvo Ausonius.

"Such insight, such intelligence, such daring, such courage," said the masked figure, "are such as are needed by a confidential agent, of the sort I mentioned earlier."

"One attached to the palace, a tenth-level imperial civil servant?"

"Certainly, but one who would report only to a given individual."

"Who?" asked Tuvo Ausonius.

"The arbiter of protocol."

"I have heard of him," said Tuvo Ausonius, shuddering.

"There would be considerable compensations, pecuniary and otherwise, involved in such a post," said the masked figure.

"I would be honored even to be considered for such a post," said Tuvo Ausonius.

"There is a serious difficulty, of course," said the masked figure. "There are the charges of peculation which, even though we both know them false, might bring about your arrest and sentencing to hard labor on a mining planet."

"Perhaps your lordship might consider sheltering me from such dangers," said Tuvo Ausonius.

"It is not impossible," said the masked figure.

"What of the matter of the slut?" asked Tuvo Ausonius.

"That matter is done," said the masked figure. "I have already cleared you of that. Your enemies, even if they wished, can no longer make use of it."

"The woman herself?"

"She is now a property," said the masked figure. "She has no legal standing, no more than a pig or dog."

"I am deeply grateful to you, your lordship."

"You are then interested in my suggestions, in the possibility of promotion, of rewards, even riches, of perquisites and favors, of various sorts, of service to the empire and palace?"

"Yes, extremely so, your lordship."

"You understand that these matters are confidential, that they may involve matters of delicacy, of state importance, and that your allegiance, devotion and service must be complete and unquestioning?"

"Of course," said Tuvo Ausonius.

"You will be contacted," said the masked figure.

"Yes, your lordship," said Tuvo Ausonius.

"In the beginning you will be on a probationary basis."

"Of course, your lordship," said Tuvo Ausonius.

"An officer will be at the guard station, at the end of the hall. He will arrange to have your clothing returned to you."

"Thank you, your lordship."

"When you receive it, I think you will discover that a letter of credit will be enclosed in the left inside jacket pocket, in the amount of a thousand *darins*."

"My thanks, your lordship!" said Tuvo Ausonius.

"In one of the pockets of your jacket," said the masked figure, "we discovered a ticket to the commissioner's auction, to be held this evening."

"Oh?" said Tuvo Ausonius.

"Perhaps you planned to attend?"

Tuvo Ausonius shrugged.

"As a matter of curiosity, of sociological illumination," said the masked figure.

"Possibly," said Tuvo Ausonius.

"You are correct that a certain slave will be put up for sale," said the masked figure.

"Oh?" said Tuvo Ausonius.

"It might be interesting," said the masked figure, "to see her exhibited naked for the men, perhaps on a neck chain, forced to move, and pose, as the auctioneer requires, knowing herself subject to his ready, even eager, whip at the least sign of unwillingness or hesitancy."

"Perhaps," said Tuvo Ausonius.

"The experience should do her good," said the masked figure. "I myself intend to attend, though you will not recognize me there."

"No, your lordship," Tuvo Ausonius assured him.

"I will have an agent bid for her," said the masked figure.

"Oh?" said Tuvo Ausonius, in disappointment.

"On your behalf, of course," he said.

"Your lordship!"

"It is nothing," said the masked figure. "That is just one of the perquisites of which I spoke."

"Thank you, your lordship," said Tuvo Ausonius.

"After the sale, return to your quarters. She will be delivered to you, hooded, by midnight."

"Thank you, your lordship," said Tuvo Ausonius.

"You will recall how she rushed upon you and struck you when you were helpless?"

"Yes," said Tuvo Ausonius.

"She will be yours, by midnight," said the masked figure.

"Thank you, your lordship," said Tuvo Ausonius.

# · · · **CHAPTER 22** · · ·

"Are you pretty?" asked the fellow.

"You can see very little through the grille," said another, irritably.

"Please feed me, Masters," she said.

"Come closer to the grille," said another, bending over the crate.

"Bring it out, farther, into the light," said another.

Three of the mariners turned the crate about and slid it out, scraping on the plating, from the wall, more under a light, fixed in the ceiling of the hold.

"The virgin seal," said one in disgust.

"Who would know?" asked another.

"They could tell, if the seal was broken," said another.

"You could lose your certification," said another.

"I am not crated, Masters!" called a feminine voice from across the hold. There was a sound of chain on the steel plating. "Content me! Feed me!"

"Be silent, if you want to keep your blanket," said one of the mariners.

"Are you pretty, in there?" asked one of the mariners, tapping on the grille with a finger.

"Some men have seemed to find me pretty, Masters," said a frightened voice, from within the locked, sealed box.

"What is your name?" asked one of the mariners.

"Whatever Masters please," she said.

"You answer to 'Flora'?" said one of the men, reading the label.

"I answer to whatever name is given me," she said. "That was my house name, in the house where I was boarded."

"I know that house," said one of the mariners, with a laugh. "They train girls there, as well."

"Are you trained?" asked one of the men.

"A little, Masters," she said. "We are trained, as Masters please."

"A trained girl," said one of the men, approvingly.

"Only a little, Masters!" said the woman.

"I am trained!" called the voice from across the floor. "Content me! I will be good! Feed me!"

"Take her blanket," said one of the men.

One of the fellows walked across the hold.

There was a tiny cry of misery.

In a moment, with a blanket, folded, he returned. He dropped the blanket to the side.

"Put the side of your face up, next to the grille," said one of the men.

The girl in the box did so.

"I can see a little of her," said a man.

"She looks interesting," said another.

"We could break the seal and claim we knew nothing of it," said one of the mariners.

"The key is here, taped to the top," said another.

"The box was logged in, and the seal checked," said one of the men. "Who has access to the hold? Do not be foolish."

The girl inside the box cried out, as one of the men kicked the side of the box, angrily.

"There is the other one," said one of the mariners.

The men turned about.

There was a sudden small sound of chain, as though a slave, perhaps finding herself regarded, had hastened to kneel, perhaps performing obeisance.

"Would you like your blanket back?" asked a man.

"If it should please Masters to return it to me," said the voice.

"Lift your head," said one of the men.

"I am hungry, Masters, please feed me," said the girl in the box.

"Be silent," said one of the men.

"Yes, Masters," she said.

The men then went, taking the blanket with them, across the hold.

The girl in the box, peeking through the grille, watched them.

They were crouching down, about the other girl. She was fair-haired and well ankled. Her left ankle was chained to a ring, set back near the opposite wall of the hold.

"I am not a virgin," she said to them.

"Bring her a little food," said one of the mariners. "She will need her strength."

Men laughed.

The girl in the box watched for a little, but then lay down, her knees drawn up, closely, in misery. She could not help but hear the cries from across the hold. She squirmed. She was helplessly heated, for she, too, was a slave. The cries were those of slave rapture, that rapture that she herself had never yet felt, that rapture mercilessly, even ruthlessly, inflicted upon one who has no choice but to submit.

Later a man came to her box and, with his boot, slid up the tiny panel at the foot of the door.

Two small pans, with the side of his foot, were slipped through the opening from the outside, one for food, which contained some broken pieces of pressed cakes of cereal, and one for water.

"Keep your box clean," he said.

"Yes, Master," she said.

## ▪ ▪ ▪ CHAPTER 23 ▪ ▪ ▪

The small slave, hooded, naked, kneeling, her wrists encircled with steel, put out her hands, following the chain running from her wrists, and felt the heavy ring, fixed in the floor, to which she, by the wrists, was chained.

It was only that night that she had been sold, and that only in a magistrate's auction, one in which a variety of items, not only women, had been offered, abandoned parcels, unclaimed trunks, confiscated properties, a captured stray dog, many such things.

She felt the ring carefully, her small fingers touching it, and holding it.

She had been exhibited naked, of course.

She had obeyed the auctioneer with perfection.

It had not been necessary to strike her, even once.

She was still reeling with what it had been like, ascending to the tall, wide, rounded block, the lights, being frightened, not being able to see the men, really, the sawdust beneath her feet, the loose metal collar with its light chain on her neck, not inhibiting her movements, the prodding of the auctioneer's coiled whip, which had snapped once and had made her cry out, almost as though she had been struck.

There seemed something terribly familiar about the ring. She put out her fingers and felt the floor about it.

She tried, defensively, to conceptualize the matter as one of having given the men a good show, but she realized that that was a self-serving distortion of what had actually occurred. Oh, to be sure, doubtless it had been a good show, but that was largely the auctioneer's doing. Putting it the other way suggested that it might have been the consequence of some decision on her part, or the result of some benevolent or defiant intention, that sort of thing. Rather she was only a property, which had been well displayed, in numerous attitudes, postures, and such. It was true, however, a little later, and as the bidding heated, she had been almost overcome with strange feelings, exciting, moving, thrilling feelings. It was then that she had, suddenly, perhaps for the first time, fully understood that she was a property, really, a wondrous, vital, excited, acutely conscious, extremely sensitive, highly intelligent, incredibly desirable property, a property that most men would find far more appealing than gold and diamonds, a property for which men might even kill. She tried to force such thoughts, such memories from her mind. Could it have been she who had behaved as the girl on the block? She could feel the heat as the men cried out. She could feel the interest and desire, like waves, such an incredible feeling, wash over her. She had had an identity imposed upon her, a clear, incontrovertible identity, but, too, this identity had seemed to emerge from within her. It was as though, for the first time in her life, she had had no choice but to be what she truly was. On the block then, there had been, at the end, only a flushed, startled, sweating, comprehending, leashed slave girl. But now, again, she was frightened. One bidder had apparently, not even audibly, but by signs from the audience, topped each bid. He had had her for a bid of forty *darins*, which was high for a girl at the magistrate's auction, and well satisfied the auctioneer, but would not have been unusual, or even high, for a typical auction of women, even in a small town. But, of course, rich men seldom attended magistrate's auctions, apparently finding them of little interest. Too, she was not even trained. But now, she realized, she no longer belonged to the city, but, presumably, to some private individual.

She now had a master!

Her fingers touched the ring, and the floor about it.

They trembled a little.

"Oh!" she cried, softly, for large, heavy hands were at her

neck, undoing the fastenings on the hood, and then they thrust up the hood, a little, revealing her trembling, parted lips, there was no doubt they were masculine hands, and they held her face. The hood was left much in place, so that it acted as a blindfold. She felt her hair, what had been loosened in the partial lifting of the hood, touched, felt, almost wonderingly, and then arranged, softly about her shoulders. This seemed to be done almost with a sort of curiosity. Her hair had been washed and combed prior to the sale, but it was a bit disarranged now, and sweaty, from its incarceration in the hood. She had also been touched with perfume, prior to being taken to the block. The perfume was perhaps a bit subtle for a slave, but then she was new to the brand. Perhaps they thought it might make her first night in chains, at the mercy of a master, easier. But that seems unlikely. It is much more probable that it was designed, in its subtlety, to encourage a master to prowl her beauty, almost as in curiosity, detecting and relishing it. It was, of course, a cheap perfume. That would be expected from a magistrate's auction. And it was also, as those versed in such matters would have recognized, a slave perfume, a perfume extracted and prepared with the vulnerable beauty of a slave in mind. She was now aware of someone, behind her, bending over her, taking in the scent of the perfume.

She did not dare speak.

She knew herself slave.

Then, in a moment, she felt a glass held softly to her lips, and tilted a little.

She tasted *kana* and was eager for more, but the glass was withdrawn.

Barely had she wet her lips.

She understood then that what she drank, and in what quantities, was no longer at her discretion, but at that of another.

Her lips trembled a little.

She heard a tiny noise, as of something being broken, a cracker, or perhaps a biscuit.

A moment later she felt a small piece of pressed cake of cereal put betwixt her lips, against her teeth.

She thought to lift her hands but, as she was kneeling, and they were fastened, she could not bring them near her mouth, not without changing her position, bending down, lying down, such things.

She opened her teeth and took the bit of pressed cake into her mouth, and ate it.

She was surprised at how sensitive her lips were, so soft, and moist, to the smallest touch. She could scarcely conjecture what it might feel like, what it might be to feel with them other surfaces, other textures, such as the body of a man.

She felt, again, the presence of a bit of pressed cake against her teeth.

Even the tiny pressure of the cereal cake against her teeth could be felt, so clearly, so precisely.

Her entire body was becoming sensuously alive, even helplessly so.

She fed.

She opened her mouth, again, lifting it, delicately, even imploringly, as she was hungry.

Surely there must be more.

But there was not.

She understood then that what she ate, and in what quantities, was no longer at her discretion, but at the discretion of another.

Indeed, whether she was to have food or drink at all, she now realized, was not at her discretion, but at that of another.

It had not been a true feeling, at all, she then realized. It had been an instruction.

She trembled.

She had learned a valuable lesson for a slave.

Suddenly, terribly frightened, she put down her hands and grasped the ring, and she then put them about the ring, seeing how it fitted into its hemispherical staple, and she then felt the heavy, solid plate, bolted into the floor, in which the staple, with the ring, was fixed, its dimensions, its shape, its height above the floor, the location and nature of the bolts which anchored it in the floor, and she then felt, even, the very nature of the floor itself, and a crack in a board, a place where something once must have scraped.

Her heart began to pound wildly.

Surely she knew the plate, the ring, the staple.

She was certain then, too, that the crack, or gouge, she could now feel was one which once she had seen.

She lifted her head, her lips trembling. She jerked at her chains, but her wrists could move only a few inches upward, as they were fastened closely to the ring.

"Yes," said a voice. "It is the same room."

She squirmed on her knees, and jerked at the chains.

Hands took the hood in their grip and pulled it wider, and then, lifting it, tore it away.

"You!" she cried.

He seemed very tall then, standing over her. In his hand was the hood.

Damp, dark hair was loose, and wild, about her head and shoulders.

"Is this some form of jest?" she asked, pleadingly.

"I suppose so," he said.

"Is this the room of my master?" she asked.

"Yes," he said.

"What are you doing here?" she asked.

"It is my room," he said.

"You are my master?" she said.

"Yes," said Tuvo Ausonius, "I am your master."

## · · · CHAPTER 24 · · ·

"No!" she cried. "Surely it is not true!"

"It is quite true," said Tuvo Ausonius. "I own you. I am your master."

A sudden, wild, almost-indescribable look, perhaps one of horror, perhaps one of misery, perhaps one of sudden, startled, unbelievable elation, or perhaps one of all three, transfused the countenance of the slave, but this was only for the briefest moment, for, in a moment, she had recaptured herself.

"I despise you," she said. "I do not want you for my master!"

"Dogs and pigs do not decide who will be their masters, nor do lesser creatures, such as slave girls," said Tuvo Ausonius.

He cast the hood to one side, to the floor.

"You are 'Sesella,'" he said, naming her.

She glared up at him.

"What is your name?" he asked.

"Sesella," she said.

" 'Sesella'?" he inquired.

"Sesella, Master," she said.

"Do not forget it," said Tuvo Ausonius.

"No, Master," she said.

"How does the word 'Master' feel on your lips?" he asked.

"Fitting," she said. She could scarcely tell what that simple sound, and its meaning, did to her, addressed to men, how it made her feel. Suddenly she felt warm, soft, moist and receptive.

"What are you going to do with that whip?" she asked, uneasily.

"Perhaps you recall," he said, "how in a basement chamber in the headquarters of the commissioner, you, not commanded, only permitted, flew at a kneeling, helpless fellow, and, somewhat ardently, even savagely, one might say, with supposed impunity, struck him, again and again."

He shook out the coils of the whip.

"That was done by a free woman, Sesella Gardener," she said. "Surely you would not punish a poor slave for something done by a free woman!"

"I see that you are highly intelligent," said Tuvo Ausonius.

"Thank you, Master," said the girl.

"But not intelligent enough," he said.

"Master?" she asked.

"It is not improper, you see, if the free woman has become the slave," said Tuvo Ausonius. "For, in that case, after her embondment, her punishment is even more shameful, being then beaten as a mere slave."

"I am small and soft," she said. "You own me! I beg not to be whipped!"

"Perhaps we should not concern ourselves overly much with what was done by Sesella Gardener, the free woman," said Tuvo Ausonius. "After all, she is gone. There is now in her place only pretty little Sesella, the slave."

"Yes, Master!" said the slave, gratefully.

"But Master has not yet put aside the whip," she said.

"But there does remain, of course, undeniably, the connection between Sesella Gardener, the free woman, and Sesella, the slave, for one has become the other."

"Yes, Master," said the girl, falteringly.

"But we need not concern ourselves, I suppose, at least not overly much, with such matters."

"No, Master!"

"But you may, in any event, be whipped whenever I wish," he said. "For example, if I feel like whipping you, I may do so."

"Yes, Master," she said.

"You understand that you are subject to the whip?"

"Yes, Master," she said.

"As a highly intelligent girl, even if not quite intelligent enough, you understand that?"

"Yes, Master."

"You may be whipped at any time, for any reason, or for no reason," he said.

"Yes, Master," she whispered.

"That helps to keep slave girls zealous," he said.

"Yes, Master," she said.

He looked at the whip, in his hands.

"Please, no, Master," she said.

" 'No'?" he said.

"No," she said.

"Why?" he asked.

"I am zealous," she whispered.

"Speak up," he said.

"I am zealous!" she said.

"Is she who was once Sesella Gardener the free woman and is now Sesella, the slave, zealous?"

"Yes, Master!"

"Who is zealous?

"Sesella, the slave, is zealous!"

He struck the whip once or twice into the palm of his hand.

"Do not whip me," she begged. "Rather let me serve your pleasure!"

"My pleasure?"

"Yes, as a slave girl!" she said.

"You would serve with such abject perfection?"

"Yes, Master! Let me on the bed!"

"Lie on your back, where you are," he said.

He took a blanket from the bed, and threw it to the floor. He then drew her down, so that her hands were up, chained over her head, as she lay. He did thrust the blanket under her.

Then he stood up, and looked down at her.

"The top button of your jacket is undone," he said.

"Yes, Master," she smiled.

"You leaned forward," he said. "Your undergarments were not those prescribed to conceal your figure. You bared your hair before me, a same, though you, too, were a same. You knelt. You dared to use lipstick. You came to this room, garbed, adorned, perfumed, in ways inappropriate for a same. There are many counts against you."

"Punish me," she said.

"Why did you come to the room?" he asked.

She turned her head to the side.

"You hate me," he said.

She looked up at him. "I can no longer play such games, Master," she said. "My feelings were troubled, and complex. I did not hate you, but what you were. From the first moment I saw you I wanted to be yours."

"As you are now?"

"Yes," she said, "as I am now!"

"But I am a same," he said.

"I, too, was a same," she said.

"True," he said.

"Can we not both know then what we have missed, what we were denied, what we have been deprived of?"

"Perhaps," he said.

He crouched down, beside her.

"Some sames keep servants," he said.

"They need never know that I am your slave, Master," she whispered.

"You would wear same garb," he said.

"Outside," she said.

"Yes, outside," he said.

"And inside?"

"We shall consider that," he said.

"And even if I am permitted clothing," she said.

"Yes," he said.

"Touch me," she begged. "The slave begs to be touched."

"Ah!" she said.

"I have never been a man," said Tuvo Ausonius.

"Perhaps Master would like it," she said.

"Perhaps," he said.

"Ohh!" she said.

"Yes, it might be interesting," he said.

"Oh, Master!" she whispered.

"I should not be touching you like this, for I am a same," he said.

"We are no longer sames," she said.

"What are we then?" he asked.

"You own me," she said, tensely. "Be kind!"

"What are we?" he asked.

"A man and a woman, a master and his slave!"

"I suppose I might find some application for you," he said, "in housework, or such."

She arched her back.

"Can you cook, clean, sew?" he asked.

"No, no, no!" she wept. "No, please don't stop!"

"Do you like being a woman?" he asked.

"Yes, yes, yes!" she wept.

"And a slave?"

"Yes!" she cried. "A thousand times 'Yes! Yes! Yes!'"

"See how you arch your back," he said.

"Do not criticize me, Master!" she begged.

"See how you squirm," he said.

"I cannot help myself, Master!" she said.

"You may writhe," he said.

"Thank you, Master!" she cried.

"The chains hold you well," he said.

"Yes, Master!" she wept.

"I have never seen a woman like this before," he said.

"Oh," she said. "Oh!"

"You are very beautiful, Sesella," he said.

"I am yours!" she wept.

"Kneel at the ring, with your head down," he said.

"I obey," she said.

"Onto your stomach," he said.

"Yes, Master," she said.

"I must rethink matters," he said.

"Master?" she asked.

He was sitting on the floor, on the blanket, near her. She was still chained to the ring.

"There are dangers in this world," he said.

"Yes, Master," she said.

"Is there such a thing as honor?" he asked.

"I do not know, Master," she said. "I am only a slave."

"I thought there was no such thing," he said. "But now I am not sure."

# · · · CHAPTER 25 · · ·

"Why is she bound in this fashion?" asked Julian.

"He bound me so!" she said.

"She broke a plate," said the house master.

"You were clumsy, Gerune," said Julian.

"The plate was slippery," she pouted.

"What punishment did you intend?" inquired Julian of the house master.

"I thought five lashes would be sufficient," he said.

"Master will never permit you to strike me!" she said.

"Why is that?" asked Julian.

"Surely Master remembers last night," she said.

"Yes," said Julian. "You are juicing well, learning quickly, and becoming an excellent slave."

"Then certainly Master will have me released," she said.

"Certainly," he said.

"Thank you, Master!" she said, casting a glance over her shoulder at the house master.

"After you have received ten lashes," said Julian.

"Master!" she cried.

But Julian had left the area.

# · · · CHAPTER 26 · · ·

"It has been long," said Julian.

"I should return to Varna," said Otto. "There is no commission, no captaincy."

"They must transmit it, they have no choice," said Julian. "They dare not refuse to grant it."

"It is time for the harvesting in the fields of the Wolfungs," said Otto.

"They can manage without you," said Julian.

"There are lions in the forests, against which I should like to test my mettle," he said.

"There are fiercer lions within the empire," said Julian.

"I have not seen them," said Otto.

"They are not easily detected," said Julian.

"I am thinking of Varna," said Otto.

"You are hungry for slave meat," said Julian.

Otto was silent.

"How is Renata?" asked Julian.

"She is coming along excellently," said Otto. "Already, at a touch, she is hot and helpless. I am thinking that she would make a lovely gift for someone."

"It seems," said Julian, "that it is a particular piece of slave meat for which you hunger, perhaps one that you have never forgotten."

Otto did not respond. He looked out of the vehicle, at the rugged terrain.

"Perhaps one that you have never even tasted," suggested Julian, smiling to himself.

"She is a lying, treacherous, meaningless slut," snarled Otto.

"But surely one who is attractive," said Julian.

"Yes," growled Otto. "She is not without her insidious charms."

"I think she has learned the collar," said Julian. "And that she is fearful."

"She should be fearful," said Otto. "She is a slave."

"I think it is her desire, even desperately so," said Julian, "to be found pleasing by her master."

"She, the treacherous, meretricious chit?" said Otto.

"Yes," said Julian. "And I think, too, it is her desire to please you."

"Slaves are often in heat," said Otto.

"If she truly betrayed you," said Julian, "I would think you might enjoy making use of her."

"She is far away, on Varna," said Otto.

"Stop the vehicle," said Julian to the driver.

The driver stopped the segmented, treaded vehicle.

They were at the height of the winding path that led to Julian's holding.

Julian stood up and looked back, over the path, and down to the road far below, lying in the valley.

"The way is clear behind us," said Julian.

"And I see no cars in the sky," said Otto, shading his eyes.

"What is the delay?" said Julian, angrily.

"Perhaps they have arrangements to make," said Otto.

"Yes," said Julian, "perhaps they have not yet completed their arrangements."

It was not easy to detect the presence of the holding as it was set in among the granite mountains. Indeed, portions of it were carved from the living rock itself.

"I thank you for the outing," said Otto.

"You should learn how to operate a vehicle of this sort," said Julian.

"I would be pleased to do so," said Otto.

"Your horsemanship is remarkable," said Julian.

"It is like flying," said Otto.

"Surely you have ridden before," said Julian.

"Only here," said Otto. "We had no horses in the village."

"Do you think you could do war from the back of a horse?" asked Julian.

"Yes," said Otto.

They were not on one of the original Telnarian worlds but one, Vellmer, within the first quadrant, not the first provincial quadrant. This holding was one of several owned by the Aurelianii, and one of some five which were designed to afford an occupant a large measure of both security and privacy.

"Why will you not wait at your ancestral home?" had asked Otto, some days ago.

"I do not want to risk it," had said Julian.

"But will the palace know where you are?" asked Otto.

"Certainly," said Julian. "They have been informed."

Julian and Otto now resumed their seats.

In a moment, the codes spoken into the receivers, the gate slid to one side and the vehicle entered the holding.

The gate, which was better than a yard thick, of layered steel, then slid shut behind them.

# · · · **CHAPTER 27** · · ·

"Where am I?" begged Flora, rising from her mattress, as the door of the cell was opened.

"On Vellmer," said the slave girl, bearing the tray, with fruit, two slices of bread, some leaves of vegetables, and drink. She knelt down and, carefully, placed the objects on the small table, some two-foot square, on short legs, rising some foot or so from the floor. There was one mat on the tiles, near the table. The cell had only one occupant. There were no chairs in the cell. The mattress was in a small frame, only an inch from the floor. Slave girls are seldom permitted to sit in chairs. Too, their bedding is usually on, or near, the floor.

"Should you not have asked me to kneel?" inquired Flora.

The girl looked at her.

"Or instructed me to do so?" asked Flora.

"I, too, am only a slave," said the girl.

Flora knelt down, on the mat, by the table. The girl was still kneeling on the other side, but ready to rise, and withdraw.

Neither was collared.

"Wait!" said Flora.

The girl looked up.

"I know I am on Vellmer," said Flora. "I was delivered to an address on Vellmer, but then I was hooded and moved, and was brought here."

"Yes," said the slave girl.

"Where am I, here?" asked Flora.

"I may not say," said the slave girl.

"Is my master here?"

"Yes."

"Who is my master?" begged Flora.

"I may not say," said the slave girl.

"I do not even know who owns me!" said Flora.

"Doubtless you will learn, when it pleases the masters," said the slave.

"Is this the house of my master?"

"No."

"But my master is here?"

"Yes."

"Who is my master?"

"I may not say," said the slave.

"Do not leave!" begged Flora.

The slave rose up, with the tray. "You are very beautiful," she said.

Flora, too, rose up. Both women were very much the same height. Perhaps Flora was the tiniest bit taller.

"You, too, are very beautiful," said Flora.

"You must be muchly favored, and a high slave," said the slave girl, "for you are gowned."

Flora wore a simple, loose, ankle-length garment of white wool. It was sleeveless. Its neckline was generous, generous from the point of view of masters, and would leave a slave in little doubt as to her bondage.

The garment of the slave girl was quite similar, being sleeveless and of white wool, and such, and differed really, only, in its length, for it came high on her thighs. It was a simple garment and displayed its wearer well. It was a common form of slave tunic.

The two garments were all the women wore.

"You are well fed, and have your own cell," said the slave girl. "You are not kenneled."

"Are you kenneled at night?" asked Flora.

"Save when I am chained at the foot of my master's couch," said the slave.

The slave girl went to the door of the cell, which consisted of heavy, vertical bars fixed in thick, lateral crosspieces. She paused there for a moment, the tray in her left hand, looking back at Flora. She then stepped outside, and closed the door.

"Wait!" called Flora.

The door shut with a heavy, unmistakable, efficient snap.

The slave girl turned, and paused, a few feet on the other side of the bars.

"Why am I being treated like this?" begged Flora, hurrying to the bars. "Why have I not been set to service, why have I not been summoned before my master?"

"I do not know," said the slave girl. "Perhaps they are readying you to be a gift."

"A gift!"

"I do not know," said the slave girl.

"That must be it!" wept Flora.

"You have been trained, as I understand it," said the slave girl.

"Only a little!" said Flora.

"I envy you," said the slave girl.

"All masters train us," said Flora.

"That is true, each trains us to his pleasure," said the slave girl.

"Then your master trains you?"

"Yes," said the slave girl. "He trains me, as it pleases him, precisely so."

"Wait!" called Flora.

The girl paused at the end of the short corridor, before the iron door there. She would knock on this and be admitted to the outer area. A little later the guard would check the cell, to make certain it was securely locked.

Flora clutched the bars of the cell door. She shook them, wildly. But there was little movement of the door.

"I was sold!" she said.

"Perhaps your master tired of you?" said the slave girl. "Perhaps he no longer wanted you. Perhaps he did not like you."

"I have been sold!" wept Flora. "Now I am on Vellmer, and am to be given away as a gift!"

"I do not know," said the slave girl.

"Do not go!" begged Flora.

"I must, I have duties," said the slave.

"Be kind to me!"

"May I call you 'Flora'?"

"Yes, yes!" said Flora.

"Do you like the name?"

"Yes," said she who wore the name.

"That was the name on your packing slip," said the slave girl.

"It was what they called me in school," said Flora.

"Your master had not given you a name?"

"No," wept Flora.

"It must be terrible not to have a name," said the slave girl.

"Yes," said Flora.

"We will say your name is 'Flora'," because that is what the guards call you," said the slave girl.

"Thank you," said Flora .

"So it will do," smiled the slave girl.

"Yes," said Flora .

"Your name is 'Flora'," she said.

"Until men see fit to change it, or take it away," said Flora.

"Yes," said the slave girl. "Such things are up to the masters."

"Yes," said Flora.

"We are powerless. We are totally at their mercy."

"Yes," said Flora.

"I must leave," said the slave girl.

"What is your name?" asked Flora.

"Renata," said the slave girl.

She had then knocked on the iron door at the end of the corridor, and in a moment was in the outer area. The door closed, and locked, behind her.

Flora clutched the bars. "I have been sold," she wept. "I am to be given away, as a gift!"

She then, sobbing, clinging to the thick bars, put her head down. She pressed the side of her face against the bars. Her tears ran against the metal.

## · · · CHAPTER 28 · · ·

"My name is Tuvo Ausonius. I believe you will find my credentials in order. I come on behalf of his majesty, Aesilesius, emperor of Telnaria. I bring, enclosed in this case, a commission, in the rank of captain, for one Ottonius, known to you, milord, and, as I understand it, a guest now in your house."

"This is he," said Julian, indicating Otto, who stood beside him.

"Greetings," said Tuvo Ausonius.

"Greetings," said Otto.

"May I introduce my colleague, Sesella," said Tuvo Ausonius.

"It is unusual for a same to have but one name," said Julian.

"Greetings," said the companion of Tuvo Ausonius.

"Greetings," said Julian.

Julian regarded his two visitors. He had surely not expected sames, not from the summer world. How severe, and gross, he thought, were their garbs, and yet, oddly, they did not seem to carry themselves as sames, nor to have the severe mien one expects of sames. Perhaps they were not sames, thought Julian, but what would be the point of disguising such matters, what would be the object of the pretense, under these circumstances?

"Your colleague appears to be a female," said Julian.

The smaller of the same-garbed pair, for a moment, looked frightened.

"Sames do not concern themselves with such matters," said Tuvo Ausonius.

Julian had an eye for women, and thought that he might detect something of interest within that bulky shielding of same garb, something of perhaps even considerable interest.

"You come, actually, I take it," said Julian, "from our esteemed friend, Iaachus, arbiter of protocol."

"It is my understanding that my mission derives most immediately from that revered personage," said Tuvo Ausonius.

"Why has there been this long delay, a delay unconscionable in a matter this straightforward, this simple?"

"I do not know," said Tuvo Ausonius. "I apologize, of course, on behalf of my superiors, for any inconvenience."

"Such considerations do not lie within the purview of your assignment," said Julian.

"No, milord."

"We do not allow just anyone in this holding," said Julian. "But you are of the Ausonii."

"That is interesting," said Tuvo Ausonius. "I had not realized that something of that sort might have mattered."

"We are particular," said Julian.

"Ah," said Tuvo Ausonius.

"Is anything wrong?" asked Julian.

"It is nothing," said Ausonius.

"You are from Miton," said Julian.

"Yes, milord."

"Why was not someone from the palace, from the summer world, from the capital world, from the administrative worlds, not given this assignment?"

"I do not know, milord," said Tuvo Ausonius.

"The same worlds tend to be isolated," said Julian, "scarcely integrated into the empire."

"We are loyal to the throne," said Tuvo Ausonius.

"Your car is below, in the landing area," said Julian.

"Yes, milord," said Tuvo Ausonius.

Julian pressed a button on the lower edge of the top of the desk in the receiving office.

There was a whirring of machinery, as though far off.

"I had expected," said Julian, "given my rank, that the commission would be brought to the holding by an imperial magistrate, preceded by twelve lictors."

"Is that the common protocol?" inquired Tuvo Ausonius.

"Yes," said Julian. "One would have thought it would have been observed by Iaachus."

"Yes," said Tuvo Ausonius.

"He is the arbiter of protocol."

"Yes," said Tuvo Ausonius, thoughtfully.

"What is wrong?" asked Julian.

"Nothing," said Tuvo Ausonius.

Julian walked to one side of the room, and looked out, through gigantic windows, onto the mountains. Too, he could see, in a small landing area below, on a shelf below, the car. Air rippled about it. Its motors were hot, running.

He then returned, to stand behind the great desk.

On this desk there lay, rather at its center, but nearer Tuvo Ausonius, a flat, black case.

"Open it," said Julian.

Tuvo Ausonius hesitated.

"Honor," said Tuvo Ausonius, "is more important than life, for life is worthless without it."

"You are a same," said Julian. "Such things are of no interest to you."

"Why do you hesitate?" asked Otto.

"You have a duty to perform," said Julian.

"Documents, treaties, charters, commissions, such things, are not ordinarily delivered in this fashion, are they?" said Tuvo Ausonius.

"No," said Julian.

"There is a time lock on the case," said Tuvo Ausonius.

"It is a simple device," said Julian. "You dial the combination, and, in ten seconds, those necessary for the internal machinery to clear the bolts, the case opens. You know the combination?"

"Yes," said Tuvo Ausonius.

"What is wrong?" asked Otto.

"Nothing," said Tuvo Ausonius.

"Open the case," said Julian.

"There are special instructions," said Tuvo Ausonius. "It is to be opened only in your presence, milord, and that of your guest, Ottonius.''

''That is that we may verify the opening of the case,'' said Julian. ''We are both present. Proceed.''

Tuvo Ausonius drew from within his jacket a sealed envelope and handed it to his colleague.

His colleague regarded him, puzzled.

''Leave the room,'' he said to the colleague.

Wildly then, bewildered, did the colleague regard him.

''Now,'' he said.

The colleague, looking back but once, frightened, clutching the paper, hurried from the room.

''Milords,'' said Tuvo Ausonius, ''I must now ask you to leave the room, as well.''

''The case is to be opened in our presence,'' said Julian.

''I must insist,'' said Tuvo Ausonius.

''You are a brave man,'' said Julian. ''What is the combination?''

''Milord?'' asked Tuvo Ausonius.

''When the combination is dialed,'' said Julian, ''not only will the mechanism be engaged, but a signal will doubtless be transmitted to your car below.''

''It is waiting,'' said Tuvo Ausonius.

''It is ready for flight, even now,'' said Julian. ''It will need ten seconds to ascend to its attack track.''

''I do not understand,'' said Tuvo Ausonius.

''I have taken precautions,'' said Julian. ''Dial the combination.''

Tuvo Ausonius, steadying the case with one hand, began to rotate the dial with his other hand.

He stopped, short of the last number.

''What is it?'' asked Julian.

''Six,'' said Tuvo Ausonius. ''Perhaps you had best leave the room.''

Julian reached over Tuvo Ausonius's hand and moved the dial to six. A small purring sound emanated from the case.

''The mechanism is engaging,'' said Julian.

Tuvo Ausonius was sweating.

''The car is rising, outside, I hear it,'' said Otto.

''Gentlemen,'' said Julian. ''I think it would be wise if we withdrew. Please follow me.''

Scarcely had the three men stepped from the room, through a concealed, spring-actuated panel in the wall behind the desk, than the room vacated was rocked with an explosion. Window glass flew outward, the desk was shattered, walls were gouged and battered, papers were scattered, and blackened and aflame. At almost the same instant a searing flash of fire from the car tore at a thick, transparent domelike shield which, by the mechanism activated by the button beneath the desk earlier, had been placed in position. The car was not a hundred yards past the dome, and was banking for a second run, when it exploded, and burst into flame, caught in steams of fire from the walls.

The screaming of Tuvo Ausonius's colleague could be heard from the outer room.

The men, half choking with dust, kicked the panel open, which was now awry on its hinges, and reentered the room.

The colleague of Tuvo Ausonius ran to him. Her eyes were wild. She gasped. It was almost as though she wished to throw herself to her knees before him.

At almost the same time several men, guards at the holding, armed, rushed into the room.

"We are all right," Julian assured them.

He then turned to face Tuvo Ausonius and his colleague.

"You are under arrest, of course, both of you," he said.

Their hands were tied behind their backs and they were conducted from the room.

"There is little left of the case," said Otto, looking about.

"The only prints on it, even on the fragments," said Julian, "would be those of its messenger."

"Milord," said a man, entering, "there is a party approaching, climbing the trail."

"They are clad in white robes," said Julian, "there are thirteen of them, twelve preceding, carrying rods and axes, and one following, bearing a scroll case."

"Yes, milord!" said the man.

"Open the gate," said Julian. "Admit them."

"Wait!" called Julian.

"Milord?" said the man, turning.

"Secure all slaves," said Julian.

"Yes, milord," said the man.

# · · · CHAPTER 29 · · ·

"What is going on?" cried Flora.

She ran to the door of her cell.

The door at the end of the short corridor had been flung open and Flora saw some five slaves being thrust forward. All were in brief tunics. All were hooded. Their hands were cuffed behind their backs. They were on a common neck chain. She was sure that Renata was among them. Small, stifled noises came from some of the hoods. Doubtless, beneath the hoods, they were gagged.

The door to her cell was flung open.

"Stand! Hands behind you!" ordered a guard.

Two guards entered the cell.

Her hands were cuffed behind her back. A gag was fixed on her, making it impossible for her to speak. A hood was drawn over her head and buckled shut, about her neck. She was then thrust from the cell. In a moment she felt a collar locked on her neck, and the draw of a chain, before and behind. She then was forced along the passage, and down a sloping passage.

In a few moments she felt damp stone beneath her bared feet, and tiny puddles of water.

She was forced to her belly. Her head was forced down. She could feel the stone of the floor through the hood, on the left side of her face. She felt the collar removed from her neck, but, in a moment, another collar, a heavier one, snapped about her neck. A chain ran from this collar to a staple, fixed in the stone. She determined this, feeling it with the side of her face, through the hood.

She felt the dampness of the floor through her gown.

She did not know where she was.

She tried to call out, or inquire, but could utter no more than tiny, helpless sounds.

She then lay there, prone, somewhere, unable to speak, in the darkness of the hood, her hands cuffed behind her, chained.

The chain on her neck, running to the floor, was a short one, only some six inches in length.

It would hold her head quite close to the staple.

Somewhere, seemingly faraway, she heard gunfire.

· · · **CHAPTER 30** · · ·

"He is escaping!" called Otto.

The magistrate was climbing the interior stairwell, leading to the parapet, that to the left of the left gate tower, as one would view the gate from within.

The magistrate clutched a scroll case in one hand, a pistol in the other.

He fired toward the portal of the left gate tower. There was a shower of stone from the wall. The muzzles of rifles protruded inward from the towers. There were marksmen, too, behind barricades, arranged on the walkways of the walls. Others had fired from the sides of the walls, and others from the external walls of the inner bailey, from gunports.

"There is no escape for him," said Julian.

The magistrate looked over the wall, and then turned back, wildly. He fired once down, into the outer yard. A tile buckled and leapt up, blackened, to Julian's right.

Then the figure on the wall, a mass of blood and fire, tumbled into the yard.

Julian lowered his pistol.

"That is all of them," said Julian.

"No," said Otto. "There is another, somewhere."

"He from the summer world," said Julian.

"There were several from that world," said Otto.

About the outer yard there were several bodies, twelve bodies, as one counted.

These wore white robes. Near eleven of them, and parts of them, their blood run on the tiles, were weapons, assault rifles which had been concealed within the bundles of rods, each with its ax.

The firing had been brief and fierce, the sudden unbundling of the rods, the revelation of the weapons, but the guards in Julian's holding had been in place and, almost instantly, almost before fingers had found the triggers of weapons, the white-clad bodies, startled, several blown open, reeling, twisting about, searching for their concealed foes, had begun to succumb to the storm of fire from all sides.

Julian considered the bodies.

"They did not have a chance," said Julian.

"One is still at large," said Otto, looking about.

"He lost his rifle," said Julian. "He is not to be feared."

"There are only eleven axes here," said Otto, walking among the bodies.

"We will make a search," said Julian.

"I do not think he will know how to use the ax," said Otto. He himself bent down and picked up one of the long-handled axes, double-headed, which had protruded from one of the bundles of rods. The bundles of rods and axes, carried before high officials on certain occasions, are an ancient symbol, one perhaps now rather familiar, almost benign and innocuous, but one once, one supposes, of the power of the state, of its might and terror, its capacity to chastise, and, if it wishes, to kill.

"Be careful," said Julian.

Otto entered the inner bailey, and made his way upward, slowly, to its parapet. He looked about himself. He saw two guards, adjusting the slings on their weapons. Other than this the parapet was deserted.

Their attention would presumably have been directed to the outer yard, below.

In the forest one notices little things when one is hunting, and many of the skills of war, of course, are much like those of hunting. Perhaps that is one reason that those who live by arms are often fond of the hunt.

A crushed leaf, the dislodgement of a twig, indicated by the tiny depression in which it had formerly lain, such tiny things, can mark a trail.

Accordingly the tiny drop of blood on the stones of the parapet required no great discernment, or acuteness, to interpret.

The opening to one of the towers was nearby.

Otto held his ax ready, in the guard position. Twice, in the arena, he had fought in labyrinth games, where the spectators, tense, silent, as quiet as though holding their breath, observed, from the height and safety of their seats, the men looking for one another, in the maze.

Sometimes they would cry out in excitement, or exultation, as contact, sometimes sudden, and brutal, was made.

Otto entered the tower, and looked up the spiral stairwell leading to its height.

The stairwells in such towers almost invariably ascend in a clockwise fashion.

One might suppose that there is no particular reason for this surprising conformity of structure, but, if one did so, one's surmise would be in error.

Most men, you see, are right-handed, and will, accordingly, handle weapons with their right hand. In this fashion one who ascends the stairwell, presumably an intruder, must, in order to employ his weapon, expose more of his body, whereas one who is higher on the stairwell, presumably a defender, in such an employment of weaponry, in virtue of the shielding of the masonry, may expose less of his body.

Suddenly the blade of an ax, from above, slashed down, diagonally, and stone spit out from the side of the shaft.

It had not come close to Otto.

Had the wielder of the ax been frantic, too eager, foolish, or had he merely intended to appear so.

Otto took another step upward, slowly.

And then another step.

"Stay away!" he heard.

Otto did not think it was wise of the man to have cried out.

The voice had sounded frantic.

Was the man frantic, or had he merely intended to seem so?

Otto did not think the man would know the ax.

But Otto did not hurry his ascent.

There was a drop of blood on the steps.

Then Otto heard the sound of steps on the tile of the level above, a different sound from that of the stone stairs.

He ascended the steps. He did this with great care. He was then at the landing. It was the highest landing within the tower. From it, three openings, each with a heavy door, led outward, onto a semicircular walkway. Two of the doors were latched. Such doors can be latched only from the inside. This provides some protection in the event of a successful escalade. Otto glanced upward. The trap leading to the roof of the tower, too, was still latched. It, too, for the same reason, could not be latched from the other side. In this fashion the defenders can keep others out, at least for a time, and cannot themselves be locked in.

"Stay away!" he heard, a scream.

It came from the walkway outside, from behind the one unlatched door.

A blow of Otto's ax cut the latch away from the door, so that it might not be latched behind him.

He drew the door open.

"Stay away!" screamed the voice.

"You!" cried the voice, in terror.

The figure stood at bay, in a tunic, its back to the parapet, holding the ax. The white robes had been torn away, and discarded. They would have been an encumbrance. They lay near the man's feet. They were bloody.

"Yes," said Otto.

It was a man he had met some days earlier, in the streets, on the summer world, the leader of those who had addressed him with rudeness.

Otto recalled another, as well, the one who had made the mistake of touching him. That one he had lifted from his feet, and thrust, not gently, against a wall. The man had sunk down, against the wall, leaving blood on it, behind him, marking his descent. That fellow now lay below, in the outer bailey, blown apart. Several of the others, too, among the white-robed figures below, Otto had noted, had been among those who had swarmed about him, and Julian, in the streets.

The man rushed at Otto, striking down, wildly, with the ax. Otto blocked three blows, two handle to handle, one with the blade of his own ax, blade to blade. Sparks flashed from the metal, showering about them.

The man backed away.

The wind, ascending the stairwell from below, swirling in the interior of the tower, swung the door a little.

The creak of its hinges could be heard.

"I once speculated that you would not stand up well against an ax attack," said Otto. "Now we shall see if I was right."

The man screamed with fear and hurled the ax at Otto.

One of the blade edges sunk deeply into the heavy timber jamb on the left side of the door.

The handle vibrated for a moment.

"I am disarmed!" cried the man.

"It was not I who disarmed you," said Otto.

"*Civilitas!*" cried the man.

"I have no intention of leaving one like you behind me," said Otto.

"*Civilitas!*" screamed the man.

"*Barbaritas,*" said Otto.

The man turned about and leapt into the crenel behind him, stood there for a moment, and then lept down.

Otto went to the wall, and looked down. The man's leap had carried him to the height of the transparent dome, some twenty feet below, now muchly scarred and blackened from the fire of the car which had brought Tuvo Ausonius to the holding. That dome, in its halves, sheltered the office and certain private chambers in the holding.

Otto watched as the man tried to keep his grip on the dome. Perhaps if he had landed higher on the dome, where its slope was less precipitous, or if he had managed to get his fingernails in some of the fissures left by the attack, things might have turned out differently.

Otto watched him, screaming, slipping slowly, inch by inch, from the surface of the dome, until, looking upward, wildly toward Otto, he fell from it, to the rocks more than two hundred feet below.

Otto then left the parapet, and descended to the inner bailey.

He had stopped only to wrench loose the ax, imbedded in the jamb of the portal, that leading to the walkway.

There was little sound then on the height of the parapet, only the whisper of the wind, and the movement of the door, swinging a little now and then on its hinges.

# • • • CHAPTER 31 • • •

Flora walked unsteadily down the hall, almost unable to keep her balance.

She was not with a guard, and on a leash, as a slave is often taken to the room of a guest, whom she is to serve. Rather she had just been told the room, and sent on her way.

Bitter tears ran down her cheeks.

How joyous she had been, but moments before.

"I have a surprise for you," had said Julian, of the Aurelianii, to his friend. "Behold! I have had her brought from Varna, and boarded, and trained, to some extent, on the summer world, and thence brought to Vellmer, now a more knowledgeable slave."

She had thought, for a moment, when she had entered, as the eyes of the barbarian giant had first looked upon her, that there had been recognition, and elation, on that often fierce countenance which she had hoped to soften with kindness, or at least with some tiny bit of consideration or regard for her, but, almost instantly, his visage, as though he had forced himself to recollect what despicable thing it was that hurried to kneel before him, the fragile, delicate slave flower in its hands, became cold and hard, cold like the wintry sheathing of dark rivers, deeply flowing, hard like stone in the month of Igon.

She had knelt, her emotions in tumult, stirred, a chaos of joy, confusion, and pain. It was he who had been her master on Varna, and now, it seemed, still was, for it was before him that she had been signaled to kneel. She remembered him even from Terennia, and the first time he had looked upon her, a look that had stripped away her dark, judicial robes, and all she wore, and had been, revealing the naked, vulnerable slave beneath. She had seized the railing behind which she stood, that she might not fall. She had fought in herself the instantaneous, almost overwhelming desire to hurry to him, to kneel and perform obeisance. How startled she had been with these feelings, how furious with herself!

Let her mother, the judge, proceed with the prosecution of the fellow!

But he had survived in the arena, and had later obtained his freedom.

Through a complex set of circumstances she, who had been an officer of the very court which had condemned him to the arena, her mother the very judge who had pronounced the sentence, had become his slave.

She dared not meet his eyes, so fierce they were upon her.

On the ill-fated *Alaria*, kneeling at his feet in the darkness, not even knowing it was he, she had become, technically, and legally, a slave. But he, at that time, had unaccountably treated her well and not enforced her bondage. Indeed, in a vital matter, pertaining to his plan to escape the *Alaria*, he had trusted her word, that she would remain silent, on this word refusing to subject her to the efficient indignities of the gag. But she had broken this word, betraying him and his party, calling out, alerting enemies. Shortly thereafter they had become separated, but each, in their own way, in different capsules, had managed to escape the *Alaria*. She had later, on Varna, come again into this possession. This time he had not seen fit to show her indulgence but had had her branded and tagged. She now wore on her thigh a mark in virtue of which there would be no mistaking what she was, a mark which would be recognized throughout galaxies.

"I thought you would be pleased," said Julian.

"She is a faithless, treacherous, lying slave," said Otto.

"Please, no, Master," she had whispered.

"She is well curved," said Julian.

"So are millions on thousands of worlds," said Otto.

"I love you, Master. I want to serve you," she whispered.

"Surely she is exquisite," said Julian.

"As are innumerable others, all for one price or another," said Otto.

"She bears the slave flower, to offer it to you," said Julian.

"She is a collared slut," said Otto. "She will offer it to whomsoever her master decides."

"I think she would offer it to you," said Julian.

"She is worthless," said Otto.

"She might bring a decent price in a market," said Julian.

"Perhaps," said Otto.

There was little doubt as to this.

The slave's handlers, who had prepared her for presentation to her master, had left little of her beauty to the imagination. Her breasts strained against the mockery of a skimpy bandeau of scarlet silk. A narrow, black, cloth cord was put twice, snugly, about her waist, and knotted, with a slip knot, at the left hip. This cord supported two narrow rectangles of scarlet silk. It also supplied a means whereby, if it were removed, she might be bound. Such features are not unusual in slave garments. A common variation on such a theme is a leather thong wound several times about the left ankle, and tied there. Is it an attractive decoration? Certainly, but it may also serve, with similar decorative appeal, as a bond. Her dark hair was bound back with a scarlet ribbon. On her neck there was a close-fitting, steel slave collar.

"Is your name 'Flora'?" asked Julian, kindly.

"In the house they call me that, Master," said the slave.

"Is it your name?" asked Julian.

"My name," she said, "or even if I am permitted a name, is up to my master."

She looked at Otto.

But he turned away from her.

"Look upon her, my friend," urged Julian.

"Thank you, my friend," said Otto, "for having seen to it that she has received some training. That will doubtless improve her price."

"Have you not been permitted in this room," asked Julian of the slave, "to offer the slave flower to your master?"

"Yes, Master," she said, gratefully.

"Look upon her," urged Julian.

Otto turned in the chair to regard the slave kneeling before him. There were tears in her eyes.

"Please, Master," she said, lifting the flower delicately, timidly, to Otto, "accept my slave flower."

"It is worth less than that of a pig or dog," snarled Otto.

She put her head down. "It is true that I am only a slave, Master," she said.

"Keep it well in mind," said Otto.

"Yes, Master," she sobbed.

Julian lifted his hand to summon a guard, who would conduct the slave back to her quarters.

"Wait!" said Otto, suddenly, menacingly.

The slave looked up, frightened. Julian turned to him, puzzled. The guard hesitated to approach.

"There is now one in the house who should be well known to you," said Otto.

"Master?" she asked.

"Do you remember the *Alaria*," he asked, "and the supper at the captain's table, with Pulendius, and others?"

"Yes, Master," she said.

"And surely you remember the purpose of your journey on the *Alaria*?"

"Of course, Master," she said uneasily. It had been to take her to Miton, where she was to be wedded. The marriage had been arranged with great attention to detail. Genealogies had been checked, credentials and records had been examined, biographies had been scrutinized, and the earnings, and likely future earnings, of the prospective groom had been calculated with care. The marriage had been arranged largely through the offices of the girl's mother and her friend, the mayor, of the small city on Terennia, which was, for the district, a juristic center. Both the girl's mother

and the mayor hoped, too, to profit significantly from so favorable
an alliance, soon following the girl to the first provincial quadrant,
and perhaps even, later, the first imperial quadrant. Pictorials had
been exchanged. The prospective groom was, of course, a same,
as was the prospective bride, a matter which was of great consequence to the mother and her friend, the mayor. That was almost
as important as the prospective groom's position and income. With
respect to the latter, he was, at the time, a level-four civil servant
in the financial division of the first provincial quadrant. The
marriage was calculatedly favorable, too, on the count of geneal-
ogy, as the prospective groom was of the 103rd degree of the
Ausonii, and the bride of the 105th degree of the Auresii. The
prospective bride's name was Tribonius Auresius, and the prospective groom's name was Tuvo Ausonius. The marriage did not take
place, of course, as the *Alaria*, as it may be recalled, failed to enter
orbit at Miton, having perhaps encountered some mishap en route.

"Two sames are currently under arrest in this house," said Otto.
"Perhaps rumors of this have reached you."

"Yes, Master," she said.

"But, too, we may regard them as guests," said Otto.

"Master?" she asked.

"One is a a female, whose name, as related, is simply 'Sesella',"
said Otto.

"Yes, Master," said the slave.

"The other is a male, whose name is Tuvo Ausonius," said Otto.

"Tuvo Ausonius!" cried the slave.

"I see the name is meaningful to you," said Otto.

"You remember something of this matter, too, do you not?"
Otto inquired of Julian.

"Yes," said Julian. "I do."

"I was to wed him!" cried the slave. "He was my fiancé. I was
his betrothed!"

"You were a free woman," said Otto.

"Certainly, Master," said the slave.

"What are you now?" asked Otto.

"A slave," she said.

"And do you not think it is fitting that a guest be shown
hospitality in a house?"

"Oh, no, no, Master!" she cried. "Please, no, Master!"

"Oh?" asked Otto.

"I hate him!" she cried. "It was an arranged marriage! I wanted
nothing of it! It was the doing of my mother and another! I hated

him! I despised him! I intended to make his life miserable, even to ruin him!''

"Surely you do not think that he is interested in wedding you now, do you?" asked Otto.

"No, Master," she said, "for I am now a slave, no more than an animal."

Otto regarded her.

"No, no, Master!" she cried.

"What is the room of Tuvo Ausonius?" asked Otto of Julian. He was told.

"How is it reached?" asked Otto.

He was informed.

"You have heard?" asked Otto.

"Yes, Master," said the slave, dismayed.

"You are sent to him," said Otto. "And take with you the slave flower. It is to be offered to Tuvo Ausonius."

"No, no!" she wept.

"Go," said Otto.

"Yes, Master," she wept.

Flora walked unsteadily down the hall, almost unable to keep her balance.

She was not with a guard, and on a leash, as a slave is often taken to the room of a guest, whom she is to serve. Rather she had just been told the room, and sent on her way.

Bitter tears ran down her cheeks.

She stopped, to put one hand against a wall, to steady herself. She feared she might fall.

She saw a guard before one door, and she counted the doors to that door. No, that was not the door. There were two sames under arrest in the house. That must be the room in which the other same, the woman was. Neither, she understood, was below, secured in cells. The guard was watching her approach. She feared she was not walking well. He must, of course, over the years, have seen thousands of slaves. She had heard the guards refer to her as "a pretty one." She was confident she would bring a better price than many, though, of course, not so good a price as many others. He was watching her approach. She tried to walk well. She did not wish to risk being struck. She had, of course, in her bondage, grown accustomed to men looking at her, watching her, considering her, speculating openly on what it might be to own her, to have her, theirs, in their arms.

When she reached the guard, before passing him, she would kneel, and bow her head.

She did so.

"Are you all right?" he asked.

"Yes, Master," she said.

"Lift your head. Straighten your back. Do not rise," he said. He walked about her.

Then, again before her, he looked at her, in detail.

It pleased her to kneel before men.

"You carry the slave flower," he said.

"Yes, Master," she said.

"You may continue on your way," he said.

"Yes, Master," she said.

She looked at the door he guarded. Behind it was one of the sames in custody, the woman.

In a moment she had rounded a corner and was no longer in sight of the guard.

I hate Tuvo Ausonius, she thought. Rather would I be thrown to guards, to be put to the tiles, to serve for fear of my very life, each to tear a petal from the slave flower, than to be touched by one such as Tuvo Ausonius.

But then she thought, suddenly, wildly, that she might master Tuvo Ausonius, manipulate him, govern him, overcome him with misery and guilt. Was he not a same? Might she not take advantage of that complex, subtle, pervasive conditioning program used on the "same" planets to deprive men of their manhood, that program so gradually instituted and promulgated, bit by bit, rule by rule, law by law, that many did not even realize it existed, that program designed not so much to challenge healthy, natural modalities of human existence as to preclude its victims from even understanding that they existed? Yes, she thought wildly to herself, there is nothing to fear. He is already demeaned, degraded, and debased, and conquered. I need not fear him. His entire world has prepared him for defeat. There is no doubt that I will be victorious!

She looked wildly about. No guard was in this corridor. There were various rooms. They would be, presumably, mostly empty, mostly unlocked. In some there must be wardrobes, or chests, containing garments. Surely guests must come to this holding upon occasion. Some must surely be free women, perhaps sisters, or relatives, of one degree or another, of the master of the house! Or perhaps there might be garments of sufficient opacity and modesty as to be mistaken for, or which would serve as, the garments of a free woman. If slaves were to serve at suppers at which free women were present, they might well be attired decorously. Surely, at such suppers, they would not serve naked, save for their collars. There must be something, somewhere!

It was in the third room that she found a chest which contained suitable robes, white, even sleeved. Too, there were hose, and even shoes, small, soft, colored, delicately embroidered. Too, there were scarves which might encircle her throat, useful in concealing a steel collar.

She thrust the slave flower in her belt, that formed from the twice-turned black cloth cord.

She then turned her attention to the chest.

It was seemingly a different woman who emerged from the room, after first carefully looking to the left and right.

Doubtless there would be a guard at the door, but the door was about the next corner, across the structure, its room well separated from that of the other same, doubtless that there might be no communication between them.

She did not think the guard would take her for a free woman. Indeed, it was altogether probably that he would recognize her. Thus, in greeting him, she must kneel. She trusted that Tuvo Ausonius would not know she had done so.

The guard, when she turned the corner of the corridor, looked up, and leapt to his feet, from the chair, having mistaken her, naturally enough, under the circumstances, for a free woman. Then, as she approached, he regarded her closely. She knelt down a few feet from him, primarily because she feared to prolong his doubt as to her status, which might irritate him, but also because she wanted to be further from the door. She lowered her head.

He stepped to her.

"Flora," he said.

"Yes, Master," she said.

"I prefer slave garb on a slave," he said. "It is more fitting."

"If we are permitted clothing," she said.

"Yes," he said.

"I am sent to the prisoner," she said.

"Never have I seen a slave so clad sent to a prisoner," he smiled.

She said nothing.

"But then he is a same," said the guard.

"Yes, Master," she said.

She went to the door, while the guard resumed his post, the chair a few feet from the door.

At the door she trembled, just for a moment, for she was a slave, of course, truly, and her charade had not been commanded by her master. Indeed, it had been undertaken without his knowledge. Her hand shook, and she thought, for a moment, to knock softly, even timidly, at the door, as befitted a helpless, vulnerable slave who had been sent to a guest, to be as though his until morning. But then, suddenly, angry with the thought of Tuvo Ausonius, and contemptuous of him, she struck the door clearly, decisively.

In a moment the door was opened.

She was taken aback a bit, for he who opened the door was not precisely what she had expected to find. Oh, it was Tuvo Ausonius all right, or bore at least some resemblance to him. That could be told from the pictorials. But those had displayed something seemingly inhibited, deceitful, venal, petulant, sullen, hypocritical, weak. The fellow who had opened the door was not only considerably larger than herself, and above average height for a male of the empire, but, more importantly, carried himself, and seemed such, as one would not expect of a same. She feared for an instant that he might not be a same, but a man, one of those creatures in the presence of which a woman could be only a woman. But, reassuringly, he wore same garb. She wished, suddenly, that she had been able to avail herself of same garb, but none, not surprisingly, had been in the rooms she had investigated.

"Tuvo Ausonius?" she brought herself to ask.

"Yes," he said.

He looked beyond her.

Had he expected another? Had he hoped for another? This angered her.

"May I come in?" she asked.

"Yes," he said.

She thrust past him, and closed the door, firmly, behind her. She noted, to her satisfaction, that the door was thick. She did not think that, given the thickness of the portal, for those of the empire's upper classes tend to be fond of their privacy, and the position of the guard, down the hall, they would be likely to be overheard. Tuvo Ausonius seemed surprised that she had closed the door herself.

In the center of the room she turned to face him.

"What is wrong?" she asked.

"Nothing," he said.

"Perhaps you hoped for a different visitor?" she said.

" 'Visitor'?" he asked.

"Yes," she said.

"Perhaps," he said.

"Do you not recognize me?" she asked.

"For what purpose have you come?" he asked.

"I am a free woman!" she said.

"I see," said Tuvo Ausonius.

"Surely you recognize me?" she asked.

"I am sorry," said Tuvo Ausonius. "I do not. Should I?"

"I am the free woman, Tribonius Auresius!" she announced.

"I do not think so," said Tuvo Ausonius. "You are too pretty."

" 'Pretty'?" she cried. "Shame, shame!"

"You are a same?" he asked.

"Certainly!" she said. "And you, too, are a same!"

"You are not dressed as a same," he said.

"That is not important," she said.

"Tribonius Auresius," he said, "was aboard the *Alaria*. It never reached Miton."

"Nonetheless, I am she!" she said.

"The *Alaria*," he said, "I have heard it recently rumored, fell to a barbarian fleet. Distress calls supposedly made that clear. Debris was also supposedly indicative. If there were any pretty prisoners taken, they were doubtless made slaves."

"Shame!" she cried. "You cannot even begin to think of a woman in such terms, even hypothetically, even in the wildest stretches of your imagination! You are a same! Such a horrifying, terrifying fate for a woman could not even occur to you!"

"I doubt that you are Tribonius Auresius," he said.

"Why?" she asked.

"You are not she," he said. "You are far more desirable, far more exciting and beautiful than she."

"Watch your language!" she cried. "But you saw the pictorials!"

"They were of a rather plain, snobbish little slut," he said, "but one who, perhaps, had some promise."

"Wicked man!" she cried.

"You escaped the *Alaria*?" he asked.

"Yes!" she said.

"And kept your freedom?"

"Yes!" she said.

"And still retain it?"

"Of course," she said.

"What is the name of the mother of Tribonius Auresius?" he asked.

He was told. It was "Cualella."

He then asked a number of complex questions, pertaining to various matters, matters the answers to which would be likely to be known only to themselves.

"I am Tribonius Auresius!" said she, at the conclusion of this inquiry.

"Your identity is established beyond doubt," said Tuvo Ausonius.

"And what would be the purpose of attempting to deceive you with respect to such a matter?" she asked.

"I can conceive of no such purpose," he said. "But I am not clear as to what you are doing here, here in this house, here in this room."

"Surely you are overjoyed to see me," she said, "your fiancée, your betrothed."

"Doubtless," he said.

"I was traveling in these mountains," she said, "and sought, and was granted, hospitality, and subsequently, in pleasant converse, our relationship emerged. At that time I did not know you were here. Our host, in his graciousness, has permitted me to visit you."

"That is surely exceedingly kind on his part," said Tuvo Ausonius.

"Though not a same, he is a gentleman," she said.

"Perhaps we might avail ourselves of this opportunity to renew our relationship."

"As sames?" she said.

"What could be more appropriate?" he asked.

"True," she said.

"I must admit," he said, "I was somewhat put off by the somewhat calculating and mercenary nature of the arrangements connected with our prospective relationship."

"One cannot be too careful," she said, "when patricians are involved."

"I was not overly pleased," he said, "that you were only of the 105th degree of the Auresii."

"Surely the 105th degree of the Auresii is comparable to, or superior to, that of the 103rd degree of the Ausonii," she said.

"Scarcely," he said.

She reddened, angrily.

"It is true," he said.

"Perhaps," she said.

"I gathered," he said, "that you had certain anticipations of the nature of our relationship, and desired to impose certain conditions upon it."

"Of course," she said.

"Absolute superiority of the woman?" he asked.

"At the very least," she said. "It must be remembered that, even though we are both sames, that we women must protect ourselves, as we are smaller and weaker than you."

"A husband has no rights which he may enforce?" asked Tuvo Ausonius.

"Not unless we permit it," she said.

"Everything is up to the woman," he said.

"Of course," she said.

"It is all on your own terms," he said.

"Yes, of course," she said.

"What of nature?" he asked.

"We have improved on nature," she said.

"I wonder," he said.

"As a same, you are not permitted to wonder about such things," she said. "It is forbidden to wonder about them."

"But what if they are absurd?" he asked.

"It is forbidden to ask such questions," she said. "Remember that you are a same!"

"Perhaps you would now like me to kneel before you, and beg your hand in marriage," he said.

"Certainly, if you wish," she said.

"That would be entirely appropriate?" he asked.

"Certainly," she said.

"I was not truly eager for the marriage," he said.

"What?" she said.

"But I thought it might be construed as a portion of my duty to the empire," he said.

"Your duty!" she cried.

"Yes," he said.

"Well, I was not eager for it either!" she said.

"Why then did you agree to the matter?" he asked.

"These things were arranged by my mother and another," she said.

"Why did you agree to them?" asked Tuvo Ausonius.

She regarded him, angrily.

"Why?"

"It was to my advantage!" she said.

"You are a mercenary little thing," said Tuvo Ausonius.

"I hate you!" she said. "Even on the *Alaria* I hated you."

"It seems your feelings were somewhat ambivalent, ranging between disgust and greed," said Tuvo Ausonius.

"I despised you."

"And do you think I would have held you in high esteem, one only of the Auresii?"

"Knave!" she said.

"What sort of relationship would we have had?" he asked.

"It would have been on my terms," she said. "I assure you of that!"

"You do hate me, don't you?" he said.

"Yes," she said.

"Why?" he asked.

"You are a weakling!" she said.

"And doubtless you would punish me for that?"

"Yes," she said, "I would have made you suffer! I was even considering ruining you!"

"Would you not then have ruined yourself, as well?"

"No!" she said. "I could have taken what I could from you, and then contracted other marriages."

"You are materialistic, indeed," he said.

She looked at him, in fury.

"Therefore, what has happened to you is surely not inappropriate."

"What do you mean?" she asked, suddenly.

"Do you wish to discuss our possible marriage further?" he asked.

"If you wish," she said, uncertainly.

"You are a free woman," he said.

"Yes," she said.

"And you would consider proposing yourself as a marital partner to a free man?"

"Certainly," she said.

"Even to me," he said.

"Possibly," she said.

"Do you know the penalties for a slave girl who lies?" he asked.

"How could I know such things?" she whispered.

"I thought you might have heard," he said.

"She would be severely punished," she said.

"That is my understanding, as well," he said.

"Such things are of no interest to me," she said.

"I thought they might be."

"No," she said.

"You are Tribonius Auresius, of Terennia, where you are an officer of a court?"

"Yes!" she said.

"You are Tribonius Auresius, a free woman, one of the *honestori*, even of the patricians?"

"Yes, of course," she said.

"Normally," he said, "one might expect those of the patricians to wear some token of their blood, a purple ribbon, even a thread somewhere. Have you such a token?"

"I did not so garb myself," she said.

"Even though traveling?"

"No," she said. "Do you have such a token about you?"

"I normally do not wear the color," he said. "I find it does not fit well with same garb, and that it sometimes tends to evoke resentment or envy."

"The lower orders are subject to such faults," she said.

" 'The lower orders'?"

"Yes."

"I admire your ensemble," he said.

"Thank you," she said.

"They are clearly the garments of a free woman."

"Of course," she said.

"As I understand it, a slave girl who dares to don such garments without the authorization of the master may be severely punished, even slain."

She turned white.

"To be sure, sometimes a master will order his slave to wear such garments, perhaps because, for some reason, he wishes to keep her true status a secret."

"Are you all right?" he asked.

"Yes, yes," she said.

"You are trembling," he said.

"I think that I will be leaving now," she said.

"You will remain," he said.

"Please, Person Ausonius!" she said.

"It is fortunate that you are not a slave girl," he said, "for a slave girl's addressing a free person by his name in that manner can be cause for severe discipline."

"Do not forget that you are a same!" she said.

"You are a free woman, are you not, even of the patricians?"

"Yes," she said. "Yes!"

"Your shoes are pretty," he said. "Remove them."

She looked at him, agonized, but she dared not disobey such a direct order, as she was a slave.

"Very well," she said.

"No," he said, "not there, there."

She rose from the bed, on which she had sat, and sat on the floor, beside the bed.

"Now the hose," he said.

He watched. Her legs were shapely.

"Now rise," he said. "Come here."

She stood small, trembling, before him.

He put his hands to the scarf, at her throat. He very gently unwrapped it, revealing the slave collar.

"Master!" she moaned, falling to her knees.

"Do you really think I cannot tell a slave, when I see one?" he asked. "How she moves, the nature of her body, little things, of which she is not even aware."

"You are a same!" she wept, looking up at him.

"No," he said. "In my arms I have held a slave. I can no longer be a same. I have tasted slave meat."

"Forgive me, Master!" she wept.

"Do you think I do not know why a slave is sent to a man's room?" he asked.

"Forgive me, Master," she said.

"So," said he, looking down upon her, "this is what has become of my former betrothed, my former fiancée, the proud, mercenary, materialistic little snip, Tribonius Auresius."

"Yes, Master," she said, fearfully.

"The collar looks well on you."

"Thank you, Master."

"What is your name?" he asked.

"I do not truly have a name," she said. "In this house I am called 'Flora'."

"An excellent name for a slave," he said.

"Thank you, Master," she said.

"It will do," he said.

"Yes, Master," she said.

"Surely your master did not tell you to appear before me in the garments of a free woman."

"No, Master," she said.

"Remove them," he said.

She hastened to rid herself of the garments of the free woman, and then there knelt before him the same slave who, earlier, had knelt before her master, she in the narrow bandeau, she of the black, twice-turned cloth cord, the bits of silk. She even, with acute self-consciousness, realizing how this must accentuate the beauty of her figure, in misery, replaced the scarlet hair ribbon.

"Aii," said Tuvo Ausonius.

"But what is that flower in your belt?" he asked.

"The slave flower," she said, "which I have been ordered to offer to you."

"Your master thinks so little of you?" he asked.

"Yes, Master!" she wept.

"Place the flower on the foot of the bed," he said. "Remove your garments completely. Remain kneeling."

"Yes, Master," she wept.

"In the corner of the room, there," he said, pointing, "there is a slave whip. Crawl to it, on all fours, and fetch it, bring it back to me in your teeth."

The slave complied.

He took the whip from her and put it on the bed, by the flower.

"Lift your wrists, crossed," he said.

In a moment her wrists were lashed together. He then tied them to the ring at the foot of the bed, a common feature in many bedrooms in the empire.

She then knelt at the foot of the bed, her wrists tied before her, to the ring.

"You thought to make a fool of me," he said. "I do not care for that."

He picked up the whip, and shook out the blades.

"I am of the Auresii!" she said.

"Are you?" he asked.

"No, no!" she said. "I am only a slave girl!"

"You came to this room under false pretenses," he said. "You dared to garb yourself without authorization in the garments of a free woman. You pretended to be free, to be the free woman, Tribonius Auresius, once my fiancée. Your speech was insolent. Many were the lies that passed your deceitful lips. By recourse to insidious psychological devices you attempted to bend me to your will. Though an animal you dared to speak of marriage. You addressed me by my name, soiling it, by putting it on the lips of a slave."

"Mercy!" she begged.

"There are many counts against you, Flora," he said.

"Forgive me, Master!" she begged.

"What I do not understand," he said, "is why you did these things."

"From what I knew of you, Master," she wept, "I loathed you. The thought of you disgusted me. My very skin crawled at the thought of your touch."

"Because you thought me a same, a weakling?"

"Yes!" she said.

"Do you think such things are true?" he asked.

"No, Master," she said. "I see they are not."

"But even if they had been true," he asked, "would they have excused your conduct?"

"No, Master!" she said.

"Is it up to the slave girl whom she will content and serve?" he asked.

"No, Master!" she said.

"It depends on whom?" he asked.

"On the master!" she said.

"Are the feelings of the slave girl of any account?" he asked.

"No, Master!" she said.

"You know these things?" he asked.

"Yes, Master," she wept.

"And yet you did what you did," he said.

"Forgive me, Master," she said.

His eye looked to the slave flower, on the foot of the bed. She followed his eye.

"Punish me," she said. "I am yours to do with as you will."

"Do you care for your master?" he asked.

"I love him," she said.

"A slave can love?" he asked.

"No woman who is not a slave can know what love truly is," she said.

"I have heard that love makes a slave of a woman," he said.

"That is why such feelings are forbidden to sames," she said, "that women not be weakened, not be placed in such chains, not be so enslaved."

"And yet," she said, "it is only in such bondage that they are truly themselves, and truly free."

"Interesting," he said.

"And think how much more so is this the case when the woman is truly slave, legally, and in all respects."

"Surely you fear the labors, the terrors, of slavery," he said.

"Yes, Master," she said. "For we cannot choose our masters, and are owned, and must serve, unquestioningly. Yet, too, in such a condition, for all its miseries and terrors, we know ourselves the most needful and open to love, the most sexual, the most free, the most ourselves."

He put aside the ship, and bent down, freeing her wrists.

"You may offer me the slave flower," he said.

Timidly, confused, she took the flower from the bed, and, kneeling before him, with two hands, lifted it to him.

"I offer you my slave flower, Master," she said.

"Stand," he said, "turn about, cross your wrists behind your back."

Startled, the slave did as she was told.

She felt her hands tied together, not gently, but rudely, tightly, behind her back. One hand still clung to the slave flower. She was tied in such a way that her hands were fastened rather at the center of the black, cloth cord, the ends of which were then brought together before her belly, and tied there, this holding her hands rather at the small of her back.

"Master?" she said.

"You have complied with the orders of your master," he said. "You have come to my room, and have offered me the slave flower."

"Master?"

"Perhaps you will come again, sometimes, to the room," he said, "and will serve me, and I will see to it that you do it well, indeed, with perfection, but now, now I think I will spare you for your master."

"I do not understand," she said.

"I do not accept the flower," he said. "I reject you. I am sending you back to your master."

"Am I not of interest?" she asked.

"Vixen," said he, "I am hastening you from the room before I cannot help myself, but throw you to the slave ring."

"Master!" she cried, joyfully.

"Once, too," he said, "you were of the *honestori*, of the empire, and a patrician."

"But not now!" she said.

"No, not now," he smiled.

He took the flower from her and thrust it in the cord at her waist. He put the bandeau, the bits of silk, and the ribbon, too, beneath the cord, but at the left hip.

He went to the door and opened it.

She regarded him, wonderingly, gratefully.

"Get out!" he said, hoarsely.

"Master!" she cried.

"Is it necessary to whip you from the room?" he inquired.

"No, Master!" she said.

At the door she stopped, momentarily, and lifted her lips to his cheek, and kissed it, lightly.

"Thank you, Master," she said.

"Now, shapely slave girl," he said, "get out!"

"Yes, Master!" she said.

"Oh!" she cried, sped forth into the hall, stung by a slap below the small of the back.

The guard looked up, from his chair, and then rose to his feet.

"She is rejected," said Tuvo Ausonius to the guard.

"Do you want another?" asked the guard.

"There is one I would like," said Tuvo Ausonius.

"Who is she?" asked the guard.

"It is not important," said Tuvo Ausonius, and retired within the room, and shut the door.

Flora hurried past the guard, to return to the lower floor.

## • • • CHAPTER 32 • • •

"Is it as she has spoken?" asked Otto.

"Yes," said Tuvo Ausonius.

Flora knelt before the table, at which were seated Tuvo Ausonius, and a seeming same, the smaller individual who had accompanied him to the holding in the mountains, Julian, who was the master of the house, and Otto, her master.

Two slaves were in attendance, who would serve the table. One's name was Renata, the other's Gerune.

The individual seated by Tuvo Ausonius, she in same garb, seemed troubled, and fearful.

It was the evening following the visit of Flora to the room of Tuvo Ausonius.

Flora trembled.

Her master has summoned her before the table.

She knelt there, naked, save for a collar, her knees spread, in the fashion of a pleasure slave, her wrists crossed, her hands tied together before her body.

Her master wished, it seemed, a full account of what had occurred in the room of Tuvo Ausonius. The slave, for example, had returned early, rejected, the slave flower thrust in the black cord, it then serving to bind her, holding her wrists to her back.

She had been taken immediately to her cell, and unbound only within it, and then had been locked within.

She had been denied her garment.

Tuvo Ausonius had not objected to the interrogation of the slave, and had graciously acceded to Otto's request that he monitor her testimony, in order to assure its absolute fidelity to what had occurred.

At times Otto's eyes had blazed with fury, and his fists had clenched on the table.

But the slave fully, tearfully, honestly, gave an account of what she had done.

"Such behavior is to be punished surely, and terribly," said Otto.

"You see," said Otto, turning to Julian, "she is utterly worthless."

"Then sell her," said Julian.

Renata and Gerune exchanged frightened glances. They, too, could be sold on a whim.

The lip of the individual seated by Tuvo Ausonius, she in same garb, trembled.

Otto turned to Tuvo Ausonius. "You are he who was most abused by the impudence of this embonded slut," he said. "What punishment do you recommend?"

The individual beside Tuvo Ausonius regarded him wildly, frightened.

"There are complicated circumstances involved," said Tuvo Ausonius. "I would recommend lenience."

Flora looked at him, wildly, gratefully.

"Show your gratitude," said Otto.

Flora sprang to her feet and hurried to kneel before Tuvo Ausonius. She put down her head and covered his feet with kisses.

"Enough," said Julian, clapping his hands. "Let us feast. Too, I have a surprise for you, my friend, Otto, later. But now, let us have food and drink."

"Slaves, serve!" said Julian, and Renata and Gerune hurried to a buffet, on which were placed numerous delicate viands and rare, precious wines.

"Shall we withdraw?" asked Tuvo Ausonius.

"By all means, remain," said Julian, "as you are both honored guests."

Tuvo Ausonius and she in same garb, with him, looked at one another.

Renata and Gerune began to place food upon the table.

Both slaves were in brief slave tunics, and collars.

"We are still, I gather," said Tuvo Ausonius, "under arrest."

"Certainly," said Julian.

"I do not think my life is worth much outside this holding," said Tuvo Ausonius.

"New identities might be arranged," said Julian.

"My ultimate allegiance," said Tuvo Ausonius, "is to the empire."

"So, too, is mine," said Julian.

Gerune placed a goblet before Tuvo Ausonius, and poured wine into it.

"I think, of late," said Tuvo Ausonius, "I have learned something of which, hitherto, I had known little."

"What is that?" asked Julian.

"Honor," said Tuvo Ausonius.

"It is my hope," said Julian, "that more in the empire will recollect it."

Renata poured wine for Otto. He lifted his hand, slightly, and she desisted.

"Master, may I assist?" asked Flora, lifting her wrists to Otto.

"Thank you, Master," she said, freed.

She hurried to assist in the serving.

Otto watched her, his fists clenched. How beautiful she was, the slave.

She returned in a moment with a plate filled with tiny cakes.

"Perhaps I should send you to the kitchen, to scour the tiles," said Otto.

"As Master wishes," she said.

"You may remain," he said.

"Thank you, Master!" she said.

Her flanks were exquisite, and the little slave, the vixen, was doubtless not unaware of that.

The individual seated by Tuvo Ausonius, she in same garb, seemed uneasy, being served by the slaves, Renata and Gerune, and then Flora. It was almost as though she was frightened to be where she was, seated, at the table.

She looked anxiously at Tuvo Ausonius, but, if he noticed her agitation, he gave no sign of it.

Julian, however, had been considering her, with some attention, and was not unaware of her lack of ease.

"Your colleague," said Julian, addressing himself to Tuvo Ausonius, "is a female, is she not?"

The garmentures, and practices, of sames are designed to minimize and obscure sexual differences.

Among sames, by intent, it is often difficult to distinguish the sexes.

Tuvo Ausonius turned to the individual at his side.

"Such things are not of interest to sames, of course," she said.

"But you are a female, are you not?" asked Julian.

"Yes," she said, "I am a female."

"It is my understanding," said Julian to Tuvo Ausonius, "that you are no longer a same." This information, of course, had emerged earlier, in the interrogation of a slave.

"That is true," said Tuvo Ausonius. "I am no longer a same."

"It seems suprising then that you would travel in the company of a same," said Julian.

"Perhaps," smiled Tuvo Ausonius.

"One might expect then that one of your station, and income," said Julian, "might own a slave."

"True," said Tuvo Ausonius.

"You understand that for purposes of security, we have kept you and Person Sesella separate," said Julian.

"Of course," said Tuvo Ausonius.

"It is not as though she were a meaningless slave," said Julian.

"Of course," said Tuvo Ausonius.

"And doubtless, as she is a same, she is simple, plain, homely, even ugly, and of no interest whatsoever."

Tuvo Ausonius looked annoyed.

The individual beside Tuvo Ausonius, she in same garb, regarded him, frightened.

"Here, Renata, Gerune, Flora," said Julian. "Parade and pose before our guest."

The slaves did so, and well, as they were slaves, and commanded. Any personal feelings they might have had were immaterial.

The individual beside Tuvo Ausonius became then quite agitated.

"There are three beauties," said Julian. "Pick any of them. She will be sent to your room this evening."

Gerune cast a wild, pleading glance at Julian.

"You do not mind, do you, Otto?" said Julian.

"No," said Otto. "They are only slaves."

Renata and Flora looked at Otto, pleadingly, but knowing they were slaves.

"None of them," said Tuvo Ausonius.

The three girls cast wild glances about, among themselves, of relief, but, too, of surprise.

"I would prefer another," said Tuvo Ausonius.

"I can summon others," said Julian. "There are some in the kitchen, some with the guards, some in kennels below."

"May I pick my own?" asked Tuvo Ausonius.

"Of course," said Julian.

"And may I offer you something?" he said.

"Of course," said Julian.

"I have something here," he said.

He snapped his fingers.

"Yes, Master!" cried the small figure at his side.

She leapt gratefully, delightedly, to her feet and began to tear away the same garb which had obscured what, in a moment, was to be delightfully revealed.

"Aii!" cried Julian.

"Superb!" said Otto.

"Ahhh," cried the slaves.

There now knelt, before the table, in a tiny tunic of red silk, and collared, a startlingly beautiful slave.

"Excellent," said Julian. "What do you call her?"

"'Sesella'," said Tuvo Ausonius.

"That is a slave name?" said Julian.

"Of course," said Tuvo Ausonius.

"But she wore same garb," said Julian.

The pretty slave put her head down, frightened.

"That seemed appropriate," said Tuvo Ausonius, "to conceal her identity and status."

"I understand," said Julian.

"Such things are not concealed now," said Otto.

"No," admitted Tuvo Ausonius.

"Would you like to resume your place at the table?" asked Julian of the exquisite, frightened slave before him.

"No, no, Master!" she said, frightened.

"Why not?" he inquired.

"I am a slave," she said. "It is more fitting that I kneel in the presence of masters."

"Let Sesella, now in her turn, parade and pose," said Tuvo Ausonius.

The slave, frightened, walked before the men.

"Interest them," said Tuvo Ausonius. "You are a slave."

The slave obeyed, pausing, crouching, kneeling, sitting, casting glances, extending a limb, calling attention, delicately, in this fashion and that, frightened, to her indisputable, marvelous, commanded loveliness.

"Excellent," said Julian.

"Splendid," said Otto.

Well, you see, was her master's property exhibited.

"Obeisance," snapped Tuvo Ausonius.

Instantly, as slaves must obey, did she assume a common position of obeisance, kneeling, her head down to the floor, the palms of her hands on the floor.

"An exquisite slave," said Julian.

"Indeed," said Otto.

"I offer her to either of you, or both, for the evening," said Tuvo Ausonius.

The slave gasped in misery. Her small shoulders shook.

"But you would like her, would you not?" asked Julian.

"Yes," said Tuvo Ausonius.

"I shall send her to your room tonight," said Julian.

From the slave there came a tiny sound, of joy.

"But are we not to be kept separated?" inquired Tuvo Ausonius.

"If she were a free woman, of course," said Julian. "But as she is not a free woman but only, as is now evident, a meaningless slave, it does not matter."

"My thanks, milord," said Tuvo Ausonius.

"Chain her well," said Julian.

"I shall, milord," said Tuvo Ausonius.

"And if her cries of ecstasy become too obtrusive you might, for the sake of the rest of others, consider gagging her."

"Of course, milord," said Tuvo Ausonius.

"Perhaps, my dear," said Julian to the slave, "you would care to assist in the serving?"

"Yes, Master!" she said gratefully. "Thank you, Master!"

The four slaves then, Renata, Gerune, Flora and Sesella, addressed themselves to the serving of the supper. Sesella seemed jealous to serve Tuvo Ausonius, hurrying to him, placing herself before others and such. The other slaves did not object. She was, after all, his own slave. Sometimes, of course, such competitions tend to be adjudicated later in the kitchen or slave quarters, which *loci*, as one might suppose, are not entirely unacquainted with biting, scratching, screaming, kicking, the pulling of hair and other such unpleasant modalities of arbitration.

Better surely the sword and spear.

"Is it thus," asked Julian, turning to Otto, "that the women of the enemy, now captives, or now slaves, would serve in barbarian halls and camps?"

"More likely, all would serve nude, save for their collars," said Otto.

Tuvo Ausonius snapped his fingers and Sesella, blushing, dropped aside her silk.

A moment later Renata, at the merest glance from Otto, discarded her slave tunic. "Yes, Dira!" she whispered. "Yes!"

Flora was already unclad, save for the band on her neck, closed by the small stout lock, in the back.

"Please, no, Master," said Gerune, standing before Julian.

"You were a woman of the Ortungs, of the Drisriaks," said Julian. "Indeed you were a princess of those tribes."

"Please, no, Master," begged Gerune.

"Would women of the empire not serve thusly at given feasts in the camps and halls of the Ortungs, of the Drisriaks?" inquired Julian.

"Yes, Master," she said, tears in her eyes.

"Strip," said Julian.

"Yes, Master," she said.

"Now continue serving," he said.

"Yes, Master," she said. "Now I know I am a slave," she said.

Later, over liqueurs, Julian called one of the guards to him.

"I mentioned to you, earlier," he said, "that I had a surprise in store for you."

"Yes?" said Otto.

The guard returned in a moment, bearing the cylindrical leather case which had been borne earlier by the magistrate, he preceded by the twelve lictors. It had been recovered from the outer bailey, where it had fallen.

Julian removed the cap and took from the case a rolled paper, bound with a ribbon and seal.

"Do you know the seal?" asked Julian.

"No," said Otto.

"It is the seal of the imperial war office," he said. He broke the seal and spread the paper, flat, it curling up at the ends, on the table.

"It is your commission," said Julian.

"Is it in order?" inquired Otto.

"Yes," said Julian. "They would not have dared, under the circumstances, it having been requested by me, not to grant the commission. Too, it would not have been issued from the war office had the authorizations not been in place. Copies of this, too, as a matter of routine, will be filed in various offices, on numerous worlds, wherever it might be thought expedient to check credentials, particularly if a breakdown in communications occurred with the capital world. In short, the commission is authentic. It is merely they had not expected it to be received. Our friend, Tuvo Ausonius, was to have seen to that, and, if that failed, the magistrate and his henchmen, serving as lictors, were to make certain of the matter."

"Make your mark here," said Julian.

A pen was brought, and Otto made a mark on the paper, where Julian indicated. Otto, raised in a *festung* village on Tangara, could neither read nor write. In this he did not differ from millions throughout the empire. His mark was a crudely drawn, very carefully drawn, very slowly drawn, spear.

"Gerune, bring drink!" said Julian.

He was standing.

Gerune hurried forward and filled the goblets of the men.

"Captain!" said Julian, lifting his goblet.

"Captain!" said Tuvo Ausonius, rising to his feet.

"My thanks," said Otto, acknowledging the toast.

The three men drank.

Though it seemed a small thing, and one is not to be blamed for thinking little of such things at the time, this was an evening, and a moment, which later assumed some importance in the history of the empire. Some have seen it as one of those mysterious hinges on which fate is sometimes, at a much later date, noted to have turned.

"It is late!" said Julian.

"Gather up your things," said Tuvo Ausonius to Sesella.

"Master?" she asked, finding the envelope which he had given into her hands earlier in the afternoon, when he had ordered her from the room, shortly before he, Julian and Otto, following Julian, had vacated the same room, which shortly thereafter had been rocked with an explosion. Sesella had placed the envelope within the same garb, but had not raised the question of its contents. If she had been a free woman it would not have been appropriate for her to have opened it, and as a slave, of course, it would have been far less appropriate. Indeed, as a slave, she would not have dared to open it. A slave knows her place, and, under certain circumstances, fears for her very skin and life. Too, it may be recalled that she and Tuvo Ausonius had been kept separated after their arrest until the supper of this evening. Little opportunity had occurred at supper to bring up the matter, and, in any event, it would not, even had she not been a mere slave, have seemed appropriate to have done so. Now, however, she lifted the envelope. Should it, whatever it might be, whatever its contents might be, be returned to Tuvo Ausonius, or should she keep it with the same garb? Obviously there was no place to keep it in the bit of silk in her grasp.

"May I?" asked Julian, extending his hand.

"Yes, Milord," said Tuvo Ausonius, reddening slightly.

Sesella surrendered the envelope to Julian and he opened it, and perused the contents.

"Person Ausonius, it seems," said Julian to the slave Sesella, now kneeling before him, "suspected the treachery of Iaachus, arbiter of protocol, or that of someone purportedly acting on his behalf. He had apparently intended to risk opening the case while unattended, in the event his suspicions were justified. But he had with him a slave, of whom, despite the fact she was a mere slave, he had, it seems, made the mistake of permitting himself to grow fond."

Sesella threw a wild, joyful glance at Tuvo Ausonius, but he glared at her, angrily, with embarrassed savagery, and she instantly lowered her head, but seemed to smile.

"These papers," said Julian, "pertain to such a slave."

Sesella lifted her head.

"Flora," said Julian.

The slave girl addressed was kneeling to one side.

"Master?" she said.

"You have had some training in the law, have you not?" asked Julian.

"Yes, Master."

"To be sure," said Julian, "given your nature, it would have been better had you been trained as a slave girl from the cradle."

"Yes, Master," she said.

"What do you think is the purport of these papers?" asked Julian.

"They are doubtless papers of manumission, Master," said Flora.

"No!" protested Sesella.

"It is clear you are from Terennia," smiled Julian.

"Master?" asked Flora.

"Do you not understand that lovely Sesella is as much a slave girl as you?"

"Yes, Master," said Flora.

"Do you think that slave girls are freed?" he asked.

"No, Master," she said.

"Do you think these are papers of manumission?" Julian asked Sesella.

"I trust not, Master," she said.

"The purport of these papers," said Julian, "is that his wealth, and estate, what they are, and certain funds supposed to have been deposited on Miton in his name, were to be used to secure you a light slavery and a kind master."

"Ah," said Sesella.

"Incidentally, Person Ausonius," said Julian, "I rather suspect that the funds supposed to have been deposited for you on Miton have not been so deposited."

Tuvo Ausonius nodded.

One who has been blasted to atoms had little need of such resources.

"What think you of the generosity of your master?" asked Julian.

"I do not know if my master knows that what he owns is truly a slave girl," said Sesella.

"Oh?" said Julian.

Tuvo Ausonius regarded her, with interest.

"The thought means much to me," she said.

"Speak clearly," said Julian.

"I want my slavery to be real," she said. "I want to know that I am a slave."

"The lightness of your slavery is not important to you?" asked Julian.

"Such matters," she said, "are at the discretion of the master. I am a slave."

"A master is to be under no obligations in such matters?"

"No, Master," she said.

"But surely you would wish a kind master," said Julian.

"I want a strong master," she said, "one who is not weak, one who will take what he wants from me, as he wants it, and how he wants it, one who will not compromise in the least with me."

"Surely you would want him to be kind?"

"Oh, yes," she said. "At least sometimes. And sometimes we hope desperately for that."

"I see," said Julian.

"But such things are meaningless," she said, "except against a background of strength, a background of leather and iron."

"Give me the papers," said Tuvo Ausonius.

Julian handed the papers, and the envelope, to Ausonius.

To the wonder of Sesella, and the others there, Tuvo Ausonius tore the papers, and even the envelope, to bits.

"I see I was too lenient with you, slave girl," said Tuvo Ausonius. "No special provisions should have been made for you, for you are a true slave girl. Should anything happen to me now, you will be merely another of my properties, to be disposed of at the discretion of others, as what you are, merely a chattel. You will take your chances, like any other slave, in the open market."

"Yes, Master," she said. "Thank you, Master!"

He regarded her.

"But I want to be yours!" she said.

"I may sell you," he said.

"No!" she cried. Then she hurried to him, and put her head to his feet. "Let me serve you that you will desire to keep me!" she said.

"I will have you serve me as few slaves have ever served a man," he said, "now that I know, fully, what you are!"

"Yes, Master," she said. "I want to serve as what I am, fully. I love you! I love you!"

He rose to his feet, and nodded to Julian and Otto.

"What of the same garb?" asked Julian.

"Burn it," said Tuvo Ausonius.

"It will be done," said Julian.

"It is unbecoming to a slave girl," said Tuvo Ausonius.

"True," said Julian.

Sesella looked down at the gray, formless heap of concealing, disguising materials thrown to the floor.

"Heel me," said Tuvo Ausonius, "slave girl."

"Yes, Master!" she said.

At the door to the room she looked back, once, at the same garb on the floor. She realized that she might never again be put in such garb. She was a slave girl and would now, presumably, be clad, if she were clad, accordingly.

"No!" said Tuvo Ausonius, suddenly, a little beyond the portal. "You will precede me."

"As a free woman?" she asked.

"No," said he, "as a female slave on whom I look at my pleasure."

"I do not know the way," she said.

"I shall direct you," he said.

"Yes, Master," she said.

"Move," he said.

"Yes, Master," she said.

She hurried on ahead then, clutching in her right hand a tiny bit of scarlet silk.

"It is late," said Julian.

Gerune hurried to Julian, and knelt before him.

"What is it?" he asked.

"You have taught me that I am a slave," she said. "I would serve you as such."

"Is this the proud Gerune, the barbarian princess, the princess of the Ortungs and Drisriaks?" he asked.

"No, Master," she said. "It is only Gerune, your slave, naked and in her collar, who begs to serve you."

He looked at her for some time.

Tears were in her eyes.

"Hurry before me to my chambers," he said. "Prepare them for love."

"Yes, Master!" she cried, and leapt to her feet, hurrying from the room.

Julian rose to his feet.

"It is the turn of Renata, as I recall, from the roster in the kitchen, to clear, and to restore the room," said Julian.

Otto looked up.

"Unless you wish otherwise," said Julian.

Otto had made it clear earlier that Renata, his curvaceous blond slave from the summer world, was to participate in the duties of the house.

"No," said Otto.

Flora looked up, startled

"What of the guard?" asked Julian.

"What of this one?" asked Otto, indicating Flora.

"But it is Renata who is on the roster," said Julian.

"Surely he should receive some compensation for his inconvenience, supervising her labors," said Otto.

"Excellent," said Julian.

The guard would presumably enjoy Renata on the tiles of the floor of the dining hall, and he might, also, if he wished, take her by the hair to the mat in his quarters. She should, however, be kenneled before dawn.

"I will want a good report on you before noon," said Otto. "I do not wish to have to have to whip you."

"It will not be necessary to whip me, Master," she said.

"If the guard should show interest in you," said Otto, "see to it that you are fully pleasing."

"I will not be able to help myself, Master," she said. "He is a man. I am a slave."

"You may begin to clear," said Julian.

"Yes, Master," said Renata, attending to the table.

"I am going to my room," said Otto.

"Master!" said Flora.

"I did not realize that it was Renata's turn on the roster," said Otto.

"It seems to have turned out that way," said Julian.

"Master, please, Master!" said Flora.

"Treacherous, lying slut," snarled Otto at the kneeling slave. "It is fortunate for you that Tuvo Ausonius recommended lenience. Otherwise you might have been thrown to the dogs."

"Yes, Master," she whispered.

Otto then turned about and strode angrily from the room.

Julian gathered up the commission from the table.

He looked down at the slave who knelt there, her head in her hands.

"It is growing late," he said. "It is appropriate then that you should either be in your cell or chained in your master's room."

"Master?" she asked.

"There is a slave rose in the kitchen," he said. "It is fresh, and beautiful."

# · · · CHAPTER 33 · · ·

The dark-haired slave knelt before Otto, in the privacy of his chambers.

A lamp, suspended on three chains, burned to one side. Heavy tapestries were about, hunting and battle scenes, but they were muchly dark now, their thick, heavily woven textures hardly discernible. There were narrow bars on the window. Shadows were cast by the massive couch.

"How dare you have come here?" had inquired Otto, who had opened the door in response to the timid knock. There, kneeling in the threshold, had been the slave.

"Master Julian has sent me," she said, frightened.

In her hands there was a silver tray, on which were a flask of wine, with a goblet, and some viands, and a flower.

"It is thoughtful of him to send me a light collation," said Otto.

He gestured that the slave might enter.

She did so, and placed the tray on a table, near the couch.

She was dressed in a brief slave tunic, much like Renata and Gerune had worn earlier.

It seemed that Julian, who had much taken her garmenting and her quarters in hand, had decided that she would no longer wear the long, sleeveless garment of wool, that which had been for so long her garment in her cell.

Otto looked away from her, angrily. Her legs were superb.

She then knelt at the foot of the couch.

"You may leave," said Otto, not looking at her.

"Master Julian," she said, "has desired that I inquire after your wants."

"You have now done so," he said. "You may now leave."

"It is late," she said. "At this hour I might be severely punished if found in the halls."

At this hour it would be normal for a slave to be secured,

perhaps in the master's room, perhaps in the slave quarters, in a cell, or kennel, such things.

"You came here upon command," he said.

"But a guard may seize me and beat me," she said.

"Inform him that you are here on the orders of the master of the house," said Otto.

"Master Julian will not wish to be disturbed now," she said.

"Then be whipped," said Otto, angrily.

"At the least," she said, "I would spend the night in close chains."

"I will bind your hands behind your back," said Otto, "and then it will be understood that you are in proper custody."

"I was being kept in a cell," she said. "But now it has been taken from me."

"You now have a kennel?" asked Otto.

"Yes," she said.

"Is it clean and dry?" he asked.

"I must keep it that way," she said.

"How large is it?" he asked.

"It is larger than the cage you keep me in on Varna," she said.

"You look well in a cage," he said.

"Yes, Master," she said.

She looked about.

"It seems Master has not slept," she said.

Otto growled with rage.

"Master?" she asked, innocently.

"May I pour the wine, Master?" she asked.

"I would have a woman," said Otto suddenly, fiercely.

She rose to her feet, unbidden, to pour the wine. Otto looked to the slave whip, on its hook, on the wall, but he did not advance toward it, and remove it from its hook.

She poured the wine. "The girls are now in service," she said, "or kenneled for the night. I suppose one might be brought up, from the kennels."

She replaced the decanter on the tray. "I am a woman," she said.

Otto cried out with rage.

She took the goblet and knelt before him, kissing it and then lifting it to him.

"I have been sent," she said, "to inquire after your wants."

"My wants," said Otto, in rage, "are well satisfied."

"What of mine?" she cried, suddenly, tears brimming in her eyes. "What of my wants?"

"They are nothing," said Otto. "They are only those of a female slave."

He turned away from her.

"Do not treat us with such cruelty!" she cried.

" 'Us'?" he said.

"Slaves," she wept. "You do not know what it is to be a woman, and a slave. You do not know what it is to be in bondage, to be property, to be owned. You do not understand how this at once makes us so vulnerable, so helpless, and yet so free and needful. Do you think we do not know the meaning of our brands, of the collars on our necks? Do you think we do not understand how it is that we are garbed as we are, and what this means? Can you not understand how such things touch us in our deepest belly, how they liberate, and inflame, our sexuality? Have you not heard how desperate we are to obey, to love and to serve, to be the most complete and perfect of women, to be mastered, and in being mastered, in our own conquest, to become most ourselves, and secure our greatest fulfillment, our greatest exultation and ecstasy? Can you not understand how we long to return to the very wellsprings of our being, to the world in which we were bred, a world of flint, of hammers and thongs? Have you not heard how slave girls, in their kennels, weep and scratch, and moan, and cry out for the touch of a man? Do you think any other woman can know the heats of one who is a slave? Can you understand what it is to be subject to sale, to know that one must please, to fear the whip, to know that one is owned? I have screamed with need, for the touch of my master, and he does not even look upon me!"

Otto turned to regard her.

"I beg kindness," she said.

"You are worthless," he said. "A thousand things have shown me this."

"Even the lowliest, and most worthless of slaves," she said, "may beg her master for his touch."

"And you do so?" said Otto.

"Yes, Master," she said. "Yes, Master!"

Otto took the wine from her.

He put it on the tray.

"Strange remarks," he said, "for one who was formerly an officer of a court on Terennia."

"That was long ago, Master," she said. She put her fingers to her collar. She lifted it, just a little, on her neck. "See, Master," she said, "I am now only your slave."

"It is true," he said.

"Yes, Master," she said.

He looked down upon the distraught beauty.

"Do not send me away, Master," she said.

"Is this behavior seemly in one who was once an officer of a court on Terennia?" he asked.

"Surely," she said, "if she who was an officer of a court on Terennia was even then a slave, deceitfully concealing the fact, which deceit she is now no longer permitted to practice, for her slavery has now been confirmed upon her, publicly, for all to see, legally, for all to know."

"Are you not ashamed?" he asked.

"No, Master, for slaves are not permitted shame."

"It is obvious that you are no longer a free woman," he said.

"Yes, Master," she said.

"You would love, and serve and obey?"

"With my whole heart, and all that I am, and might be," she said.

"Surely you lie," he said.

"No!" she wept. "Cannot you see the transformation which has taken place in me, that I am now collared, am now a helpless slave, that I am owned, and you are my master, and that I love you!"

"Lying slut," he snarled.

"Then hate me," she wept. "Abuse me! Tie me to a ring and whip me, if you wish! But do not neglect me! That is the most cruel of all!"

"Do you not find me attractive, even a little?" she asked.

He cried out with rage.

"Master?" she asked, frightened.

"Yes," he cried. "I find you attractive, slave slut! If I did not know you, do you think I would not ride a thousand leagues to capture you, to put a rope on you and run you beside my stirrup? Do you think I would not, having merely glimpsed you in a public place, have followed you, and scouted your residence, and entered it, and stolen you? Do you think I could have rested before you were safe at my feet, on my chain? Do you think I would not break walls, subdue cities, and fight armies to own you?"

"To own me!" she cried.

"Yes," he said, angrily.

"Master!" she cried, delighted.

"But I do know you!" he cried. "I know how meaningless, and petty, and treacherous, and worthless you are!"

"Then treat me as your enemy," she said, "and subdue me! Teach me my defeat!"

"Bitch," he said.

"You are a barbarian," she said. "Do you think I do not know how you view women of the empire? As booty, worth only a pittance as slaves!"

"How can you know this?" he said.

"Do you think that slaves do not know who are their rightful masters, and that they do not long for them?"

He glared at her, savagely.

"I am yours," she said. "Put me mercilessly to your pleasure. I beg it!"

He turned away, his fists clenched.

"I have been trained to please," she said. "I am sure you will find me suitable. My tongue has been educated. I have been taught the use of my hair. I can cater to the most refined taste, or to the most savage taste!"

"You are a true slave," he said.

"Yes, Master," she said.

"If your kennel is so spacious and pleasant," he said, "perhaps you should soon go to it."

"It is still a kennel, Master," she said.

He turned, again, angrily, to face her.

"And doubtless one too good for such as you," he said.

"Yes, Master," she said.

"Perhaps I shall speak to Julian," he said, "that a crate, or tiny bitch cage, may be arranged."

"As Master wishes," she said.

"What more could a slave want?" he asked.

She turned a little, putting her fingers on the furs with which the massive couch was bedecked.

"These are softer, Master," she whispered.

"Turn them down," he said.

"Yes, Master," she said, rising.

"With your hands clasped behind you, with your teeth," he said.

"Yes, Master," she said.

When she had completed her task she knelt again, at the foot of the couch.

"You have brought me a light collation," he said. "You have turned down the bed. You may now leave."

"Master!" she wept, pleadingly, looking up at him.

He put his hand upon her.

"Master!" she begged.

"It is well," he said, "that there is no nether closure in a slave tunic."

"Yes, Master," she sobbed.

He pointed to the door.

She rose to her feet and went slowly toward the door. She paused at the door, weakly, defeated, leaning her head against the stout, dark wood.

He looked to the tray on which was the goblet, the decanter of wine, the viands, the slave flower.

She was sobbing.

He heard the latch lifted.

The door had opened only a little, little more than a crack, to let the slave slip through, when she jerked her hands back, alarmed, as the door was thrust shut again, loudly, with fury. She turned, frightened, her back against the wood, looking up at the gigantic form that loomed over her. Otto's arms were over her shoulders, the palms of his hands flat on the door. His hands then were lowered to her shoulders, to the slave tunic there. Angrily he tore it down, away from her arms, to her hips. For an instant it seemed she would have darted her hands to her breasts, as though, in sudden embarrassment, to cover then, but, just as suddenly, she recalled she was before her master and put her arms down, a little behind her, their palms against the heavy dark wood of the door. Her eyes were frightened. He turned about and strode to the other side of the room. He turned about, again, and studied her, she standing there, against the door, in the light of the lamp, hanging from its tiny chains, hooked to a beam in the ceiling. There was a glint of the warm lamplight on the band on her neck, the steel of her collar. Her long dark hair was behind her shoulders.

"Yes," he said. "You are a pretty slave. Let us see the rest of you."

"Master!" she protested.

Then she slipped the shreds of the slave tunic away.

She stood with her back against the wood, the palms of her hands, too, flat, back, against the wood.

"You are a pretty slave," he said. "Why should you not be used, like any other?"

"Are you too good for use?" he asked.

"No, Master!" she said.

"Turn about," he said. "Bolt the door."

Two heavy bolts, one after the other, were thrust home, securing the great door.

"Kneel there," he said, "facing me."

"Proud woman of the empire," he said.

She shook her head, negatively.

"Now only a slave," he said.

"Yes, Master," she said.

"Here," he said, pointing to his feet, "crawl, on your belly."

She went to her belly, and crawled to his feet, where, her head down, she covered them with kisses.

"You are afraid, aren't you?" he said.

"Yes, Master," she whispered.

"On all fours," he said. "Go to the tray. Fetch the slave flower in your teeth."

She went to the tray and, turning her head, delicately, managed to grip the stem of the flower in her teeth. She then backed to where he stood, and put down her head, and placed the flower at his feet, between them.

"You offer me the slave flower?" he asked.

She lifted her head, tears in her eyes. "Yes, Master," she said.

"Pick it up, again, in your teeth," he said.

"Yes, Master," she whispered. Then she had the stem between her teeth, the flower to the left side of her lips, the base of the stem to the right.

She lifted her head to him, the flower between her teeth.

"You again offer me the slave flower?" he asked.

She nodded, tears in her eyes.

"And more properly this time?" he said.

She nodded, again, and lifted her head even more, proffering the flower.

To her consternation, he crouched down before her, and pried open her teeth.

"You do not offer it to me," he said, angrily. "I take it," he said. He tore it from her mouth.

She shuddered.

"On your knees, hands clasped behind you," he said. "Draw the furs to the floor, at the foot of the couch."

She looked at him, wildly.

"One such as you surely did not expect the dignity of being used upon its surface, did you?"

She shook her head, tears in her eyes.

"With your teeth, of course," he said.

She drew the furs from the couch.

She then, on all fours, as he stood to one side, her head down, using only her teeth, as she knew she must, spread them carefully.

She knelt to one side.

He snapped his fingers, and pointed to the furs. "On them, slave girl," he said.

Obediently she crawled to the furs.

He dropped the slave flower down, beside her.

He arranged her, as he wished.

"Master?" she said, as her small wrists were locked in the cuffs of chains, one to each side, above her, behind her.

"I have waited long for you," he said. "Ever since the court on Terennia."

"And I have waited long for you, my master," she said. "Ever since the court on Terennia."

He crouched down beside her, and put the slave flower again between her teeth, but it did not remain there long.

"This will be done quickly," he said. "Then I will teach you what it is to be a slave."

"Oh!" she cried.

He pulled the flower from between her teeth and cast it to the side.

"Your slave flower has been plucked, my dear," he said. "That can be done but once, and now, among knowing men, you will have even greater value as a slave."

"Yes, Master," she whispered.

It was long that she lay in his chains, and in this time she experienced feelings, and ecstasies, which she had not even understood were possible, and further knew that in them she had only begun to sense what might await her, could only begin to dimly sense new dawns, rising on new worlds, far seas, distant horizons, beckoning continents of sentience, realities toward which she wished to race, but knew that she must in any event follow, whether she wished to or not, in the chains of masters.

"Already you writhe well," Otto commented.

"I am totally yours, my savage master, my barbarian Lord!" she wept.

"That is known to me," he said, "slave girl."

"More! More! Do not stop!" she begged.

"I shall do as I please," he informed her.

"Yes, Master!" she wept.

"This is what you are good for," he informed her.

"Yes, Master!" she wept. "But I want to serve you, too, in all ways, totally, helplessly!"

"You will," he informed her.

Toward morning it was necessary to gag her.

When the sounds of the rising of the house were audible in the corridor, Otto rose and dressed. He looked down at the slave, who was curled on the furs, and looking up at him. She was no longer gagged, and the only bond now on her was a chain which ran to her left ankle, fastening her to a ring at the foot of the couch.

She looked away from him, trembling.

Yes, he thought, it seems possible that she has the makings of a good slave.

# · · · CHAPTER 34 · · ·

Otto and Julian breakfasted upon a terrace, one outside the office which had suffered much damage in the explosion. The seared, protective dome, which could withstand most strafing blasts from atmospheric craft, had been returned to its sheath. The morning was bright, and the air crisp. The mountains, which could be seen over the terrace, were striking in the sunlight. On the tops of some distant peaks there was snow, some of which lingered throughout the year.

The breakfast was being served by a barbarian slave girl whose name was Gerune, who now wore the simple, short slave tunic which was common to women of her condition throughout the empire. When not serving she knelt to one side, to be ready if aught was desired.

She was clearly a beautiful slave, and was becoming well trained.

Earlier this morning, before breakfast, Julian and Otto had bid farewell to a citizen of the empire and his slave. They had left in a road vehicle, and the citizen had had in his possession new papers, which were excellently done, and unlikely to provoke suspicion at almost any checkpoint. His purse was also filled with coins and certain letters of credit, and introduction. He wore clothing of a sort common in the empire, at least among the upper *honestori*, the patricians and such, a tunic and robe. These were not ostentatious and were not likely to attract undue attention. The slave who accompanied him wore slave garb, in this case, Serian slave leather, which her master had picked out for her. This was a combination of garment and harness, which held her hands buckled in cuffs behind her. She was also leashed, which leash ran to the ring on the thick leather collar, part of the harnesslike garment. No identificatory papers were required for her, no more than for any other animal. There was, however, required for her, a health certificate. This was kept by the master. It primarily attested that, at the time of the preparation of the certificate, the slave had been found free of communicable disease. She might, thus, be legally transported among worlds.

Julian and Otto looked up from their coffees, as I shall call them. One, favored by Julian, was *feldis*, a steaming, bluish-black liquid brewed from the *feldis* lichen. It was popular in the navy, particularly on long interstellar fights. He did not care greatly for *kemac*, brewed from the stewing of *kemac* leaves, popular at the court. The other, sipped by Otto, was *oris*, a bitter, black fluid generally served hot, as well. It was brewed from the *oris* root, found only on Sybyl II. It was expensive, and rare. Otto did not find the taste displeasing. Many, and diverse, thought Otto, are the riches of the empire.

"Slaves," announced the guard.

He had approached, being preceded by two slaves, Renata and Flora. They were naked, and each had a whip tied about their neck, and their hands were thonged behind them. They both knelt, head down, before the table.

Each, as we may recall, had been consigned to duties in the house. In this regard, they were both now being presented before Julian. Julian put down his coffee.

"Was Renata satisfactory?" Julian asked the guard, he to whom Renata's custody had been given the preceding evening.

"Yes, milord," said the guard.

"She worked well?"

"Yes, milord."

"And did you require slave use from her?"

"Yes, milord."

"How was she?"

"A slave, milord," he said.

"Totally?"

"Yes, milord."

"Excellent," said Julian. He then regarded the kneeling Flora. "As I recall, my dear," he said, "you were sent last night with a light supper to the room of my friend, Otto, and were to see to his comfort and needs."

"Yes, Master," she said.

"Was everything satisfactory?" Julian asked Otto.

"Yes," he said.

"And did you require slave use from her?"

"Yes," said Otto.

"How was she?" asked Julian.

"She is already muchly needful," said Otto. "And I think that, in a matter of even days, she will be helplessly so, and will crawl, and whine and beg, and will do anything for the touch of a master."

"You found her satisfactory then?" said Julian.

"Yes," said Otto, "for a new slave, one whose slave flower was only recently plucked, one at this stage in her development and training."

"Excellent," said Julian. He then turned to the guard. "Take the slaves away," he said. "To the kitchen."

"Yes, milord," said the man.

The two slaves rose quickly to their feet, and turned about.

"Wait," said Otto.

The party hesitated.

"That one," said Otto. "Give her ten lashes in the kitchen."

Both slaves trembled.

"The one with dark hair," said Otto.

Renata visibly relaxed and Flora stiffened, in bewilderment, and apprehension.

"You were not satisfied?" inquired Julian.

"That is not it," said Otto. "It is merely to remind her that she is a slave."

"Excellent," said Julian.

He then waved his hand, and the party left the terrace, the slaves preceding their guard.

"She will doubtless be twice as diligent tonight," said Julian.

"When I next call her," said Otto. "Tonight, I think I will call Renata."

The men then returned to their coffees.

"Abrogastes will grow ever more dangerous," said Julian.

"You would have me recruit on Tangara, among the Otungs," said Otto.

The Otungs were one of the five tribes of the Vandal nation. They are not to be confused with the Ortungs, which was a secessionist tribe from the Drisriaks, one of the eleven traditional tribes of the Alemanni.

"Yes, but alas," said Julian, "for my hopes in this matter have been frustrated by the long delay in the delivery of your commission."

"In what way?" asked Otto, puzzled.

"The time is no longer ripe," said Julian, wearily. "It had to have been done earlier."

"Why?" asked Otto.

"Because, on Tangara, among the Otungs," said Julian, gravely, "this is now the Killing Time."

"I have heard of that," said Otto.

"It is too dangerous to go there at such a time," said Julian.

"I will leave immediately," said Otto.

"As you wish," said Julian.